FULL CIRCLE

BY

Deborah Fezelle

Published 2020 by Shorehouse Books
Printed in the United States of America

Cover by

Wendy Prince

ISBN-13: 978-0-9600085-9-9

"The wheel is come full circle, I am here."

KING LEAR, Act 5, Scene 3

The Nick McDeare Series

THE EVIL THAT MEN DO

A WALKING SHADOW

FULL CIRCLE

For Mom

Special thanks to:

Cynthia Dickason-Scott, Marilyn & Kevin Wells, Nancy Sonner,
Kathryn Fasbender-Bos, Joshua Grenrock, Kelly Kerry

&
Meagan Martino

PROLOGUE

Andrew Brady was technically dead. Murder was a sudden way to exit this life, especially for a thirty-three-year-old healthy male. It was a shock to the system, a yanking from the real world to the great beyond in a split second. Maybe that's why Andrew's spirit hovered over his family from the day he was physically taken from them. Two and a half years ago.

Andrew originally returned for revenge, prodding his estranged older brother Nick to go after his killer. An award-winning investigative reporter and author of six best-selling suspense novels, Nick McDeare was the right man for the job. But Andrew's manipulation didn't stop there. He also orchestrated his brother falling hard for Andrew's widow Jessie. No easy feat for a confirmed bachelor like Nick, but all too easy when a gem like Jessie was involved. Andrew wanted Jessie and their young son Anthony protected and loved. And despite Nick's checkered past with the ladies, he could fill his brother's shoes in a way no other man could.

After achieving his goals, Andrew assumed his time tethered to earth had drawn to a close. Yet here he still was. He could no longer communicate with his family in dreams, his usual MO. The rules had changed, and so must his methods. He had to find new ways to get through to people. And this time he'd use his considerable acting skills. He would impersonate a man he knew well. He had the man's voice down, and he knew his history with Nick. It would be a challenge, but Andrew was confident he could pull it off. After all, dead or alive, he was Andrew Brady, Broadway star. And he had the Tony Award to prove it.

This time there were several items on his to-do list.

And he knew exactly where to begin.

Katrina 'Kat' Gillingham.

*

Lake Placid, New York

Kat was scared. She'd never been afraid of anything in all of her twelve years. She and her mom Olivia were the Dynamic Duo, facing the world fiercely, bravely. But that began to change eight months ago when her mom was diagnosed with cancer.

Cancer. Kat hated the word. It should be written in black ink. It should never be spoken out loud. It should be erased from the dictionary.

Kat stood in the hallway outside her mom's hospital room while the doctor talked to Olivia privately. Rosie, her mom's best friend, leaned against the wall, a protective arm around Kat, looking just as frightened.

Kat hated hospitals. She hated the smell of vinegar and disinfectant, the metallic clicks and beeps of machines, the cold sterility of the walls and floors. Her mom didn't deserve this. She didn't deserve to lose her beautiful blond hair because of 'treatments.' She didn't belong here with all these sick people, with all the tubes in her arms and the nurses calling her 'dear,' treating Olivia like a helpless child. Kat's mom was tough and funny and—

The doctor appeared. "You can go in. But not for long. She needs rest."

Kat flew to her mother's side and took her hand, Rosie on her heels.

"What ... what did the doctor say?" Rosie murmured.

Olivia stared at the ceiling. "Not good news." She swallowed with difficulty, a tear splashing onto her cheek.

Kat had trouble finding her voice. "What do you mean?"

Olivia's eyes slid to Rosie. A silent communication passed between them.

"Tell me the truth, Mom. You've always been honest with me."

Olivia continued to stare at her friend. "Time is short, Rosie. Send the letter I gave you to Nick McDeare."

"Who's Nick McDeare?" Kat squeaked, terror consuming her.

Olivia licked her cracked lips and tried to squeeze her daughter's hand. "Your father."

*

Late that night Kat researched Nick McDeare on her laptop. It was a welcome diversion from the grief threatening to choke her. Her mom was going to—No. She wouldn't think about it. The doctors were wrong. They had to be. Everything would be fine. Life would continue as usual.

Kat shivered and tried to shake the feeling she was being watched. She gave the room a quick scan. Nothing. Of course.

Back to this man who was supposed to be her father. Why did her mom hide him from Kat all these years? She asked Rosie this question when they returned from the hospital. Between bouts of tears, Rosie explained that Olivia had indulged in an affair with Nick McDeare after losing her husband in a car accident. It wasn't a serious relationship, just something to drown out her grief. That's all Olivia told Rosie. Nothing, really.

So Kat decided to do a little detective work on her own.

Nick McDeare must be a real loser.

She froze, catching movement in her peripheral vision.

Kat peeked over her shoulder.

The rocker was swaying.

*

Nick McDeare stared at the bedside clock. Three AM. Why was he still awake? He looked over at his wife, Jessie, who had drifted off hours ago. Flaxen hair. Alabaster skin. Pale lashes dusting her chiseled cheeks. Her measured breathing filled the silence of their darkened bedroom. That, and the snores of Hamlet, the Siamese cat stretched between them.

For hours Nick had stared at the ceiling, flipping from side to side and punching the pillow. Occasionally the cat opened one turquoise eye and gave him the feline glare. Nick glared back.

This was ridiculous. Throwing the covers back he paced to the window, staring out at New York City.

Even the city that never slept was quiet at this hour. The brownstones lining East Seventy-Fifth Street were dark, the sidewalks deserted. A lone cab crept by, looking for a stray passenger. Rain splashed against the window, dampening Nick's spirits even more. If only he could shake this sense of … what? He couldn't even describe his anxiety.

Nick had every reason in the world to be happy. He had a beautiful, talented, loving wife. An eight-year-old son he adored. A successful and celebrated career. The dark days were over, thank God. There would be nothing but sunny times ahead. Finally.

Yet Nick felt a groundswell. A shaking to his core. He had learned the hard way to listen to his gut.

Something was building all around him. Massive change was coming.

And Nick knew he was in the bullseye.

CHAPTER 1

Three Weeks Later

Sunday in New York City. A day of lingering over the *Times*, eating a sumptuous breakfast, watching a game on TV and sitting down to a traditional Sunday dinner. Nick McDeare had done most of those things, but his heart wasn't in any of it.

He sat in front of his laptop in his second-floor home office, his manuscript forgotten, staring out the back window of the East Seventy-Fifth Street brownstone. His home now. At one time his brother's home. His murdered brother, Andrew. The family home of Nick's wife, Jessie. Formerly Andrew's wife.

To the outside world it looked like Nick stole his dead brother's life. Which couldn't be further from the truth. Nick and Jessie were pushed together by Andrew's industrious spirit, a ghost who showed up in Nick's dreams, as real as if his death had been a prank. If that didn't sound crazy enough, Andrew guided Nick to his killer.

A cardinal landed on the windowsill, peering in at Nick. What was it they said about a lone cardinal? Wasn't it supposed to be the spirit of a loved one checking up on you? Snatching a leaf on the slate sill, the bird flew off. Probably building a nest. Couldn't care less about Nick. So much for that theory.

Autumn had come early to the city. It was only mid-September, but the leaves were already crimson and pumpkin. The air was crisp, a relief after the humidity of summer in the concrete metropolis. Nick was grateful for the splash of nature in the brownstone's back yard.

His focus drifted down to a framed photo on his desk. His adopted eight-year-old son, Anthony. Jessie and Andrew's son. With his dark hair, Anthony looked enough like Nick to be his legitimate offspring. The boy's piercing blue eyes were pure Jessie, however. Nick's eyes were unique. Large, amber and drooping at the outer

1

corners. Exactly like Andrew's eyes. It was what told the world they were brothers, despite being raised separately as children.

Nick's gaze shifted to another brownstone abutting the back yard. The dark windows of the ground floor apartment gnawed at Nick's gut. Its tenant, Lt. Lyle Barton, NYPD, had been killed in the line of duty last January as Nick had watched. Killed by a monster, Gianni Fosselli, who had made all their lives a nightmare. Killed while rescuing Anthony from the madman's clutches. Nick had immediately avenged both Lyle's death and Andrew's murder with a single bullet to Gianni's heart. If Fosselli even had a heart.

Hamlet, the Siamese cat, stretched across the back of his desk. Nick absently gave him a few strokes, eliciting a jealous whimper from the dog at his feet. Monty, a black Portuguese water dog, was theoretically Anthony's dog, but with the boy spending the weekend at his friend Zane's house, the dog had attached himself to Nick. Hamlet hissed at the canine interloper. The cat hated the dog. Monty, however, loved the cat, thinking of Hamlet as his personal chew toy.

Nick ran his fingers through his thick dark hair, tendrils spiking back onto his forehead. Frustrated, he forced himself to concentrate on his manuscript, almost finished. A Pulitzer Prize winning investigative reporter, Nick had written six best-selling suspense novels. This one, *THE SILVER LINING,* was to be his finest, a tribute to Lyle. The only true friend Nick ever had. It should be a joy to finish, the story already laid out by cold hard facts. Yet Nick was losing his passion for it. He'd rather have Lyle here with him, the two of them chasing down their latest target, searching for clues, brainstorming. The thrill of the hunt. And the satisfaction of getting their man. Nick had worked alone in his early investigative work. Until Lyle. Together, they were unstoppable. Now he was alone again.

A swooshing sound made him jump. Nick spun around, scanning the room with a professional eye. His stack of unopened mail had fallen to the floor from its cubbyhole by the door. He glanced at the cat and the dog, still in place, staring at the mail. Hamlet's whiskers were taut with tension, his fawn-colored fur forming a mohawk down his back. Monty's jowls were curled, a low growl rumbling from deep inside him. What the hell?

Nick approached the scattered envelopes on the polished wooden floor. Glancing around, he spotted a heating vent directly above him. That must have caused it. The furnace kicked on, trying to chase the chill from the old house, and blew the mail to the floor.

He picked up the stack and returned to his desk. He couldn't remember the last time he opened his mail. Weeks, probably. Not much of it made it to his office, most of it filtered first by his agent and then by Mary, their housekeeper. Housekeeper? That was a joke. Mary was mother to them all and ran the house.

One letter caught his eye. The return address was Lake Placid. At one time Nick spent time up there, working a case.

He ripped it open. A photograph of a young girl was tucked inside. Staring at the picture, an electric current shot through Nick. He knew what this was about before he even began to read:

Dear Nick,

Maybe you don't remember me. I hope I'm wrong, that I left some sort of lasting impression on you. Just in case you're drawing a complete blank ...

You and I knew each other pretty well many years ago. I was the lead reporter for the local paper here in Lake Placid when you came to town to investigate two brutal murders. We had a good time together, you found our killer, and then you left, both of us content. I wanted nothing from you but some great sex and to maybe learn a little from a master sleuth. Ah, the best laid plans ...

I'll get to the point. Our fling produced a child. At first, I planned on having an abortion, but I quickly changed my mind. If you recall, I'd lost my husband in a car accident the previous year, my parents were dead, I had no siblings, no family at all. I always wanted a baby, but my husband had been sterile. The idea of finally having a child to raise appealed to me, and I wanted to do it on my own. I had a good job, lived in a small town, a great environment for children.

I didn't tell you about our daughter because, well, I didn't want to trap you into something you never asked for and probably wouldn't want. You told me you had a son from your first marriage, and I thought the last thing you needed was some surprise offspring from a quickie affair. If I was wrong, I apologize. Katrina and I have had a good life. I told her that her father was a good man who passed through town, and I never saw him again. When she asked for a name, I told her I couldn't remember. It's the only time I ever lied to my daughter, but I didn't want her showing up on your doorstep unannounced one day. Now here I am doing it for her.

If you're reading this letter it means my health has taken a downward turn, and I don't have long. I'm writing this while I'm still able to, and my friend, Rosie, will hang onto it and eventually see that you get it. You see, I have breast cancer, and my doctor fears it's spread to my lymph nodes. Which means Kat will need a home. Rosie can't take her in. She cares for her elderly mother who has Alzheimer's, and she's a single parent with six children of her own. So you're my only option. More importantly, I believe children belong with family.

I've kept up with you over the years, relatively easy with how much press you get. I know you lost your son a few years back to leukemia. I'm so sorry, Nick. Death can be vicious. But let me congratulate you on your recent marriage. I've always been a fan of Jessica Kendle. She's an amazing talent. I saw her on Broadway in a fabulous musical with her husband shortly before he was killed. I wish Kat could have seen the two of them, Andrew being her secret uncle, but I had to leave her at home. My trip was mostly business.

Your taking in Kat may not be the best idea for a newlywed, and if it's impossible please be honest with me. If you don't want her but take her anyway, she'll know it. She's smart and intuitive. I'd rather she took her chances with a foster home that truly welcomed her than feel she was in the way with you.

Katrina just turned twelve. She's a straight-A student, talented in the arts – she's studied ballet, voice and piano for years - but her dream is to be a writer and/or a journalist. I guess she takes after both of us. She has a natural curiosity and a surprising command of the language at such a tender age. Kat's an extraordinary girl, and that's not just motherly pride speaking.

I've enclosed a recent picture of her, along with relevant phone numbers to reach me or Rosie. As you can see, Kat looks very much like you, but you still might want to have a paternity test done for legal reasons that could crop up down the road.

This is the last thing I ever thought would happen. I expected Kat and I would live out our lives in cozy Lake Placid, very content. But life has a way of kicking you in the gut, doesn't it? How does that John Lennon lyric go? "Life is what happens while you're busy making other plans."

No matter what, I wish you nothing but the best. May your life be filled with happiness and laughter whether Kat is a part of it or not ...

Olivia Gillingham

Nick turned his attention back to the photo. The girl had shoulder-length sandy hair, a strong nose, a radiant smile ... and large amber eyes that drooped at the corners.

Nick's eyes.

His instincts told him to run. As fast and as far as he could get from Kat Gillingham.

*

"I'm going for a run." Nick said to his wife as he came down the back stairs to the large, airy kitchen. Dressed in sweats, Monty on his heels, he grabbed the leash and collar and attached it to the dog. Without another word he headed for the hallway. A moment later, Jessica McDeare heard the front door slam.

Jessie sat at the vast island running down the center of the homey kitchen, making a salad. "Hello to you, too, Nick." Her husband always got like this when he was working against a deadline. His latest novel was due in a matter of weeks.

Nick's dedication to jogging and exercise put Jessie to shame. She should be working out in the fifth-floor gym. Then she dismissed the notion. Starving herself and exercising twenty-four/seven was what she did when she was working. After her big success on Broadway last winter, earning her a second Tony Award, she deserved a break. She wanted nothing more than quality time with her husband of nine months and her son.

Jessie glanced at Mary, who was basting the pork roast. Mary Bodine was a statuesque bronze woman, surrogate mother to them all, the only mother Jessie could really remember. She was tough and sarcastic but also soft-hearted.

The front door slammed again. Mary's nephew Willie appeared in the doorway. An ex-cop, Willie was tall with a muscular build and handsome as hell. He had the same quiet strength and gentle touch Mary exuded. With his eye-catching looks, Jessie felt he could easily be a stand-in for Denzel Washington. Willie was now Nick and Jessie's driver and security guard and was considered family. "Picked up Anthony."

As if on cue the small boy trudged into the room, heading straight for the fridge. He pulled out his favorite power drink. His next stop was the cookie jar.

"Hold it," Mary ordered. "Dinner in an hour."

Sighing dramatically, Anthony headed for the back stairs.

"How was your weekend at Zane's?" Jessie added cucumbers to the greens.

"Great. We went to the movies with Luci."

"Luci? The woman who works in your school cafeteria? How did she end up at Zane's?"

"It was her birthday and she didn't have anyone to spend it with so we invited her. She bought us popcorn and sodas and candy and then Zane's mom invited her for dinner and we played games and laughed so hard—" he paused for a breath "—I want you to invite her for dinner sometime, okay?"

"Uh, sure, I guess so."

Satisfied, Anthony hurtled up the stairs.

Willie backed towards the archway. "Vince just got here, so I'm heading out." He swung into the hallway and disappeared. Vince was their overnight security guard, relieving Willie. The perils of being celebrities in a dangerous world demanded round-the-clock protection.

"Willie seems down." Jessie added shaved parmesan and kalamata olives to the salad. "Everything okay with him, Mary?"

"LeJeane threw him out. After two years. What's wrong with women these days?" A heavy sigh accompanied Mary's disapproval, followed by mumbling under her breath. "She found someone with more credit cards and spare time." More mumbling. "So now he's looking for a place to live. Everything's out of his price range." A shake of the head as she shoved the pan of apples into the oven. "Nick's not in the best of spirits either."

Jessie retied her blond hair into a ponytail. "He's been down for weeks. I thought he was finally coming to terms with losing Lyle, but I guess not."

"That kind of thing comes and goes, honey. You know that better than anyone. Maybe you two should get away. Take that honeymoon you were robbed of. Or go down to your villa in St. John."

"Good idea. We need some time alone. I'll mention it to him."

*

Luci Ruiz hated her job at the Grantham Academy, a private school for the rich and privileged kids of New York City. At forty-five years of age, she deserved better than working in a lunchroom. There was only one bright spot in her entire day. One reason for tolerating this demeaning job.

Anthony.

Luci knew all about Anthony's history. Everyone knew the story. Nick and Jessica McDeare were famous. Their drama was international news. How Jessica had borne a son by Gianni Fosselli. How she kept the truth from both the boy and Gianni, insisting he was Andrew Brady's son. How Gianni had taken his revenge when he'd learned the truth, killing Andrew. How Gianni had kidnapped the boy, hiding him away in Ohio. And, finally, how Andrew's brother Nick had interceded and put Gianni Fosselli in his own early grave. McDeare had then adopted Anthony, giving the boy his name.

The details made Luci sick. Anthony was such a sweet boy and deserved better parents. He needed people who loved him and would protect him from the glaring publicity. Luci saw how the other kids taunted Anthony because of his notorious parents. Nick McDeare had a reputation that would make a whore blush.

So Luci took a special interest in Anthony. She brought him treats and showered him with praise. Having almost no family of her own, she centered her world around the boy, their relationship the only bright spot in her dismal existence.

She had plans for Anthony. Big plans.

*

Nick nodded to Vince, their nighttime security guard, sitting in his parked car in front of the brownstone. Stretching his legs, Nick set off across East Seventy-Fifth Street. His mind was reeling, and a jog usually organized his thoughts. At Fifth Avenue he weaved his way across the busy street. Taxis honked. Buses belched their noxious

7

fumes. Monty seemed oblivious to the chaos, happy to be outside and getting exercise.

Entering Central Park, Nick picked up speed, the images in his brain a staccato beat keeping pace with him. Kat. A daughter. He had a daughter. Her eyes. His eyes. That distinguishing trait. Her mother. Olivia. Not the usual clinging vine Nick romanced. Olivia was tough. Smart. Independent. She didn't fall for his one-liners. Threw his flattery back in his face. Laughed at his chicanery. Nick enjoyed their time together. If she hadn't been planted in Lake Placid their relationship might have gone somewhere. Nick chuckled. Who was he kidding? A lasting relationship wasn't on his dance card after his first marriage failed. Until he met Jessie."

Dear God, Jessie! How would she feel about Kat? Would she be able to mother a young girl who was the offspring of one of Nick's affairs?

Nick blew out a breath and pumped his legs harder, trying to pound the images from his mind. He circled the Reservoir and turned back towards home, Monty trotting at his side. Still, the young girl beckoned to him.

Halting, Nick bent over, breathing hard. It was no use. He couldn't wish Kat away, no matter how hard he tried.

He pulled out his phone and speed-dialed his attorney.

*

Lake Placid, New York

Kat sat up and blew her nose. Rosie's couch was lumpy, not ideal for a substitute bed. But her own bed, her own house, was already cleaned out and packed up with a 'For Sale' sign out front. This image brought on a fresh round of tears. She was an orphan without a home. She was also becoming a cry-baby, someone she loathed. But she couldn't stop the waterworks. She missed her mom.

The day had been a living hell. She suffered through her mother's funeral that morning, followed by a houseful of acquaintances at Rosie's. Most were from her mom's newspaper, people she didn't know well or like. People who said all the wrong things.

"Your mother will always be with you, Kat, in your heart."

I don't want her in my heart. I want her by my side.

"You must be excited about finally meeting your dad."

I'm not.

8

"Who is he, by the way?"

Wouldn't you like to know, you old motormouth!

"At least you won't have to worry about money. That house will go for a fortune, being right on the lake. I heard someone already made an offer."

I don't want the money. I want my mom.

"Rosie didn't mention your dad's name. Do I know him?"

From what I've read, everybody knows him. Except me.

"Your mama was so proud of you. She loved you so much."

I want my mom!

"Why haven't you met this man before? Where does he live?"

In a land far, far away. Why don't you all just leave me alone?

The infamous Nick McDeare, the mystery man who was the talk of the funeral, called Rosie last night. Unbelievable timing. He got the letter and wanted to have a paternity test done. Which meant tomorrow Kat was having blood drawn. She hated needles and she hated hospitals and she hated Nick McDeare.

Kat begged Rosie to let her live with her. She wouldn't be any trouble. She'd help with Rosie's kids. She'd give Rosie all the money coming to her, money she didn't want.

Rosie said no. She belonged with her dad now. It was what her mother wanted.

Kat added Rosie to her hate-list.

Sniffling, she slumped against the pillow, exhaustion finally overtaking grief. As sleep descended, a comforting hand stroked her hair.

Kat jerked awake and glanced around. Someone had touched her hair.

But she was alone.

She would always be alone.

Welcome to your new life, Kat.

*

Ten Days Later

"There's something I have to tell you, Jess."

Jessie froze. Those words usually meant trouble. "I thought we agreed. No more secrets."

"It's not a secret." Nick filled their snifters with brandy. They sat across from each other in the kitchen's breakfast nook, the others in bed. It was becoming their nightly ritual, this special time together when the house was silent. "I just didn't want to discuss it until I was sure."

"Sure about what?" He wouldn't look at her. "You're scaring me, Nick."

"I'm sorry. I don't mean to." He blew out a breath. Whatever it was, it was obviously eating away at him. Which caused Jessie's fear level to rise. "A couple weeks ago I got a letter from … a former lover of mine." He tugged a folded envelope from his pocket and handed it to her. "Read this. It explains things better than I can."

Swallowing hard, Jessie opened the letter and read.

There it was. Her greatest fear. Nick had a daughter. A child conceived during his wild years of catting around. Before Jessie met him. Before they fell in love.

"Olivia died a couple weeks ago." He pulled out a photo and slid it across the table.

Jessie stared at the picture of Katrina. The girl was the image of Nick. Her eyes. Her nose. The long cheekbones. The dimple in her chin. But she had Andrew's fair hair and skin tone.

Nick took a gulp of brandy. "The paternity test came back this morning. Kat's mine. I knew she would be."

Jessie felt like she was free-falling. She couldn't take her eyes off the photo.

"With her mother dead," Nick continued, "she doesn't have anyone but me." He stared at her, waiting for a response. "Jess?"

"So … um … you've decided to take her?"

"I don't think I have a choice." He reached for her hand, rubbing her fingers. "Tell me what you're thinking."

Jessie tried to organize her swirling thoughts. She felt light-headed and nauseous. A twelve-year-old girl. Becoming part of their family. A child Nick created with another woman. "I need to know …how you feel about it, Nick."

He shrugged. "I keep trying to picture it. Another child in this house, a virtual stranger. The question is how do YOU feel about it?"

Suddenly there wasn't enough air in the room. "I don't know … I-I need some time to get used to the idea."

"We don't have much time. I talked to Rosie this morning. She thinks Kat will adjust better if we move quickly. Apparently, she's not doing well."

Jessie pulled her hand away and rubbed her forehead. "But, Nick ... we just got our life back. The whole Gianni Fosselli nightmare is over. We've settled into a healthy routine. Anthony's finally doing well. Gianni put him through so much— My God. Anthony. How will he feel about this? We have to think about him."

Nick nodded. Another slurp of brandy.

"There must be other options for the girl," Jessie pressed. How could there be no one in Kat's life but Nick? A complete stranger?

"I'm Kat's only family."

"There have to be aunts, uncles, cousins. Someone other than you. Do some snooping. You're the famous Nick McDeare, ace investigator."

"I did. Olivia was the only child of deceased parents. Who had no siblings. There's no one, Jess."

This couldn't be happening. Not after everything they'd been through. "Why does something always ruin things when we finally have smooth sailing?"

"Ruin things? Is that what you think this girl will do?"

"I don't know what I think." Her voice, along with her frustration, rose. Her stomach threatened to rebel. Nick's past had dropped a bomb on their lives. "I knew it. I just knew it." she said, mostly to herself. "This was bound to happen. I wonder what other wives do when their husbands spring their illegitimate offspring on them?"

"Stop it, Jessie. You knew my history from the beginning."

She didn't want to stop it. She wanted the whole problem to go away. "You had to figure a child was going to turn up on your doorstep one day, Nick. You can't screw around for a decade and not expect to pay for it. The world doesn't work that way."

He sat back and glared at her. "Well, you're certainly the expert on the subject. You screwed around with Gianni and got pregnant. If Andrew hadn't come to your rescue and raised Anthony as his own, you would have been in the same situation as Olivia and Kat. At least Kat is legitimately mine."

"Why are you attacking Andrew? He didn't do anything wrong."

"Of course he didn't." His tone was sarcastic. "Andrew's always the saint. I'm always the sinner."

"In this case? Yes."

11

Jessie could see Nick's anger. He started to rise, his movement awkward, his arm knocking over the decanter of brandy. The amber liquid spilled into her lap.

Jessie surveyed the mess and shook her head in disgust. "Great. Just great." Feeling like she was going to be sick, Jessie fled for the stairs and their bedroom.

CHAPTER 2

Nick grabbed some towels and mopped up the brandy. What in the hell just happened?

Something had hit his elbow, jerking his arm forward, resulting in the spilled brandy. Or was it a muscle spasm? It damned well didn't feel like one.

After washing down the table and floor, he headed up to the master bedroom. Jessie was in the bathroom, the door closed. He wrapped his knuckles on the door. "Jess?" Was she sick? He heard coughing. "Jess, you okay?"

She emerged, a robe wrapped around her, a towel pressed to her lips.

Nick took her hand, leading her to the bed. He dropped down beside her. "I'm sorry, honey. About all of this."

"And I'm sorry for the awful things I said. It just came spewing out of me. I couldn't stop it." She turned to Nick. "We both made mistakes in the past. Beating each other up about it only makes it worse. Our situation is what it is. We can't change things now. So no more dredging up ancient history. I promise if you promise."

"Promise." He lifted her chin and traced her lips with his thumb. "Maybe bringing Kat here isn't a good idea."

"What choice do we have? You said it yourself." Her eyes bore into his. If only he could disappear inside those two pools of crystal blue water and shut out the world. "That letter said Kat would go into the foster system if you don't take her. I know what that's like, Nick. Andrew was going into the system if Dad didn't take him in when your mom died. He was twelve, exactly Kat's age. You were lucky to be adopted at birth by loving parents."

Lucky? If my mother hadn't been forced to give me up when I was born, Andrew and I would have grown up together. Jessie's dad

13

would have taken us both in. Instead, we were raised separately, only reconnecting shortly before Andrew was murdered. We were robbed of so many years together.

"Dad and I checked out the foster system," Jessie continued. "It's awful. Kat could end up living in a house with ten other kids. She could slip through the cracks. Do you want to be responsible for that?"

He didn't. It would gnaw at him for the rest of his life. "So we take her?"

*

Jessie paced to the front windows. How could she deny Nick his daughter? If Anthony were taken from her, she'd want to die. Parents and children. A bond like no other. Nick had already lost one child, his son from his first marriage. Jeffrey had died of leukemia at the young age of ten. That loss nearly destroyed Nick. Now he had a second chance. With a daughter.

Nick sidled up to her. "What do you want me to do, Jess?"

She looked up at him. In the dim light from the streetlamps she could see he was masking his feelings. Nick McDeare, former loner, still found it hard to bare his soul, even to his wife.

"It won't be easy for her – or for us – if we take her in," Jessie began. "I remember what I was like at twelve. A monster. Hormones raging. Wanting to be treated like an adult but technically still a kid. And this girl will have anger issues. She just lost her mother. She'll want to blame someone." She ran her hand up his chest. "She'll probably resent the hell out of you, feeling like you abandoned both her and her mother. Can you handle that?"

Nick nodded, but he didn't look happy about it.

If anyone would understand how Kat felt, it was Nick. After a lifetime of bitterness towards Chelsea, his birth mother, Nick finally forgave her when he learned the truth: she regretted giving him up and searched for him until the day she died. But Jessie sensed Nick still had lingering anger, despite being adopted by good parents. Would Kat be the same way?

She brushed a lock of hair from Nick's forehead and ran her hand down his cheek, the bristle not unpleasant. Pressing her lips to his, she kissed him. He tasted of brandy, and his skin carried the scent of musk. He oozed rugged masculinity with a hint of vulnerability. It sucked Jessie in every time. "Call Rosie," she whispered. "Say yes. We'll make it work."

14

"You're sure?"

She nodded. "She's your daughter, Nick. She belongs with you. With us. Tomorrow I'll tell Mary, and you tell Anthony. You're best with him one-on-one. Then go get the girl."

He pulled her close, his hands circling her waist and sliding further down. "I love you, Jess." He kissed her with passion, sparking a familiar tingle.

After lighting the logs in the brass grate, they kindled a different fire in the big bed, disappearing inside each other.

*

"So how do you feel about it, Bongo?" Bongo. Nick's pet name for Anthony. Invented by Andrew.

They'd been tossing a football in the backyard for an hour. Now they sat on the back steps, enjoying the bright sunshine on this chilly Sunday morning.

"Well ..." Anthony dropped his head back onto his shoulders and stared up at the sky. "I always wanted a brother or sister."

Good. This was going well so far.

"She'd be my real sister?"

"Of course."

"But you adopted me."

"And that made me your father." Nick stretched his long legs out in front of him and leaned his elbows back on the stairs. "Kat is my daughter from a former relationship. You're my son from my relationship with your mom. You're both my kids. So that makes you sister and brother."

Nick could see Anthony's brain computing the words. "Got it." The boy imitated Nick's pose, which always amused him. "I got a couple questions."

"Shoot."

"How does Mom feel about it?"

Smart kid. "She's okay with it. She's more concerned about how you feel."

"So if I'm good with it, she is, too?"

Nick nodded. "What else?"

"Well, um ... will this change things with you and me?"

"What do you mean?"

"I'll have to share you with Kat – that's her name, right?" Again, Nick nodded. "Will you still have time for me?"

Nick straightened up. "Anthony, that won't ever change. Ever. I love my time with you. We'll still work on your photography. And baseball and football. And piano. That's a promise. You know I never break a promise. But," Nick paused, choosing his words carefully, "I'll spend time with Kat, too. Just the two of us. And there will be things the three of us share, and things the two of you share that don't involve your mom or me. That's the way a family works."

"We'll still be a family? Even though we come from different places?"

"Families have all kinds of definitions." Nick sat forward and clasped his hands. "So. Are you good with this? Any more questions?"

Anthony looked down at his own stubby hands, twirling a special ring around on his finger. A ring that had belonged to Nick's son Jeffrey. Nick loved how much it meant to Anthony.

A grin broke across Anthony's face. "When will she get here?"

Nick gave his son a bear hug, both laughing. "A couple days. I'm flying up to Lake Placid to get her tomorrow."

*

Every Monday five women arrived to clean the brownstone under Mary's direction. Today the third-floor bedrooms would get special attention, and Jessie was in charge. She was giving one of the large front rooms to Kat.

Nick left around noon for Lake Placid. He'd stay overnight, returning tomorrow with Kat. He asked Jessie to go with him, but she thought Kat should get to know her father a bit before she met the rest of the family.

Poor Nick. He looked nervous as hell.

Jessie spent the day focused on getting things ready for Kat's arrival. When the doorbell rang repeatedly late that afternoon, she dropped everything and hurried downstairs. Someone was incredibly impatient. Maybe Nick changed his mind and came back today. In any case, why not use his key?

Swinging the massive door open she got the surprise of her life.

Her old pal Abigail Forrester pushed past her. "Thank God I'm finally safe!"

*

Luci Ruiz stacked the trays on the cafeteria line. Scanning the lunchroom for Anthony, she spotted him sitting with his friend Zane.

Reaching under the counter for the strawberry tart she baked last night, Luci approached the boys' table.

"... and she'll be here tomorrow, Zane. A sister. I have a sister!"

Luci halted at Anthony's words. Her jaw dropped.

"Are you nervous about meeting her?" Zane was eating an apple.

"Hi, Luci." Anthony took another bite of his sandwich. "What's wrong?"

"... Nothing. Did you say ... you have a sister?"

"Yeah. She's my dad's from a long time ago."

Luci swallowed her bile. Nicholas McDeare was a degenerate. But to bring one of his bastard children to live with sweet, innocent Anthony was too much.

*

Nick pulled the rented SUV in front of a bungalow on the outskirts of Lake Placid. The house was small but tidy. Geraniums bloomed in decorative pots. Shrubbery hugged the perimeter. The paint looked fresh. The shutters, clean.

Nick had borrowed Bill Rudolph's private jet and pilot for the one-hour trip. Bill was a well-known Broadway producer and close friend of the McDeares.

Taking a deep breath, Nick approached the front door. Before he could knock, it swung open. A pretty woman with auburn hair and dark green eyes greeted him, a young child in her arms. "Mr. McDeare? I'm Rosie. Come in."

"Thank you." Nick stepped inside, surveying the tiny living room. Another child jumped up and down in a playpen. An elderly woman sat in a wheelchair, a tray table beside her, staring at the TV.

"This is my mother," Rosie said, making the introductions. The older woman didn't seem to hear her daughter. Turning to a young girl framed in the kitchen archway, she announced, "And this is Kat."

Katrina Gillingham stared back at Nick, her mouth a thin straight line. Dressed in an oversized turquoise tunic and black leggings, she was tall for her age, long and lean. Her straight sandy hair brushed her shoulders. Bangs framed her amber eyes. She was striking, the kind of girl who would stand out in a crowd.

"Kat, this is Mr.—this is your father."

Nick smiled at the girl. "Why don't you call me Nick for now?"

A pause. "Hello." Her lips barely moved. No smile. No life in those familiar eyes.

A brick wall would have shown more emotion.

*

A spectator in her own drama, Kat sized up Nick McDeare. He was taller in person than he looked in his photos. And he obviously worked out. Broad shoulders. Dark thick hair, spikes brushing his forehead. Classic bone structure. Small mouth with a dimple in his chin. And his eyes. Kat's eyes. There was something exotic about the man's looks and demeanor. Dads weren't supposed to be exotic. They were supposed to be ordinary, even boring, with a jovial smile and an "aw, shucks," persona. He didn't even dress the part. Dads wore trousers. Tacky golf shirts. Polyester jackets. Nick McDeare wore tight-fitting jeans, a maroon turtle-neck sweater and a black leather jacket.

Rosie had morphed into a gushing, blushing, fawning bundle of chatter in the man's presence. Kat was embarrassed for the woman.

What happened to the no-nonsense adult who told me I'd have to go live with strangers?

Rosie prattled on about Kat, her intelligence, her ballet, her piano lessons, her literary prizes, what she liked to eat, her exercise routine, even her childhood illnesses.

A test will follow. A failing grade means I get to stay here.

"And over here is what she wants to take with her. The things she's keeping from the house are in storage. The attorney will give you the key and code."

I'm not a baby. I can take care of my own things.

"The attorney, Mr. Lublow, is expecting you. There are papers to sign. Also financial arrangements to be made. The house sold a week ago, and Mr. Lublow has set up a trust for Kat. Here's his address."

"Thank you." Nick McDeare flashed a dazzling smile. Rosie melted under the man's gaze.

What an operator. Nick McDeare knows how to turn on the charm.

"What time is your flight?" Rosie asked.

"It's a private plane. We're not leaving until tomorrow."

A private plane? And why tomorrow?

"We'll be at the Mirror Lake Inn tonight."

"Wow, fancy! Aren't you lucky, Kat?"

Daddy Warbucks was showing off. She wouldn't give him the satisfaction of being impressed.

"Better than sleeping on my couch again."

Please shut up, Rosie.

"You're very quiet, Kat," the man said.

She shrugged. She wasn't about to welcome this man into her life with open arms, no questions asked. An absentee father who suddenly materialized, who decided it might be a hoot to have a daughter for a while? Like a stray puppy from the pound.

No. He'd have to earn her respect first.

If that was even possible.

*

"I had to get out of L.A. fast," Abbie explained to Jessie. Needing a drink, she hurried to the study, pouring an oversized Sherry. Flipping a hand through her mane of mahogany hair, she took a gulp and plopped down on the couch. "I packed so fast I'm not even sure what clothes I brought."

"What's going on, Abbie? You weren't supposed to be back until February at the earliest." Jessie poured her own Sherry and sank into Mary's recliner.

"That's how long I figured the job would take. But it fell apart yesterday."

"You look crazed. And destitute. I've never seen you travel in rags before."

"That's how panicked I was." Jessie was right. Abbie was usually a fashionista. "This is what I was wearing when he discovered I was a private investigator."

"Who discovered?"

"Joey." Abbie leapt up, pacing. "I was a fool to get involved with him. And I fell hard, Jessie. Damn my affliction for Italian men. He's the last, I swear!"

Mary appeared in the doorway. "Abbie! Good Lord, girl, what are you doing back?"

"Sit down, and I'll tell you both what happened."

"I will. As soon as Jessie gets out of my chair."

*

Nick transferred Kat's suitcases and boxes to the back of the SUV while the girl said goodbye to Rosie. When she joined Nick in the front seat she looked like she'd been crying.

"You okay?"

She nodded, reaching into her shoulder bag for a tissue.

Nick started the ignition. "We'll stop at the attorney's office first. Then maybe there's somewhere you'd like to go before we head to the hotel?"

Kat shook her head.

She was too quiet. Nick fished for something to say that would crack the wall of ice between them. He turned to face her. "I know this is hard for you. It's not easy for me either. We're family ... but we're strangers."

She remained silent. Then ... "Why are we staying at the hotel tonight? Why not just go straight to New York?"

"I thought we should spend some time together, just you and me, before you meet the rest of the family. I thought it might make it easier for you."

"Easier?" She snorted and looked out the side window. "You have no idea."

He turned off the car. "You think I don't know how you feel? How alone? What it's like to--" Damn. He took a deep breath. Stay calm, he reminded himself. Just stay calm. "Look, I realize you don't know anything about me yet---"

"Wrong. I know everything about you," she mumbled.

"Really?" he asked sarcastically. "How? We just met."

"The internet. It loves you."

So she'd researched him. Of course. She was curious. But the internet had a vulgar habit of trashing his history. "Don't believe everything you read."

"I know how to sort fact from fiction."

Was this girl really only twelve? Thirty-year-old women didn't have her command of the language. He folded his arms. "Go ahead then. Tell me."

"What?"

"The facts. About me. Just the facts."

She crossed her arms, a mirror image of him. "Okay ... You were adopted by an Air Force surgeon, an admiral, and his wealthy wife. You grew up all over Europe and the Far East, living in mansions and going to the best schools. Your adoption separated you from your biological brother, Andrew Brady, for most of your life." She looked over at Nick. "Would you like more?"

"Please."

"You've been married twice, first to a woman named," she scrunched her face, trying to remember, "Lyndsay. One son, Jeffrey, who died of leukemia when he was ten. You weren't around much during his illness and it destroyed your marriage. You've dated every famous model, actress, beauty queen, waitress or … well, just about every woman you met. Then you married Andrew's wife, Jessica, and adopted her son, Anthony. Anthony is really the son of Gianni Fosselli, someone Jessica had an affair with. Andrew pretended Anthony was his son—"

"Enough."

"Am I wrong?"

She wasn't wrong. But she was twisting the truth. And she was cold. Almost mean. He'd heard enough.

A noise in the back seat jolted them both. Nick looked over his shoulder. His overnight bag had fallen to the floor. On it's own. The SUV hadn't moved.

"That's weird." Kat glanced at Nick.

He agreed. Weird. Like the brandy spilling the other night.

"Let's go."

*

"Well," Abbie began, drawing out the suspense. Where should she begin? She couldn't disappoint her captive audience. Jessie and Mary knew why she went back to California. Her Uncle Pete needed her on an important case. Pete had trained Abbie as a private investigator three years ago. She'd learned enough to return to New York and help Nick and Lyle Barton capture Gianni Fosselli, Andrew's killer. Andrew had been her bestie since they were small kids. So when Pete called, Abbie moved. She owed him everything.

"Do you need an overture to start playing?" Mary's sarcasm drew a scowl from Abbie.

"Always the drama queen," Jessie teased.

"Look who's talking!" Abbie took a gulp of Sherry. "Okay. The guy I was investigating killed his wife Dora and got away with it. And he's a cop. A detective."

"Oh my God, Abbie, that's dangerous." Jessie, queen of the understatement.

"No shit, Sherlock. Anyway, I look a lot like his wife. The type he's attracted to. So my uncle planted me in a bar that Joey frequents after hours."

"Joey?" Jessie's eyebrows shot up. "Doesn't sound Italian, your usual Romeo of choice."

"Joseph Evenatti. I told you he was Italian ten minutes ago. Weren't you listening?" Abbie rolled her eyes. "Why do I waste my breath? I swear I'm done with the Meatball Brigade. Never again. Never! Not after this."

"Focus, Abbie. Focus. Tell us what happened."

"Well, of course he took the bait. I'm the best at reeling in a fish. We dated, got close. You know. The usual. I started staying at his place, which gave me opportunity to search for clues."

"Didn't you learn anything from your experience with Gianni?" Jessie shrieked.

"Look, I do what I have to do. Anyway, I'd search when he was working. But he surprised me last night and came home early. Found me going through his stuff."

Abbie's cell rang. A number she didn't recognize.

*

Kat trailed behind Nick as he checked them into the Mirror Lake Inn. Everyone in the lobby, particularly the women, gawked as they passed by. Moses McDeare parting the seas.

The pudgy girl behind the desk appeared flustered to be in Nick's presence. "I-I have your reservation right here. I just need a credit card."

Flashing that masterful smile, the idol obliged.

"We're THRILLED to have you staying with us, Mr. McDeare. You have the BEST of our family suites with a STUNNING view of the lake and mountains. And your dinner reservation is all set." Dragging her eyes away from Nick, she studied Kat. "This must be your daughter. She looks like you. Hello, Sweetie." Her voice dripped with condescension.

Without a word Nick turned on his heel and strode to the elevators. Kat sprinted after him. They rode up in silence. Nick's sudden anger squashed any conversation.

Their two-bedroom suite was on the top floor. Kat deposited her bag in one of the rooms and slumped down on the old-fashioned four-poster bed. She wasn't used to this kind of luxury. Moving to the window she looked out at her hometown. That silly woman was right. The view was spectacular. The sun hung low over the Adirondacks, a blanket of lavender velvet as far as the eye could see. The fading light turned the lake below a deep blue, a spray of dancing diamonds on its surface.

Kat shivered. The room was unusually cold.

A circle of fog appeared on the window glass, spreading outward. Condensation on the outside? She touched it lightly. It was inside.

The circle continued to move. Expanding and contracting. Expanding and contracting … as if someone were breathing on the glass.

Kat instinctively backed up.

"Ready for dinner?" Nick's voice made her jump.

*

Abbie stared at her phone, waiting for the call to go to voice mail. She never answered a call from a number she didn't recognize.

No message. Hmm.

"Is there anything to eat?" Abbie headed for the kitchen. "I'm starving."

Monty bounded down the stairs, greeting Abbie with a sloppy lick of her hand. "Hey, buddy, I was wondering where you were. You want food, too, right?"

Jessie had followed her to the kitchen. "Abbie, I'll try again. Focus. What happened when Joey found you going through his things?"

Abbie grabbed some brie from the fridge and went to the pantry for crackers.

"Hold it right there." Mary could move like a roadrunner when she wanted to. "Give me that cheese." She snatched it from Abbie's hand. "It's for Kat."

"Who?" Abbie got a knife from the drawer and sliced off some ham from a roast on top of the stove. She tossed Monty a sliver.

"Kat," Jessie said. "Nick's daughter."

Abbie spun around, stunned. "What???"

"Dammit, Abbie, I'll tell you about Kat after you tell us the rest of your story. You're A.D.D. is getting worse."

"I do not have Attention Deficit Disorder!"

"My brain is short-circuiting from your verbal U-turns."

23

Abbie took a bite of ham. "Okay, okay. Ooh, this ham is delicious, Mary."

Mary looked at Jessie and rolled her eyes. "No A.D.D. huh?"

"Well ..." Abbie admitted, "Maybe when I'm tired, okay?

Her cell rang again. Same number. Abbie pushed IGNORE and shoved the phone into her pocket. "So. Where was I? Oh, right. When Joey caught me, I made up an excuse, a damned good one, but he didn't believe me. He grabbed my purse, went through my wallet and found my PI license. Things got ugly. Fast. He slammed me against the wall and was choking me. He was cursing and threatening to kill me. Honest to God, I thought I was going to die, Jess. He was too strong for me. I finally managed to knee him and got the hell out of there. Broke all speed limits. Which means nothing in California. I thought I was home free until I realized he followed me. I was terrified. I couldn't go to the cops. He was one of them. So I went to my uncle's who met him at the door with a shotgun."

"You have to give up your PI work, Abbie. I wish Nick would give it up, too. It's too dangerous. I worry about you both."

"Oh yeah, I'm done. Which means back to lipstick modeling." She waved a hand, dismissing the subject. "Anyway, Uncle Pete snuck me out the back door and put me on the red-eye to New York immediately."

"How do you know this ... Joey ... didn't follow you?"

"I don't."

"Great." Mary shook her head. "Now we're all in danger."

Abbie's cell shrilled again. She clicked on, waiting in silence. Nothing. The caller hung up.

CHAPTER 3

The Taste Bistro of Mirror Lake Inn was high-brow and definitely not Kat's taste. They were led to a table by a hostess who swished her butt, bounced her boobs and flicked her mane of fried peroxide hair. File the woman under 'overkill.' Once again Nick drew everyone's focus. "Wait a minute." Nick halted.

"Yes?" Betty Boop brushed her chunky monkeys against him. This was getting embarrassing.

"Is there a table that's a little more private?"

A cheesy smile parted her red lips. "Of course, Mr. McDeare. Follow me." The vaudeville act resumed, ending at a table partially obscured by foliage. Nick sat down, his back to the room. The woman sashayed away.

Kat cleared her throat. "Am I ruining your reputation?" It was obvious Nick didn't want to be seen with her.

"Hmm?" Nick's nose was buried in the menu.

"Am I – as they say – cramping your style?"

He looked up, frowning. "What are you talking about?"

"Having a daughter in tow doesn't attract the female population."

"Attract—? Why would I want—? God, kiddo, are you even capable of speaking like a twelve-year-old? Your vocabulary—"

"You didn't answer my question."

Nick tossed his menu onto the table. "I'm married, remember? With a son."

"You were married before. With a son. And it didn't stop you from—"

"This is an insane conversation to be having with a child. If you ARE a child and not some carnival midget Rosie pawned off on me in place of my daughter. Do your friends talk like you?"

"I don't have friends. My mom was my only friend."

"Your mom?" He paused, nodding to himself. "Ah. I get it now." Kat couldn't read his expression. "No wonder you're so—"

"Don't you dare say anything bad about my mom! She was—"

"Whoa. I didn't mean—"

"You're ashamed of me, aren't you?"

"Ashamed? Why in the hell—heck—would you think that?"

"You can swear in front of me. Don't talk down to me! Mom swore. I've heard it all."

"Why would you think I'm ashamed of you?"

"Because when that lady at the desk was checking us in, she asked if I was your daughter, and you didn't answer her. You got angry instead."

Scrubbing a hand over his face, he looked skyward. "Kat, Kat, Kat," he mumbled under his breath. Leaning forward, he met her eyes. "I didn't answer her because it was none of her business. And I got angry because I'm tired of it."

"She was just being friendly."

"Maybe. But when your life has been dissected publicly for too many years you get very protective of your privacy. That's all. Unfortunately, it's something you're going to have to deal with, too. Both Jessie and I are in the public eye. We've kept Anthony out of the spotlight, and we'll protect you the same way."

Nick's words and tone were far from what she expected. And for some reason she believed him.

"As for your mom, she was a good lady. I have nothing but praise for her."

"Then why did you ...?"

"Leave her?" She nodded. He exhaled slowly. "Didn't she explain any of this to you?"

"All she told me was my dad was a nice man she knew briefly. I didn't even know your name until right before she—when it was too late for explanations. She was really, really sick and ..."

He shocked her by reaching across the table for her hand. She withdrew it, folding her hands in her lap.

"Look, Kat." His voice was low, soft. "I know you want to make me out to be the bad guy. But there are no villains in this story. Your mom and I had a wonderful time together a long time ago. And that's all we wanted from each other. She lost her husband a year earlier and was still mourning him. She was a good reporter, and we worked well together. We laughed a lot. Drank too much. It was fun. I think that was what she needed at the time. Something to help her forget her grief."

Again, Nick McDeare surprised her. But could she trust this version of the man? "Did you ever see each other again?"

He sat back, crossing his arms. "About a year later I had a book signing in Burlington, Vermont, and called her. Got her voice mail and never heard back. I didn't understand her silence then. I do now."

"She didn't want you to know about me, right?"

"In her letter – the one Rosie sent me – she said she wanted to raise you alone. And she had every right to do that. You can read her letter when we get to New York if you'd like. Maybe it will explain things better than I can. It helped Jessie to understand."

"You showed my mom's personal letter to your wife?"

"Of course. This situation affects her, too. Do you want to read your mom's letter?"

It would be hard to read her mother's words, see her handwriting. But she desperately wanted to see that letter.

Kat nodded. All she seemed to do today was nod. Like some stupid bobblehead.

"Let's order."

*

Dinner was a simple meal, eaten in the brownstone's breakfast nook. Ham. Scalloped potatoes. Green beans. And biscuits. After gobbling everything in sight, Anthony snuck Monty some ham and disappeared upstairs to his computer games.

"And you're okay with this, Jess?" Abbie asked. "Taking this girl into your family?"

Jessie nibbled on a biscuit, her stomach upset. "She's Nick's daughter. His responsibility. And he's my husband. What choice do I have?"

"You have a choice."

"Can we drop the subject please? It's done. She'll be here tomorrow."

"God, and I was going to ask if I could stay here for a while. My apartment sublet goes through next March."

"That reminds me," Mary said. "I want to talk to you about Willie. He's having trouble finding a place to live and I thought maybe he could stay in--"

"Sure, Abbie." So much for Jessie and Nick getting some alone time. "Stay here. Why not?" Jessie took some plates to the sink. "And, Mary, have Willie come here, too. We're running a B&B and take in all strays."

"You okay, honey?" Mary joined her.

"Never better." If only her stomach would settle down.

*

Despite being exhausted, Kat couldn't sleep. Staring out the picture window at the lights of Lake Placid, it finally hit her she was leaving this peaceful town for good. The only home she'd ever known. Tomorrow she would move to a large noisy city and live with a houseful of strangers. Saying goodbye to Lake Placid was like saying goodbye to her mother all over again.

Kat dropped her head against the cold glass and sobbed. She missed her mom so much her heart literally ached. If only she could have her mother here one last time. She wanted to talk to her about Nick McDeare. She had so many conflicting impressions of the man.

As she dried her tears, an idea formed. Grabbing her laptop, Kat crawled back into bed. Jeez, this room was freezing. There must be something wrong with the— The air system turned on. Kat heard the click, then felt the swoosh of warm air flowing across her. What was going on? She hadn't touched the thermostat. Maybe Nick ...? Oh, who cared? Her fingers were finally defrosting.

Anyway, back to her idea. She would pretend her mom was simply away, out of town for a while, like when the newspaper would send her on assignment, and she'd write her a ...

Dear Mom,

First of all, I miss you. SOOO MUCH. And I need you. You taught me to believe in God, to rely on my faith. Well, I'm angry with God right now. If He's so good, why did He take you from me? Why am I being forced to go and live with a stranger who is supposedly my father? Nothing makes sense.

Nick McDeare is a puzzle. One minute I can't stand him. The next I can't figure him out. What did you ever see in him? I mean, yeah, I guess he's good-looking. Was that it? He doesn't seem like what we'd

28

call a 'nice' man. He has a quick temper, he's judgmental, and sometimes he's downright rude.

I'm scared, Mom. Tomorrow we go to New York, and I'm going to have to get along with Nick's wife and son. I don't want to meet new people. I don't want to make small talk and smile when I don't feel like it. Mostly, I don't want to become part of a new family. I want my life to go on as it used to. With you.

Wherever you are, Mom, help me through whatever tomorrow brings ...

Your Kat forever

*

Nick poured himself a bourbon from the mini bar. Stretching across the bed he called Jessie. "Save me," he whined when she answered.

Her laugh lifted his spirits. As always. "Start talking."

"Kat's a piece of work. With a mouth to match."

"Sounds like a chip off the old block."

He grinned. "Maybe. You'll be the judge."

"Tell me about her."

"She's hurting. And lashing out. Just like you predicted. She's going to need a lot of TLC."

Silence.

"Jess? Did you hear what I said?"

"Sorry. Abbie was talking to me."

"Abbie? What's she doing there?"

"She turned up late this afternoon with quite a story. I'll let her tell you when you get home. She's staying for a while, so we'll have a houseful. Oh, one more thing. Mary wants us to offer Lyle's apartment to Willie. Apparently, he's having a hard time finding something he can afford without moving two hours away."

Lyle's place ...

Do it, man.

A voice. Nick heard a voice. And not just any voice.

Lyle Barton's voice.

What the hell?

"Nick? ... You there?"

29

"Uh, yeah. We'll talk about it when I get home tomorrow. Love you."

*

Kat was overwhelmed. When overwhelmed, she remained silent. First the private plane, then being met at the New York airport by a limo. Nick said Willie, the driver, was part of the family. Curiouser and curiouser, as Alice said.

The drive into Manhattan was a blur of steel and concrete and crowds and noise. Horns honked. Traffic crept. Pedestrians had no rules. Streets were rutted. Nick didn't seem bothered by any of it.

The car stopped in front of a slate gray stone home, five stories tall, on East Seventy-Fifth Street. A shiny black fence surrounded the miniature front – what did you call it? – Terrace? Slab? – and the front door matched the fence.

They climbed the front steps, and Nick unlocked the door, swinging it open. Kat stepped into an entryway. Ahead of her was a long hallway with a flight of stairs on the left leading to the second floor. At the far end of the hallway Kat saw a winterized back porch with wicker furniture and hanging plants.

"Come in," Nick urged.

She followed him down the hallway, taking her time, surveying everything. A plush beige living room on the right with thick carpeting, a fireplace, expensive furniture and a baby grand. Wow. A baby grand! On the left was a dining room, too medieval for Kat's taste, with a heavy long oak table, a fancy chandelier and polished wooden flooring. A small bathroom was tucked under the stairs.

Moving on, Kat encountered her first comfortable room. A den or study. It looked lived-in, even a little worn. There were wall-to-wall bookshelves, a bar, a recliner and an overstuffed sofa and chairs. There was also a large screen TV and another fireplace. But the focus of the room hung over the fireplace. An enormous oil painting of two men, one obviously Nick. They were both wearing a tux, both had their heads tilted towards each other, as if they were in the middle of a conversation.

"That's Andrew and me." Nick stood beside her.

"I don't understand. From what I read, you never met, only talked on the phone."

"That's right. The artist painted it using photographs of each of us. It was a gift from Jessie."

30

"Andrew's fair ... like ..."

"Like you. But we all have the same eyes."

Staring at the painting, Kat focused on Andrew. It was sad he died so young. Like her mother. He seemed alive in the painting. "He was a jokester, wasn't he?"

"How'd you know?"

"There's a—I don't know—a twinkle in his eyes, like he's keeping some hilarious secret from everyone."

"Very observant. Jessie says he laughed all the time, was outgoing and fun to be around."

You're very different from your brother, aren't you, Nick McDeare?

"We're as different as night and day."

Shocked, she looked up at him. He was watching her.

"It's what you were thinking, right? How different Andrew and I are."

He just totally freaked her out. He could read minds?

"Andrew's the saint. I'm the sinner. Now you know the family secret."

You're jealous of your brother. Is that why you married Andrew's wife and adopted his son? And now live here in your brother's home?

"Come on." They crossed the hall and entered a large cheerful kitchen. There was an enormous island down the center and another flight of stairs leading to the second floor. A built-in breakfast nook was perched under a picture window overlooking the back yard. Throw rugs covered the natural wood floors. An enticing aroma wafted from the oven.

"Hey, where is everyone?" Nick shouted up a flight of stairs in the kitchen.

"Nick?" A far-off female voice.

"You're early." Another female voice. Deeper.

A woman skittered down the stairs. She was stunning. Too stunning. Like a Barbie doll. Petite, blond. Huge blue eyes. Gorgeous figure. Jessie, of course.

She looks as phony as Mom looked real.

The woman halted, staring at Kat. "Wow. She has Andrew's coloring."

I'm another person in the room. You can talk directly to me.

31

"We've covered that subject." Nick glanced at Kat.

"But-but she looks like you. Your faces are the same. And she's tall like you. It's amazing."

What am I? A prized heifer at the county fair? So much for a warm welcome.

Kat knew how to play the game. Her mother had interviewed dozens of actresses over the years. Kat had met most of them. They were all the same. Plastic. Self-centered. And vain. "I thought you'd be taller. Mom said most women who work on Broadway are willowy," were her first words to Tallulah.

Jessie opened her mouth to say something, then closed it again. It was like watching a balloon deflate.

"Jessie's not 'most women'," Nick said pointedly. "Have you ever seen a Tony Award? She has two."

Interesting. Jessie can't defend herself. You do it for her.

Turning to his wife, Nick asked, "Where's Abbie?"

Who's Abbie?

"Asleep. We were up most of the night, talking. I doubt we'll see her today. She ate everything in sight and then crashed. I hate her. She never gains an ounce."

Yep. Vain. Obsessed with her appearance.

The chauffeur materialized, carrying two boxes. "Where do I put these?"

"I'll show you." Jessie shot Nick a look that Kat couldn't decipher. "Thanks, Willie. Come on." She led the man up the stairs.

Nick turned to Kat. "Lose the attitude, kiddo."

"She talked about me like I wasn't standing right in front of her."

Nick's glare softened. A little. "Come on. Let's get your suitcases."

So the great Nick McDeare isn't above carrying luggage. Too bad the same can't be said for his Tony-Award-winning wife.

*

"You did a great job in here, Jess." Nick watched as Kat surveyed her new bedroom. The queen-sized bed. The multiple dressers. The matching bookshelves. The old-fashioned desk in front of the windows with a rocker beside it.

"Thanks." Jessie opened a far door, flipping on a light. "You have your own bathroom and dressing room through here." She joined

Nick as Kat continued to pace around the room. "I hope you'll be comfortable in here, Kat."

"It's nice. Thank you." Her voice was flat. Unemotional.

"Well," Jessie continued, "I'll let you settle in." She squeezed Nick's hand before leaving the room.

The girl went to the windows and stared down at the street. She looked so small in the high-ceilinged room. This must be intimidating for her, coming from such a quiet town to a bustling city. To a family of strangers.

Hamlet wandered into the room with all the dignity of a lion king. He leapt up on the desk and rubbed his fawn fur against Kat. "Who's this?"

"Hamlet. He's been miserable since being displaced by the dog."

"What dog?"

"Good question. Mary must have put Monty in Anthony's room so he wouldn't jump all over you."

"Who's Mary?"

"That's me." Mary's timing was always impeccable. "And you must be Kat. Boy, do you look like Andrew when he was your age. Of course, you're much prettier. Anyway, I just wanted to say hello and tell you if there's anything you need, just ask me. I'm looking forward to having a good long talk with you one of these days. You're exactly what this house needs. More kids. It's been too long. Well," she said, backing up, "I have to check on my chicken." She was gone as quickly as she appeared.

Nick chuckled. "Typical Mary. To-the-point. A huge heart. Mother to us all. She pretty much raised Jessie and Andrew. By the way, Andrew moved in here when he was exactly your age."

"Why? What happened to his--your mother?"

"She died unexpectedly. Andrew had no one else, so Jessie and her father took him in." It suddenly struck Nick. The parallel history of Andrew and Kat.

Nick knew Kat was thinking the same thing. For a fraction of a second, the girl looked scared. And just as quickly, her armor snapped back into place.

Kat stroked Hamlet, who was in ecstasy. He rolled onto his back, all four legs in the air. His purring could be heard across the room.

"Looks like you've got a roommate. He and Anthony used to be inseparable. But since Monty arrived – Monty's a Portuguese Water Dog – Hamlet's become a loner." Nick ambled to the door. "Come down whenever you're ready."

Jessie was in the kitchen, not looking happy. Nick put his arms around her. "What do you think?"

"Too early to tell." Jessie sighed. "I got the impression she didn't like me very much."

So did Nick.

Damn. Problems already.

*

Kat methodically put her things away under the watchful crossed eyes of Hamlet. She placed the framed photo of her mom by the bed, some books on the shelves, her blown-glass piano on the desk and her ballet shoes on the bedpost.

"Hi." Kat spun around.

A young boy with a mop of dark hair and enormous blue eyes stood in the doorway. A huge dog with black curly fur squatted beside him. "I'm Anthony."

"I figured."

The dog suddenly darted across the room and leapt on the bed, terrifying Hamlet. The cat wailed and took off, circling the room with the dog in pursuit.

"Stop it!" Kat shrieked. "Get your dog to stop. He's scaring Hamlet."

"Hamlet's used to it, but—Monty, NO!"

The dog halted but licked his chops at the cat. Hamlet hissed in response from the top of the bookshelves.

"Come here, boy." Anthony patted his thigh. Monty slinked over to his master and sat. Anthony turned his attention back to Kat. "You look like Daddy."

This again. "Well, he's my dad."

"No, I mean my first dad. Andrew."

I need to know more about Andrew.

"You look like Dad, too.

Like mother, like son.

"How do you like your room?"

"It's okay."

"What's the matter?"

"Nothing."

Anthony stared at her. It was as if he were studying her. She wished he'd stop. He backed towards the door. "Well ... see you later."

He was gone, the door closing with a click. She was alone. Finally.

Kat went to the bookshelves and reached for Hamlet. He came willingly into her arms. "It's okay, sweetie. You're okay." She held him close, feeling his purr. "I won't let anything happen to you. Promise."

Movement caught her eye.

The door swung open again.

By itself.

*

Nick took his usual place at the head of the table, the roast chicken and a carving knife beside him. It was a new tableau in the dining room: Anthony and Kat on his right; Jessie and Mary on his left. Monty made the rounds, hoping for dropped morsels and stray scraps.

Kat looked miserable. She sat back, her hands folded in her lap.

"I hope you like chicken," Mary said. "I need to learn your taste in food."

"It's fine."

"This heaping plate of chicken is for the human vacuum cleaner here." Nick winked at Anthony. "You'll have to tell me how much you want, Kat."

"Just a little."

The tick-tock of the hall grandfather clock filled the silence.

Jessie passed Kat the mashed potatoes. "Your mother's letter said you're a ballerina."

The girl nodded.

"And you sing?"

Again, a nod.

Jessie exchanged a frustrated glance with Nick.

"Would you like to keep up with your ballet training?" she continued.

"How? I've been with the same teacher from the beginning. She coaches the Olympic ice dancers."

"Well, a friend of mine was with the American Ballet Theater for years. She's danced all over the world. She retired and now teaches. Interested?"

Kat shrugged.

"I'll call Susie tomorrow. We also have a gym on the fifth floor. I had a barre installed up there because I—well, I do some dancing myself."

Jessie exchanged another look with Nick, who picked up the baton. "What about piano?" he asked. "Did you take lessons?"

Kat swallowed a bite of chicken. "Yes, but I hated the teacher. She was old and had a voice like a fire engine."

Anthony found this hilarious.

Nick chuckled. "So you won't miss that."

"Dad could teach you," Anthony piped up. "He's teaching me."

"You play?" Kat seemed surprised.

"My mother's a concert pianist. She taught me."

"Nick's good. You should hear him." Mary passed the zucchini to Kat. "Here, child, you need veggies."

Silence again.

Nick helped himself to more chicken, tossing a piece to Monty. "Jessie and I thought you could take this week to settle in before starting school next week.

Kat froze, her fork halfway to her mouth. "School? You mean go to school in an actual building?" Nick nodded. "I-I was home-schooled."

"It's an excellent private school," Jessie explained. "We did a lot of research before choosing it for Anthony. He loves it."

"No I don't."

"Since when?" Nick asked.

"The kids are mean, and the teachers don't do anything about it. There are cliques, and they're awful to Zane and me. They make fun of me because—Anyway, I hate it! I'd do anything to get out of there. Zane, too."

Nick caught Jessie's eye. They weren't prepared for this.

"Anthony," his mother said, "attending school is important. You need friends. A social life outside of the home. Extra-curricular activities teach you how to work with others. You learn life skills that will carry you into adulthood. You don't want to end up a loner with no--"

"Honey--" Nick put a hand on her arm to stop her.

"—social skills and --"

"Jess, please--"

Kat slammed her napkin on the table. "I won't go to school. And you can't make me." Leaping to her feet, she ran from the room.

"Kat, please," Nick began. "Wait— Dammit." Frowning at Jessie, he tossed his own napkin on the table and sprinted after his daughter.

CHAPTER 4

The October night was brisk. Too brisk. J, as his New York friends called him, was used to warm California weather. 'J'. A single letter. So cool ...

Cold. It was too damned cold. Shivering, he pulled the lambswool collar up around his ears and stuffed his hands in his pockets. He must have been out of his mind to leave the balmy coast of Los Angeles for this slab of arctic cement.

Who was he kidding? J came back to New York for revenge. In this era of twenty-four-hour news cycles, his story was already forgotten. He, however, would never forget. Not until she got what was coming to her.

Receding further into the shadows, he continued to stare at the East Seventy-Fifth Street brownstone. He pictured her inside that house, moving from room to room, feeling secure in her sanctuary. Let her feel safe for now. The bitch.

She deserved what was coming. She knew too much. Had exposed him.

He'd done his homework. Was caught up on her New York life. He knew her Achilles Heel.

That's where he would attack.

*

Nick knocked on the locked bedroom door. "Kat?"

"Leave me alone."

"I want to talk to you. Please." He waited.

The lock turned. He slipped inside. Kat sat down in the rocker, cuddling Hamlet. Nick eased into the desk chair, collecting his thoughts. "Look, Jessie only wants the best for you--"

"Are you defending what she said? Jessie insulted my mom." Kat sniffled, her eyes red from crying. "She made me sound like some

38

loser who can't handle herself with people. Which put the blame on Mom for home-schooling me."

"You said yourself you don't have any friends." He kept his voice gentle.

"Did you have friends when you were my age?"

"Don't change the subject. We're not talking about me."

"I told you I researched you. You were an Air Force brat. Lived all over the world. Never in one place long. Not exactly conducive for making friends."

Damn. She knew exactly how to get to him. It was uncanny.

"Your silence says it all."

"Okay, I was a loner. I'll give you that."

She flashed a smug smile, pleased with herself. "Your parents were your friends. Just like Mom was my friend." She buried her face in Hamlet's fur.

Nick shifted in his chair, searching for the right words. "My story is complicated, Kat. I was … smart. Advanced. I graduated from high school before I was sixteen. College students didn't want to hang out with a kid my age."

She looked up at him. "Checkmate."

"What do you mean?"

"I have the same problem. I test two grades ahead of my age. The older kids resent me because I'm smarter than them. Which is why I was home-schooled."

Memories flashed through Nick's mind. Long buried memories. He shoved them away. Back into the locked vault of his past.

"I get it, Kat. I do. I promise to give the subject of your schooling serious thought." He sat back, crossing his arms. "In return I'd like a favor."

She waited, her expression cautious.

"Don't take everything Jessie says the wrong way. This is awkward for all of us. Her heart's in the right place. You'll see as you get to know her better."

"She doesn't want me here."

"Of course she does."

"She doesn't. Why would she? I remind her of your past."

Uncanny. Olivia's letter said Kat was intuitive.

The girl stared at him, her lips a firm, thin line.

And stubborn. She was stubborn as hell. He'd get nowhere arguing with her.

Kat focused again on Hamlet, rocking him like a baby.

Nick had done all he could tonight. Reaching into his pocket, he handed her Olivia's letter. "Keep it. It's a beautiful letter."

After a beat she took it, running her fingers over the envelope.

"Night, Kat." Nick moved to the door, looking back.

The image of her so still, cradling the cat, staring at that letter with tears in her eyes burned itself into his brain. Her implacable facade had crumbled, leaving in its place a lonely little girl who yearned for her mom.

*

Anthony couldn't sleep. He called his friend Zane to tell him about Kat. Then he watched Monty chase the streetlamp shadows around the bedroom, crashing into the wall a couple times. He heard his mom come up to bed a while ago. Still, he was awake.

"Hey, Bongo, it's late. You should be asleep." Dad sat down on the bed.

"Tell me about it."

"What's wrong?"

He sighed. "Kat. She doesn't like me."

"She doesn't know you. Give her time. Then she won't like you." Dad chuckled and tickled him.

"Stop it. Stop! I'm too old for that now." Anthony's laughter faded. "She doesn't want to know me."

"That's not true. She's just missing her mom." He straightened the bed covers. "Remember how you felt when Andrew died?"

Anthony nodded. "Sad. Really sad."

"But you still had your mom. With Kat - on top of being sad about losing her mom - she didn't have anyone. She was all alone."

"She has you."

"Yes, now she does, but—she has to deal with all of us, be part of a family she doesn't even know. She's scared, Anthony. We have to give her time."

He thought about it. If he lost his mom and dad and had to go live with strangers he'd be miserable. "I didn't think of it like that. I'll be nice to her. Promise."

"You are so smart, Anthony. Have I told you that lately?"

"Tell me again."

"You're smart. And I love you."

Anthony reached up for a hug.

"You're too old to be tickled, but not too old for a hug?" Nick wrapped his arms around his son, squeezing hard.

"I won't tell if you don't. And I love you, too, Dad."

Monty whimpered and crept towards a spot near the window. His whimper morphed into a soft howl. It stopped abruptly, and he laid down, his gaze glued to the same spot.

"Monty?" Anthony patted the bed. The dog didn't move. "Come here, boy." Nothing. "What's wrong with him, Dad?"

"Uh, you know dogs. They see things we don't."

"Like a spirit? Like when Daddy Andrew used to visit you or me?"

"Andrew's gone for good. You know that. We have to accept it. Monty probably just saw a shadow or something. 'Night, Bongo. Get some sleep."

*

Jessie heard Nick tiptoe across the darkened bedroom and into the bathroom. His nightly ritual of washing his face and brushing his teeth.

When she felt him slip into bed she rolled over. "I'm awake."

"So's Anthony."

He pulled her into his arms and pressed his lips to her forehead. "Am I the only one who's exhausted?"

"You're the only one who's had time to get used to our new family member."

"I'll tell you what I told Anthony." He yawned. "She's scared. Her whole world has changed overnight. She'll come around. We just have to be patient."

Jessie snuggled against his neck. He smelled of soap and toothpaste, such a comforting scent. "Nick, I'm sorry. I didn't mean to upset Kat. But I'm not going to back down on school—"

"We'll figure it out." Another yawn.

"I mean it, Nick. Kat has to go to—"

"Abbie's certainly wound up. I was surprised to find her at the table when I came back down."

So he refused to discuss school. He could be so damned stubborn. Fine. She'd corner him tomorrow. "I think those cell calls are upsetting Abbie.

41

"She's really scared of this guy in L.A. That's not like Abbie. Maybe I should look into it for her."

"You've got enough on your plate with Kat. Plus, finishing your book. Please don't go running around chasing a stalker."

"I'm an investigator, Jess," he mumbled. "Remember?"

"And what should we do about Lyle's apartment and Willie?"

Silence.

"... Nick? ... Nick?"

"... Hmm?"

"Willie. And Lyle's place?"

"Can we talk about this tomorrow? I'm dead."

"Sure, Scarlet. Tomorrow. At Tara."

*

Dear Mom,

Nick gave me the letter you sent him. I loved everything you said, but it made me cry. I just miss you so much.

I'm here in New York with my new 'family.' I don't know what to make of them yet. One thing's for sure – Jessie, Nick's wife, doesn't want me here. Nick says she does, but I know she doesn't. Anthony, the little boy, seems like a typical kid. No opinion of him yet. And there's someone named Mary. Supposedly the mother of the house. She seems nice, but I don't really know her yet. My one true friend is a cat named Hamlet. He was tossed aside when Anthony got a dog. Hamlet and I have a lot in common. He's with me now as I write this.

Nick seems to be trying, but he's still a puzzle. He can be really nice – like giving me your letter – but I think he gets frustrated with me. Just like you always did. I'm trying to keep an open mind, but after everything I read about him, I just don't know if I can trust him.

I'm trying hard to imagine how you'd respond to all this, but I can't hear your voice, and that makes me even sadder. For the last few weeks I could hear you in my head, but tonight? Nothing. What does that mean? I need to feel you're watching over me. I love you, Mom ...

Your Kat forever

*

42

"Do you want me to look into this guy, Abbie?" Nick asked the next morning, munching on a banana. "What's his name ... Joey—?"

"Joseph Evenatti."

"Another Italian?"

"Would you all please stop with the 'Italian' crap? Anyway, he's a cop. I tried to get access to his department history, but I hit a brick wall."

"No surprise there." Willie leaned on the island, waiting to take Anthony to school. "The department keeps it under lock and key except in rare circumstances."

"Murdering your wife isn't rare circumstances?"

"Was he tried and convicted?"

"He wasn't even arrested. But he's still a suspect. Which is why the wife's sister Claire hired my uncle and me to find some evidence."

"Maybe I can get that history. I'm still in touch with my old partner, Roger."

"I forgot!" Abbie said. "You're an ex-cop."

"Let me see what I can find out."

What the hell? Nick tossed the banana peel in the trash. Abbie accepted Willie's help but not Nick's? A renowned investigative reporter?

Mary handed her nephew another muffin. "Come for dinner tonight. I won't take no for an answer."

Anthony galumphed down the stairs. "If Kat doesn't have to go to school, why do I?"

Kat was a few steps behind Anthony.

Jessie had her nose buried in the newspaper and didn't see Kat. "Don't worry. She'll join you next week."

Kat halted mid-step, staring at Jessie.

School again. Damn. Nick changed the subject. "Hungry, Kat?"

Still staring at Jessie, Kat shook her head.

Mary held out a basket of muffins. "I made my famous orange muffins. Try one. You don't want to hurt my feelings."

Kat half-heartedly accepted a muffin. "Actually, I wanted to ask you something, Mary. Could I have some supplies for Hamlet in my room? A litter box. Maybe a couple of bowls--"

"In your room?" Jessie looked up. "That cat really makes a mess. Which is why we keep his litter in the basement."

"I'll be responsible for him, including cleaning up after him. My room seems to be his safe haven." Glancing at Anthony, she added, "Poor thing."

"That's fine," Nick said, ignoring Jessie's glare.

"Well," Mary began, "since you tried one of my muffins, I'll set it up for you. Then it's all yours. Anthony, your cereal's waiting."

"I want a muffin." Anthony snuck a look at Kat, nibbling on her own muffin.

Nick swallowed a smile. The boy was imitating his older sister already. "I'm going for a run."

"You're jogging?" Kat asked. "Can I go, too?"

"I guess so. But dress warmly. It's cold out there today."

"When you finish your run," Jessie said, "we need to talk about—" she glanced at Kat, then Willie "—several things."

Nick knew what was on Jessie's mind. School. This could get ugly.

*

Jessie sat with Mary and Abbie in the breakfast nook. Abbie was polishing off the muffins. Jessie's stomach was upset again.

Kat trotted down the stairs, dressed in a midnight blue jogging suit and running shoes.

Abbie leapt up. "Hi, Kat. We haven't been formally introduced. I'm Abbie, old family friend. You're beautiful, by the way. And I envy your height. I have these stubby little legs."

"Nick's waiting for you by the front door," Jessie supplied. "And Mary and I want to know what your favorite food is."

"My favorite? Japanese, probably. And I like fish."

Mary grinned. "You just made your father's day. Japanese is his favorite, too."

"One more thing, Kat," Jessie added. "I called my friend who coaches ballet. She'd like to come over tomorrow afternoon and meet you. See you dance?"

"Fine."

Nick appeared in the archway. "Let's go."

"Japanese for dinner tonight," Mary announced.

"Fine."

Father and daughter disappeared down the hallway.

"It's uncanny." Abbie grabbed another muffin. "She's a mini-Nick."

44

"Yep." Jessie's stomach was about to revolt. "Right down to the 'Fine.'"

*

"Better stretch first," Nick instructed Kat.

"I'm not stupid." She began to work her legs.

"Right. I forgot." He pulled two woolen caps from the front closet. "I'm pretty dogged when it comes to jogging. I hope you don't slow me down."

I hope you don't slow ME down. "I used to jog with Mom every day."

"So you haven't run in a while? Since she ..."

"Some. Not as much."

"Okay." He plopped a cap on his head and one on hers. "Tuck your hair up under it." He opened the door, and they stepped outside.

"Why do we have to wear these?"

"To remain anonymous."

Of course. Your celebrity.

Monty bounded down the hall towards them. "Not this time, Monty." Nick rubbed the dog's head. "I'll walk you later. Go on. Back inside."

They left the brownstone, trotting towards a park. "Is that Central Park?"

"And this is Fifth Avenue. I usually run in the park." They clipped across the busy street and entered the park a few blocks down. "We'll keep it slow until you find your rhythm."

It didn't take long to settle into an easy gait. Kat breathed deeply, enjoying the brisk air. The park was kind of pretty, almost making her forget she was in a huge city.

"Ready to step it up a bit?" Nick asked.

"Sure."

They jogged in unison. Kat was blessed with long legs and was almost able to keep up with Nick. Or maybe he eased off in deference to her. Whatever. She was just grateful he didn't feel the need to talk. As he guided her from path to path, she took in her surroundings. Lots of grass and stone. People walking their dogs, jogging, sitting on benches reading newspapers. They rode bicycles, rowed small boats on a lake, even flew kites. She passed a carousal and too many statues to count. There were mimes, musicians and opera singers entertaining for spare change. Carts sold coffee, donuts, hot dogs, popcorn and cold drinks.

"That's enough. Let's slow to a brisk walk as we head home." He led her towards Fifth Avenue. "You did well. What did you think of the park?"

"It's different. There's certainly nothing like it in Lake Placid."

"That's true about most things in New York. It's like a foreign country."

"Did it take you long to get used to it?"

"I was born here, so I guess it's in my blood. Before moving back here a couple years ago I lived in Washington D.C. Another foreign country."

Plus all those cities around the world.

"Do you jog every day?" she asked, a bit winded.

"I try to. Sometimes work doesn't allow it."

"Work?"

"My writing. I'm finishing my seventh novel right now."

"Right. I haven't read them."

"You're a little young for them."

"I'm not a little young for anything, remember?"

"You are for my books."

"Why? Are they full of sex and violence?"

"Kat, I know you're advanced for your age, but you just turned twelve. My books aren't appropriate for a twelve-year-old."

We'll see.

"Don't even think about it."

"What?"

"Sneaking my books."

Wow. Maybe he could read minds after all.

"No," he continued, "I'm not a mind reader."

This was getting bizarre.

*

Mary locked eyes with Abbie as she knocked on the powder room door. "Jessie? Honey? You okay?"

Jessie opened the door, a towel pressed to her mouth. "I must have the flu. I haven't felt well for two days."

Abbie put an arm around her friend. "I think you're making yourself sick over Kat."

Jessie said nothing as they returned to the kitchen.

"I'm calling Dr. Chao." Mary reached for her cell.

"Don't bother. There's nothing he can do."

"Jessie," Abbie sat her down in the breakfast nook, "I've known you forever. You can't fool me. This whole thing with Kat is upsetting you. I know it would upset me. Maybe you should reconsider having her here."

"I can't, Abbie. She's Nick's daughter. She belongs here."

"Jessie's right." Mary looked up the doctor's number on her phone. "I'm calling. Maybe the doctor can give you some pills to calm your stomach. And everything will work out with Kat. Trust me."

*

Luci Ruiz always left home early in the morning. She hated her tiny apartment and spent as little time as possible there. Often her first stop was the drug store. She'd become friends with the pharmacist, Raoul, even flirting with him. He was born in Columbia but had been in the United States for thirty years. When Luci confessed she was originally from Chile, a bond formed. He complimented her olive skin, her dark, shoulder-length hair, her almond-shaped eyes. Luci was hungry for attention and basked in his compliments.

Leaving the Bronx, she would take the train into Manhattan, going for long walks before heading to work at the school. Always, always she ended up on East Seventy-Fifth Street. Anthony's home had a magnetic pull for her.

If only she could get inside that house. Or even look through the windows. She wanted to know how he lived, what his bedroom was like, to meet his dog. But it was impossible. A security guard protected the house day and night.

On this particular morning, McDeare and his bastard child came out. They looked like criminals with those wool hats on their heads. A beautiful black dog joined them briefly. That must be Monty. Luci watched as McDeare shoved the poor creature back inside. What a monster.

Luci had an idea. Hiding behind a delivery truck, she snapped pictures of them with her cell. As they began to jog, Luci did her best to keep up with them, taking photo after photo. Out of breath, she halted and looked at the gems in her phone.

Her smile morphed into a laugh, then to a cackle.

What a brilliant plan!

*

"Where are you off to?" Nick kissed Jessie on the cheek as he and Kat swung into the kitchen. "Sorry, honey. I'm sweaty."

"The doctor."

"What's wrong?" Nick felt her forehead. It was cool.

"An upset stomach. Probably just the flu." Jessie squeezed his hand. "Abbie's in her room contacting every lipstick client who ever hired her."

"Why lipstick?" Kat asked.

"Abbie's lips used to be famous, featured in every glamour magazine on the market. She's hoping they still are."

Nick watched Jessie dash down the hallway.

"She doesn't look or act sick," Kat observed.

Nick was thinking the same thing. But Jessie's trip to the doctor meant no argument about Kat's schooling. For now, anyway. "Listen, kiddo, I don't want you to jog alone. It's not safe. And this is not an 'age' thing. Jogging alone is taboo for Jessie, too."

"It's not an 'age' thing. Just a 'sexist' thing."

Nick rolled his eyes. "Call it what you want. I don't care about all that crap."

"Why am I not surprised? You're not exactly the epitome of today's modern man."

"What the hell does that mean—"

"Such language in front of a twelve-year-old!"

"You said your mom swore—" She was doing it again. Pushing his buttons. With the precision of a computer programmer. "About the jogging. I mean it. You either join me or use the machines up in the gym."

Mary plodded down the stairs. "I just set up Hamlet's home-away-from-home in your bathroom, Kat. Lunch will be ready in an hour. You can help yourselves and eat wherever you want. But I want all dirty dishes put in the dishwasher afterwards, got it?" She glared meaningfully at Nick.

"Are you insinuating I'm a slob?"

"I'm not insinuating. You ARE a slob."

Nick poured some coffee and headed upstairs. "Grabbing a shower, then I'm not to be—"

"—disturbed. I know," Mary finished as he reached the landing. "Did you hear that, Kat? When Nick's door is closed, we leave him to his work."

He was glad Mary remembered to tell Kat about the closed door. Not that she'd be pounding on it anytime soon.

Mary bellowed up the stairs. "Don't forget I need your help with dinner."

Right. Japanese tonight. Yum.

*

Luci glanced around the school kitchen. No one would notice if she disappeared for a few minutes. Lunch was almost over.

She grabbed her treat for Anthony and approached him as he ate with Zane. "For you." She placed a small basket in front of Anthony. "A peanut butter pie. And some stewing bones for your dog."

"Wow, Luci, thanks! We can have it for dessert tonight."

"Where's your new sister?" Luci gathered the trays on the table. "Didn't she come to school today?" After she jogged with the degenerate, Luci added silently.

"She's not coming to school till next week."

"Why not?"

He shrugged. "Dad says she's dealing with a lot."

Luci inwardly cringed at Anthony calling Nick McDeare 'Dad.' A man like McDeare didn't deserve a boy like Anthony. He didn't deserve any children.

"It's scary for her," Anthony continued, "not knowing anyone."

So the girl was scared? She didn't look scared earlier that morning.

Too many games being played in that sick house.

Poor Anthony.

*

Jessie sat back as Willie guided the car home. Her mind jumped from subject to subject, never staying in one place for long.

Her doctor did a thorough exam, taking blood and urine samples. Dr. Chao said she was stressed to the max. Maybe Abbie was right. Kat was upsetting her more than she would admit. Was suppressing her feelings irritating her stomach? Was she developing an ulcer? Was that what the doctor wasn't telling her?

Dr. Chao said he'd call when he got the blood work back. He sent her home with no prescription, just a strong recommendation of rest and serenity.

Fat chance. Not with a manipulative twelve-year-old and eager-to-please daddy in the house.

CHAPTER 5

Nick gave up on his manuscript. He'd been staring at the same page for hours. He just couldn't concentrate. Hearing the fresh fish being delivered, he headed downstairs. Might as well get to work on dinner. Mary was making the rice, so Nick attacked the fish.

Kat came downstairs, carrying her lunch dishes. She rinsed and stacked them in the dishwasher. Wandering to the island, she watched Nick's handiwork. "What are you doing?"

"Cutting the fish for sushi."

"Nick's an ace in the kitchen, especially with Japanese." Mary handed Kat a bowl of jumbo shrimp. "How about making it a family affair and cleaning these? They're for tempura."

Finished, Nick put the fish in the fridge and grabbed the sirloin. "And this is for negamaki. Ever had it?"

"Thin slices of beef wrapped around scallions, right?"

"In a tangy sauce. Don't forget the sauce."

"And we're having gyoza," Mary added.

"Dumplings. I always order them."

"You know your Japanese." Nick was impressed. "What about yakitori?"

"Chicken and scallion skewers."

Mary whistled. "You are definitely your father's daughter. We're also having fried tofu. And spicy edamame, which Anthony hates." Mary shook her head. "Anthony and vegetables, a lifelong battle."

The front door slammed. Jessie was home. "What did the doctor say?" Nick wiped his hands.

"He ran a bunch of tests and said I have to watch my stress level. I'll know more when the tests come back."

"That's what's causing your stomach problems? Stress?"

"Apparently. Any soup left from lunch, Mary? I think I'll take a bowl upstairs and sleep for a bit. I tossed all night."

*

Kat cleaned the shrimp and vegetables for tempura. She also breaded the tofu and made the sauce for it, following Mary's instructions. Nick watched her while he made the negamaki and yakitori. Then they assembled the sushi together.

Abbie joined them, becoming part of the sushi assembly line. "Maybe I can get a job in a Japanese restaurant," she whined. "My days as a lipstick model are apparently over. I'm considered over the hill at thirty-six. It's outrageous."

Kat wiped her hands on a wet towel. "Is it okay if I play the piano?"

"Sure." Nick put the sushi in the refrigerator. "We're finished here."

Kat slipped into the living room and opened the keyboard of the baby grand. What a gorgeous piano. She began to play the Chopin piece she'd been working on the past year. Op 9 No 2. She was rusty, not having played in weeks. She started again. And again. Frustrated, she dropped her hands in her lap.

"You're trying too hard." Nick slouched in the connecting doorway from the study, hands in his pockets. In that pose he didn't look anything like a dad. More like one of those models for men's cologne. Which was why it was impossible to think of him as her father. He was a celebrity, like his plastic wife. "You're good. Very good," he continued, approaching the piano. "You may not have liked your teacher, but your talent overcame her."

"I practiced a lot on my own. I-I don't know what's wrong today."

"Different piano. Different surroundings. It matters. Look, you know the piece, so forget about the notes. Close your eyes and go someplace else. Really go there. Go on. Close your eyes." She did as she was told. "Now try again. Feel the music. Let it come from inside you."

*

"Is that Kat or Nick playing?" Mary asked Abbie.

"It has to be Nick. What twelve-year-old can play like that?"

"Maybe the daughter of Nick McDeare, master pianist?"

"No way." Abbie got to her feet. "Come on."

They crept to the connecting den door.

"Good Lord," Mary whispered, "it IS Kat." The young girl sat at the piano, eyes closed, intent on what she was playing. Chopin. Nick played it often.

Nick, standing behind Kat, spotted them. Putting his finger to his lips he shooed them back to the kitchen.

Mary said a silent prayer of thanks. That look on Nick's face as he watched Kat play ... This girl was having an impact on him, no doubt about it.

The front door slammed. Didn't anyone know how to close a door quietly?

Anthony and Willie swung into the kitchen. Monty bounded down the stairs to greet them. "Luci made us a peanut butter pie for dessert." Anthony held up a basket.

"Peanut butter?" Mary made a face. "We have a pear tart for tonight."

"But she made it special."

Abbie reached for the basket. "Tell you what, sport. Let's have a piece of that pie right now." She avoided Mary's glare. "Ew, what's this?"

"Bones for Monty."

Abbie passed the bones to a disgusted Mary and pulled out the pie. Her cell rang. Glancing at the screen, she pocketed it. "Want some pie, Willie?"

"I never turn down anything peanut butter."

"Dad's playing the piano?" Anthony's eyes were glued to the pie.

"Your dad's giving Kat a lesson."

"I want one, too." He started for the living room.

"Anthony, no. Your turn tomorrow." Nick needed this time with his daughter.

Anthony pouted until Abbie handed him a slice of pie. "Where's Mom?"

"Napping. I'm going to check on her now."

As Mary mounted the steps, Abbie's cell rang again.

*

"You're a natural, Kat. You got to me." Nick sat down beside her on the bench. "That's the point of the arts. To touch people. We take all our bottled-up feelings and express them in different forms.

Your music and ballet. Jessie's acting. My writing. If we're successful, we tap into an audience's emotions. Whether it's two people or two thousand. The arts bring out our passion. If you have no passion, find another career." He had her full attention. "So. You're gifted at the piano. And, I presume, ballet. But your mom said your true love is writing."

"Maybe. I don't know." She looked up at him. "Were you always driven to be a writer?"

"Driven? No. Did I always have a passion for writing? Yes. Two different things."

"What's the difference?"

"Drive is about achieving a goal." Nick fingered the keys lightly. "Passion is what fills you up. Makes you whole. Something that forces you from bed in the morning, that defines you. I wrote my first short story when I was Anthony's age. And the next day I wrote another one. And another. Do you see?"

"I think so." She stared at the keys. "Are you passionate about the piano?"

"Mmm … In a different way."

"Would you play something for me? I really want to hear you play." She stood up and moved away from the piano, giving him room. "Please?"

"I haven't played in weeks." Nick took his time, thinking for a moment, then began to softly play Beethoven's Moonlight Sonata. It reminded him of his teen years, of late nights alone in Japan while his parents were out or slept upstairs. He closed his eyes and was transported back to that time. The soft breeze billowing the Chantilly lace curtains. The scent of cherry blossoms in the Ming vase. The stillness of the Tokyo night. And a scruffy mutt named Haywire snoozing at his feet.

He finished, sitting quietly as reality came back into focus.

"That was incredible," Kat whispered. "Why didn't you follow in your mom's footsteps? Become a concert pianist?"

Nick could hear his mother's words, urging him to pursue the piano. "No. Writing was my true passion."

Kat sat back down beside him. "This is a talented family, isn't it?"

"And your talent is part of it."

53

A man's soft laugh was heard in the distance, startling them both.

"What was that?" Kat peered around, clearly spooked.

"Probably ... Anthony's TV upstairs. He must have left his door open."

"It didn't sound like it came from upstairs."

"This is an old house."

Nick knew exactly what that was. Who it was.

Andrew.

*

Jessie wasn't in the mood for Mary's prying. She threw her legs over the side of the bed. "I told you, I'm fine. Just stressed. I have to take it easy."

"Take it easy? Uh-huh."

"I hate when you imply I'm lying."

"Jessie, I've known you since you were a little girl. I don't imply. I know when you're lying. You can fool everyone but me."

"Stop it, Mary. I mean it. Nick's piano music calmed me down, and now you're riling me up again."

"It wasn't Nick playing. It was Kat. Looks like she inherited her dad's talent."

Jessie pressed her fingers to her temples, a small headache forming. Kat.

She wasn't supposed to stress about Kat. But she shouldn't suppress her anxiety either. If she was upset, she should let it out. But she didn't want to antagonize or hurt Nick. What a mess.

She felt Mary's analytical gaze on her. "Mary, stop worrying. I'll be down in a little while."

"Uh-huh."

*

Abbie cut herself another slice of pie. She could eat the whole thing by herself, it was that good. "I'm a peanut butter addict."

"Me, too." Willie swallowed before continuing, "Listen, I did some snooping on your Joey Evenatti. Roger, my old partner, says he's been out sick a lot in recent months. Otherwise, his record is clean."

Abbie's cell rang again. Same number. She pushed IGNORE. "Was he sick the day his wife was murdered?"

"No. I checked. But he was out of the precinct for hours at a time that day. What's with the calls, Abbie?"

"He did it. I know he did it."

"Abbie. The calls?"

She sighed. "Someone's calling and not leaving messages. I answered once, and he hung up."

"You think it's Evenatti?"

"I don't know. Maybe." She needed to lighten the mood. "Tell you what. I'll bet you ten peanut butter pies he's guilty."

An easy smile spread across Willie's face. He was a handsome man. Angled cheeks that dimpled when he grinned. Perfect bronze skin. And dark green eyes. Funny. Abbie had never noticed before.

"I'll take that bet." He scooped another bite of pie. "Anyway, Roger's going to keep an eye on him for me. And you need to keep a log of those calls."

Nodding, Abbie finished her pie and took her plate to the sink. "Tell me something, Willie. Why'd you leave the force? You were a detective, right?"

"And I'd just made captain." He blew out a long breath. "Why'd I leave? Basically, burn-out. I'd put in over twenty years. I'd seen horrendous, awful things. Evil exists, believe me. I was losing faith in humanity. But the final straw was—" He shook his head. "This can't interest you."

Abbie sat beside him. "What was the final straw?"

He took his time. "Roger was out for a month following surgery, so I was riding with a young guy who'd just made detective. Manny Lopez. Good cop with a beautiful wife and a baby on the way. Anyway, we got word of a bank robbery in progress and were the first on the scene." He paused, lost in the memory.

"What happened?"

"I took two bullets. In surgery for hours. They tell me I was lucky."

"And your partner?"

He swallowed hard. "Died at the scene." Clearly embarrassed, he took his plate to the sink.

Abbie wasn't sure what to do. She wanted to reach out to him, but it didn't seem appropriate. "... And then this job came along?"

He faced her. "I did some security work for a while. Hated it. So I was glad to get this job. I've known this family my whole life. I love them, really."

"We all do, believe me."

*

Jessie pulled Nick into the study before dinner and closed the doors. "Nick, we have to talk--"

"Jessie, you won't believe what happened this afternoon while Kat—"

"No, Nick, we're not talking about Kat now—"

"This isn't about—"

"NO."

He backed away from her. Confusion, followed by anger, flared in his eyes. He strode to the bar and poured a bourbon, draining the glass in one swallow.

Jessie forced herself to calm down. "You've been procrastinating for days, but we have to make a decision about Willie taking Lyle's place."

He poured another bourbon.

"Honey, I know how much you still miss Lyle, but that place has been sitting empty for eight months. We own the space. Let's make good use of it. Willie's done so much for us. And it would be convenient for both him and us if he lived there."

Silence. A Nick McDeare trademark.

"Why do you want to keep it empty?"

He took a swig of bourbon.

"For God's sake, say something. I hate when you go silent on me. Willie's here for dinner. It's the perfect time to tell him."

The study doors opened. Mary looked from one to the other. "Nick? I need you to start frying the tempura." She returned to the kitchen.

"Nick, please. Let's settle this."

More bourbon.

"Dammit, Nick, say something, or I'm bringing it up at dinner. I'm tired of waiting for you."

Nick drained his glass and slammed it down on the bar. "Do whatever the hell you want." As he strode from the room, his empty glass shattered, shards raining down on the bar and floor.

*

Dinner was interesting. Kat loved the food, but she loved watching the family dynamics more.

There was a lot of talk about Willie taking some apartment behind the brownstone that had belonged to Nick's friend, Lyle Barton.

56

Jessie was all for it. Nick was all about his sushi. Willie kept asking Nick if he was okay with it. Nick assured him he was. Kat didn't believe him.

Abbie volunteered to clean out the place for Willie. It hadn't been touched since Lyle died. What was that about? Kat kept watching Nick. He looked annoyed. And sad. This friend must have meant a lot to him. Hard to imagine Nick McDeare having a friend. He gave off such a loner vibe.

Anthony wanted to know when they were having someone named Luci over for dinner. Jessie dismissed the subject. There was enough upheaval in the house right now. Luci would have to wait.

Upheaval? Obviously she was talking about Kat.

Anthony next asked if Zane could spend the weekend with them. It was his turn to have his friend here, he insisted. Jessie squelched the idea, but Nick gave his permission. This was followed by a measured look between Nick and Jessie.

There was definitely something wrong between the two of them tonight. There were no little smiles or deferring to each other or using words like 'honey' or reaching out for occasional touches. They both looked angry.

Mary was the mediator. Switzerland. She wanted everyone to get along. She did her best to keep the conversation going, but Jessie kept starting little brush fires. Nick was mute, his plate of food the center of his universe.

Helping herself to more edamame, Kat caught Nick's eye. His face remained placid, but there was the hint of a smile on his lips. Before she could stop herself, she smiled back. She glanced at Jessie, who was watching the two of them. Kat's smile faded.

*

Nick was barely holding onto his temper. He methodically ate his food, but he wasn't enjoying it, and that made him even angrier. He loved Japanese, and it was a lot of work to make. But Jessie was getting on his last nerve. He caught the others sneaking glances at him. Too bad. At least he was still sitting here. Taking it from his wife.

His mind kept flashing back to what happened earlier in the study. That glass breaking, long after he set it down. And as he left the room, someone whispered "Stubborn" in his ear. Andrew. First he heard Lyle in Lake Placid. Now he heard Andrew. And that laugh in the living room when he was with Kat. That was also Andrew. He didn't imagine these things. They were real.

They ate in silence for a while, and Nick breathed a sigh of relief. They were going to get through the meal after all.

He watched Anthony take some edamame, again imitating his sister. If Kat got Anthony to eat vegetables, that alone was an advantage to having her here.

"Kat," Anthony said, making a face at the taste of the edamame, "I can't wait for you to come to school with me. You'll meet Luci and—"

Nick interrupted. "We'll talk about school tomorrow."

"Procrastinating again?" Jessie's sarcasm brought the room to a standstill. Chopsticks and forks froze over plates. Mouths halted mid-chew.

Nick put his chopsticks down, folded his napkin, pushed his chair back and stood up, all with a controlled rage. He'd had enough. "I'm going for a run. Come on, Monty."

*

Jessie was waiting for Nick in their bedroom when he got back from his run. She was determined to clear the air. "We need to talk, Nick."

"I don't want to fight." He went into the bathroom.

"Neither do I, so we have to talk this out." She followed him.

Tossing his clothes in the hamper, he stepped into the shower.

"Can I please have just one minute of your attention?" she pressed.

"Give me a second, okay?"

She stormed back into the bedroom. They'd been having problems since Kat set foot in the house. It stopped tonight.

Dizziness swept through her, and she reached for the bed, sitting down hard. She had to calm down.

The bathroom water turned off. Nick appeared, a towel wrapped around his torso, his wet hair slicked back. "Well?"

Deflating, she started to cry. Her emotions were raw, her stomach churning.

"Jessie, what's wrong?" He was beside her, his arm around her. "Please, honey. Tell me what's going on with you."

"With ME?" she sniffled. "Let's talk about what's going on with you."

"I'm fine."

"No, Nick, you're not fine." She wiped away her tears." You won't listen to me about Kat's schooling. You refused to even discuss Willie taking Lyle's apartment. You overturned my decision about Zane staying over--"

"Overturned your decision? Do you hear yourself?" Nick dropped his arm. "Since when is everything that goes on around here your decision? It should be OUR decision. You did the same thing with Luci coming to dinner." He stood up and paced away from her. "As far as Kat's schooling, what makes you an expert on the subject? School is a sore spot for her. If you'd take the time to listen to her, you'd know—"

"She's only been here twenty-four hours. When was I supposed to listen to her?"

"Maybe instead of taking your nap today?"

"Dr. Chao said—"

"Yeah, yeah. You're stressed. Who isn't?"

Anger swiftly replaced tears. "Don't you dare make fun of me, Nick. I deserve better from you. I've done everything I can to make your daughter feel welcome in this house. To understand how important she is to you. Would every wife do that in my situation? I don't think so."

His eyes narrowed. "You can't stand the fact that I had a kid with someone else. Well, I'm sorry, Jess. It happened. And you resent Kat because of it. You're taking your anger out on a twelve-year-old girl."

"I resent Kat because she's been the center of your universe since she popped up on your radar screen. And I'm angry at you, not her!"

"This is ridiculous. I'm sleeping in one of the third-floor bedrooms." Tossing his towel, Nick threw on jeans and a sweater and left the room.

What just happened here? He wouldn't even try to understand how she felt about the situation with Kat, and that wasn't like Nick. He would defend his daughter, no matter what.

Jessie dropped her head, frustrated and confused. What more could she do to make Kat's transition easier? To make Nick happy? Everything she did only infuriated him.

The answer was simple. Nothing.

*

Kat was at her bedroom desk when she heard noise in the hallway. Peeking out, she saw Nick disappear into one on the other bedrooms. Wow, that must have been some fight. She wasn't used to adults fighting.

Returning to her desk, she stroked Hamlet, warming himself under the desk lamp. Opening her laptop, she began to type.

Dear Mom,

It was a day of discovery, both good and bad. Nick and I spent a lot of time together. He took me jogging this morning. It's bizarre, but we're evenly matched as joggers. We both have long legs, good stamina, and we like silent running.

This afternoon I found out he's somewhat of a chef. I helped him make a Japanese dinner, and it was actually fun. Afterwards, he gave me a piano lesson. I was practicing my Chopin, and I was stuck. He gave me great advice. Then he played Beethoven's Moonlight Sonata for me. I've heard that piece since I was five years old. I even learned it a few years ago. But I have NEVER heard it played better. It's interesting, being part of such an artistic family. It's giving me insight, helping me understand where my passion for the arts originates.

The jury's still out on my opinion of Nick, though. He's a chameleon, changing with the wind. Is he a loner? A womanizer? A devoted husband? A disciplined writer? Or a man who speaks through music? Maybe he's a little of each. An enigma. I just don't see him as my father.

Mary is my favorite. A nice lady. Of all the people in this house, she's the only one I'd call normal. Her nephew Willie is nice, too. Another regular person.

They have a friend staying here named Abbie. She's colorful, a flamingo in a houseful of wrens. Well, Nick's not a wren. He's more like a hawk. Anyway, Abbie says whatever pops into her brain, has a gorgeous figure even though she eats everything in sight, and she's hilarious.

Anthony? No opinion yet. He's just a kid, and you know how I feel about kids.

Finally, there's Jessie. She spent the morning seeing a doctor who told her she's stressed. Then she slept all afternoon while everyone else prepared the Japanese meal. She was awful at dinner, mean to Anthony, rude to Nick. He ended up leaving the table and going for a run. Jessie McDeare is a prima donna. Everyone dances to her needs. She hardly talks to me because she doesn't want me here. From what I've read, Nick can have any woman he wants. Why did he choose this woman? It's a mystery ...

Your Kat forever

*

Nick couldn't sleep. His anger with Jessie had dissipated, replaced by questions. What could he do, if anything, to make this transition easier for all of them? Why was Jessie having such a hard time accepting his daughter? Hell, Kat was conceived long before Nick and Jessie knew each other. Jess should understand better than most. She had her own illegitimate son with Gianni.

Discovering he had a daughter, having Kat here on a daily basis, working with her at the piano, making a Japanese meal together stirred up ancient memories. Images flashed through Nick's mind. The ten-year-old boy sitting alone in an oversized house. The twelve-year-old reading his short stories to a dog named Haywire. The fourteen-year-old sneaking into the kitchen of Fujiyama to watch an ancient master create sushi.

Damn. Memories were destructive. They resurrected dark times, kicked you in the gut and served no purpose.

Rolling over, his thoughts turned to Andrew. That voice. He'd know it anywhere. If only Nick had been able to tell Jessie about Andrew when they were in the study before dinner. But she was too intent on farming out Lyle's apartment.

Lyle ...

Nick yawned, finally drifting off, thinking about his friend ...

I'm here, McDeare.

... about McGowan's, the cops' bar Lyle took him to in Hell's Kitchen. They ate the best—

—corned beef on rye with horseradish and mustard—

61

"—and half-sour pickles," Nick mumbled.

Take your daughter there. Tell her about your life. Let Kat be a friend as well as a daughter. She's up to the task, believe me. She's got your genes in her ... Are you hearing me, McDeare?

CHAPTER 6

Jessie sat across the island from Susie Jacobs. Her old friend hadn't changed a bit since their days at Juilliard. She still had long thick, curly locks, though they were now speckled with premature gray. She still wore a dozen necklaces, turquoise stones gleaming in the daylight. And she still had a dazzling smile, long limbs and a fluid grace.

"So," Susie said, "where's your famous husband?"

Jessie hadn't laid eyes on Nick since she got out of bed hours ago. Mary said he went for an early run with Kat, then retreated to his office to work on his book. "Working on his latest novel. Maybe you can meet him later."

"And where's this prodigy of yours?"

"Kat? Well, we don't know she's a prodigy. That's what we want you to tell us. There's a barre up in the gym on the fifth floor. Also a dance floor. She's waiting for you up there. And Susie," she added, "be honest. You don't owe me a thing. If she doesn't have the stuff, so be it."

"Okay," Susie said, scooping up her dance bag and twisting her curls into a knot. "Time to find out what I'm dealing with."

Alone, Jessie bit at a hangnail. She debated going up and trying to straighten things out with Nick, then nixed the idea. She wished she had someone to talk to. But Mary was in the basement doing laundry. And Abbie had gone with Willie to clean out Lyle's place.

*

Abbie scrubbed down the interior of the refrigerator, its noxious contents in a sealed garbage bag.

"What's this computer?" Willie called from the study. "It looks like police equipment."

Abbie got to her feet and joined Willie. "It is. Lyle got it installed from Midtown North."

"Awesome." Willie sat down at the console and typed. "I'm in. The system still takes my password. Roger covers that for me." He pulled up Barton's files. "My God, all this info on Gianni Fosselli. His entire life is on this computer. Should I delete it? He's ancient history now."

"My instincts say keep it. Gianni's like one of those monsters in scary movies who never dies."

"Abbie, he's dead. Nick shot him. He made sure Fosselli was dead."

"Keep it until I'm convinced he hasn't sprouted a new appendage that can wreak havoc on us." Her cell rang.

Willie took the phone. "Hello? ..." He shook his head. "Hung up. I need to find out who owns that number."

Abbie didn't want to talk about it. "Okay, back to the business. What to do with Lyle's things."

"Right." He shut the computer down. "I started making stacks. Clothes. Photos and other personal items. Household things."

"Good. I want to finish in the kitchen, then I'll help you. Have you started in the bedroom yet?"

"No. I ... hate this. Going through a dead man's things."

Abbie hated it, too. Especially since she knew Lyle Barton so well. She found his bottle of Scotch in the cupboard and instinctively put it back. As if he would ever need it again. "This is going to be hard on Nick, but we have to give him the personal stuff. He's next-of-kin since Lyle had no family when he died."

*

Nick was finally able to get some solid work done on his manuscript. His editor needed it by next Tuesday, five days away. The publisher wanted it on the shelves for Christmas. Nick would be shocked if that happened, but the publishing world was changing.

One last chapter to finish, followed by fine-tuning the entire manuscript. He needed to bury himself in this office through Monday.

He was hungry, craving a corned beef on rye. And he couldn't shake a hazy dream he had last night. It stayed annoyingly on the fringe of his subconscious. Lyle was in it ...

"Nick." Jessie shouted for him. "NICK!"

He shot out of his chair. When she used that tone, something was wrong. Flying down to the kitchen, he found Jessie staring at the open *New York Post.* "Look." She pointed to pictures and an article on Page Six.

What now? She slid the paper across the island to him. And there it was.

Three photos of his jog yesterday with Kat, one outside the brownstone. The headline: *Child Bimbo or Bastard Child?*

It was déjà vu. Similar photos of Nick and Jessie appeared in this same paper shortly after Nick first came to town. The accompanying article had been full of ugly and false innuendo about the two of them. Worse, it desecrated Andrew's memory. They jumped through hoops to fix things then, for Andrew's sake, but he'd be damned if he'd do it again. "It's garbage. Damned garbage!"

"What do we do about it?" she asked in a small voice.

"Nothing." He hurled the paper into the garbage. "We ignore it."

"But you have to tell Kat—"

"No. I don't. And I don't want you telling her either. Small cracks are starting to show in her armor. Who knows what something like this would do?"

"But we can't just pretend we never saw it."

"Wanta bet? I'm sick of it. You and I are fair game for those bottom-feeders. It's part of our job descriptions. But I won't let them do it to our kids."

A woman came down the stairs, interrupting them. Jessie introduced her as Susie Jacobs, ballet coach. "Where's Kat?" Nick asked.

"Working on the combinations I taught her."

Jessie offered Susie a cup of coffee. "No thanks. I have a class to teach in an hour. Let me get right to the point. Katrina's had stellar training. She has great feet, soft hands, perfect posture. And she picks up quickly. I would love to coach her. My suggestion? She begins by taking class three times a week, plus occasional private coaching sessions with me. We can reassess after a month or so."

"What did Kat say?" Nick asked, pouring himself some coffee.

"She wants to think about it."

"Think about it?" Jessie looked at Nick, shocked. "What's to think about? A great ballerina like Susie Jacobs wants to take her on and she'll think about it?"

Nick mentally counted to ten before speaking. "I think it's smart."

"So do I," Susie said. "She told me a little of her situation. Quite a lot for a twelve-year-old. I'd rather she makes sure she's committed before wasting my time. Maybe it's too soon for something like this. Maybe she'd rather wait a couple of months until she's more settled."

"Exactly," Nick agreed, avoiding Jessie's glare.

"Anyway, I have to run. I'll see myself out. I gave Kat my number. She'll take it from here." She blew a kiss at Jessie and jogged out of the kitchen.

When the front door slammed, Jessie turned her fury on Nick. "Do you have any idea who that woman is? How lucky Kat is to even have Susie Jacobs take a look at her? She turns down dozens of students every week because they're not up to her standards."

"You heard Susie. It's Kat's decision." Before Jessie could say another word, he climbed the stairs, two at a time.

Back in his office, Nick flopped down in his desk chair, spilling coffee all over himself. He was furious with his clumsiness, furious with Jessie, and furious with that rag, *The New York Post*. It was exhausting to be this angry. And there was no time for exhaustion. Nick had a deadline looming.

His phone thrummed. A reporter from *The Washington Post*, a friend. Probably wanted to know about those photos. Word traveled fast among the media. Another call came in. And another. Nick turned off his phone.

Enough.

*

"So when do I come for dinner?" Luci watched Anthony gobble the sugar cookies she baked for him. The cafeteria was almost empty, afternoon classes about to start.

"Mom said," Anthony explained between bites, "things have to settle down first."

"I don't understand."

"Kat," Anthony choked on a cookie.

"Careful." Luci clapped him on the back until the cookie went down. "I can't come because she's there?"

"Just for now. But soon. See, Kat's ... Dad says she's going through a lot, and we have to try to help her. She's only been here two days."

Nick McDeare's bastard child came before Anthony's needs and wants. It made Luci sick.

"Don't worry," Anthony added, "It'll work out. Promise."

Luci wasn't so sure. She knew all about McDeare's selfish desires.

The bell rang. "Gotta go. See ya." Anthony sprinted out of the cafeteria.

Luci went to her locker and pulled out *The New York Post*. She bought it on her way to work this morning. The pictures helped erase Luci's feeling of helplessness where Anthony was concerned. She knew the paper would print them.

At least she was trying. At least she was doing SOMETHING.

*

"Done." Abbie dropped the last bag of Lyle's belongings on the back porch. "I'll ask Jessie about donating the clothes and household stuff to the Salvation Army. And I'll give this bag of personal items to Nick."

She joined Willie in the kitchen, who just put the garbage out front, including the bare mattress Barton slept on. They'd been there all day, with the exception of Willie picking up Anthony at school.

"You can tell a lot about a person when you go through their things." Willie leaned against the kitchen island.

Abbie pulled the bottle of Scotch from the cupboard. "Shall we? I saved a couple glasses. The only two that weren't chipped."

"Barton was a typical cop. Bare bones."

"And a man of few words. Like Nick." She poured them each some Scotch. Staring at the amber liquid, she suddenly felt sad. "To Lyle Barton," she whispered. They clinked glasses and drank. "You know, I think Lyle was the only true friend Nick ever had."

"He's taken his death hard."

"Nick feels responsible." Abbie swirled the Scotch around in her glass. "He thinks if he and Barton had never met, Lyle would be alive today. Barton was getting nowhere on Andrew's case until Nick blew into town. Together, they took a lot of risks going after the nefarious Gianni Fosselli. I ought to know. I helped them. And when they finally caught up with him, it cost Lyle his life." She was on the verge of tears. Abbie adored Lyle Barton.

"Abbie." His voice soft, Willie forced her to look at him. "Barton was a cop down to his bones. A cop's cop. Sure, when Nick came along they had the perfect marriage—"

"Marriage?"

"Partnership. For cops it's like a marriage. Or so they tell me.

"You've never been married?"

Willie shook his head. "I came close with LeJeanne. But that's a story for another day. Anyway, Lyle was all about getting his man, with or without Nick." He shrugged. "In the end, he got him. Case closed."

"You need to say all this to Nick."

"Nah. He'll figure it out for himself."

"I'm not so sure. Nick is hurting. Which is why I'm happy Kat came along. She's exactly what he needs at exactly the right time."

Hearing a sound in the study, they peeked into the room.

The computer had been off all afternoon as they worked on the apartment.

But it was on now.

And Gianni's files were front and center.

*

Jessie sat in the breakfast nook, sipping a cup of tea. Her phone buzzed non-stop. Probably friends and reporters asking about the *Post's* photos. All calls were sent to voice mail.

She hadn't laid eyes on Nick since their earlier fight. He didn't come down for lunch. Now it was dinnertime. She glanced at Mary, her nose buried in a crossword puzzle, glasses perched on her nose.

Willie and Abbie came in through the back porch and sat at the island. "We got it done," Abbie announced. She looked tired.

"Was it awful?" Jessie asked.

"It was filthy and cluttered and depressing. But it's ready for a new chapter."

"Yep," Willie said. "Now it needs furniture and stuff."

"Stuff?" Abbie's eyebrows shot up.

"My favorite word. Can apply to anything and everything."

"Well then you need a boatload of stuff."

"Willie, before you spend a fortune, check our storage on the fourth floor," Jessie suggested. "You'll find a ton of stuff. Take what you want."

"Got any ghostbusters up there?" There was a look of mischief on Abbie's face.

"I told you," Willie whispered. "It's an old computer. With glitches. And I'm not sure I shut it down the right way earlier.

Mary tossed her puzzle aside. "Dinner's ready. Help yourself. Pot roast, new potatoes and carrots on the stove. French bread in the oven. Salad on the counter."

"You're a godsend, Mary." Abbie grabbed two plates, handing one to Willie. "Where's Nick?"

Jessie shrugged. "Working. I assume."

"I have something for him. I'll take it up after I fill my stomach."

*

Nick pushed away from his desk and rose, stretching. He finished the last chapter. Now he needed a break before he began to tweak.

Ambling to the window he looked across at Lyle's apartment. Abbie and Willie had been over there all day, but now the place looked deserted. It was dusk already, the days getting shorter. Another year was almost over. And what a year. A wedding. A kidnapping. A senseless death. And a new daughter.

There was a knock at the door. Abbie poked her head in. "Don't mean to disturb you."

"You're not. Come on in."

She was carrying something, which she handed to him.

"What's this?"

Abbie sighed. "Some of Lyle's things I thought you'd want."

Nick looked down at the black plastic bag. This was what a life amounted to. A small garbage bag of belongings. He nodded, not trusting his voice. Abbie surprised him by throwing her arms around his neck and hugging him. "I miss him, too." Her voice was hoarse, emotional.

Nick held her tight. The three of them had been through a lot together as they searched for Gianni Fosselli.

She pulled back, looking up at him. "You okay?"

He didn't respond. He couldn't.

"You will be. Fate intervened, sending you Kat."

Let Kat be a friend as well as a daughter. That hazy dream again.

"Well," she said, backing towards the door. "I'll let you get back to work." And off she went.

Nick sunk down into the chair, fingering the bag in his hands. Whatever was in here, he knew he wasn't ready for it yet.

*

Jessie was curled into the wicker couch on the glassed-in back porch. Hurricane lamps cast the room in a soothing golden glow.

Mary had taken plates up to Kat and Nick. The girl hadn't left her room since her ballet audition that morning. Nick was buried in his work. Willie went back to his mom's. And Abbie was soaking in a hot tub.

Her chin cupped in her hand, Jessie stared out the windows at the darkness. She hated winter, with its short days and bitter cold. She had hoped a New Year's Eve wedding would change her dislike of the season. It hadn't. Anthony had been kidnapped by Gianni Fosselli at the wedding, turning a celebration into a devastation. Yes, winter was a gloomy season.

Jessie's eyes came to rest on Lyle's apartment. If it wasn't for Lyle, Anthony wouldn't be sleeping upstairs right now. Lyle and Nick. Lyle gave his life so she could have her son back. Nick wasn't the only one who missed their friend. She missed his calm voice, his sense of order, the balance he brought to his friendship with Nick. Nick was fearless, volatile. Lyle was steady, cautious.

"Jess?" Nick stood in the doorway. "Can we talk?"

"Sure. I want to, in fact." She was relieved to see him.

He sat down beside her. "I'm sorry. I hate fighting with you."

"Me, too, Nick."

He leaned over and kissed her. It had been too long since she felt his lips on hers. "So," he began, "should we start by talking about Kat's schooling?"

"Sure. But you have to promise not to get mad at me."

"Promise."

Jessie curled her fingers through his. "Okay." She took a deep breath. "You know I registered Kat for school before she even got here. You agreed she would attend Anthony's school."

"That was before—"

"Just hear me out, okay?" He nodded. "Children need friends. A school provides an education and a social life. Both are important for their development. Here's my proposal. We send Kat to school, like we

70

agreed. For a month. If she doesn't like it after a month, we talk about home schooling."

"For both kids. You heard Anthony. He hates that school. We can't have one child home-schooled and not the other."

They locked eyes, at an obvious impasse.

"Okay. Both kids," Jessie relented. "Are we agreed?"

He formally shook her hand. "Agreed. I'll get the brandy. To celebrate."

"Not for me." He halted, a surprised look on his face. "My stomach."

He was back immediately, brandy and snifter in hand. One swig and he groaned with satisfaction. "About Kat." He stretched his legs out in front of him. "Do you mind if I tell her? It's going to take some convincing."

"I'd be thrilled if you'd do it. Otherwise, I come off as the wicked stepmother."

Nick chuckled. "Situation resolved." He brought her palm to his lips, his tongue doing an old familiar dance, sending a tingle down her spine.

"I'm sorry if you think I've been difficult about Kat, Nick," she whispered. "I don't mean to be. I guess I just need time to get used to another child in the house. Especially one that isn't mine."

She felt Nick stiffen. "Anthony isn't mine."

"You know what I mean. It's different with Kat and me."

"Why?"

She released his hand. "Kat's your daughter with another woman. Someone you had an affair with. And that takes some getting used to."

Anger crept into his eyes. "Anthony's your son with another man. Someone you had an affair with. And it didn't bother me at all."

"You're kidding, right?" She straightened up, stunned. "You're actually saying you weren't jealous of Gianni Fosselli?"

"I was not jealous of Gianni Fosselli."

"You were so jealous you were spitting bullets!"

"I was not. Why would I be?"

"Because Anthony was his son. Because Gianni was still in love with me."

Now Nick straightened up. "And people accuse ME of having an inflated ego. You have me beat by a mile."

"That's a horrible thing to say!"

"I was convinced Gianni Fosselli killed Andrew. That was the extent of my feelings for the man. Period. Jealousy never came into it." He laughed and shook his head.

Jessie leapt up. "Come down off your throne. You were jealous. Period. Maybe you don't remember because jealousy isn't part of your usual repertoire."

Nick got to his feet. "That's right. I don't get jealous. Ever. You, however, are a walking example of jealousy right now."

Jessie headed for the kitchen. "I'M jealous?"

"YOU'RE jealous." Nick followed her.

"Of what?"

"Of Kat. Of her mother. A woman I haven't laid eyes on for a decade. It's ridiculous."

"I'm ridiculous?"

"If the shoe fits ..."

"Damn you, Nick. DAMN YOU!"

Mary appeared on the stairs. "Hush. I could hear you from my room. Right down the hall from Kat. Which means she heard you, too."

Nick's eyes became slits. "Good job, Jessie." He pounded up the stairs, almost knocking Mary over.

*

Dear Mom,

It's been another weird day, some of it good, some of it awful.

Nick and I jogged again early this morning. It was just like yesterday — a long quiet run in the cold air. I loved it. When we finished he took me to his favorite English bakery, Great Expectations. I had a scone with clotted cream for the first time. I actually liked it, even though the thought of eating anything clotted is revolting. Nick's traveled all over the world, so he has adventurous taste in food. He's spent a lot of time in England, London in particular. The way he described it made me want to see it one day. And taste it. He said the world makes fun of English food, but he loves it. Their sausage is his favorite — called bangers. How funny!

Later this morning I met with a ballet coach who watched me dance. Susie Jacobs is a famous ballerina, and she was so complimentary of my technique. She wants to take me on, which is thrilling, but I need some time to get used to my new family and home before I get involved in anything else. Still, I'm pretty sure I want to study with her.

There's something odd going on around here. I began to think this house is haunted until I remembered I had some bizarre episodes right before I left Lake Placid. One night I thought someone was stroking my hair. And at the hotel it looked like someone was breathing on the window. I hoped maybe it was you watching over me. But then yesterday when Nick and I were playing the piano we heard a man's laugh. Nick tried to tell me it was Anthony's TV upstairs, but that's impossible. Crazy, huh?

I spent the afternoon doing something that would probably make you mad. I know it would make Nick mad. I snuck one of his novels from the study and read it up in my room. He told me I was too young for his books, but after the way he described England I was curious about his writing. His plots are thrilling, full of surprises, and his characters are rich and full. You CARE about them. If only I could write like him!

I was so busy reading I forgot about dinner. Mary surprised me and brought a plate to my room. We talked about Nick a little. She said he enjoys having me around. I think he's just getting used to me. But am I getting used to him?

A few minutes ago I heard a horrible fight between Nick and Jessie. They were screaming at each other. It was about me. And you. Jessie hates that he had a child with another woman. She's jealous, and she never even met you! You are more than she will ever be, Mom.

I wish Nick was a single father. I think our chances would be so much greater with Jessie out of the picture.

Your Kat forever

CHAPTER 7

Nick spent the morning working on his manuscript. It was Friday, his Tuesday deadline getting closer. Needing a break, he went in search of Kat. He found her in the fifth-floor gym, dressed in a leotard, her hair in a tight chignon. Humming, she worked at the barre. On pointe. Wow.

She didn't see him at first. He remained in the doorway, admiring her. Hard to believe this lithe, graceful creature was his daughter. That they shared the same gene pool was a mystery to him.

Hamlet reclined on the windowsill. The cat had attached himself to the young girl. Two loners found solace in each other's company. Hamlet gave Kat someone to love.

Haywire sat at Nick's feet as he wrote. The dog slept at the foot of his bed. He made Nick laugh when he felt like crying ...

Seeing Nick, Kat stopped dancing. "What?"

He approached her. "I don't know anything about ballet, but it looks like your gift for the piano has some serious competition."

She looked down. Was she embarrassed by his compliment? "Thank you."

"I want to talk to you about school."

Kat sighed dramatically and turned away. Shades of her Uncle Andrew.

"I know how you feel, Kat. But I think you should give it a shot."

"In other words, you're caving to Jessie."

Nick's eyes narrowed. "I don't ever want to hear you speak about Jessie in that tone again. Understand?" He waited.

She nodded. Imperceptibly.

"For the record, I didn't cave. I weighed the pros and cons. I want you to try it. For one month. You never know. You might like it. But if you hate it, we'll talk about home-schooling." Truth be told, he made some calls that morning about a tutor. One name kept coming up, so that problem was solved. "One month. Then we reevaluate. Okay?"

Another slight nod.

He won this battle, a tough one. The first in what was sure to be a long line of skirmishes. Nick would take them one at a time. "What about ballet? Have you decided to train with Susie?"

Kat turned her steely gaze on him. "I'm weighing the pros and cons."

Such a mouth on the girl. He wanted to wipe that smirk off her face. "One more thing. Put my book back in the study."

"Did you search my room?" Her indignation was over-the-top. Andrew would applaud her dramatic flair.

"Of course not. You know how I feel about privacy. I checked the bookshelves. *RED ROVER* is missing." He hoped his own smirk reflected hers.

"Do you want to know what I think of it?

He said nothing, turning on his heel and heading for the door.

"I wish I could write like you."

Nick couldn't help smiling. His first compliment. "One day I suspect you'll surpass me," he mumbled to himself.

*

Anthony's friend Zane Harwell arrived that afternoon, staying for the weekend. Jessie was fond of Zane, with his gray eyes and spikey blond hair. He was polite, quiet and highly intelligent. Nick seemed to have a special bond with the boy. With all children. He knew how to talk to them. How to reach them on their level without talking down to them. Jessie was jealous. She freely admitted it.

Despite the cooler temperature, Nick fired up the backyard grill, making burgers for the boys and steaks for the adults. Mary provided seasoned French fries and corn on the cob, frozen from the sweet crop of the summer. Willie and Abbie supplied pumpkin cheesecake from Goldblatz Gourmet Delights.

Jessie and Nick had an unspoken agreement to put aside their fighting in front of the kids. She pretended all was well in the House of McDeare. Anthony and Zane were boisterous. Abbie was loud. Willie and Mary, chatty. And Nick and Kat, quiet. After dinner, everyone retired to the study. Nick lit a fire in the grate, the first of the season, and excused himself. His manuscript wasn't going to write itself, he declared. Jessie had been through enough deadlines with Nick to know his work took priority right now.

Kat said an early good night. Probably didn't feel comfortable without Nick, her security blanket, in attendance.

Zane surprised them by producing a Ouija board, a recent birthday gift.

Abbie proclaimed it was perfect for a spooky Friday night and began to explain to Willie how it worked.

Jessie didn't think it was a good idea. She believed in spirits, of course, because of Andrew. So did Nick and Anthony. Maybe that was why she feared using the board. "I'm not sure this is appropriate for kids."

"Mom," Anthony drew the word out and rolled his eyes. "Zane's mother gave it to him. She doesn't think there's anything wrong with it."

"Come on, Jess, it's harmless." Abbie was already unpacking the board. "No one really believes a piece of wood can conjure up spirits. It's just for fun."

"Zane," Jessie sat down next to the boy, "I appreciate your bringing it. I do. But I'd rather we found something else to do. How about watching a movie?"

"I'm going to ask Dad." Anthony leapt up.

"Anthony, no! Your father can't be disturbed—"

The boy was gone, hurdling up the kitchen stairs.

Irritated, Jessie followed her son.

*

J spent his days looking for an apartment. Damn, the city had gotten so expensive. Whenever he needed a break, he made his annoying phone calls to Abigail Forrester. He knew the calls would drive her crazy, but she deserved more, much more. And he was working on it.

J got a good laugh out of the photos of McDeare and his kid in the *Post*. The pictures must have caused major hysteria in that deranged house. He'd be willing to bet there were a dozen more mini-McDeares running around out there, waiting to explode on his doorstep.

Karma was a bitch.

*

Nick ignored the knock on his office door. The family knew his work rules.

Another knock. "Dad, it's me." Anthony used his quiet voice. As if that made a difference. "I gotta talk to you. Please."

Nick unlocked the door. "I'm working, Anthony."

"I'm sorry, Dad. Really sorry. But Mom won't let us play with the Ouija board Zane brought. His own mother gave it to him, so what's the big deal?"

Jessie burst into the room. "Anthony, you know you're not to disturb your father when he's working."

"Dad, please. Zane saved the game specially for tonight."

Nick slumped back into his chair. He was familiar with Ouija boards. Jessie was overreacting. "A Ouija board is just a game, Jess. It can't connect with the spirit world. It's all hype. I don't see any harm in the boys playing with the board, especially if the adults are in on it, too."

Anthony clapped his hands and skipped from the room, proclaiming victory all the way down the stairs.

Jessie glared at Nick. "Just once I wish you'd take my side."

"I did. Kat's going to Anthony's school."

"Right." Her voice dripped with sarcasm. "If she's going to school, why did you spend the morning looking for a tutor?"

What in the hell? Did Jessie listen at his office door? Was she eavesdropping now?

"What, no witty quick-fire response?" She left the room, slamming the door.

*

When Jessie didn't return to the study, Mary took charge. They played with the Ouija board, paying no attention to the rules. Questions flew in rapid succession. Answers made no sense. There was a lot of laughing and cynicism.

Then Anthony asked about Andrew. The board spelled out I-M H-E-R-E B-O-N-G-O.

Mary shut the game down. "Who wants to watch a scary movie?" She shot Abbie a meaningful look.

Abbie got the message. "Come on. Let's make popcorn." Abbie and Willie hustled the boys to the kitchen.

A chill danced down Mary's spine.

Bongo.

The family wasn't aware that Mary knew all about their dark secret. That Andrew's spirit had returned to this house for a brief period

77

to guide Nick to his killers. And to bring Nick and Jessie together. Did they think Andrew would return without spending time with Mary?

Mary knew everything that went on in this house. Always had. Always will.

A framed photo fell over on the mantel, making Mary jump. After the incident with the Ouija board, she was jittery. Picking up the photo she sucked in her breath. It was a picture of Andrew planting a kiss on Mary's cheek at her fiftieth birthday party.

Mary chuckled. "Welcome back, Andrew. I've missed you."

*

The weekend flew by for Nick. Time passed quickly when you didn't have enough of it. He put in fourteen-hour days, working late into the night.

He wasn't able to spend any time with the boys, something he always enjoyed. And his jog with Kat was interrupted by a swarm of reporters. When they were accosted as they tried to leave the house, Nick decided to use the back way out, through Lyle's apartment. It was an old trick, employed when they wanted to escape unnoticed.

Walking through Barton's place was difficult. Abbie and Willie were painting, the rooms stripped of everything familiar. Only the police computer remained. Boxes of supplies and furniture waited to be unpacked. And Barton's bottle of Scotch sat on the kitchen island.

Nick saw little of Jessie that weekend. He ate his meals in his office and went to bed long after she was asleep. Truth be told, he was tired of being angry with her. He could barely remember what they were fighting about. They needed to call a permanent truce.

If they ever ran into each other again.

*

Dear Mom,

It's late Sunday night. Anthony's friend Zane finally went home. There are already too many people in this house. Another kid was one person too many.

I didn't see much of Nick this weekend. His deadline for the new book is Tuesday morning. When we left the house to jog, some reporters approached us. Nick shoved me back inside before I could make out what they were asking. We used a back way out, which felt very 'secret agent.' When I asked Nick what the reporters wanted, he brushed it off.

So I went online to see what it was about. Sure enough I found pictures of Nick and me jogging, with articles insinuating I'm either his bastard daughter or one of his bimbos. I don't know why Nick didn't tell me about this. Doesn't he know you can't keep anything secret, not in this era of Twitter and Instagram and Google? Was he trying to protect me, like he promised before we left Lake Placid? He warned me about incidents like this, but I didn't think I'd be of any interest to anyone. I was wrong. I have to admit I don't like being the target of gossip. I'm used to our simple life, Mom. How I wish I could click my heels together and we could go back to that golden time.

Tomorrow I have to go to that school. I'm going to hate it, I know I will. But I'll keep peace between Nick and Jessie and give it a try. Not that peace seems to be an option for them. All they've done since I got here is fight. I've been spending a ton of time in my room, staying out of the way. I have Hamlet for company, and that's enough for now. He doesn't want anything from me but unconditional love, and that's easy to give. He's the sweetest little thing.

Your Kat forever

*

Nick made sure he was downstairs Monday morning when Kat left for school. He knew she was dreading it.

Mary went out of her way and made the girl a special lunch. Crab salad, croissants and exotic fruit. Anthony was excited to have company in the car that morning. Willie lounged against the island, waiting to drive the kids. And Jessie was silent.

Abbie was still asleep. Now that Willie's place was finished, she'd probably revert back to sleeping until noon.

Nick hoped against hope that Kat would like the school. But if she didn't, he intended to keep his word and have her home-schooled. He never broke a promise to a child.

"I wanted to tell you something all weekend, Dad," Anthony said between bites of cinnamon toast, "but you were never around. When we were playing with the Ouija board, Daddy Andrew said he was here."

Nick choked on his coffee. "What?"

"And he called me Bongo."

79

Jessie turned her steely blue eyes on Nick. There was no mistaking her expression: I told you so.

Thinking quickly, Nick turned back to Anthony. "Abbie was probably goofing on you. Everyone knows your nickname's Bongo."

"You think? ... Maybe ... I'll ask her."

Knowing Anthony's attention span, it would be forgotten by noon. But just in case ... Mental note to self: warn Abbie. Without telling her the truth.

Andrew was back in the house.

*

J woke up that morning with an extra bounce in his step. Today was the day he put his plan into action. The beginning, anyway. It should go off without a hitch. He would make no mistakes. Leave no fingerprints behind. Nothing that could be traced back to him.

It all hinged on one phone call.

When J placed the call, he was thrilled to be put right through. "Harry? Hi. This is a blast from your past ..."

*

Kat decided to eat her lunch alone in the school's stone courtyard. Anthony and Zane had invited her to join them in the cafeteria, but she wasn't ready to be associated with the McDeare family yet. To the other kids she was Katrina Gillingham, new student from Lake Placid.

So far, the day was a bust. Reporters followed their car that morning. Willie managed to outrun them, speeding through yellow lights. Anthony thought it was a hoot. Kat was sure they'd be killed. Unfortunately, she made it to the dreaded school in one piece.

As she followed some pencil-pusher down the busy hallway, heads turned, fingers pointed, conversations halted. Apparently, new students were unusual in this expensive haven. After meeting the headmaster in his office, Kat wasn't sure which she preferred – the reporters' trashy questions or this nerdy man with the pathetic rug and coke-bottle glasses who looked like he sucked lemons for a living. What she really wanted to do was run.

Her first two hours were taken up with testing. The results were predictable. She was joining the ninth-grade class.

Here we go again. Only now I'm dealing with teen bitches.

"Kat?" Anthony interrupted her solitary lunch. Zane and a foreign-looking woman were with him. "This is my friend, Luci. And this is my sister, Kat."

The woman nodded. "Hello, Kat."

An accent. Spanish?

"Hello."

Silence hung in the air.

"Luci's coming for dinner soon."

Great. More people in the house.

"She's a good cook. She makes me special things all the time."

And your point is ...?

"Do you like the school?" the woman asked.

No. I hate it.

"I guess so."

Turning away, Kat resumed eating.

"Well," Anthony said, "meet you after school."

Kat eyed Luci as the trio went back inside. There was something about that woman that gave her the creeps.

As she gathered her empty containers she heard high-pitched laughter. A group of girls stood a few yards away, their heads together, watching her and whispering.

Great. She'd just been outed as a McDeare.

Thanks, Anthony.

*

Working at his desk, Nick heard Kat come up the stairs. She was home from school. Hurrying to the door he was in time to see her turn down the third-floor hallway. He'd give her a few minutes, then go up to see how the day went.

Anthony met him on the landing, milk and cookies clutched in his fists.

"How was school, Bongo?"

"Awful. One of the football players stuffed me in a locker."

"Did you report him?"

"Yeah. Mr. Yablonski didn't do anything. Just told the jerk not to do it again."

"You want me to talk to the headmaster?"

"It wouldn't do any good. I hate that school." He went to his room and slammed the door.

Nick climbed the stairs and knocked on Kat's open door. "How'd it go?"

She sat on the bed, her legs tucked beneath her. Hamlet was on her lap. "Just as expected. I tested two grades ahead, so that's where they put me."

"Nicholas, we're going to move you ahead in school. You're not properly challenged with kids your own age."

"In the older classes, they teased me about being smart. They treated me like I was some kind of freak."

"You're a freak of nature, McDeare. What fifteen-year-old takes college courses?"

"And then when they realized—" She looked down at the cat, stroking him.

"Realized what?"

"Nothing."

"Tell me."

She looked up at him. "That I'm your daughter, they gave me crap about being a bastard all afternoon."

"My dad told me you're adopted, McDeare. Which makes you a bastard."

"And don't tell me not to use those words. They're perfect words to describe what happened."

Damn. It wasn't Kat's fault she was his daughter. "I'm sorry, Kat."

"Please don't make me go back. Please!" She looked ... anguished. Another perfect word. "I'll do anything not to have to go back there tomorrow."

He hated himself for what he was about to say. What he had to say. "Give it more time. Maybe the kids will come around." Even he didn't believe what he was saying.

"They won't. Being smart and your illegitimate daughter is unforgiveable in their eyes."

Nick wanted to punch a wall.

Kat turned away, reaching for a textbook. "I have a lot of homework."

At the door, Nick glanced back at the girl. Hamlet licked her cheek with his scratchy tongue. Kat buried her face in the cat's fur.

Haywire sensed his dark mood, pawing Nick and licking his face.

Deborah Fezelle

Nick returned to his office and forced himself to finish his work. But the thought of his daughter upset over something that was no fault of her own haunted him for the rest of the night.

*

Kat sat morosely in the back seat as Willie pulled the car in front of the school.

"Come on, Kat." Anthony scampered to the sidewalk, waiting for her. Dragging herself from the car she followed Anthony towards the door.

In an instant she was surrounded by reporters, all asking questions simultaneously. She pushed through them, only to be confronted by the same girls who taunted her yesterday. Backing up, she ran into the reporters again.

Tossing her books on the sidewalk she broke free, sprinting down the sidewalk. Hearing Anthony call her, she glanced over her shoulder. He was running after her, his short legs pummeling the pavement. "Kat, wait for me!"

Rounding a corner, she halted, catching her breath. Anthony caught up with her. "Why'd you run?"

"I'm not going back in that school. Ever." Spinning around, she put more distance between the school and herself.

Anthony was right on her heels. "If you're not going back, I'm not either." With a burst of speed, Anthony raced past her. "Come on."

Kat couldn't let him run off by himself. He was too young. Annoyed, she chased after him.

*

Willie leapt out of the car the moment he saw what was happening to Kat. By the time he reached the girl he was too late. The two kids had taken off down the street. Realizing they were too far ahead of him, Willie's only choice was to follow them in the car.

Grabbing his cell, he speed-dialed Nick.

*

Jessie clicked off her cell. The doctor got the blood tests back. He wasted no time telling her the news. She needed to alter her diet and activities immediately.

A million emotions coursed through her. She worried about Nick's reaction. What would he say? Their lives were altered again. With one phone call everything changed. Would they ever have

83

stability? Be able to settle into a routine without wondering what other surprises lurked down the road?

She had to tell Nick. She couldn't put it off.

*

Nick reread the dedication in his book: 'For Lyle Barton. The quintessential cop and friend.' *THE SILVER LINING* was ready to fly. He pushed SEND.

Finishing a manuscript was always bittersweet. He lived with the characters for months, sometimes a year at a time.

Nick pulled the last sheet of paper from his battered typewriter. Finished. He was proud of himself. How many thirteen-year-olds wrote a novel? Closing the box of cherished pages, a wave of sadness swept through him. He gave the characters life. Now he had to say goodbye to them. They had become old friends.

Nick's cell thrummed. Willie. "What's up?" Listening, his fear grew by the second. "I'm on my way. Don't worry. I'll find you."

Leaping out of his chair, he collided with Jessie in the outer hallway.

"Nick, I have to talk to you."

"Not now. Later, okay? Promise." He tried to keep the panic out of his voice as he brushed past her.

"But it's important."

"Jess, I don't have time--"

"It's Kat, isn't it?"

"Yes. Now I have to go. I'll be back as soon as I can."

*

Jessie watched Nick dash down the steps.

Running off to rescue Kat. Or comfort Kat. Or show Kat how much he loved her. Kat would always come first with him. Always.

Before his wife. Who needed him now more than ever.

Before his son. Who couldn't survive losing another father.

Dragging herself to her bedroom, Jessie dropped onto the bed. She felt alone and scared.

CHAPTER 8

"Willie, where are you exactly?" Nick was in the back of a cab not far from the school, cell pressed to his ear.

"I'm double-parked at Seventy-Third and Riverside."

Two minutes later, Nick climbed into Willie's car. "Where are they?"

"I'm sorry, Nick. I lost them. I saw them turn down this block. I've driven around the area, and no sight of them. Damn."

"I may know where they are. Come on." He got out of the car and led the way into Riverside Park. As they trekked north a few blocks, his cell rang.

It was Jessie. Panicked. "Nick, Mr. Yablonski called from the school. Kat and Anthony ran away. They never came into the school."

"I know. I'm on it. Please don't worry. They're together, and Anthony knows the neighborhood."

"This is where you were going when you ran out of here? Why didn't you tell me?"

"There wasn't time. I have to go, Jess. I'll keep you updated." He clicked off. "There they are." He nodded towards a bench near the Hudson River. Anthony and Kat sat staring at the water.

*

"Dad brings me here sometimes when we need to talk." Anthony explained. He looked sideways at Kat. "Why'd you run away? Why didn't you run into the school? Or back in the car?"

She shrugged. "I just wanted to get away. I didn't care where I went." She glanced at him, her dislike obvious. "The mystery is why you came along."

Anthony felt a stab in the pit of his stomach. "Why do you hate me?"

"I don't. I don't know you."

"You don't want to know me."

Again that awful glance at him.

"What did I do?"

"Nothing. Stop asking questions." She seemed angry. She was always angry.

"It's not my fault you had to come live with us. And it's not Dad's either. Why can't you be nicer?"

"You don't understand."

"Then explain it to me."

"I lost my mom, okay?" She was definitely angry now.

"I know. And that's sad. I know how you feel. I'm still sad Daddy Andrew died."

"But you had your mother. I don't have anyone."

"You have your dad. And that makes you lucky, because your dad is the best in the whole world. I should know. I've had three."

"Three?"

"Gianni, Daddy Andrew, and now Dad. And I lost Lyle, too."

"Who is this Lyle?"

"Dad's best friend. He was the whole family's friend. He died saving me when Gianni kidnapped me. So I'm not just sad, I feel guilty, too, and that beats just being sad by a lot."

*

"Should we bring them home?" Willie asked.

"They're talking," Nick whispered, as he and Willie hid behind a large tree. "Let's not interrupt. See where it goes." He hoped the kids would bond. Kat needed a friend, someone who didn't use a sandbox for a toilet.

"I'm sorry, Nick. About not getting to Kat sooner back at the school. It happened so fast, it surprised me. I don't know where those reporters came from. They weren't there when the kids first got out of the car."

"It's not your fault, Willie. If you couldn't get to them, no one could." Right now he could rip those media vipers apart.

*

Jessie sat at the kitchen island with Mary, nibbling on a piece of toast. She was furious with Nick. Not only had he withheld the news about Kat and Anthony from her in the first place, he hung up on her when she asked him about it on the phone. This wasn't like Nick. Or maybe it was. The old Nick. Secretive and thoughtless. The bachelor who answered to no one.

"Honey," Mary said, pouring herself more coffee, "let it go. The kids will be okay. Nick will see to it."

"It's not the kids, Mary. It's Nick. Our marriage is in trouble. And the timing couldn't be worse."

"You're certifiable. If there's one marriage that's not in trouble, it's yours."

"We've been fighting non-stop. Everything sets him off. Except Kat."

"It's not Nick. Well, it's not only Nick." She forced Jessie to look at her. "I know you talked to the doctor. And I know what he told you."

"You know?"

"Of course. When are you going to learn I know everything that goes on in this house? With everyone." She reached over and squeezed Jessie's hand. "Tell Nick. Trust me, it will put an end to your fighting."

*

"Everybody talks about Lyle like he was some kind of saint," Kat dug through her purse for gum. "And whenever his name comes up, Nick looks like he lost his best friend."

"I just TOLD you he was Dad's best friend!" Anthony rolled his eyes dramatically. "Dad didn't have friends before Lyle."

Nick said he didn't have friends when he was a kid. He said nothing about being friendless as an adult.

"It took Dad and Lyle a long time to get close. In the beginning they fought a lot. But Lyle ended up being Best Man at the wedding."

Okay, Nick's friend died. That doesn't compare to losing a mother.

"Dad's lost too many people. His son Jeffrey. His brother Andrew. And then Lyle. I think losing Lyle was too much for him."

A son, a brother and a best friend.

"I know about Jeffrey," she said. "He was ten when he died. The articles I read said Nick was too busy with his books to spend time with his son."

"That's not true!" Anthony was red in the face. "Dad loved Jeffrey, and Jeffrey loved Dad." He stuck out his left hand. "See this ring?" He pointed to a thick gold band with a sizeable diamond in the middle. "Dad brought it back from Africa for Jeffrey, and when Jeffrey

87

died, Dad gave it to me." He slipped it off his finger. "He even had our initials carved on the inside. So don't say Dad didn't have time for him. Yeah, he was working and had to travel, but he saw Jeffrey all the time. And for your information, I only saw Dad cry twice. When he told me about Jeffrey. And when Lyle died."

Wow, this kid really loves Nick, and Nick isn't even his blood father.

Anthony stood up and dug in his pocket. "I'm hungry. I have twelve dollars. Let's get some pizza. There's a really good place near here."

*

J met his old pal Harry for lunch. First, they gossiped about old friends. J was relieved to learn that nothing had changed. They both still hated the same people. It made his task that much easier.

After an hour of catching up, he swung the subject around to his mission. His request was innocent enough, at least that's the way he made it sound to Harry. And it dealt with a person they mutually loathed. As expected, Harry was happy to oblige and made the call immediately. J's meeting was set up for tomorrow. Drinks at the Golden Calf Bar on Madison.

J picked up the tab over his friend's protestations. A little extra insurance, so-to-speak. Harry was the tightest S.O.B. J had ever known.

Back out on the street, J put part two of his master plan into play, making a quick call. Another old friend was thrilled to hear J was back in town. A favor? Sure. Anything for such a valuable client.

The day was a total success.

*

Nick called Jessie to update her. He got her voice mail. "Just want you to know the kids are okay. We'll be home soon." He clicked off, angry she wouldn't pick up. She was probably listening as he left the message.

"Quick, hide, Nick. They're coming this way."

Feeling ridiculous, Nick sidled around the massive tree with Willie, trying not to be seen by Kat and Anthony as they passed by. Next the cops would probably show up and arrest them for stalking children. Backing up, he stepped in a pile of—Dammit!

Nick scraped the sole of his shoe against the tree, but it was pointless. The entire shoe had sunk down into--

"Come on, Nick, or we'll lose them— What are you doing?"

Nick cursed. "Some dog left me a care package."

"I don't think that's from a dog."

"What the hell else would it be?"

"A horse?"

"Shit."

"Exactly."

A woman walking her poodles stopped and stared at Nick. "You're Nick McDeare, aren't you?"

Nick inwardly groaned. "Sorry, lady. I get mistaken for that crud all the time." He whispered to Willie, "Let's get the hell out of here."

*

"This is Dad's favorite pizza place. Costello's. We always come here after we hit some balls in the park."

Kat wasn't impressed. The place was a hole-in-the-wall. There were only two small tables, and both were taken. The pock-faced guy behind the counter handed her a huge slice with pepperoni. She'd never seen pizza sold by the slice, and this slice was the size of an entire pie back in Lake Placid. "How do you eat this thing?" She had to balance it with both hands.

"Like this." Anthony folded his slice over and ate it like a sandwich. "This is how New Yorkers eat pizza."

Kat gave it a try, taking a big bite. She grabbed some napkins to wipe the juice – or grease? – dripping from her mouth. Whatever it was, it was fantastic.

"Like it?" Anthony asked, his mouth full.

Kat nodded and took another bite. She couldn't stop shoving the mega-hit into her mouth. The pizza was off-the-charts outstanding!

*

Nick and Willie ducked inside a Korean vegetable market across the street from Kat and Anthony. Nick tugged the visor of his new Knicks cap further down on his forehead. There would be no more sightings of Nick McDeare today.

"That pizza looks great," Willie said.

"It is." Nick's stomach growled. He skipped breakfast that morning to get the book off to the editor. He'd kill for a slice of Costello's right now.

"Did you notice Anthony showed her how to eat the pizza?" Willie chuckled.

89

"I noticed." The odor coming from Nick's shoe was gagging him.

"God, what's that smell?" Willie crinkled his nose. "Is that your shoe?"

"Shut up."

Willie looked around. "Let's get out of here. You're starting to attract flies."

As they moved away from the rows of fresh goods, Nick hit a wet patch of flooring and skid into a counter. Hundreds of Brussels Sprouts cascaded to the floor. Willie stepped on one of the slick sprouts, going down hard, taking Nick with him. Nick felt a sharp pain shoot from his hip down to his toes.

The owner, a small woman with a gold front tooth, began to screech in Korean, shaking her fist at them. Nick offered to pay the lady, but she was having none of it. Grabbing Willie by the jacket, the two men hit the street again.

Nick glanced over at Costello's.

No kids.

*

Anthony and Kat progressed uptown, stopping at a bakery on the way. Anthony insisted she try a black and white. This time Kat paid, surprising Anthony when she pulled a twenty from her purse. Kat was equally surprised to discover a black and white was a giant cookie, half with vanilla icing, half with chocolate. Yummy.

Their journey ended on a shady cross street full of historic brownstones. Anthony pointed to a tidy dwelling with geraniums growing in pots on a windowsill. Kat loved geraniums. "That's where Dad and Daddy Andrew's mom lived," he said importantly, chocolate and vanilla icing outlining his mouth.

"Andrew and Nick lived there, too?"

"Just Andrew. Dad's the oldest and was adopted when he was born."

"I read he was adopted, but I couldn't find out why."

"His dad didn't want him."

Didn't want him?

"But he wanted Andrew?" she persisted.

"Nope. He didn't want him either. But their mom refused to give up another baby. So she kept Daddy Andrew. And that's when their father left."

"Did he ever come back?

Anthony shook his head. "I don't understand not wanting your kids. Dad and Daddy Andrew wanted me, even though I'm not theirs. Dad even adopted me."

"I read that Nick and Andrew finally met right before Andrew was—"

"You read a lot."

"I was curious about Nick. And the internet is a gold mine of information."

"They found each other, but they never met." Anthony finished his cookie, wiping his mouth with his hands, then his hands on his pants, "They only talked on the phone."

"Right. I forgot."

Hard to imagine finally finding a long-lost brother who dies before you have a chance to meet.

"So what made Nick and Andrew finally go looking for each other after all those years?"

This was interesting. Anthony was plugging the holes in Nick's history.

"Jeffrey's leukemia. Dad thought maybe his birth family could be a match for Jeffrey, whatever that means.

It means Jeffrey needed a bone marrow transplant.

"So Dad went searching. He checked out every adoption agency he could find. But by the time Dad and Andrew found each other, Jeffrey was dead."

Nick's search was useless. He found Andrew too late. Nick ended up losing his son. Then his brother.

"I like what Dad said to me about it. He said ... finding his birth family ended up not being about saving Jeffrey. It was about Jeffrey saving Dad. See, Dad was all alone. He didn't have any family anymore."

Just like me. When Mom died I didn't have any family. Or so I thought.

"What happened to Nick's adoptive parents?"

"Nothing. They're over in Europe somewhere. I never met them."

"They didn't come to the wedding? Or to meet you and your mom?"

"Huh-uh."

Weird.

*

As she took the subway back to the Bronx, Luci was close to tears. It was all over school that Anthony and the brat ran away. If only she knew Anthony was okay. But the school wasn't giving out any information. And she couldn't call Anthony's home, even if she had a phone number.

Stopping at the drug store to pick up her allergy meds, Raoul saw that she was upset. Turning the counter over to his partner, he took Luci for coffee. Coffee turned into dinner, and they talked for hours. About their neighborhood. About their favorite food. About the pharmacy business. About life in general.

When he asked questions about her homeland, she told him her memories were too painful to discuss.

The last thing Luci wanted to talk about was Chile.

*

Nick and Willie finally spotted Anthony and Kat a few blocks north on Columbus Avenue. Thank God the kids kept stopping to eat, or the adults wouldn't be able to keep up with them. Nick's hip was killing him, and Willie had done something to his foot.

Seeing Anthony take Kat down a side street, Nick couldn't help smiling. Anthony was obviously explaining some of Andrew and Nick's history, starting with their mother's home. Was Kat curious? Or were they just killing time?

"I'm starving, Nick. Let's get a hot dog from that vendor back there on Columbus."

Nick looked longingly at the Sabrett cart on the busy street. Yep. Three dogs with mustard, sauerkraut and barbecued onions.

"Damn." Willie pointed. "The kids are heading right towards us."

The famished duo leapt into the lower entryway of a brownstone. Crouching behind some garbage cans, Nick massaged his aching hip.

*

"Do you think the school called Nick and Jessie?" Kat stopped to rub her heel. She shouldn't have worn these boots today.

Anthony turned his cell back on as they retraced their steps to Columbus Avenue. "They haven't called. Or texted. And the school hasn't tried to call either. Where's your cell?"

"It finally died. I have to get a new one."

"Wouldn't Mom and Dad try to reach us if they thought we ran away?"

"Definitely. The school must think we're out sick."

"Which means we won't be in trouble. So what do we do now? School will be out soon. Willie will come pick us up."

Kat had an idea. "We'll hide and wait until school lets out. Then we'll—"

"—blend in with the other kids!" Anthony let out a whoop and pumped his fist.

"Right. Brilliant, huh?"

"We make a good team, Kat."

She shot him a half-smile. He earned it. Sort of. "We still have an hour. Let's get a hot dog. There's a cart over there."

"Sabrett. You have to try one with mustard, sauerkraut and barbecued onions. That's how New Yorkers eat them."

*

Jessie sat at the island with Abbie and Mary, a cup of untouched tea in front of her. "Where are they? They should be home by now."

"Stop worrying," Abbie's nose was buried in today's *New York Times*. "Nick won't let anything happen to Anthony. And Willie must be with him. He never came back after driving the kids to school."

"Abbie's right." Mary spread the last of the garlic basil butter on the ciabatta.

"Oh my God." Abbie looked up from the paper. "Bree won a Pulitzer Prize. For her reporting on those women who escaped from the Taliban."

"What?" Jessie asked.

"Breanna Fontaine. You remember her. Nick's old friend."

Yes, Jessie remembered Bree. Another of Nick's old girlfriends, but this one had some sticking power. Brianna relocated back to New York last year, claiming she was tired of her global stints as a reporter for the *Times*. Just in time to help Nick, Lyle and Abbie in their pursuit of Gianni Fosselli. And do her best to win back Nick. "So what? Nick has a Pulitzer."

"It's a big deal, Jessie. And didn't Bree help Nick on his Pulitzer story? When they were working together in Hong Kong?"

"I don't remember."

"I'm sure Bree told me she and Nick—"

93

"Enough about Bree!" Jessie leapt to her feet, toppling her stool. Her sudden burst of anger made her light-headed. She dropped back down and laid her head on her arms.

"I'm sorry." Abbie pushed the paper away. "I didn't mean to—"

"I'm sure Bree married her photojournalist by now," Mary said, shooting Abbie a warning look. "What was his name again? ... Yves ..."

"Yves Leveaux," Abbie supplied. "One hot Frenchman."

"You okay, honey?" Mary lifted Jessie's head and stared into her eyes. "I want you to go upstairs and lie down. Come on. I'll take you. Come on."

Jessie pulled herself to her feet and let Mary help her up the stairs. She loved Mary, but she wished it was Nick with his arm around her.

Sexy, funny, compassionate Nick.

Jessie's Nick. Not Bree's.

*

"Okay," Kat directed, "we hide here until we see Willie." She pulled her collar up and tried to huddle under an eave of the building. It was starting to rain.

Anthony pointed to a cart across the street. "Look, there's the pretzel guy. Will you buy us two? I spent all my money on the pizza. I'm gonna have to come up with a story for Mom about that twelve dollars."

"A cart just for pretzels? How dumb. You can buy a bag of pretzels anywhere."

"They're not THAT kind of pretzel. You'll see."

Kat gave Anthony the money. He returned with two large soft pretzels smeared with mustard. "This is awesome, Anthony." It was the best pretzel she'd ever eaten.

"See? New York has some great things."

"Looks like it. Food, anyway."

Hearing the school bell ring, they stuffed the last of the pretzels in their mouths and got into place. Anthony grinned at his sister. "I haven't had this much fun in a long time."

*

94

Watching Kat and Anthony eat everything in sight made Nick even hungrier. His stomach felt hollow. To make matters worse, a light rain had turned into a deluge.

It was obvious what the kids were planning. They would make it look like they'd been in school all day. The little shits. He'd play along. So would Willie. Make them think they got away with it. Wallow in their successful scam. For a moment anyway.

Nick hailed a cab, dropping Willie at the car before heading home.

Where he would wait. And pounce.

*

Hearing the front door slam, Mary shook her head at Abbie. "I'm going to give everyone in this house a lesson on how to close a door properly."

Nick burst into the kitchen, tossing his drenched Knicks cap on the island. "I'm starving, Mary. What do you have to eat?"

"Hello to you, too, Nick. And I hope you didn't trail water all the way down the hall."

"Nice hat-head." Abbie chuckled.

Mary produced bread, cheese, ham and mustard. "Here. Knock yourself out. Where are the kids?"

"Willie's bringing them." Nick shoved a piece of ham in his mouth. "And not a word that we're on to them. Got it, both of you? NOT ONE WORD!"

"On to what?" Abbie asked.

"Before I forget, Abbie," Nick slapped a sandwich together, "if Anthony asks you about the Ouija board—" He stared at the *Times* on the island. "Bree won a Pulitzer?"

"Yeah," Abbie said, "for that expose she did—"

"What's that smell?" Mary crinkled her nose.

"Yeah, what's that foul odor?" Abbie asked. "Did Monty have an accident?"

Mary came around the island. "What in the world...?" A wet dark footprint tracked into the kitchen from the hallway. Hurrying through the archway she saw the trail led from the front door. "Nicholas McDeare, what's on your shoe?" Mary shouted.

His mouth full, Nick looked at the floor. "Sorry." He took his shoes off.

"Throw those things out the back door right now!"

Nick did as she asked.

"Why are you limping?"

"Long story."

The front door slammed. Mary winced.

The kids swung into the kitchen. Willie brought up the rear. Slowly.

"What stinks?" Anthony asked.

"You're limping, too?" Mary asked her nephew.

Willie looked guilty. Very guilty. "Must've slept wrong."

"On your foot?"

Willie backed towards the door leading to his place. "Have things to do. Want to come, Abbie?"

"You bet." Abbie followed him.

Mary turned to Nick, who barely swallowed before taking another bite. "You need to go upstairs and talk to your wife."

"In a minute." He was reading the article on Brianna Fontaine.

"Now!"

"I need food first."

"After you talk to Jessie."

Nick slid off the stool, shoving the last of the sandwich into his mouth. "How was school?" he asked the kids, his mouth full.

"Horrible." Kat followed him up the stairs. "You have holes in your socks. Want me to alert the media?"

*

Nick found Jessie propped up in bed, earbuds in, listening to music. Setting her iPod aside, she stared as he approached.

"You're mad, aren't you?" Nick began.

"I'm trying not to be. What happened to your hair? And you're wet. And limping."

"It's nothing." He shook out his hair and stripped off his soaked jeans and socks.

"What about the kids? Are they wet and limping, too?"

Nick snorted. "They're fine. More than fine." Off came the wet Baltimore Ravens sweatshirt.

"I've been so worried."

"I'm sorry, Jess." He dug clean jeans and a sweater from a drawer in the dressing room and tugged them on. "It all happened so fast. There wasn't time to explain." He crawled across the bed, favoring his sore hip, and plopped down beside her. "Do you want to hear about it?"

"Later. They're okay. That's all that matters."

Nick leaned back against the headboard, suddenly tired. "Mary said we need to talk. Is it about the kids?"

"No." She fingered her rings, twirling them on her finger, an old nervous habit. Not a good sign.

"The doctor got my tests back today."

Something was wrong. Very wrong. Nick's chest constricted. "And?"

"I guess I'll just say it outright."

"For God's sake, Jessie, you're terrifying me."

"I'm ... pregnant, Nick."

CHAPTER 9

"God, Jess, you just gave me the scare of my life." He stared at his wife, her words sinking in. "You're pregnant? You're sure?" She nodded. "But I thought you couldn't—"

"—They didn't say I couldn't with my condition, just that the odds were stacked against me. In fact, they called Anthony my miracle baby." She looked up at him, her blue eyes threatening to overflow with tears. "Looks like I get another miracle." She sniffled. "Are you happy?"

"Am I—Are you kidding? I'm thrilled!" My God. A baby. Jessie was pregnant with their baby! "Did you think I wouldn't be?"

"Maybe. I mean, a couple years ago you had all the freedom in the world. Now you're strapped with a wife and three children."

Nick threw his head back and laughed. "Two years ago I was alone. Now I have a family." He couldn't stop laughing. "Oh, honey, come here." He wrapped his arms around her, pressing his lips to her forehead. A baby.

*

Jessie nestled against Nick's shoulder. She felt better than she had in weeks. They were having a baby. And Nick was ecstatic! "I kept telling Dr. Chao he must be wrong. But he said the test doesn't lie." She looked up at her husband. "He also said I have to be careful. He called it a high-risk pregnancy. When I was carrying Anthony, I had so many problems and came close to miscarrying. I ended up in the hospital the last month."

"I'll make sure you're careful. Even if it means bedrest for nine months."

"I have an appointment with a specialist on Thursday."

"I'll go with you." Nick laughed again. Jessie couldn't remember the last time she saw him this happy. "Does anyone else know?"

"Only Mary. Nothing gets by her." She pulled him closer. "But I don't want to tell anyone else, especially the kids. Not until I'm past the first trimester. Just in case."

"Damn. The kids." He released her and sat up. "I have to talk to them about what happened today. But I don't want to leave you right now. Care to join me?"

"And ruin the utter joy I'm feeling? I'll pass. But tell me this much. Was Kat the instigator?"

"Yes. But it wasn't her fault. The press was all over her. And the other kids were giving her crap about my past. She's miserable."

Jessie sighed. She didn't want to fight about this anymore. "Home-school her, Nick. Just do it."

"It's the right decision, Jess. You'll see. What about Anthony?"

It was time to surrender. She was outnumbered.

"Him, too."

*

Nick leaned against the bookshelves in the study. Kat and Anthony sat on the sofa. Anthony wouldn't look at him. Kat met his gaze, a stubborn glint in her eyes. "Tell me about school today."

Anthony sidled a look at Kat and fidgeted.

"You know, don't you?" Kat said. Anthony tried to shush her, but Kat waved him off. "Forget it, Anthony. We're busted."

Anthony dropped his head, a replica of Monty when he was scolded. "I'm sorry, Dad."

Kat folded her arms. "I'm not going back to that school."

"I'm very angry with you both. What you did was wrong. You could have been hurt." He looked meaningfully at Anthony. "Or kidnapped. I don't want either of you to do something that stupid again. Understand?" He waited. Raising his voice, he asked again, "Do you understand?"

After a beat, they both nodded, Kat defiantly.

Nick dropped down on the ottoman. "I talked it over with Jessie. After what happened with those reporters today, we decided to home-school you both."

Anthony leapt to his feet with a whoop. "Zane, too?"

"We didn't discuss Zane. That will be up to you. Talk to him. See if he'd like to join you. I know Zane's on scholarship at Grantham, so if it's a question of money, I'll be happy to pay. We owe him after his help with your kidnapping."

"Can I call him right now?"

"Go."

Both kids headed for the door.

"Not you, Kat. We need to talk."

*

"Abbie, this is delicious." Willie took another bite of the linguini with white clam sauce. "I didn't know you could cook."

They were eating in the breakfast nook in Willie's kitchen, a smaller version of the one in the McDeare house. Abbie ordered in groceries and whipped up a meal for them. She hoped to make Willie feel at home in his new place, now that he was finally living here.

"Well, I'm not Mary or Nick in the kitchen, but I can throw a meal together when I want to. Do you cook?"

"Not at all. I survive on take-out and the generosity of friends."

"Here. Have some of this." She passed him the garlic bread.

"Mmm. Smells great." Willie broke off a piece of the bread. "I looked into those phone calls for you. They're from a throwaway phone."

"So it's a dead end. Which means I just keep ignoring them." Abbie twirled some pasta on her fork. "Tell me about LeJeanne."

Willie chuckled. "Where did that question come from?"

"I'm curious.

"Are you always this straightforward?"

"Usually. Does it bother you?"

"No. I'm the same way. But I don't switch subjects at the speed of light."

Abbie grinned. "Jessie razzes me about that all the time. But back to LeJeane. Tell me about her. How long were you together?"

"A couple years."

"Did you love her?"

He choked on his bread. "You give 'straightforward' new meaning." He chewed, thinking. "I thought so. But I don't miss her as much as I thought I would. Starting over bothers me more than anything. I'm getting a little old for it."

"How old ARE you?" She played with her salad. "I'm thirty-six."

"You look younger." Willie dredged some bread in the clam sauce. "I'm forty-one."

"Same age as Nick."

"Mmm-hmm … So I told you about LeJeanne. What about you? Ever been married? Or in love?"

Abbie pushed her pasta around on her plate. "Never married. But in love hundreds of times." She chuckled. "Or so I thought. I always fall for Italian men. The kind who are demanding and take you for granted."

"Why?"

"Why? Why did I fall for them? A shrink once told me I keep trying to recreate my father, who was Italian. He was also callous and controlling."

Willie put down his fork and stared at her.

"What?" she asked.

"It's just that … you're beautiful. You're outgoing, Smart and funny. You could have anyone you want."

Abbie wasn't used to so many compliments from a man. In fact, she could count the genuine compliments she received over the years on one hand. "You're just being nice. But thank you."

"I meant every word." His voice was soft, his eyes warm as he stretched his palm across the table. "I'm straightforward, remember?"

Abbie hesitated before slipping her hand into his. A jolt shot up her arm.

Her cell shrilled, shattering the moment.

*

Kat waited for Nick to start talking.

You're going to punish me, right? You can't confine me to the house. I never go anywhere. Lock me in my room? I already live in there. Take away my T.V.? I don't watch television. My cell? Dead.

"I believe that home-schooling is the right decision. But I also think you need more than school. And don't roll your eyes at me."

Did I roll my eyes? It must have been involuntary.

"What about ballet? If you're as good as Susie says you are, you shouldn't interrupt your training."

Ballet? That's my punishment for running away from school?

"This isn't a punishment, Kat."

How does he do that?

"I understand why you bolted today. What you did was dangerous, but I get it. Ballet is a different subject. The arts are important. I think you should continue to train. And I'll work with you on piano. Okay?"

This man was a constant surprise.

"Okay."

"What about your writing?"

"Could you teach me?"

"I don't think it's a good idea. These are your formative years, when you find your own voice. Let me look for a creative writing class. It will force you to write all the time. That's how you learn."

"Did you take classes when you were my age?"

"Lots of them."

"Okay.

"I called a tutor I found a few days ago and told him home-schooling is a go. He'll be here tomorrow afternoon to meet with us and set up a schedule."

You planned on my being home-schooled all along. I knew it. You sent me to that school just to keep the peace with Jessie

Nick stood up. "One more thing. No dinner tonight for you or Anthony. That's your punishment."

"Fine." Kat shot him a triumphant smile. "I'm stuffed anyway."

*

"The lamb was fantastic, Mary." Nick poured himself some brandy.

Mary dropped a chai tea bag into a steaming mug and handed it to Jessie, who was on her cell. Nick's sunny mood was infectious. The new baby changed everything. "This is a good day."

"Yeah?" Abbie stood in the archway, windblown and damp from her trek across the backyard. "What'd I miss?"

Mary glanced at Jessie. The baby had to remain a secret for a while. "Just my award-winning rack of lamb."

Jessie clicked off her cell. "That was Bill." Bill Rudolph was Broadways' most successful producer and Jessie's benefactor. Like a father to her. "I didn't realize how long it's been since we talked." She turned to Mary. "He and Marcie are coming for Thanksgiving again, by the way. Anyway, he's thinking about reviving *EARLY SPRING* next fall and wondered how I felt about playing Daniella again."

"And how do you feel?" Nick nuzzled his wife's cheek.

"I'm definitely interested. It would be weird to do it without Andrew, but it's such a great role." She looked up at Abbie. "Where were you tonight?"

"I made pasta for Willie and me."

"You cooked?" Jessie looked incredulous.

"Stop it. I can cook. When I want to." She reached for the decanter. "No brandy, Jessie?"

"I don't even think I even want tea. I'm tired." Jessie kissed Nick. "Stay. Enjoy your brandy. I'll see you upstairs."

*

Luci was depressed tonight.

She hadn't seen Anthony since yesterday. A day without Anthony was a day not worth living. The weekends were torture without him. Which was why she'd gotten herself invited to Zane Harwell's house a few Saturdays ago. She knew telling Anthony it was her birthday would work. It had been so much fun. Mrs. Harwell made Luci feel welcome in her home, like she was part of the family.

She'd done all she could to get invited to Anthony's home for dinner. Her patience was wearing out. She had to get inside that house. Once her foot was in the door, she'd find a way to make it permanent.

*

Nick drained his snifter and stretched, rubbing his back. He was stiff from his jaunt with Willie. And his hip was killing him.

He filled Mary and Abbie in on the antics of the day. Abbie said Willie didn't want to talk about it, that it was too embarrassing. Nick agreed. In hindsight, they came off as morons. Still, it was hilarious.

Abbie's cell rang. She shoved it in her pocket. "Don't ask," she said to Nick. "Willie's taking care of it. I'm going to bed."

Willie again? Instead of Nick's expertise? He rose, swallowing his annoyance. "Me, too."

"Wait a minute." Mary lowered her voice and waited until Abbie was out of sight. "I want to give you some advice. Privately." She leaned closer and whispered, "Better get out your suit of armor."

"Meaning?"

"In all my years I've never seen a more difficult pregnant lady than Jessie. You're going to need patience. Lots of patience. We all will."

Nick paused. The past few weeks replayed in his mind. The fights. The bitter silences. The sarcasm. "You mean, worse than—"

"Much worse."

"So she's—"

"—a pain in the ass. Consider yourself warned."

*

Willie sat at his computer, staring at the screen.

Damn. Abbie's Joey Evenatti had disappeared. MIA for days. Digging further, he discovered that most of Evenatti's family lived in Manhattan and Queens. The man had been born in Flushing. He could be right here in the city. Abbie had cause to be afraid.

Willie called his old partner, asking for a favor. He wanted a money trail. Maybe credit cards would turn up something. His password wasn't authorized to access that information. Roger said he'd get back to him in a couple days. In the meantime, Abbie didn't need to know.

Taking his glass to the kitchen, Willie refilled his Scotch. He had to buy some gin, his drink of choice.

Wandering aimlessly into the living room, he listened to the silence. The place seemed empty with Abbie gone. Barton must have gone bat-shit-crazy when he was here alone. The walls screamed out for noise. Voices. Laughter.

Abbie.

He kissed her. As she was leaving, he kissed her. He didn't know what made him do it. He had no right. In a way, working for Nick and Jessie meant he also worked for Abbie.

Damn. What had he been thinking? But she kissed him back. Didn't she?

Chuckling, he realized he was thinking like a teenager. "Well, golly gee, I wonder if she likes me. Did she kiss me back?"

Reaching for the remote he flicked on the TV. There had to be a football game on. Wasn't there always a football game on?

Anything was better than listening to all this quiet.

Or talking to himself.

*

"Anthony?"

The boy stood at the window, staring out into the darkness. Monty lounged on the bed, his rawhide bone planted between his teeth.

"Bongo? Something wrong?" Nick sat at the desk.

104

"I thought I heard Daddy Andrew."

Andrew again. "What did he say?"

"He was humming. That famous song from his last show."

The theme of *HEARTTAKES*. Andrew's last Broadway musical before he was murdered. "You're sure he was humming that song?"

"Maybe not. I was kinda upset about something else when I heard it."

"Upset about what?"

Anthony sat in the rocker. "Zane's mom said no about home-schooling. She said Zane needs to play soccer with the other kids. And work on the school paper. But Zane only likes that stuff because we do it together."

"Maybe I can convince her."

"Zane says nothing will change her mind. He wants me to be home-schooled without him. He said this'll get me out of that school for good. I told him I wouldn't do it without him, but he kept saying he'd be fine."

"So what are you going to do?"

"I'm going back. Zane won't be fine, Dad. If I leave, the guys will take it out on him. Why are they so mean to us?"

"I think one of the reasons they pick on you is because of me, because of my past. I wish I could erase it, for your sake, but I can't. But they also focus on you because you're gifted in a way they don't understand. You're an excellent photographer. Your pictures are always in the school paper. You even had some photos printed in a national magazine. They're jealous."

"What about Zane? Why him?"

"Zane's there on scholarship because he's smart, smarter than all of them. You two aren't like the others. Being different is good. You march to your own drummer. One day you'll sell your photographs for five grand a pop, and those kids will be working in some depressing cubicle."

"You're a loser, McDeare. You'll always be a loser. Someday I'll be rich and running a multi-million-dollar corporation. You'll be dirt-poor and still writing garbage nobody reads."

"Zane and I, we protect each other, Dad. I can't leave him there alone. He's my good friend. Heck, if it wasn't for him, you and Lyle might not have found me at Gianni's."

Nick nodded. Zane was instrumental in providing a clue that helped them find Anthony – tracking Gianni through Monty. A rare Portuguese water dog.

"So I'm going back to school tomorrow. Do you see, Dad?"

Nick smiled. "I see, Anthony. I also see what a big heart you have."

Heart. Andrew humming *HEARTTAKES*.

Was his brother sending him a coded message?

*

Jessie roused when Nick slid into bed beside her. She reached for him, curling into his arms. "There are three of us in this bed now," she whispered. "I'm so in love with you, Nick."

"Good thing, since we're having a baby." He slid down and kissed her stomach.

"So did you and Mary manage to keep our secret from Abbie? She has a way of getting at the truth."

"We were good little soldiers." Moving up, he nibbled at her ear, his tongue sending goosebumps down her body. "By the way, Mary told me ..." He buried his lips in her neck.

"What? ... What did Mary tell you?"

"Never mind." He moved down to her breastbone.

"Tell me. What did Mary say?"

"She said ..." Nick's hands caressed her breasts, his thumbs— she shivered with pleasure. "... that you can be difficult ..." His lips took over, his hands beginning a new journey. "... when you're pregnant."

"Difficult?" Jessie abruptly sat up, accidentally slamming her knee into Nick's chin. "She's crazy."

"What the--?" He, too, sat up. "You're lucky I didn't—"

"What made her say that"

"Maybe she remembers what you were like when you were carrying Anthony." He rubbed his chin. "I think you broke my jaw."

"I was NOT difficult. Andrew even said—" She suddenly remembered what Andrew said. "Never mind. Forget it."

"Now you want to forget it? Could it be that Andrew agreed with Mary?"

"I said forget it." She glared at Nick.

He raised both hands in surrender. "Whatever you say, dear. That's my mantra from now on."

"Oh, stop it." The submissive expression on his face made her laugh.

"Whatever you say, dear." He traced her cheek with his thumb, those lazy amber eyes meandering down, further down, all the way to—"Come here." In one swift move he slid her beneath him, covering her mouth with a slow, achingly slow, long deep kiss. His taste was salty, his scent pure masculinity. This man could arouse her in a heartbeat. It seemed an eternity since they'd made love ...

She pulled out from under him and sat up again.

"Okay," he sighed. "What now?"

"You're not going to like this. In fact, you're going to hate it. Dr. Chao said ... well, he told me ... it's about sex, Nick ..."

*

"Okay, Abbie, spill," Mary said. "What's on your mind?" Mary knew exactly what was on Abbie's mind.

"Mmm, nothing really."

"Okay, don't tell me. Who am I? Just a woman who's loved you for years."

"Don't make me feel guilty, Mary."

"Me?"

"You. The queen of guilt-trips. Besides, I can't tell you this."

"It's Willie, isn't it?"

Abbie looked down, rubbing her brow.

"Honey, what are you afraid of?"

"He's such a nice man, Mary. And I'm—well, I have a history I'm not too proud of."

"So did Nick," she said pointedly. "And so did Jessie. Remember Gianni Fosselli and Carl Wexley? Everyone has a past."

"And another thing. I don't want to get involved with Willie and then decide it's not right for me. You know how I am, changing my mind every twenty seconds. I don't want to hurt him. He deserves better."

"Listen to me, Abbie. Life is short. Happiness is fleeting, especially in this family. When good fortune comes along, you have to grab it, because it may not pass your way again. And if it's right, who says you'll change your mind? But you'll never know if you don't give it a try." She winked and pushed her weary self off the stool. "Now I think I'll sneak a plate up to Kat. Against Daddy's orders."

"You have such a good heart, Mary."

107

"Just like my nephew."

*

Kat stood at her bedroom window. She'd heard humming coming from outside. Someone walking down the street? She didn't see anyone. The melody was haunting. Beautiful. She couldn't get it out of her mind. Returning to her desk, she hummed the tune.

There was a knock at the door. Mary brought her a tray of lamb, rice pilaf and sautéed winter squash. "Don't tell your daddy, okay?"

"I won't. Thanks, Mary." Kat fed Hamlet a tiny piece of lamb. "Hamlet thanks you, too."

"I heard you humming your uncle's song. The one from *HEARTTAKES*."

HEARTTAKES? Hamlet pawed Kat, wanting more lamb. She tore off another little piece. "Are there any recordings of Andrew in that show?"

"Sure. It was recorded for PBS."

Kat broke into a smile.

*

Nick lay flat on his back, staring at the ceiling. Jessie slept beside him, her cheek resting against his shoulder, her leg tossed casually over his thighs. Did she have any idea what she was doing to him? Time to buy her flannel pajamas.

Dr. Chao must be wrong. No pregnancy was that risky. Rules for sex? Sex didn't have rules. That's what made it fun. He would confront the specialist about it on Thursday.

Frustrated, he stuffed his hand behind his head and stared down at his wife.

Mary's warning came back to him.

I've never seen a more difficult pregnant lady than Jessie.

Great. He would be living with a scorpion for the next nine months.

Wondering when she would sting.

CHAPTER 10

Finn Cagney couldn't be more Irish if he were a leprechaun and spoke with a brogue. He was an adorable man with thick shiny silver hair, deep jowls, dimples and saggy bright blue eyes that literally sparkled. Mary liked him immediately.

He sat at the island, sipping coffee and complimenting her orange muffins. "My wife died a few years ago," he explained, "right after I retired from teaching. No kids or family to speak of. With her gone I had too much time on my hands, so I decided to tutor. I like it. Call my own hours and choose my students."

"I apologize again for keeping you waiting. Mrs. McDeare is resting – a special situation - and Mr. McDeare is running late from a meeting with his agent."

As if on cue, the front door slammed and footsteps hurried down the hallway. Nick swung into the kitchen. "Mr. Cagney, I am so sorry. My lunch ran late and—"

"Please. Call me Finn."

"And I'm Nick." He poured himself some coffee. "So. Where do we start?"

They discussed a schedule, settling on mornings, leaving the afternoons for Kat to pursue her artistic endeavors. Plus, Finn gave a lot of homework. He believed in making children think for themselves.

"Kat has dreams of being a writer," Nick added, "so you might want to put some focus on English and literature courses."

After agreeing on the fee, it was time for Finn to meet his student.

*

Kat stepped into the sitting room of the fourth-floor VIP suite. She'd never been up here before. Beyond this large and airy room was a lavish bedroom.

"Come on in, young lady." The man standing by the terrace door was not what she expected. Hearing her tutor was an older man she pictured a dried-up, old-school taskmaster. This man looked like he'd break into a jig at any minute.

"Mr. Cagney?"

"Please. No last names. We're going to be spending a lot of time together. You're Kat, and I'm Finn." He looked around the room. "Pretty nice digs, huh? So. Tell me about yourself. Also, what do you like to snack on? Judging from that nice woman downstairs, I expect we'll be eating as much as we'll be studying."

A grin spread across Kat's face.

*

At Jessie's request they ordered in Chinese for dinner. She was craving spicy eggplant. Also curried shrimp. Abbie was MIA, probably with Willie again. Jessie needed to schedule some serious girl-talk with her friend.

Dinner was eaten in the breakfast nook. Jessie was pleased to find Kat in a good mood. The girl loved Finn and talked about him quite a bit. Anthony, on the other hand, was subdued. She knew he wasn't happy about returning to school, but his reason was admirable. Nick was quiet. Too quiet. He pushed his food around his plate with his chopsticks, eating very little.

"How'd the meeting with your agent go, Nick?"

"You know Liz. Demanding. Linden Publishing is putting a rush on my book to get it out there in time for the holidays. Which means a book tour from Thanksgiving to Christmas. I'll have some TV interviews in New York, but I'll pretty much be gone a month."

Jessie deflated. A month? She was pregnant. She needed him around, not off promoting his book. And he was leaving her here with Kat. Could she handle the girl on her own?

"I'm in London the week before Christmas." He looked pointedly at Jessie. "I was hoping you could come with me."

Jessie's heart soared … then plummeted. The doctors would never let her travel that far and for so long.

Her cell thrummed. Bill Rudolph's office. An odd time for them to call.

Nothing prepared her for the news she received.

Bill, her sweet friend, her benefactor, was dead.

*

110

When Willie asked Abbie where she'd like to go for dinner, she picked The FusterCluck, a homey pub with booths and stained-glass lamps. Also the best fried calamari in New York. "You didn't have to buy me dinner just because I cooked you a meal."

"I didn't. I just thought it would be a nice change of scene for you."

"It is." It felt good to be out in New York again. They exited through Willie's place. If Joey was watching, he'd focus on the McDeare home.

Abbie ran her finger around the rim of her martini. "Never had gin before. I like it."

"Be careful. It's the hangover king."

"You don't seem the type to get drunk."

Willie looked perplexed. "I think you have a skewed image of me. I'm no angel. I was a druggie when I was a kid. Heroin. PCP. Even dealt the stuff."

"What made you stop?"

"A neighborhood cop threw me into a cell for three days. Scared the hell out of me, telling me about all the lonely males waiting for me in prison. Eventually he set me up in a program that got me off the stuff."

"Is that why you became a cop?"

"I actually wanted to be an attorney. Split my time between the force and getting a degree. But I couldn't swing law school financially, so I focused on moving up in the department."

This man was not only nice, he was smart.

Their food arrived. Fried calamari. Honey-glazed chicken skewers. Nachos. Onion rings. And stuffed baked-potato skins. "Now you know my secret," Abbie declared. "I'm a junk food junkie."

"The food of the gods," Willie agreed.

Over coffee, a woman approached. She had dyed dark red hair, dangly earrings and wore a ton of eye makeup. "Read your palm? Only ten dollars."

"When did this place hire a fortune teller?" Abbie was annoyed.

"I'm not a fortune teller. I have a gift. Ask the owner. Or that man over there." She pointed to a middle-aged man across the aisle.

"She's good," the man said. "I was a non-believer until Adriana here. You won't be disappointed."

"Go on, Abbie. Why not? Just for fun." Willie winked. "My treat."

Adriana pulled up a chair and stared at Abbie's palm. "You've been away ... out west ... your work ... dangerous work ..." Again she studied Abbie's palm. "There's a man ..." She looked up at Willie. "Not this man ... someone you were involved with ... he's in trouble ... no, he wants to cause you trouble ... he's in his thirties or maybe early forties ... J ... J.E. .... Do those initials mean anything to you?"

"Joey Evenatti," Abbie and Willie said in unison.

*

Kat was the first one downstairs the next morning. Other than Mary, of course, who was reading *The New York Times*. "Good Lord, child, what are you doing up at seven AM?"

"I start with Finn at nine. And Nick promised to jog with me before school. What are you reading?"

"Article about Bill."

"Who is this 'Bill'?"

Mary sipped her coffee. "Bill Rudolph was the biggest producer on Broadway. He discovered Andrew and Jessie when they were young and made them both stars. When Broadway awarded Bill a Lifetime Achievement Award last year, Jessie presented it to him. Your dad and Jessie got married in his Long Island home, and Bill walked Jessie down the aisle. He was family in this house."

"Wow. No wonder Jessie was upset last night."

But did she have to be so melodramatic? He was a friend, not her dad. Jessie never let an emotional moment go to waste. Typical actress.

"How did he die?"

"Heart attack."

"Was he old?"

"Seventy. But a young seventy. And in good health, which makes this surprising."

Seventy-year-old men die of heart attacks every day. What's surprising is a thirty-seven-year-old mother dying of cancer.

Nick came down the stairs. "Ready, Kat?"

*

Because of the early hour, Nick avoided the park. Instead, they ran the neighborhood, which was already bustling with early morning

112

activity. They ended, once again, at the English bakery, Great Expectations.

"A favor, Kat? Jessie's hurting right now because of Bill. Try not to push her buttons, okay?" She's also pregnant, but you can't know that yet.

"Push her buttons?" Kat was the picture of innocence.

Nick sighed, not in the mood for dueling semantics. "You know what I mean."

"Okay, okay." Kat spread her scone with the clotted cream and blueberry preserves, groaning with pleasure. "I love these."

Nick was pleased. Not everyone loved English food. Jessie hated it.

"Are there any English restaurants in New York?"

"A few. And some great English grocers. I'll make you an English breakfast one morning."

Her eyes lit up at the prospect as she took another bite.

An idea struck Nick as he watched his daughter.

*

The next day, Jessie dragged herself from bed for her appointment with the specialist. Depressed about losing Bill so suddenly, she wanted to stay in bed and shut out the world. As promised, Nick went with her.

Dr. Lindstrom, a man easily in his seventies, was a renowned physician celebrated for his old-world skills and near-perfect success rate. When Jessie voiced her worries, he shushed her. "If you follow my instructions, you'll have a healthy baby."

Jessie had a deep fear of losing this baby. Maybe it was just that losing Bill reminded her how fickle life could be.

Jessie and Nick went over Dr. Lindstrom's instructions as Willie drove them home.

"No alcohol. No soda. No sugar," Nick read.

"No traveling. Which means I can't go to London with you. I knew it."

"How would you feel if I took Kat? She's falling in love with all things English." He'd obviously given this some thought. He suggested taking Kat too quickly.

Hmm. A week without the young girl around the house … "Fine with me."

Jessie continued down the list. "Here it is." Nick asked the doctor about sex. Lindstrom seemed embarrassed and told them to read the instructions.

"How can a gynecologist be uncomfortable talking about sex?" Nick shook his head. "The guy wouldn't have a job without it." He read the page and looked up at her. "He's joking, right? What does he expect us to do? Lay there like a couple of rocks?"

"It doesn't say we can't have sex, Nick."

"It says 'occasional sex, with limitations.' And it says 'no overexertion.' How do you have sex without overexertion?"

"Well, you certainly can't," she muttered under her breath.

"I heard that. And I'm not the dancer in the family."

"No. But you sure turn into the gymnast—" Jessie suddenly realized the window was open between the front and back seats. She felt her face heating up.

Was Willie laughing?

Nick was, dammit. He slid down in the seat and gazed out the car window, trying to hide his amusement. "God, I love it when you blush, Jess."

*

"We need to talk, Abbie." Willie put the last of the silverware in the dishwasher.

As a rule, Abbie hated any conversation that began with that sentence. It was usually bad news. "You hated dinner, right? Roasts aren't my specialty. It was raw. I should have played it safe and made chicken.

"Dinner was fine. Come here. I want to show you something." He led her to the computer in the study and pulled up a screen.

"My God," Abbie whispered, "Joey's credit card charges."

"Yep. He used the card multiple times a day. In Manhattan and Queens."

"That fortune teller … Joey's here. And he's watching me."

"Maybe. Maybe not. He's from New York, Abbie. His family's here. There's something else." He scrolled down the screen. "The charges stopped three days ago. And he hasn't been back to work in L.A. I checked."

"But I'm still getting the calls. What does this mean?"

"It means I start looking for him. Visit his family. Ask some questions."

114

"Take Nick with you. There's safety in numbers."

"Nick won't want to go—"

"He's bored, now that his book is finished. He lives for a challenge. Take him with you. And no matter what you say, I'm going to Bill Rudolph's funeral. I knew Bill for over a decade, and I'm tired of hiding."

*

Bill Rudolph's funeral was the following Sunday. Despite Nick's objections, Jessie insisted on going. For one thing, she was scheduled to speak at the service. The New York theatrical scene knew how close Jessie and Bill were. The press would ask questions if she didn't show up.

On the way to the church, Nick fussed over Jessie until she wanted to scream. "Please, Nick," she whispered. "I'm okay. Are you going to be like this for the next—" She stopped herself in time, glancing at Abbie.

Nick's eyes clouded over. He turned away, staring out the car window. She obviously angered him. She didn't mean to. But today was about Bill. Only Bill.

Jessie got through the eulogy, despite her tears. Afterwards, she approached Bill's wife, Marcie, and his partner, Harrison Alder, to offer her condolences. She'd always been close to Marcie but never cared for Harrison. And she got the feeling it was mutual.

As she, Nick, Abbie and Willie headed for the car, trying to dodge reporters, she heard a familiar voice call out to her. Turning, she came face-to-face with Josh Elliot, her former leading man.

"Hello, Jessie. It's great to see you again." Josh talked as if nothing was wrong between them. As if he wasn't involved in a nefarious plot to hurt her during the run of their Broadway show last year. He bankrolled the stage manager, George Penfield, to sabotage her, smearing her prop with ricin. Thankfully, the ricin was discovered, and Penfield went to jail. But Jessie had smelled another rat in the mix and uncovered Josh's involvement. In lieu of jail and out of deference to Josh's long friendship with Andrew, she made a deal with him. If he left town permanently, she'd keep quiet. So Josh walked out on the play, without giving notice, and moved to LA., infuriating Bill Rudolph.

"I'm shocked to see you here," Jessie said with contempt. "Last I heard, you were doing *Circus of the Stars* or some other nonsense out in LA."

"I did what I had to, like every actor." He grinned. At one time that grin was worth a million dollars. He'd done his fair share of television commercials. Until word spread that he had a falling-out with Bill Rudolph. Bill was one of the most influential voices in the business. Or he had been. Jessie swallowed, refusing to cry in front of this hypocrite. This waste of space.

Nick took hold of Jessie's elbow. "Let's go, Jess."

"Nice to see you, too, Nick." Josh's voice was saccharin sweet. "Abbie, you're looking a little plump. Pregnant?"

"Go to hell, Josh."

"Bill's gone now," Josh said smoothly to all of them. "Let's leave the past where it belongs. In the past." He nodded as if he didn't have a care in the world. "See you around."

Jessie ran for the car, ignoring Nick's caution. She wanted to be home in bed. She wanted to take care of this little baby growing inside of her.

She wanted to forget about the ugliness in the world.

*

Nick took refuge in his office. Jessie went back to bed, giving him much-needed peace and quiet. Josh Elliot's sudden appearance brought out the scorpion in his wife. Nick intended to keep his distance today.

After making a few calls, he went in search of Kat. He found her in the study, watching *HEARTTAKES*. She was at the end of the recording, the moment when Andrew sang the showstopper. Nick paused in the doorway.

Anthony said he heard Andrew humming this song the other night. Nick listened closely to the lyrics, hoping to discern a hidden message from his brother: Every person who touches us on our journey through life lays claim to a piece of our heart. Instead of the heart diminishing, it rejuvenates. Out of heartbreak comes compassion. Out of loss comes wisdom. Out of death comes life.

To Nick, the song was nothing more than a pile of platitudes. In life, you put one foot in front of the other and just got on with it. If Andrew was trying to communicate through predictable lyrics, his spirit risked a predictable exorcism.

The recording finished, Nick came around and sat beside his daughter.

Kat dabbed at her eyes. "So beautiful."

Nick remained silent.

"Andrew was so talented. I can't believe he was my uncle."

"What'd you think of Jessie?"

Kat shrugged. "She was good."

Nick swallowed a retort. This antagonism between Kat and Jessie was irritating. He'd stay out of it. For now.

"Did you want something?" Kat flipped off the T.V.

"Several things. First, I just ordered you a new cell phone. It'll be here tomorrow. I also enrolled you in a creative writing class. A friend is teaching at the New School in January. Drake Gideon. He writes contemporary novels."

"I've heard of him. He's big time, right?"

"As opposed to me. Small time."

"Well, he's famous AND teaches. You're—"

"Just famous."

"If you say so."

The girl could banter with the best of them. "Bring three short stories you've written to the first class. You'll get more details later."

"Got it. Wow. Drake Gideon. I'm excited."

"Give it up, Kat. I'm not biting. Now, next subject. Do you have a passport?"

"Yeah. I got one for a trip to Italy Mom and I were supposed—" She looked away.

So her mother planned on taking Kat to Italy. He'd been thinking about a little jaunt to Italy himself. It might be needed for the next book. But first things first. "How'd you like to go to London with me?"

Kat's face changed in a split second. "Are you serious?" Nick nodded. "Oh wow, Nick! But I thought Jessie—"

"No. She's not going."

*

"Jessie?" Abbie stood in the bedroom doorway.

"I'm awake. Come on in." Jessie was propped up in bed, a washcloth pressed to her forehead. "I've wanted to talk to you for days. What's going on with you and Willie?"

"Wow. That's getting to the point."

"Sorry. I'm desperate for girl talk." Jessie tossed the washcloth on the nightstand. It wasn't helping her headache one bit.

"I'll tell you about Willie after you confirm something for me. You're pregnant, aren't you?"

Jessie's jaw dropped. "Willie told you."

"No! What— Willie knows? You told Willie and not me?"

"Of course not. I think he overheard—Never mind. So how'd you find out?"

"I figured it out for myself. It wasn't hard. Your upset stomach. Your moods and quick temper. No brandy the other night. Since when do you turn down brandy? No coffee in the morning. You're living in bed." She shrugged. "It all adds up to pregnant."

"It's a shocker, isn't it?"

"It is. But I'm thrilled for you both!"

*

"Could I talk to you for a minute, Nick?" Willie interrupted his conversation with Kat.

Nick followed Willie onto the back porch. "What's up?"

Willie explained about Joey Evenatti. "My pal Roger gave me some family addresses. Abbie insists you go with me."

So Abbie finally wanted his expertise. About time she came to her senses. "Sure. I'm not busy right now."

*

"Now that we've established I'm pregnant, what's up with you and Willie?"

Abbie had trouble looking Jessie in the eye. This was a tough subject to dissect. "I don't know, Jessie. He's a wonderful man, and we have fun together."

"It sounds like there's a 'but' in there."

Abbie shrugged. "I'm confused."

"Is it because he's black?"

"No! Good God, no. You know I don't see color."

"Then what?"

"He's so different from all the bad-boy Italians I date. I'm afraid of hurting him." Abbie sat on the bed, tucking her legs beneath her. "When we got back from the funeral, he asked about Josh."

"Oh." Jessie nodded. "Did you tell him the truth?"

"Yes. He deserved the truth." Abbie had been involved with Josh for months. Until she learned of his deception in the Jessie plot. "And I told him Josh used me to get to you. Which is also the truth."

"How did he react?"

Abbie shrugged. "He knew about Gianni. I think he accepted it as part of the job I was doing. Plus, Gianni's dead. Today he came face-to-face with someone from my past."

"I understand how Willie might feel. I'm confronting Nick's past every time I look at Kat. It's not easy."

"But you're coming around, right?"

"Trying to."

"It's weird," Abbie said, almost to herself. "I'm afraid of getting involved with him. And at the same time I'm afraid of losing him."

"You just described my feelings about Nick in the beginning. Which should tell you something."

*

It was already the end of October when Nick set off with Willie to search for Joey Evenatti. The fall was zipping by, beginning with Kat's entry into their lives.

Since it was routine for Willie to drive him everywhere, Nick said nothing to Jessie about their investigation. Nick didn't consider their search dangerous, but in her current state of mind, Jessie would worry anyway. She didn't need that kind of stress.

They spent two weeks working their way down the list of family addresses, checking them off after each interview. A few said Joey had stopped by, others said they hadn't seen him. No one had seen or heard from him in over a week.

Nick found Willie interesting. There was more to the man than Nick realized. He obviously had been a good cop, and his style was similar to Barton's. His soft-spoken manner made people trust him, but he could become the aggressor in a heartbeat, if needed. As for Nick, he adapted to the witness.

They pursued every lead, to no avail. Joey hadn't returned to L.A., and there was no further activity on his credit card. Joey Evenatti had disappeared into thin air. It was frustrating, but Nick was happy to be on the hunt. It had been too long.

They stopped for lunch each day, Willie as adventurous as Nick when it came to food. "A cop learns to eat whatever and whenever,"

Willie joked. "You never know when you'll get your next meal." They were in a tiny Peruvian restaurant in Jamaica, Queens.

As they rose from the table, Nick accidentally bumped into a waiter carrying a tray of steaming entrees. Food and drinks went flying. Apologizing, they hustled out of the packed place, their clothes stained with empanadas and Piscol.

Nick squished as he walked. "What is it with you? Every time I'm around you I end up acting like a buffoon."

"Yeah, like it's my fault you crashed into that waiter." Willie wiped the green sauce from his face with his sleeve. "And stepped in dung in Riverside Park." His cell rang as they walked to the car. "Bodine ... When? ... Okay, thanks." He clicked off. "Joey Evenatti was just found in Prospect Park. A dog dug up his remains."

CHAPTER 11

By mid-November, Kat settled into a routine with school and ballet. She spent her mornings with Finn, discussing life as well as the curriculum. He gave her a ton of homework, but Kat didn't complain. He was the best teacher she ever had.

To their delight, Mary always sent up breakfast. Pancakes. Waffles. Yummy omelets. Canadian bacon. Home fries. And her magnificent orange muffins.

Most afternoons Kat was at ballet. Surprisingly, she made a friend, her pas de deux partner, Bertie Castro. A few years older than Kat, Bertie was tall with long legs and a wicked sense of humor. Of Puerto Rican descent, his real name was Hubert, but everyone called him Bertie. No one, he explained, wanted to go through life answering to Hubert. Worse, he had a sister named Mabel and a dead brother named Stuart. His parents must have hated kids, marking them for life with such awful names. Kat assumed Bertie was gay, a given in her world of ballet.

She invited him to dinner one night, and he hit it off with the whole family. Well, maybe not Jessie, who said little. Nick, on the other hand, engaged with Bertie, obviously finding him as interesting as Kat did. When Nick told him he'd met Baryshnikov, Bertie was in awe. Mikhail Baryshnikov was Bertie's idol. Nick took him upstairs and showed him photos of the two of them.

After that, Nick McDeare could do no wrong in Bertie's eyes.

*

With Joey Evenatti dead, Abbie thought her life could get back to normal. But the calls continued, confusing her. Who was doing this? Maybe it was a robocall.

She spent most evenings with Willie. They worked on his apartment, went to the Meadowlands with Nick and Anthony for a

Giants game, saw a few movies and shared dinner several times a week. But there were no more kisses. No more handholding. Willie was warm and kind, but there was a chasm between them now. Ever since she told him about Josh. It ate away at Abbie. She finally broached the subject one night after dinner at his place.

"What's happened between us, Willie? I thought we were getting close."

"We are close." He put their dishes in the sink.

"You know what I mean."

"Not really."

"Now I'm embarrassed." She got her coat and started for the door. "It's late. I should go—"

"No, wait." He grabbed her arm. "You're right. I do know what you mean." Abbie waited. "Look, I don't think it's a good idea if something develops between us."

"Is it the black-white thing?"

"Of course not."

"So it's because of my past. With men. It's okay. I understand." She again headed for the door.

"Would you please sit down and let me explain?"

"You don't have to explain. I get it."

"No. You don't." He took her hand and led her to the breakfast nook, sliding in across from her. "When I met Josh and realized he was someone you were involved with ... and then there's Gianni ... I mean, Josh is a big-time actor. Gianni was a famous restaurateur. Who am I? An ex-cop. A security guard and chauffeur. Come on, Abbie. It's ridiculous."

This was the last thing Abbie expected to hear. "You think Josh and Gianni are better than you?"

"Not better. Just in a different category. I can't compete with that."

"You're right. You can't. Gianni is a murderer and a kidnapper. Josh is a disgusting snake who tried to harm my best friend."

Willie's lips curled into a smile. "Well, when you put it that way ..."

"You're worth a hundred Joshes or Giannis. So put that out of your mind. But Willie, I want to be honest with you. This, this thing between us scares the hell out of me."

"I scare you?"

"Not you. Me. I'm scared of me."

"I don't understand."

"I don't think I do either. I'm attracted to you. I admit that. But I'm so stupid when it comes to men. I don't want to hurt you."

Willie leaned forward. "I'm a big boy, Abbie. And tough. I can handle anything. The only thing I'm afraid of is missing out on a good thing when it comes my way."

They stared long and hard at each other.

"How about," Willie whispered, "we make a pact? We live for today. Not tomorrow. That way there's no pressure. Deal?"

"Tomorrow isn't promised anyway. I learned that the hard way." Abbie nodded. "Deal."

*

A week after Joey Evenatti's body was discovered, the California authorities arrested Joey's sister-in-law, Claire, for his murder. She tried to hide her tracks, driving across country instead of flying and only using cash. Her mistake was being spotted when she hastily buried the body in the park.

With the Evenatti case solved, Jessie made Nick promise there would be no more investigations. "If anything happened to you, Nick, I don't know what I'd do. And what about Kat? What would happen to her if you got yourself killed?"

"This is my career, Jess. What I do."

"Writing novels is your career. Isn't that enough?"

"It should be. It's not. Look, nothing's going to happen to me."

"I'll bet Lyle said the same thing."

Nick winced at her words.

"Think of the baby. Please. Promise me."

Damn. His wife knew exactly how to get to him: bring up Lyle and the baby.

Having given Jessie his word, Nick was now bored. He spent his days plotting out his next book, helping Anthony with his photography, giving Kat piano lessons and working out in the upstairs gym.

With Jessie growing more irritable every day, Nick gave her space. At night he rubbed her back, her feet and anything else he could get his hands on. She was now more than three months along and beginning to show. They planned on waiting until Christmas to tell the kids about the baby, but it was getting harder to hide Jessie's pregnancy. Thanksgiving became the new reveal date.

Andrew was silent these days, making Nick wonder if he'd been there at all. Or maybe everything was going according to his brother's plan, so his pushy interference was no longer needed.

*

As November flew by, Luci spent more and more time with Raoul. He'd leave the pharmacy around five and meet her for dinner at a little Spanish cafe near her apartment. Eventually they began going back to her place.

It had been years since Luci had been with a man. Raoul helped fill the empty hours when she missed Anthony. She felt no love for the man, but she was grateful for the attention. He often brought her flowers or inexpensive jewelry. He never stayed the entire night. When Luci asked about it, he confessed he lived with his elderly mother.

A week before Thanksgiving, Luci's fondest wish was granted. She was invited to Anthony's home for dinner.

*

On a Sunday in late November, New York saw its first snowfall of the season. Large downy flakes drifted to the ground, coating the street and bare branches in a layer of marshmallow frosting.

Nick was happy to put his feet up in the study and read the three city papers with Jessie. A fire in the grate warmed them. Mary's muffins filled them.

Mary sat in her recliner, reading *The Daily News Magazine*. Abbie and Willie worked on *The Times* puzzle. The kids were upstairs, doing whatever kids did on a lazy Sunday.

"Oh. My. God." Jessie sat up straight, lowering the paper. "Josh Elliot is going to play Andrew's role in *EARLY SPRING*. It says Harrison Alder hand-picked him for the part. Bill must be spinning in his grave."

"How did that happen?" Nick tossed the sports section on the floor. "Elliot was banned from Rudolph Productions,"

"He was banned with Bill. Obviously, Harrison feels differently."

"Maybe he doesn't know about Josh's involvement with the sabotage at the theater."

124

"Maybe. Harrison had nothing to do with the production end of the show back then." She threw the Arts and Leisure section on the coffee table.

"Has Harrison contacted you about playing Daniella again?" Abbie asked.

"Nope."

"Do you still want to do it?"

"Not with Josh in the show. I'll call Harrison tomorrow. Josh is not going to step back into the New York spotlight as if nothing happened. Especially playing a character Andrew made famous. And I'll tell Harrison what I told Bill, that I'm interested in revising my role. But not with Josh. It's Josh or me."

"A no-brainer." Abbie drained her coffee mug.

"Abbie has news," Willie prodded. "Go on. Tell them."

Abbie struck a pose. "The Yarborough Company called me. I have a go-see tomorrow for a new lipstick line."

"I thought Yarborough only did toothpaste and things like that," Jessie said.

"Yeah. Toothpaste, mouthwash, whitening. Now they're branching out into lipstick with," she puffed up her full lips, "a soothing balm."

"Congratulations," Nick said. "To both you and your lips."

*

On the morning of the interview, Abbie took her time, using her special lip creams and sprays, applying layers of lipstick. She poured herself into a Christian Siriano butterscotch-gold pants ensemble and spent two hours on her hair.

She sashayed out to the car, feeling on top of the world as Willie drove her across town to Madison Avenue.

An hour later, she hurled herself back into the car beside Willie. She was furious. No, enraged. "The doofus who interviewed me told me I was too old. My lips have too many cracks. Too many cracks! He's blind. I wanted to kick that suite of offices into cow country, I was so mad. And then I learned the truth."

"What truth?"

"In the long hallway outside the reception room? Tons of framed photos of their supposedly famous talent. I didn't really look at them on my way in. But on my way out I was curious. Who were these 'younger' people? You'll never guess whose picture was front and center."

"Tell me."

"Josh-the-bastard-Elliot. That's right. Josh's fingerprints are all over this, and I'm going to prove it."

"Abbie ..." Willie stared out the front windshield, a pensive look on his face. "That fortune teller said J.E. We thought she meant Joey Evenatti. Maybe she meant—"

"Josh Elliot! Damn. I'll kill the steaming sack of—"

*

"Nick, I just got off the phone with Harrison Alder." Jessie stormed into the kitchen from the study.

What now? Nick had been tiptoeing around his wife all morning. She'd been in a foul mood since she got out of bed - on the wrong side, obviously.

"He told me I'm too old for the role. Too old!"

"Calm down, Jessie."

"Don't tell me to calm down. He's insane. I am not too old to play that role."

"He just came right out and said you're too old?"

"Yes. He almost sounded happy about it. He and I never really got along, but I made a lot of money for that organization. I deserve better."

The front door slammed. Abbie and Willie hurried into the kitchen.

"It's Josh Elliot!" Abbie announced.

"What is?" Nick asked.

Abbie told them about her interview. "Too old! Do you believe it? I know Josh is responsible. And he's probably the one who's been calling me. The calls started around the time Josh came back to New—"

"Harrison Alder," Jessie interrupted, "just told me I'm too old for the role in *EARLY SPRING*."

"Good God, Josh again!" Abbie started to pace. "He's known Harrison for years. They went to college together – or high school – or something like that. He calls him 'Harry' and Harrison calls Josh 'J'."

Jessie dropped onto a stool. Nick didn't like how she looked. Pale and tired. "Harrison resented the relationship Bill and I had. He made that clear over the years. I'm sure he loved kicking me to the curb."

"Josh once told me," Abbie plopped down beside Jessie, "Harrison couldn't wait for the day to take over when Bill finally retired."

"He got his wish by default. Bill didn't retire. He died. So Harrison takes over and the first thing he does is give Andrew's old role to Josh," Jessie said. "I have to lay down. This whole thing is making me sick." She grabbed a bottled water and climbed the stairs.

Nick's mind was processing the situation, and he didn't like what he was thinking. He pulled out his cell and speed-dialed a number. "Marcie? It's Nick. Could you call me as soon as you get this message? I need to know what Bill's schedule was on the day he had the heart attack. Thanks."

"What are you thinking?" Willie asked.

"How far would Josh go to get a role he wanted? Or for revenge?"

*

As they waited to hear from Marcie Rudoloph, Abbie's impatience ate a hole through her stomach. She filled the void by raiding the fridge. Leftover roast beef. Shrimp salad. Camembert cheese. Homemade chocolate mousse.

When Marcie called back, it took every ounce of restraint not to rip Nick's cell from his hands. Abbie tried to decipher the gist of the conversation, but Nick McDeare, man of few words, was a man of few words on the call.

Nick finally clicked off, making notes on a piece of paper.

"Well?" Abbie wanted to throttle him.

"The day Bill had his heart attack he met Elliot for drinks at four o'clock. Harrison Alder convinced him to see Josh."

"And when did Bill die?" Willie asked.

"Less than two hours later."

"A coincidence?" Abbie asked with sarcasm.

"I don't believe in coincidence."

"So what's the plan?" Willie asked.

Nick paused, a determined look creeping across his face. He marched into the hallway, Abbie and Willie on his heels.

"Where are you going?"

Nick opened the front door. "To have a little chat with Harrison Alder."

Willie grabbed his coat and sprinted after Nick.

*

Nick strode into the main office of Bill Rudolph's production company in midtown. The executive secretary recognized him and hurried over. "Mr. McDeare, how nice to see you. What can I do for you?"

"Is Alder in?"

"Yes, but he's—"

Nick headed straight for Bill's old office, which now sported Harrison Alder's name on the door. He entered, despite the protestations of the secretary.

Alder sat behind Bill's antique desk, feet up, on the phone. At the sight of Nick, he swung his feet to the floor and clicked off.

The secretary hurried around Nick. "I'm sorry, Mr. Alder, I tried to—"

"It's okay, Caroline. Mr. McDeare is always welcome here."

Caroline looked from one man to the other before backing out of the room.

Nick turned to the suit behind the desk. "Tell me, Harrison," his voice was smooth, almost silky, "when did you make a deal with the devil?"

Alder rose and slid his hands into his pockets. To keep them from shaking? "I'm not fond of riddles, Mr. McDeare. Speak plainly, please."

"You want plain? Fine. Josh Elliot. He's a loose cannon. A danger to anyone who works with him. He almost killed Jessie with ricin."

"That's not what I heard."

"Then you heard wrong."

"Look, I admire your loyalty to your wife, but your accusation is mere speculation."

"Wrong. It's fact. Here's another fact. Josh had drinks with Bill Rudolph hours before he had his heart attack. Jessie and I know better than anyone how far Elliot will go to get what he wants."

"Which is?"

"Revenge. And a role in a play."

Alder stared at Nick, his watery eyes unblinking. It was hilarious to watch the moron flounder for a response. "I haven't a clue what you're talking about."

"It's a good thing you're in the production end of the business because you're a lousy actor."

"I'd like you to leave."

"I'm sure you would

"Don't make me call security."

"Better start looking for a good defense attorney." Nick headed for the door.

"Are you threatening me?"

Nick slid his hands in his pockets and looked over his shoulder at Alder. "My target is Josh Elliot. But you might end up as collateral damage."

"And what exactly do you think you can do, McDeare? Write a bad review?" He laughed.

"Don't kid yourself, Alder." Nick shot him the look that never failed to instill fear in the guilty. Half smirk. Half I-know-more-than-I'm-revealing. "My reputation is well documented. After exposing Andrew Brady's killer, going after you and Josh Elliot is bush league."

He left a clearly shaken Harrison Alder alone in his office.

*

"Where is everyone?" Mary asked, back home after calling BINGO at the senior center.

Abbie was polishing off a roast beef and camembert sandwich. Her second. "Kat's upstairs with Finn. Jessie's laying down. And Nick went to talk to Harrison Alder."

"What?" Jessie stood at the top of the stairs.

Abbie didn't like the look on her friend's face. Jessie was ticked. "He, uh, found out Josh Elliot met with Bill the afternoon of his heart attack—"

"Found out how?"

"He called Marcie."

Jessie pounded down the stairs. Mary scooted out of her way. "He bothered Marcie Rudolph, asking questions about her husband's death?"

"She was fine with it. Really. See, we believe Josh had something to do with Bill's—"

"Wait a minute. You think Josh killed Bill? That's crazy. And what does Harrison have to do with it?"

"Nick thinks Harrison may be in on it. And Nick's theory isn't crazy. Look at the facts, Jessie. Bill dies suddenly, a man healthier than most of us. Enter Harrison, who offers Josh a plum role on Broadway. Exit you and me, insults flying, told it's time for support hose and dentures. This is so like Josh. It's his revenge."

Jessie paced around the island. "I can't believe this. Nick goes off half-cocked on his own to confront Harrison without asking me first."

"Actually, Willie went with him."

Jessie turned her fury on Abbie. "Stop talking. Just stop talking."

"Jeez," Mary said, "I go away for two hours, and all hell breaks loose."

*

"Well?" Willie asked as Nick climbed into the front seat of the car.

"They're definitely in cahoots with the role in the play. That much was obvious to me."

"What about Bill's death?"

"My gut says yes but proving it won't be easy. We need your police computer."

"I don't have access to everything. And I don't want to ask Roger for any more favors."

"Damn. We need that computer." Nick scrubbed a hand over his face, frustrated. "Only the police would have—" An idea hit him.

Fifteen minutes later they walked into Midtown North, Barton's precinct house. Nick greeted Lyle's old friend Harry Steinmetz, the desk officer, and introduced Willie, explaining he was a retired cop. "I need a favor, Harry. When are you free?"

"Give me a minute to talk to the boss. Then we can grab some lunch."

Against his will, Nick's eyes were drawn to a large framed photograph on the wall behind the desk. Dressed in full uniform, Lyle Barton stared back at him. Below the picture was the flag from Lyle's coffin, folded and under glass.

Harry swung around the corner with two men. One was a tall, burly dark-haired man, the other shorter with a barrel chest and graying hair. "Nick, you remember Mario Manganaro. He's Chief of Detectives now. And his partner, Bernie Loman."

The men shook hands. Barton's former go-to man, Mario was one hell of a cop. So was Loman. "Harry said you need a favor. Let's go to McGowan's for lunch."

Walking into McGowan's again wasn't easy. It was Barton's favorite pub, owned and populated by cops. The memories were bittersweet for Nick. He could still see Lyle in the back booth, a sandwich in one hand, a draft beer in the other.

I can feel my arteries hardening, McDeare. Who gives a shit, right? You only live once. But if you do it right, it's enough.

"Nick? ... NICK?" He looked up into the weathered face of Gil O'Brien, the proprietor of McGowan's. Gil clasped Nick's shoulder and expressed his sorrow over Barton's death. "Lyle and I went back decades. One of the best cops I ever saw. It was a tragedy, what happened to him." Thank God the food arrived, interrupting Gil's soliloquy.

Over mile-high corned beef sandwiches, Nick explained to the three men who their target was and what they suspected he did.

*

Harrison Alder was furious. As soon as McDeare left his office he called Josh Elliot and filled him in on the surprise visit. "Dammit, Josh, if you did anything to Bill—"

"Calm down, Harry. You're overreacting. You know me better than that." Elliot sounded cool and calm. Maybe Harrison WAS overreacting, but McDeare's visit rattled him. "McDeare is firing blanks. He's just pissed because you shut his wife out of the production. Jessie's not used to the word no."

"You damned well better be right." He clicked off.

Harrison waited years to take over the reins of this company from Bill Rudolph. If Josh Elliot was lying, Harrison would toss him to Nick McDeare and sleep like a baby that night.

*

Josh Elliott folded the classifieds and left the restaurant. A light snow fell as he headed back to his hotel. He needed to find an apartment, and he didn't want to live anywhere but Manhattan. The outer boroughs just weren't up to his standards. After all, he was a Broadway star.

131

The call from Harry Alder nagged at him. Harry was such a worrier. An ignorant worrier, thank God. Josh hadn't told him what really happened that afternoon with Bill Rudolph.

When Josh met Bill in the Golden Calf Bar, he ensured his future.

Harry didn't need to know the details.

And Nick McDeare would never be able to prove a thing.

This time, Josh left no fingerprints, real or metaphorical.

CHAPTER 12

"I owe you." Nick walked Steinmetz to Willie's front door.

"Anything for you, Nick. Mario feels the same way. Lt. Barton would want us to help."

Nick rejoined Willie at the desk in the den. Steinmetz had set up full police access on the computer. "So what'd you find on our pal Josh?"

"No priors as an adult. Teenage records expunged, which could mean something. His only health problem is bad eyesight."

"What about Bill's death?"

"Let's see ..." Willie pulled up a new screen. "An autopsy was requested by his wife. It's sealed. We'll have to talk to the coroner."

"Bill was seventy years old," Nick mused. "A cardiac arrest isn't out of the ordinary for someone that age. They may not have looked for much."

"The autopsy will tell us what we want to know. And the coroner will remember the details, given Bill's celebrity."

"Okay, we've got the computer. And I know you're licensed to carry. What about your shield?"

"It says RETIRED. But I'm now attached to Midtown North as a temporary assist officer.

Nick collapsed into the stuffed chair. "Hell, you may not need any of it. Maybe I just hate Elliot so much I'm willing him to be guilty of killing Bill."

"It's possible."

"No," Abbie stood in the kitchen doorway, surprising them both. "Nick's gut is never wrong. Josh had something to do with Bill Rudolph's death." She joined Willie at the desk. "So where do we start?"

"We?" Nick asked.

"You think I'm going to let you guys do this alone? This is personal. He came after me, too. And you're about to leave town for a month."

She was right. Next week was Thanksgiving. Then he was gone. He looked at Willie. "Abbie can help while I'm away. This can't wait."

"So it's settled," Abbie said.

It would kill Nick not to be actively involved, to have to trust Willie and Abbie. He cursed his dueling careers.

"Mary sent me over to get you." Abbie picked up their empty coffee mugs. "That friend of Anthony's from school – Luci? – is coming for dinner tonight." She disappeared into the kitchen. "And, Nick," Abbie shouted. "You better talk to Jessie. She's furious you went to see Harrison."

Great. The last thing he wanted to do was fight with Jessie.

*

"You should have talked to me first, Nick." Jessie tried not to shout. She closed their bedroom door, aware of their dinner guest downstairs. "This is about my career. You confront a producer about some idiotic notion—"

"It's not idiotic, And I had a talk with him. That's all."

"I know you, Nick. You confronted him."

"It depends on your definition of confront."

"Don't play word games with me. What exactly happened?"

Nick shrugged. "I warned him about getting involved with Elliot."

Jessie slumped onto the bed, her head in her hands. She was getting another headache. "You had no business interfering in my career."

"Josh Elliot may be responsible for Bill's heart attack."

"You don't know that for sure."

"You're right. I don't. But I sure as hell am going to find out."

"And that's another thing," Jessie continued, her voice rising. "You promised you wouldn't get involved in any more investigations."

"I shouldn't have made that promise. This is about my work, Jessie." His voice level matched hers. "You just told me to stay out of your career. Well, you stay the hell out of mine!"

"Leave it alone, Nick. Please. Knowing Alder, he's already planted an item in the gossip columns about your visit." She leapt to her feet. "I can see the headline. NICK MCDEARE DEFENDS THE LITTLE WOMAN."

"I don't understand you. A man you considered a second father may have been murdered, and all you care about is gossip?"

"Of course not! You know how much I loved Bill—"

"Sorry, Jess. I won't drop it." He turned away. "And you shouldn't want me to." He strode from the room, the bedroom door banging against the wall.

*

Kat's stomach was upset before she even sat down for dinner. She'd been shivering for hours. The atmosphere of the meal only made it worse.

Luci, Anthony's friend from school, was their guest. Tonight the woman looked almost pretty. Dressed in a matching print skirt and sweater, her thick dark hair was released from its tight bun and fell around her shoulders. And she was wearing makeup. But no matter how much she spiffed herself up, Kat didn't like or trust Luci. There was just something about her ...

Nick and Jessie were obviously fighting again. Nick focused on his food. Jessie picked at hers. Neither of them looked at each other. Abbie and Willie whispered together about someone named Josh, whoever he was. Anthony talked non-stop, thrilled to have his friend over for dinner. What was it about Luci that Anthony loved so much? And what was it about Anthony that attracted this strange middle-aged woman?

Mary politely asked Luci questions. The woman dodged most of them, only talking about work. "There are going to be layoffs," she said. "Since I'm the newest, I'm sure I'll have to go."

"I'd hate it if you weren't at school." Anthony finished his mashed potatoes and reached for more. "Mom, can we hire Luci? She could help Mary."

Jessie pushed her chair back. "Would you excuse me?" Providing no explanation, she left the room. So rude.

"Dad?" Anthony pursued. "Can we hire Luci?"

"It's up to Mary."

Mary cleared her throat, looking uncomfortable. "We'll talk about it."

Kat had heard enough. "I'm sorry, Luci," she mumbled, making a feeble attempt at manners despite her dislike of the woman, "but I'm going upstairs, too. I don't feel well."

"What's wrong?" Nick wanted to know.

"Upset stomach."

"I'll come check on you soon."

*

Nick found Kat shivering in her bed. Hamlet snuggled against her, a feline heating pad. Feeling her head, Nick knew she had a temperature. He grabbed a heavy quilt from the closet and covered her with it. She was silent, watching him.

Sitting in the overstuffed chair by the bed, he pulled out his cell. "Mary? It looks like Kat has the flu. She needs your magic touch."

Mary appeared ten minutes later with hot tea, large bottles of water and ginger ale, a thermometer and a liquid flu remedy. She took Kat's temperature. "Over a hundred and two. No wonder you don't feel well. By the way, Nick, it's time we got the house intercom fixed. I don't always have my cell with me."

"I'll take care of it tomorrow."

Nick stayed with Kat when Mary left. Just when he thought she was asleep, she sat up, looked around as if she didn't know where she was, and hurried to the bathroom to be sick. After hesitating, Nick followed her, rubbing her back and wetting a washcloth for her. She looked so pale and vulnerable. The scene was replayed over the long night, dredging up memories of Jeffrey that Nick wished would stay buried.

"Daddy, I'm going to be sick." Jeffrey had no color in his face as he turned to Nick in the car. "Sick ..." Nick swerved to the side of the road. Having nothing else to use, Nick held out his hands as his son threw up.

Towards dawn, Kat's breathing became steady, and she seemed to fall into a deep sleep. Hopefully, the worst was over.

Exhausted, Nick headed down to the kitchen and put on a pot of coffee. Sliding into the breakfast nook, he watched as streaks of orange lit the eastern sky.

"I love sunrises, Daddy." Jeffrey was propped up in the hospital bed, staring out the large window as the sun came up.

"What about sunsets?"

Jeffrey shook his head. "Sunsets are endings. Sunrises are beginnings. They're happy. Even the color is bright and cheerful."

It was the last sunrise Nick shared with his son. The next day he was on a flight to London for book signings and to accept an award.

The doctors had assured him Jeffrey's leukemia was heading into remission. It wasn't. A week later, Nick got the call that Jeffrey had died.

"Kat will be fine." Mary sat across from him, handing him a mug of coffee. "All kids get sick."

Nick nodded, still staring out the window.

"You're thinking about Jeffrey, aren't you?"

Nick took a sip of coffee.

"Kat's not Jeffrey, Nick. She's tough. Like you. She may look like a kid, but I have my doubts. That's a little adult in a kid's body."

For the first time in hours, Nick smiled.

As usual, Mary was right.

*

Realizing Nick never came to bed, Jessie went looking for him the next morning. She found Mary in the breakfast nook, but no Nick. "Where is he?"

"Kat's sick. He's sitting with her."

Of course. Kat. "You'd think he'd sit with his sick pregnant wife. Nick cares more about that girl than anyone else."

"No. He cares more about you than anyone else."

"Not lately."

"Right now he's a daddy with a sick daughter. Try to understand." Mary leaned across the table. "Do you remember how you felt when Anthony was kidnapped? Your whole focus was on Anthony, not Nick. As it should have been. You know better than anyone about the special love between a parent and child. That's how Nick feels about Kat. And he's going to feel the same way, probably more, about that baby you're carrying."

"More?"

"Because you and Nick made that baby. He didn't love his first wife or Kat's mother the way he loves you."

Jessie rubbed her eyes, suddenly feeling small. "You're right, Mary. I know you're right. It's just that I need him now more than ever, with the baby coming. And Kat seems to get all his attention."

"That's because it's new for Nick. He's trying to prove himself to her. Just give it time. I know it's not easy, suddenly having to share Nick with his daughter. But everything will sort itself out, I promise."

*

Dear Mom,

I just had the worst flu ever. I was SICK! And guess what? Nick took care of me. REALLY took care of me, even when I was sick in the bathroom. Whenever I woke up, he was sitting by the bed. One time he was sound asleep and snoring. Who would have thought Nick McDeare could care so much about a sick kid? And wouldn't his adoring female fans be shocked to know that Nick snored!!!

There's something else, Mom. The whole time I was sick I thought there was someone else in the room besides Nick. A man. He was silhouetted in the window, so I couldn't see him clearly. Mary said my temperature went up to a hundred three before it broke. Being so sick, maybe I was hallucinating?

Anyway, I'm much better and anxious to see what kind of Thanksgiving they throw around here. No matter what, I'll miss you.

Your Kat forever

*

A McDeare Thanksgiving wasn't a mere day. It took place over a week. And it always brought with it surprises.

Nick retreated to his office for the duration, out of the way of the chaos in the kitchen. From his lofty perch, Nick categorized the holiday into food groups. On Monday, Violet, Mary's sister and Willie's mother, arrived. Thus began the baking of the pies. Tuesday brought the aroma of breads baking and vegetables being prepped. Wednesday was Nick's favorite. The turkey broth simmered on the stove all day, the base for tomorrow's gravy. Nick would creep downstairs every few hours, where Mary would slip him a seasoned giblet.

Despite her lack of culinary skills, Jessie always helped in the kitchen. Mary's curses were heard on a regular basis, also the sound of dropped pans and breaking china. But this year no one – absolutely no one – dared to shoo Jessie from the kitchen. Everyone tried their best not to antagonize her, knowing she could turn on them in a New York minute.

Nick and Willie called the coroner's office to schedule an appointment that week. Unfortunately, the man who performed the autopsy on William Rudolph was out of town, not due back until Christmas.

They also wanted to interview the bartender at the Golden Calf Bar, where Josh met Bill for drinks. He, too, was unavailable, on vacation through Thanksgiving. Which meant Nick had to turn the task over to Willie and Abbie while he was on his book tour. He cursed the timing, but his hands were tied. He was contracted to do publicity for his new novel.

Because Nick wasn't running around pursuing Josh Elliot, Jessie thought he'd backed away from the investigation. In her eyes, he took her objections to heart but didn't want to admit defeat. Nick found her assumption amusing. Whenever she mentioned it, he said nothing, content to keep the peace. Besides, he technically was out of it until Christmas, so why argue now?

With time on his hands, Nick spent the week shopping online for Christmas and perfecting the plot for his next novel. Linden Publishing wanted an outline by early February.

On Wednesday morning Nick accompanied Jessie for her sonogram. "Everything looks good," Dr. Lindstrom assured the anxious parents.

"What about the sex of the baby?"

"You want to know?"

"Yes!"

*

Luci was ecstatic. Mary called to say she was hired. Anthony must have nagged until she gave in. Luci gave her notice at the school, happy that her foot was finally in the McDeare door. Despite only working three days a week, the pay was twice her former salary, so it was a win-win. Luci was determined to make herself invaluable, to inspire Mary to lengthen her work week. Only seeing Anthony three days in his home instead of five at the school wasn't good enough. She wanted more. Much more.

Her starting date was the week after Thanksgiving. Perfect timing. Anthony said Nick McDeare would be out of town. The less she saw of that man, the better.

Luci assumed she'd spend Thanksgiving with Raoul, but his mother wasn't well. He couldn't leave her by herself, he explained, and she wasn't able to have guests. Desperate, Luci called Mary, explaining she'd be alone and offering her services for the holiday. She secretly hoped Mary would take pity on her and invite her for dinner. Sadly, neither would be happening.

So Luci sat alone in her tiny apartment, feeling sorry for herself. Happy Thanksgiving.

*

"I'll call you back after I talk to Nick." Kat clicked off her cell and hurried down to Nick's office.

Nick and Jessie stood at the window, their heads together. Anthony sat on the floor with the ever-present Monty. "Good timing, Kat," Nick said. "I was just going to buzz you on the intercom. We have something to tell the two of you." He looked at his wife. "Go ahead."

Oh God, what now? Whatever it is, my news is more important.

Jessie was beaming, unusual for the grumpy woman. "You're going to have a baby sister. I'm pregnant."

"Really?" Anthony squealed, leaping up.

"In early May," Jessie said.

"Yippee! Someone to boss around."

Monty, too, leapt to his feet and jumped up on Jessie.

"Monty, no!" Nick yelled. "Get down." He pulled the dog away from Jessie.

"Sorry, Dad. He's just excited. Come on, Monty. Let's call Zane and tell him." He hugged his mom and dashed out of the room, Monty on his heels.

Kat looked from Nick to Jessie.

I'm supposed to be happy, right? I'm supposed to say something.

"Congratulations." She managed a wide smile, summoning her acting skills.

Nick won't care about anyone but that new baby. His love child with the love of his life. I'll just be in the way.

"Well. I better get back to the kitchen," Jessie said, "No matter what Mary says, she needs me." She squeezed Nick's hand as she left the room.

Kat turned to Nick. "I have a HUGE favor to ask. Bertie just called. His parents had a major fight, and his father beat up his mother pretty bad."

"Did he hurt Bertie?"

"Not this time. When Bertie got home from ballet and saw what was happening, he took off. He says it's no use trying to shield his mother anymore because she won't press charges. Apparently, this happens a lot."

"Where's Bertie now?"

"Walking around. Trying to figure out where to go. He usually stays with Susie when this happens, but she's away for Thanksg—"

"Have him come here."

"Really? That's what I was going to ask. You're sure?" Nick nodded. "What about Jessie?"

"She'll feel the same way. He can stay as long as necessary."

Kat exhaled. "Thank you. Thank you so much. I'll call him back."

"Does he have clothes?"

"I think just his ballet gear."

"Tell him to meet me in The Men's Store at Bloomingdale's in a half hour."

*

"Mary, stop yelling at me." Jessie was tired of being ridiculed. Even Abbie and Willie were teasing her. "I'm not a total idiot in the kitchen."

"Says who?" Mary glared at her. "You're making twice the work for me."

Nick hurried down the stairs. "One more for dinner tomorrow. Bertie."

Jessie's eyebrows shot up. "Bertie? Since when?"

"Since his father beat up his mother."

"Oh, God, the poor kid." Mary shook her head.

"You're okay with this, right?" Nick asked Jessie.

"I, well, I guess so. Do you think his father will come after him? Could there be trouble?"

"I don't think his father will even know Bertie's gone."

"It worries me, Nick."

"Stop it," Mary admonished. "Bertie is a good boy. I know people. And why celebrate Thanksgiving if we can't help someone in need?"

Normally Jessie would open her door to anyone who needed help. But she had the welfare of this baby to consider now. And Bertie coming here after a domestic problem worried her.

"I'll be back soon." Nick hurried down the hallway.

"Where are you going?" Jessie yelled after him.

The only answer was the slamming of the front door. "He's the most secretive man," Jessie murmured.

A pan of broth near Jessie fell to the floor.

Seeing Mary's rage, Jessie backed away. "I didn't touch it. I swear!"

"It just leapt off the island by itself?"

"Yes!"

*

After staying for a buffet dinner at the brownstone, Abbie and Willie went back to his place to watch the Knicks game. They lounged on his couch, sipping brandy. Willie had stocked the bar that morning.

"It was a nice day," Abbie reflected. "I've always loved your mom, but I'm not sure how she feels about me."

"All that matters is how I feel about you." He changed the subject "What do you think of Bertie?"

"I like him. A lot." Abbie curled her legs beneath her. "Bertie has such a positive attitude, which is amazing considering—"

"His home life, yeah. There are way too many families out there like Bertie's. But there's always one kid who's a survivor. Who learns from it and finds success in life. That's Bertie. I'd bet money on it."

"It was nice of Nick to buy him those clothes. Nick is such a softy when it comes to kids."

"Nick is complex. He can't be labeled."

Abbie looked up at Willie, who was staring off into space. "Where are you?"

"Hmm?" He met her eyes. "Sorry. I was thinking ... Nick says more with silence than he does with words. I'm starting to be able to read him now."

"He's so different from Andrew. The moment a thought hit Andrew's brain it was out of his mouth. I guess Nick got used to speaking through his novels."

142

"How astute of you," Willie whispered.

"Astute?" Abbie whispered back. "How very 'Webster's Dictionary' of you."

They both laughed softly. Willie bent down and kissed her with a sweetness that surprised her. She responded, curling her arms around him.

"Stay tonight, Abbie. Stay with me."

She wanted to. She did. But she was still scared to take that leap. Why was she so hesitant? It wasn't like her. Hell, she even slept with some targets in her investigations. What was so different about sleeping with Willie? "Soon."

*

Thanksgiving dinner was a gourmet feast. Nick scanned the table in admiration. Mary and Violet had outdone themselves this year. Roast turkey, glazed ham, cornbread and sausage stuffing, mashed potatoes, brandied cranberries, brown-sugar sweet potatoes with pecans and marshmallows, spinach soufflé, Brussel sprouts with bacon and bleu cheese, buttered corn, pecan rolls and homemade Italian bread with sweet butter.

As everyone dug in, Nick looked around the table. Two faces were missing, two empty chairs tugged at Nick's heart. Lyle Barton and Bill Rudolph.

Bertie laughed at something Finn Cagney said. Two new faces for this holiday. Nick wondered who would be sitting here next year. If any of them would be sitting here.

"I'm sorry, Nicholas, sweetheart, I have a concert in Vienna over Thanksgiving, and your dad has to fly to Johannesburg. A difficult surgery only he can perform. Priscilla will see that you have a proper turkey dinner. You understand, don't you? That's my good boy. Next year we'll all be together, I promise."

Shaking off his dark thoughts, Nick carved the turkey. The meal was a raucous one with jokes flying and laughter filling the old house. Mary and Violet were showered with well-deserved compliments, and everyone groaned when it was time for pie. Still, the pumpkin, mincemeat, apple and chocolate silk pies disappeared, along with a gallon of ice cream.

After dinner, Nick, Anthony, Kat and Bertie walked Monty. It was a chilly night with a clear sky and a bright moon suspended over the East River. People were beginning to decorate for the holidays. They were all catching the seasonal spirit.

Back home again, Nick was conned into playing the piano, and everyone gathered around, singing. Nick chuckled at the Norman Rockwell tableau, at the Thanksgiving cliché they became today. Two years ago, he couldn't have pictured it. Hell, thirty years ago he ...

The meal, purchased from the American gourmet shop in town, was dry and colorless. The dining room table was vast and lonely. Even Priscilla, the housekeeper, ate in the kitchen with the cook. Only Haywire kept Nick company. He made sure the dog got half his turkey.

Nick's reverie was interrupted by Kat and Bertie. They were singing a duet, their gorgeous voices a perfect blend. Another art form in which his daughter excelled? Where were her shortcomings? What were her failures? Everyone sucked at something.

When Kat and Bertie finished, they were rewarded with well-earned applause. Everyone was impressed.

Everyone, it seemed, but Jessie.

Late that night, in the darkness of their bedroom, Nick asked Jessie about it. "Did you like Kat and Bertie's singing?"

"Sure."

That's all she was going to say? "I thought they were—"

"Nick, I'm tired. It was a long day. 'Night, sweetie."

CHAPTER 13

When Kat came downstairs the next morning, she discovered that Nick had followed through on a promise: an authentic English breakfast greeted her, laid out on the sideboard in the dining room.

Digging in, Kat sampled everything. Cumberland sausage (which Nick called bangers), grilled onions, streaky bacon, fried eggs, creamed mushrooms, baked beans, sliced tomatoes and scones with clotted cream and strawberry preserves. Also, orange juice and English teas.

Kat adored the sausage, having two helpings. Everything was delicious, but the sausage was her favorite. "Wait until you taste the real thing in London," Nick teased. "These are just knock-offs."

Bertie also seemed to love everything, going back for seconds. Anthony was copying Kat and Bertie, eating whatever they ate. And giving a ton to Monty. What a funny little kid he was. As kids go.

Jessie poured herself some juice, ate nothing, and retreated to the kitchen. She seemed to excel at being rude. Kat couldn't keep up with the woman's moods. During dinner yesterday, Jessie was chatty and at times funny. Then last night around the piano, she was moody and sullen. Was this normal behavior for a pregnant woman?

Whatever. Kat was tired of it.

*

Jessie and Nick were in their private sitting room, lounging on the couch, shopping online for the baby. Jessie loved this airy space, overlooking the back yard. One whole wall was devoted to photos and magazine covers of Jessie and Andrew's celebrated careers. Over the couch hung Nick and Jessie's wedding photo, Anthony standing between them. They decided a large corner of this room would serve as a nursery until the baby was older.

"Why the sad face?" Nick asked.

"I feel old."

He slung his arm around her. "How can you say that with our baby growing inside you?" He rubbed her stomach.

"I was thinking about Kat and Bertie. They're tomorrow's Broadway stars."

"You're a mega-star. Talent like yours has no expiration date."

Jessie pulled Nick close. "You always know how to make me feel better." He was leaving in a few days, and she dreaded it. No. She wouldn't think about that now. She wanted to enjoy their time together and talk about the baby. "I've been thinking about names for this little one ... How do you feel about Andrea? In honor of Andrew."

"I don't know ... What about Chelsea?"

"Mmm ...I'm not a fan of naming a baby after a location."

"You know it was my mother's name. And Andrew's."

"To be honest, I never liked that name."

"... Andrea, huh? ... Andrea ... I think there are too many names that begin with 'A' in this family."

"I definitely don't like Chelsea."

"Well, that's the end of that for today." He stood up and stretched. "We've made a dent in what we need for little What's-Her-Name. Let's go find Kat and Bertie. I want to see them dance."

She couldn't believe what she was hearing. They finally had time alone. No kids. There were things that needed to be decided right now about the baby, with Nick gone for a month. "Kat and Bertie? Of course. Don't focus on our baby. Focus on Kat and Bertie."

Nick physically deflated. "I don't want to fight, Jess."

"Kat and Bertie are all you care about this weekend."

His hands on his hips, Nick stared at the floor.

"You'd think Bertie was your own son."

Turning away, he headed for the door.

"Poor Anthony. He can't get your attention for even five minutes. Since Kat arrived, he's forgotten."

Nick halted, breathing hard. "Don't—" he faced her, his voice low, "don't ever say that to me again. EVER." He stormed out of the room.

Jessie shook her head.

"There are none so blind as those who will not see."

The wedding photo behind Jessie's head fell to the floor. She shrieked.

If the couch hadn't broken its descent, it would have crashed down on her head.

*

"I wonder why Nick wanted to see us dance?" Kat asked Bertie. They were in her room, watching videos on YouTube.

"And why all the questions about my school and training?"

"Nick can be a mystery." Kat stroked Hamlet, who was curled around the desk lamp.

"Why do you call your dad 'Nick'?"

Kat was surprised by Bertie's question. "Because he—he doesn't feel like my father. It would be weird to call him 'Dad'."

"I may not know what it feels like to have a real dad, considering the disgusting specimen I'm stuck with," Bertie slung his leg over the arm of the rocker, "but I sure know one when I see one."

"At least you've known your father your whole life. I've known mine a whole five minutes."

"Girl, you are way off-base. I'd trade my lifer-father any day for yours."

"No, you wouldn't. Not if you knew everything about Nick."

"You mean all that shit about women? Don't look surprised. I troll the internet, just like you. Let me ask you something." He leaned towards her. "Has Nick screwed around even once since he got married?"

Kat shrugged.

"There you go. I bet he hasn't. So cut him a break. If he wasn't there your whole life, it wasn't his fault. He didn't know about you. And before you go getting all up in my face, I'm not blaming your mom. She made a choice. And when Nick found out about you, he made a choice."

Kat didn't like this conversation. "Let's drop it, okay?"

"No. Look, I get how much you miss your mom. I do. I get it. But you are so lucky to be here. In this house. With your dad. He's one of the good guys, Kat. He brought you to New York and gave you a family. You're home-schooled, and you have ballet and soon you'll have a writing class. He's taking you to London. TO LONDON! And look what he did for me. He opened his home to me. He bought me clothes. I've eaten better in the last two days than I've eaten in my whole life. He didn't have to do any of that. He did it because I'm a good friend of his daughter's."

"Okay, so he's given you and me things. That's easy for him. He's rich."

"Man, you just don't get it. Let me tell you something. When we were singing last night, I was watching him. I don't know him well, but his face was, I don't know, he was like so proud of you. Or ... I don't know. I can't describe emotion. But there was emotion on his face, believe me."

"Well, whatever he was feeling, IF he was feeling something, it will all change when the new baby comes. That's where his focus will be. The child he created with the love of his life."

"You're wrong, Kat. Nothing will change with the new baby. He'll love all of you equally. Just like he loves you and Anthony equally right now."

She fought what Bertie was saying. She fought it hard. But it made her think. Nick's love for Anthony was obvious, but he didn't let it interfere with the time he spent with Kat. Still ...

"You are the most stubborn girl I've ever known!" Bertie pretended to choke her, making her laugh, rousing Hamlet, who came to her defense, claws unsheathed, making them both laugh. "Chill, cat, I won't hurt her."

Bertie kissed the top of her head. "I'm going to bed. See you manana."

*

It was almost midnight. Nick stretched out on the sofa in his office, a bourbon propped on his stomach. He planned on sleeping here.

For a day that started out beautifully with an English breakfast, it sure went to hell fast. When he realized Jessie was going to pout in the sitting room all day, he decided to make the most of his dwindling time at home.

He spent a few hours up in the gym with Kat and Bertie, talking and watching them dance. They were incredible ballet dancers, talented and disciplined. He also found out more about Bertie. The boy was fourteen and lived in a hellish home with an abusive father and an enabling mother. His older brother died from an overdose, and his younger sister ran with a gang. He was an okay student, just sliding by in a dilapidated public school in the Bronx. Susie Jacobs discovered him when he was ten, performing on the street for spare change. She took him under her wing, gave him free ballet classes and let him stay with her when needed. Bertie was one tough kid.

Nick spent the rest of the day with Anthony and Monty, just kicking back. They did some shopping, picking out Christmas gifts for the family. Best of all, they went to the park with slices of Costello's pizza, tossing balls to the dog. Jessie's stinging words about Nick and Anthony still burned a hole in his stomach. Time with his son was at the top of Nick's list. Always.

"Nicholas, can't you see I'm busy? Don't bother me right now."

"Please, Dad. Just for an hour. I need help with fielding balls."

"Take your dog and go outside and play. It's a beautiful day."

Damn. Why were these memories resurfacing?

There was a knock on the door. Jessie. "Can we talk?"

"Sure." He swung his legs to the floor as she sat beside him.

"I'm sorry, Nick. I don't know why I say half the things I do these days. Maybe it's my pregnancy. Maybe it's that I'm upset because you're leaving. Just know that I'm so, so sorry."

"I understand, Jess. But you have to understand something. Don't ever question my devotion to Anthony. He's my son, and I'd give up my life for him. Hell, Lyle Barton DID give up his life for him. That bullet was meant for me."

"Don't say that. Please don't remind me." Her eyes welled with tears. "I love you so much, Nick. And I need you. This baby needs you."

Nick pulled her into his arms. They sat back. "I don't want to leave you or our baby right now, but you know I don't have a choice. It's in my contract."

"Our careers. Our damned careers. The curse of a career in the arts versus a personal life. Artists have been struggling with it for centuries."

"We're not like most artists, Jess. We'll show them how it's done."

Jessie broke down crying. Nick pulled her closer, kissing her forehead, wishing he could make it right. But he was stuck. And he hated it.

*

Dear Mom,

Other than missing you – REALLY missing you – it's been a pretty good Thanksgiving. It's been great for Bertie to spend the holiday here, and it's been great for me to have him here. He has a way of seeing things clearly, and he makes me think. He talked a lot about Nick tonight, about how lucky I am to have him as my father. But Bertie comes from a completely different background than me, so ANYONE looks better to him than his own father. He made me question my reluctance to accept Nick as my dad. He doesn't understand that I only had a mother my whole life, and that was all I needed. Now with you gone I don't know what I need. I'm so confused, Mom. I admit Nick has been good to me. And I see the way he is with Anthony – they have a great relationship. Am I closing myself off to the possibility of having that same kind of relationship with Nick simply because I don't understand or trust it? I've been acting on instinct with Nick. I think it's the only way to go.

Your Kat forever,

*

Late Sunday night, Nick was in his office packing when there was a knock on the door. "Do you have a minute?" Bertie asked.

"Sure. Move those things and sit down." Nick sat across from him. "What's up?"

"I'm heading over to Susie's in a few minutes. I, uh, just wanted to thank you. For everything. Letting me stay here. The clothes. The food. The fun. This has been the best Thanksgiving ever. I can never repay you—"

"You don't have to. I wanted to do it." Nick sat forward, elbows on his knees. "Look, you're Kat's friend, and we've grown fond of you around here. Our door is always open. When you need a place to stay, you have one."

Bertie patted his heart. "Thanks." He rose. "It, uh, may not be my place to say this, but hang in there with Kat. She's grieving for her mom and doesn't realize yet how much you mean to her. But she's starting to. I saw it this weekend. She told me she's worried about ... She thinks you'll be all about the new baby and forget about her. I, uh, probably shouldn't have told you ..."

"No, your instincts were right." Nick swallowed, thinking about what he said. "Thanks, Bertie."

"The way I see it, it shows she cares about you." Bertie slipped out the door, closing it behind him.

There it was.

150

This year's Thanksgiving surprise.
More like a miracle.

*

The reviews of *THE SILVER LINING* were glowing, and the book shot quickly to the top of the *New York Times Best Sellers List.* "Nick McDeare's finest work." "Another page turner." "A character-driven thriller with McDeare's signature surprise ending." "This book will haunt you for weeks."

Nick's book tour began with a ten-day swing through the south, followed by a week in the Midwest before a long West Coast stint. His schedule was hellish, keeping him running from early morning until late at night. Saying the same things in interviews, sitting for hours in bookstores, signing books and schmoozing became tedious. He usually enjoyed meeting his fans. Not this time. He wanted to be home. He missed his family and worried about Jessie and Kat.

The parameters were set before each interview as to what he was willing to discuss. His marriage to Jessie had been international news, so the subject was allowed. But any mention of children was off-limits.

In his rare time off, Nick went Christmas shopping. He couldn't resist buying toys for the baby. Of course someone took a picture of him holding an oversized stuffed bear, and it hit the internet immediately. Which meant more questions he'd have to dodge. Nick and Jessie were waiting until the new year to make a public announcement about the baby.

The highlight of his day was talking with Jess each evening. She'd fill him in on the daily activities of the household, making him long for home.

"How are you getting along with Kat?"

"I hardly see her. When she's not with Finn or at ballet, she's in her room."

Not seeing each other was better than the two of them fighting. "How's the baby? How are you sleeping?" Nick drained his bourbon and poured another from the mini-bar.

"The baby's fine. But I'm not sleeping well. I miss you."

Nick stretched out on the hotel bed. Yawning, he propped the pillows behind his head. "Where are you right now?"

"In bed."

151

"Okay. Close your eyes and pretend I'm right beside you. Go on, do it ... Now imagine I'm kissing your ear, my tongue ..."

Thirty minutes later, his bourbon forgotten, Nick was sound asleep.

*

Jessie missed Nick. The house was lonely without him, and so was the cavernous bed. Their nightly phone calls helped, but she wanted him home. Period. The entire routine of the house went out the window without him around. The dining room was dark, their meals eaten in the kitchen or on trays upstairs.

Anthony's friend Luci came to work for them Tuesday through Thursday. She helped Mary with—? Jessie didn't actually know what the woman did. But Anthony was happy, and that was all that mattered. Truth be told, Mary was getting older and could probably use the help.

Most days were uneventful. However, two incidents stood out during this time.

Jessie awakened one morning with pain in her abdomen. It wasn't excruciating, and it didn't last long. Worried, she paid Dr. Lindstrom a call. The good doctor said it was just the baby repositioning herself, and Jessie shouldn't worry. Relieved, Jessie put it out of her mind, not bothering to tell Nick. What good was worrying him when he was far from home? Besides, everything was fine.

The second incident was far scarier.

One evening, Kat came down to the kitchen, upset. Bertie had gone home after ballet and had a confrontation with his father. The man went after the boy with a knife, chasing him into the street. Bertie couldn't reach Susie and wanted to come to the McDeares.

Jessie didn't know what to do and wished Nick was home. While she was sorry for Bertie, she feared Bertie's father would follow him here. She couldn't risk endangering her baby. "I can't, Kat. I'm sorry, but he can't come here."

"Why? He's in trouble. His dad could hurt him, even kill him."

"If he had the time to call you, he's okay."

"You don't know that! How can you be so cold-hearted?"

Jessie was stunned by the girl's disrespect. "What did you say?"

"You heard me. You're cold-hearted. If Nick was here, he'd say yes."

"Well, he's not here, and I'm in charge."

"I hate you. I really hate you! What did Nick ever see in you?" She ran back up the stairs.

Jessie rubbed her throbbing temples. This was the kind of stress she was supposed to avoid. When she looked up, she found Mary glaring at her. "What Kat said to you was wrong. Very wrong. And I'll tell her so. But you should have let that boy come here."

"I won't put my unborn child in danger. I'm sorry, Mary. My number one priority is my baby."

She decided not to tell Nick about it. He'd only jump to Kat's defense. The girl came off looking like the Angel of Mercy.

And Jessie? The Wicked Witch of the West.

"I'll get you, my pretty. And your little cat, too!"

*

Luci used her time wisely at the McDeare house. Mary gave her minor tasks, busy work, which annoyed her. How could she make herself invaluable if all she did was water plants and do the laundry? She could do Mary's job with her eyes closed. Then it hit her. If Mary were to have an accident ... The only problem was that Mary seemed to watch her constantly. So did McDeare's demon spawn.

While Luci plotted, she kept her eyes open. It didn't take long to discover the McDeare woman was pregnant. The whole idea was revolting. And poor Anthony would be shoved into the background with a legitimate McDeare heir hogging the attention.

That baby was a disaster in the making.

The last thing this world needed was another rich, pampered, entitled brat.

*

Willie and Abbie paid a visit to the bartender at the Golden Calf. Jamal Baptista had been on duty the day Josh Elliot met Bill Rudolph.

"I'd like to ask you some questions," Willie began.

Jamal didn't bother to look up from washing glasses. "And you are ...?"

"Captain Willie Bodine, NYPD." He held up his detective's shield.

Jamal looked the shield over carefully. "Retired."

"On special assignment."

"How do I know that?"

"Look, Jamal," Abbie said, "you're not in any trouble. You were on duty when a meeting occurred here in the bar—"

"I don't listen to conversations." Jamal turned back to the glasses.

"We'll have to come back with Nick," Abbie whispered to Willie. "The name McDeare always opens doors."

Jamal spun around. "Nick McDeare? The reporter? The writer?"

Willie chuckled. "For someone who doesn't listen to customers you have amazing hearing."

"You come back with Nick McDeare, and I'll see what I can do to help. I'm studying journalism at NYU."

*

Nick had his own incident during an hour-long interview with a national magazine show in L.A. Eileen Hemmings was supposedly up-and-coming and the buzz of the town.

Nick had warned her: hands off any talk of children. Halfway through the show, she went there. "On a personal note, you've had a young girl living in your home since early fall. Twelve-year-old Katrina Gillingham from Lake Placid, New York." She paused. Nick knew what was coming. "Is she your daughter, Mr. McDeare?"

Nick hated these talk show hacks looking for a 'gotcha' moment.

"She's your daughter, isn't she? And a little birdie told me your wife, Jessica Kendle, famed Broadway star, is expecting a baby."

Ripping his mike from his jacket, he tossed it on the table. "You knew the rules." Rising, he spun on his heel and left the studio. The click of his shoes on the tile floor was the only response her audience would get.

It was all over TV and the internet the next day. His publicist was apoplectic. Eileen Hemmings' star rose higher, and she was wanted on every talk show in America. Nick's agent Liz called and chewed him out, yelling about breach of contract and how angry Linden Publishing was. Nick shut her up quickly. "That woman deserved it. And Linden can't buy this kind of publicity. You know it. I know it. And Linden knows it. This will only sell more books, Liz."

*

Kat didn't see Nick's interview. She didn't even know he was supposed to be on TV. Her fellow ballerinas were her source, peppering her with questions the moment she walked into the studio.

Bertie came to her rescue, dragging her away from the gaggle. "Don't let it get to you. They're just curious."

"Why do people care? I don't get it."

"Because he's Nick-Fucking-McDeare, Kat. Ex-bachelor numero uno. A celebrity. You're his kid from his old catting-around days. Sorry. No pun intended. But you know what? I bet once everyone knows, they won't care anymore."

When Kat got home she asked Jessie about it.

"I watched the interview," Jessie said. "It was pretty dramatic."

"You knew Nick was going to be on that show? Why didn't you tell me?"

"I, well, it was on pretty late. I'm sorry, Kat."

Angry, Kat ran upstairs to search for the interview on the internet. As she was watching it, Nick called to warn her about the fallout. "Hang in there, kiddo. This, too, shall pass. I'm sorry to put you through this."

"I'm okay. I just wish Jessie told me you were going to be on T.V. Then I could have watched it and been prepared. I got slammed at ballet."

Silence. "Jessie didn't tell you? ... Well, it's not her fault. I should have told you myself. I'm sorry I haven't called before this. My schedule's been brutal. It won't be long now before I'm home. Then we're off to London."

Typical Nick. Making excuses for his sorry wife.

*

Josh Elliot was on top of the world. He found an apartment in the trendy East Village. He was about to shoot a toothpaste commercial for Yarborough. And he had the leading role in a Rudolph Productions musical which would open in the fall.

There was no more talk about Nick McDeare. In fact, he read that Nick was on the west coast promoting his book.

So much for all those threats.

Nick McDeare couldn't touch him.

*

Nick finally came home late on December twelfth. His New York schedule was a nightmare, beginning the next day at five AM with a steady stream of morning shows. He ran from appointment to appointment, counting the days until he boarded the red-eye to London with Kat.

155

There was no time to help decorate for Christmas. No time to interview the waiter at the Golden Calf. No time for the kids. And almost no time for his wife. Exhausted, he fell into bed at night, asleep within minutes. He knew he was disappointing everyone in his life. He desperately needed quality time with Jessie. Now he would be in London for a week.

He couldn't wait until this was all over and life could get back to normal. Whatever that was.

When he finally boarded the plane with Kat, he settled into First Class and promptly fell asleep. When he opened his eyes hours later, they were landing at London's Heathrow Airport.

CHAPTER 14

Dear Mom,

I'm in London! It's the end of our first day, and I'm still too excited to sleep. I've now been up for thirty-five hours straight. Nick, on the other hand, slept through the entire flight across the Atlantic. Can't say I blame him. His two days in New York before this trip were pretty bad. He was hardly home at all. People think writers have such glamourous lives, but I'm learning there's so much work that goes into being successful the average person never sees.

Anyway, we're staying in his friend's flat (that's what they call an apartment over here) in what Nick calls the posh Mayfair neighborhood. We're very close to the West End, so it's incredibly busy all the time. This flat is awesome with the rooms in a mixed-up arrangement on various floors – strange, but fun. Nick says his friend is a writer who travels all over the world (what Nick used to do before he got married), and he rents the place out whenever he's away.

We were met at the airport by some stiff old guy from Linden Publishing, plus a publicist and a car and driver. Linden is based here in London. Nick is their most successful author, so he's getting the red-carpet treatment (my observation, not Nick's). We went immediately to an early morning breakfast reception at Linden's headquarters. I made a pig of myself with the bangers and scones. We left there around nine because Nick had an interview with the Sunday London Times, followed by a book signing.

It's interesting to watch Nick when he's working. He's professional but courteous to anyone who wants to talk with him. Women drool all over him, but if he notices he doesn't show it. He's protective of me, keeping me at his side all the time. When people ask who I am, he has an amazing way of avoiding the question without appearing like he's dodging it. It's an art, I swear!

What was left of the day was ours. Nick bought a silly hat to disguise himself and took me on a walking tour of London. Westminster Abbey, Parliament, Big Ben, Buckingham Palace, The Tower of London, Hyde Park, Covent Garden, Ten Downing Street (where the Prime Minister lives). Okay, we cabbed a few times. He said we can go back to any of these places later in the week so I can really study them. Linden can get us passes. We went into St. Paul's Cathedral, and I lit a candle for you. What a gorgeous church.

We ended our jaunt in Piccadilly and the West End, the center of the theatrical world in London. So exciting!

Nick got message after message from famous restaurateurs, inviting us to dine in their establishments. Gordon Ramsay. Rainer Becker. Rick Stein. But Nick said he wanted us to eat in some of the smaller places, old haunts that aren't so commercial. He wants me to experience London like a native. Tonight he took me to his favorite Indian restaurant for dinner. It was a small out-of-the way place that Nick said has been around for decades. The owner greeted Nick like an old friend. It was my first taste of Indian food. Not sure I like it, but we had fun.

Oops. Nick just asked if he could talk to me. Have to go. Wonder what this is about? More later ... K

*

Jessie sat with Mary, Abbie, Willie and Anthony in the study, the TV tuned to the BBC channel. Nick had been gone less than forty-eight hours, but she missed him horribly. He called early that morning to discuss what they were about to watch on television. It was now mid-afternoon in New York, but it was evening in the U.K.

She was anxious about Nick's interview with his old friend Myra Colmes. He met sixty-eight-year-old Myra when he was living and working in Hong Kong, and Jessie met her at their wedding. Nick said she was the most honorable journalist he'd ever known. Which was why he decided to sit down with her now.

The opening credits rolled. The camera focused in on Myra. "Good evening. Tonight we spend the entire hour with an old friend of mine. One of the most successful authors in the world, his novels are translated into a dozen languages. Nick McDeare has also earned a Pulitzer Prize for his investigative reporting. Tonight we discuss his newest novel *THE SILVER LINING*, a story inspired by NYPD detective and Nick's good friend, Lt. Lyle Barton. The book has gotten raves around the world, many calling it his finest work. And in a BBC exclusive, Nick will put to rest the current batch of gossip swirling around him and his celebrated wife, actress Jessica Kendle McDeare."

*

It was a good interview, Nick's best of his book tour. He felt at ease with Myra. After spending forty minutes discussing his book, it was time to get to the reason he was in this studio tonight.

"Change of subject. Nick," Myra said. "You're the current trend on the internet and talk-show circuit. There's been speculation about a young girl living in your home. This culminated a few weeks ago when you had a nasty run-in with Eileen Hemmings in LA. She asked about this girl. You refused to answer and walked off the set."

"That's right."

"You told me when we scheduled this interview that you wanted to clear the air on the subject. Why me? And why now?"

"It's time." He crossed his legs and took a moment. "Myra, you and I have known each other for years. You knew me back in my bachelor days. You were also at my wedding to Jessie and know how strong my marriage is." Nick paused and looked down.

"Go on."

"The young girl is my daughter, Katrina. I knew Kat's mother well. At one time we had a relationship. I didn't know about Kat until recently when her mother passed away. That's when I brought Kat to New York, and she's now part of our family." He cleared his throat. "One more thing. Why I got so angry during that LA interview. Eileen Hemmings broke the rules we set before the interview. My wife and I are in the public eye. We're fair game with the press. Our children are not. All Jessie and I ask is that the media respects their privacy and leaves them alone."

"I couldn't agree with you more, Nick. Bravo. Now please don't jump all over me when I talk about your children briefly before we close the subject for good. I see that you brought Kat here to London with you."

Nick laughed. "I did. She's here with me tonight." He glanced at Kat and was surprised to see her smile at him. "I'm having fun showing her London. You know how much I love this city."

"And you have a son, right? Your brother Andrew's boy."

"Yes. I adopted him a year ago."

"Why didn't you bring him along?"

"He's a little young to appreciate London. One day I'll bring him."

"And where's Jessie?"

"At home. Taking care of Anthony. And hopefully taking good care of herself. We're expecting a baby in May."

"Which explains the photo of you in the toy store."

"Right."

*

On her way home from the McDeares, Luci stopped by her apartment to get the cake she baked for Raoul last night. Today was his birthday. He could take it home and share it with his mom.

She wanted to spend the evening with him, but he told her he had to be with his mother. She didn't have long to live, he explained, and his birthday was important to her. Raoul promised to come to Luci's place tomorrow for a special celebration.

Luci entered the drug store and headed for the back pharmacy. Raoul stood in front of the counter with a middle-aged woman who kissed him lightly on the mouth. Luci froze in place, hidden behind a display for disposable diapers.

"See you at home, sweetie," the woman said. "The kids have a surprise for you before we go out to dinner, so don't be late."

Backing up, Luci fled the store. She threw the cake in the gutter and hurried home, fighting tears, feeling like a fool.

*

Nick's next three days were busy with interviews and book signings. Still, he and Kat had time to explore the famed city, often not returning to the flat until late at night. Neither of them was interested in sleep, so they took advantage of every spare minute.

160

Nick learned Kat loved history, so they spent hours in the British Museum. They went to Greenwich and the Maritime Museum. To Hampton Court where Henry VIII lived. Her favorite historic site by far was Churchill's War Rooms where the prime minister directed the British forces during WWII. At the end of each day they dined at one of Nick's favorite restaurants, always free of tourists, always with interesting cuisine, and always with an owner who knew Nick.

Nick's final three days were looser, with only one PR event per day. He and Kat continued their exploration, combing the city on foot, taking hundreds of pictures along the way. Kat wanted to record everything, even the food. They spent hours in dusty bookstores and always stopped to enjoy the street performers and artists, thinking of Bertie. Kat bought kitty treats and fed the dozens of stray cats who lounged on stone walls or huddled in ancient doorways.

They visited one of Nick's favorite spots, Cecil Court, also known as Bookseller's Row. Snow started to swirl as they explored the quaint shops along the turn-of-the-century street. Like a scene from a Dickens' novel, Nick expected to encounter Bob Cratchit or Scrooge himself as they meandered from shop to shop. Kat seemed as enchanted with this hidden gem as Nick had always been.

Ultimately, they took shelter from the weather in an exotic tea shoppe. The amber glow from the stained-glass lamps made the tiny and cluttered room feel homey. Kat made friends with the elderly man's ginger cat Oscar, named for Oscar Wilde, feeding him biscuits and letting him sit on her lap.

Onward they went, filling the days, cruising up the Thames and riding the tube to outer boroughs. They embarked on a pub crawl, sampling the bangers. They strolled along the waterfront eating fish and chips, drizzled with vinegar and wrapped in paper.

They shopped for Christmas gifts in out-of-the-way antique stores and artsy boutiques. They window-shopped in the department stores, never going in, enjoying the Christmas decorations. When Kat fell in love with a down duvet and its wine-colored cover in one of Harrod's holiday windows, Nick went back the next day and got them for her, shipping them home for Christmas.

Seeing London through Kat's eyes reawakened Nick's passion for the city. After so many years, he took too much of it for granted. Kat saw it from a fresh perspective. Nick was sorry they were returning to New York tomorrow.

Then guilt overwhelmed him. He missed his wife and son.
But he loved every minute of this trip.

*

Kat fell in love with London. Someday she wanted to call this magnificent city home.

The days ticked by quickly, every moment filled with one discovery after another. Nick showed her HIS London, the city he grew to love over his lifetime. And because he loved it, he made her love it, too. For the very first time since she moved to New York, she felt a connection to the man who was her father.

On their last day, Nick surprised her with a tour of the Royal Ballet School, followed by tickets to THE NUTCRACKER. Afterwards they had dinner at a little Japanese restaurant in a residential section called Islington. The owner, another old pal of Nick's, made them special sushi, using ingredients Kat had never heard of. It was delicious.

"I don't want to leave," Kat told Nick. They sat at a table by the windows. Ice etched the glass, reflecting the old-fashioned streetlamps. "I even love the weather."

"We'll come back. Promise. I'll set another novel here."

"Your next one?" she asked, her face lighting up.

"I used London a few years ago, so I have to wait. The next one—" He paused. "I haven't even told Jessie this yet—I want to set in St. John."

"The Caribbean? Why?"

"We have a villa down there. We'll take you there soon. You'll love it. But that's not my reason. Organized crime is rampant in the Virgin Islands. That's what I'll write about."

"Can't you write about London first?"

Nick laughed. "No. But I love how you love London. And your passion for this city has made me want to write about it again. So thank you." He slid a piece of sushi into his mouth."

"You're thanking me?" She was genuinely surprised. "I'm the one who should be thanking you. For bringing me here. I can never repay you for this amazing week."

"You never have to repay me, Kat. This is what dads do. Or what we're supposed to do. Open your eyes to new horizons. Trigger your imagination. Make you want to reach higher, go further than we did ourselves."

"I know you're a writer when you say things like that."

"... Hmm? Oh. Didn't mean to go all artsy on you."

"No, I meant it as a compliment." She grinned. "I know. You're not used to compliments from me."

He grew silent, staring out the window.

"Is something wrong?" she asked.

He didn't answer. Kat thought maybe she was prying and went back to eating her sushi.

"I have an old friend," he said quietly. "Brianna Fontaine. Great reporter. Works for *The New York Times*. Bree was in Hong Kong with Myra and me. She's been traveling, which is why you haven't met her yet."

Again, he was silent, lost in thought.

"What about her?" Kat prodded.

He moved his plate aside and put both elbows on the table, knitting his fingers together. "She told me once that I'm easier with kids than I am with adults. That I connect with them better."

"And?" Wow, she had to pull the words out of him.

He shut down. "Nothing. Forget it. I guess I'm tired and rambling."

"Rambling? You?" She laughed. "Trust me, I would never associate the word 'rambling' with you."

His eyebrows shot up. "Run out of compliments?"

She, too, must be tired because she couldn't stop laughing.

"You know," he added, finishing his sake, "you're not exactly a babbling brook yourself."

"Babbling brook?" She was laughing so hard she could barely get the words out. "What in the world is a babbling brook?"

"It's—Damn!" He rubbed his eyes, chuckling.

"You're showing your age when you say things like that."

"Ouch. That hurt."

"Oh, please," she said with sarcasm. "You're the coolest dad I ever saw."

He froze, a look of surprise and satisfaction on his face. "Well, well. That's the first time you referred to me as your dad."

"Oops. My mistake." She laughed again, hoping he knew she was teasing.

He did. "You can be such a brat."

"That's what Mom always said."

"A wise woman. Come on. Let's get out of here. Tomorrow we go home and see how the other baby is doing."

Kat flipped a piece of sushi at him. It hit his forehead and tumbled down his shirt, leaving a soy stain on its descent. Nick looked from the stain to Kat. "Mary will not be pleased."

She dissolved into laughter again.

Nick tried to keep a straight face. He failed. "Like I said. A brat."

*

Anthony was lonely. He missed his dad. He even missed Kat. His mom was always laying down. Mary told him never to disturb her when she was in her bedroom.

He spent most of his time in his room with Monty, working on his Christmas project. He liked the days Luci was in the house. He'd follow her around when he got home from school, helping her with her jobs. She looked tired. And sad. When he asked what was wrong, she told him she was having trouble sleeping. He shouldn't worry, she said. It would pass.

Anthony still hated school. So did Zane. But there was nothing they could do about it. Mrs. Harwell refused to let Zane be home-schooled. At least Anthony was spending the coming weekend at Zane's.

So Anthony galumphed through the week, counting down the hours until he could go to Zane's. And until Dad and Kat got home.

*

Kat waited with Nick and Willie in the Baggage Claim at JFK. It was late afternoon, a light snow dusting the gray December landscape outside the picture windows. The weather didn't help her mood. She missed England already.

Her cell rang. "Kat, It's Susie. Are you still in London?"

"Just got back. Why?"

"Are you alone?"

"Nick's with me."

"Good. Put me on speakerphone … I just got a call from Bertie. He's in the ER at Jacobi in the Bronx. His dad really did a number on him this time. The police were called. So was Child Protective Services. I'm of no help. I'm in LA."

"We're on our way," Nick said.

"I know Jacobi," Willie added. "It's a half hour away."

164

"Where's the damn luggage?"

*

As Willie drove them to the hospital, Nick called Jessie to explain why they'd be late getting home. She didn't sound happy, but it couldn't be helped. Hanging up, he looked at Kat. "Bertie had to know Susie was in L.A. And that we were back today. Why didn't he just call us?"

"Probably because of last time."

"Last time?"

"Jessie didn't tell you?"

"Tell me what?"

Kat sighed. "Bertie's dad went after him with a knife when you were on your book tour. Jessie wouldn't let him come to the house."

"Why?"

"She said it was because of the baby."

"Where did he end up going?"

"Nowhere. He slept on the street."

"On the—!" Nick ran a hand through his hair and turned away. Fuming, he stayed silent all the way to the hospital.

Bertie sat on a gurney in a cubicle as a nurse wrapped heavy tape around his chest. He looked like hell, his face bruised, one eye swollen shut.

It was past midnight. A full moon. They came out of nowhere on the deserted Tokyo road, surrounding Nick. At fourteen he was tall. His jogging kept him in shape. But he was no match for these guys.

"He has two broken ribs," the nurse said. "Possibly a concussion. He needs to be watched closely for twenty-four hours."

"It looks worse than it is," Bertie mumbled.

"Don't make light of it, young man," the nurse said. "You were beaten badly." She touched Bertie's shoulder and left the room.

The first blow broke some ribs. Nick heard them snap, felt the pain. Someone laughed, a high cackle. The cackle morphed into a thick Boston accent. "Kick him in the head. He thinks he's going to be a hotshot writer." A different voice, husky, warned. "Stop. We don't want to kill him."

At some point Nick lost consciousness.

A middle-aged woman with a clipboard stood near the bed. Ms. Clipboard was from Child Protective Services. "Are you related to Bertie?" she asked Nick.

"A close friend."

"I see. Well, obviously Bertie can't go home. I'm taking him to a group home tonight until we can sort this out."

"No," Nick said. "Bertie will come home with us."

They told Nick later he was saved by a stranger in a pickup truck. The man's shotgun scattered the attackers like ants. He dropped Nick at the hospital and disappeared into the night.

"I can't release Bertie to you— not until we can check you out."

"Look," Nick said, his patience wearing thin. "I think you know who I am."

"I—uh—I … Of course, Mr. McDeare."

"Then you know my wife and I can provide a safe place for Bertie until you – how did you put it? – sort this out?"

The woman hesitated, then said, "Let me make a phone call." She left the room, her sturdy shoes squeaking with each step.

Nick's parents never came to the hospital. They were at the American hospital in Paris where his father was performing surgery. Nick was alone when he told the authorities what happened. His memory was foggy, due to his concussion. They took notes and left. That would be the end of it.

His parents didn't call either. Instead, they spoke to Priscilla, the housekeeper, who assured them Nick was fine.

Nick wasn't fine.

He was angry. And determined. He'd make the scum who did this pay.

Ms. Clipboard squished back into the room. "It took some doing, but I got temporary approval. Where can we contact you?"

Nick withdrew a business card from his wallet, adding his cell number to it. He stuffed the card into her hand and his wallet back into his pocket. "So, we're finished here?"

"Uh, no, Mr. McDeare. You need to fill out some papers." She shuffled through her clipboard, then through her briefcase. "Ah, here they are." She handed him two long questionnaires to fill out and sign.

Nick scanned them, put his 'John Hancock' on both and shoved them into her hand. "Now we're done."

"Mr. McDeare, you have to--"

"Lady, I just got off an eight-hour flight from London. I'm jet-lagged and tired. I'm a man who believes in rules and laws and follows

166

them. Not today. Call me tomorrow and I'll be happy to give you all the information you need. Let's go Bertie."

*

Kat looped her arm through Bertie's on the drive home. They had the back seat to themselves. Nick chose to ride up front with Willie.

Kat was blown away by what Nick had done for Bertie. "I loved the way Nick stuck it to that woman," she whispered. "And it's the first time I've seen him use his celebrity to get his way."

"So," Bertie winced from his pained ribs, "you admit you were wrong about Nick." Kat's eyebrows shot up in a question. "When you first told me about Nick you said he wallowed in his celebrity."

"I did?" Bertie nodded. "Then, yeah, I was wrong. You know, he hid from his celebrity in England, too. He bought this ugly lavender baseball cap that said 'London' on it and wore it the whole time so he could hide from people." She chuckled. "He looked like such a dork, but I loved it. He'd take it off when we ate, and he had the worst hat-head. When I said it was a hairstrosity he started carrying a pocket mirror so he could fix it." She laughed hard at the memory. "London was so much fun."

London. She was in London less than twelve hours ago.

Now she was back in New York. In the McDeare brownstone. With Jessie.

Let the hostilities begin.

*

Luci canceled Raoul's birthday celebration, telling him she had to work. She'd be in touch soon. Angry at the world, she spent those sleepless nights plotting. At long last, she had a plan that would make everyone pay, including the McDeares.

When she met Raoul at the pharmacy a few days later, she announced she was pregnant. As expected, he was upset. The bastard. He explained he couldn't afford children right now, that she had to get rid of the baby. He'd find a way to help pay for the procedure.

"I won't go through that." Luci's tone had turned to ice. "You know I'm undocumented. You think I can go to a nice clean hospital or a skilled doctor for an abortion?"

"You mean you want to keep the baby?" he whispered.

"No. The solution is in your hands. You're a pharmacist. Get me an abortion pill. And something to help me sleep. A few months' supply."

167

"I could lose my license. You need prescriptions from a doctor. For both. I-I can't do that."

"You will do it. Or I'll tell your wife and kids exactly who you are."

CHAPTER 15

After settling Bertie into his room, Jessie went in search of Nick. She found him in their bedroom, unpacking.

"That poor boy looks terrible. I don't understand how a father can do that to his son." Jessie took Nick's unused clean shirts to their dressing room.

Nick was silent as he tossed dirty clothes into the hamper.

"It's a good thing Bertie left those new clothes you got him here," she continued, eyeing him as she came back into the room.

Nick continued to unpack, barely acknowledging her presence.

"Okay, what's wrong? What could I have possibly done to tick you off in the fifteen minutes you've been home?"

He finally looked up at her, his eyes accusatory. "Tell me something. Did you refuse to let Bertie stay here when I was away on the book tour?"

She breathed a sigh of relief. "Oh, that."

"Oh, that?" he mocked.

"What difference does it make? Bertie's upstairs, safe and sound."

"NOW he is. But he was in danger back then, and you did nothing to help him? He ended up sleeping on the street, Jessie. On the street!"

Kat never told her Bertie ended up on the street. Instead, she tattled to Nick. "Bertie's father came after him with a knife. I was afraid he'd follow Bertie here and harm the baby. Or Anthony. Or any of us."

Nick threw a dirty shirt towards the hamper. "Have you always lived a privileged life? Do you ever come down from your Ivory Tower and get a taste of life beyond the castle gates?"

Nick's words sliced through Jessie like a hot laser. "Have you forgotten my husband was murdered?"

"I haven't forgotten. Some ugliness finally touched you. You no longer had Andrew to take care of you. Or your father. Or Gianni. You were on your own with a son who needed you. So what did you do? You hid in this house for two years."

"Where is this coming from?" she gasped, feeling like she was sucker punched. "Is this about Bertie?"

"Yes, it's about Bertie. The kid needs someone who gives a damn. He's only fourteen years old, for chrissake! And when he needed us, you said no."

"I was afraid for our baby. OUR baby. Where are your priorities?"

"Are you accusing me of not caring about our baby?"

"No. I just—" Jessie turned away, hands on hips, trying to make sense of this. "You've been gone a month. You're finally home. We're together. We're having a baby. And you want to pick a fight about Bertie, someone else's child?"

"Don't turn this around on me."

"But it IS about you. It's always about you. You and the kids. Kat was one thing, but now you've latched onto Bertie. What's lacking in you, Nick, that you feel the need to save all the children in the world?"

"Don't be ridiculous. I try to help one kid--"

"Is it because you still feel guilty about Jeffrey? About not being there when he died?"

"Don't go there, Jess."

"It's Jeffrey, isn't it? I'm right."

"Jeffrey has nothing to do with this."

"Doesn't he? Something is driving you with Bertie, Nick."

"It's called compassion! Try it sometime." Hurling his dirty clothes to the flor, he started for the door. When he halted abruptly, Jessie glanced over her shoulder.

Mary stood in the doorway, shock etched on her face. "I just wanted to tell you … dinner in a half hour."

*

Nick pushed past Mary and strode down the hallway, passing both Kat and Anthony on the way. Escaping into his office, he dropped into his desk chair.

Jessie's words gnawed at him.

What's lacking in you, Nick, that you feel the need to save all the children in the world? Is it because you still feel guilty about Jeffrey? About not being there when he died?

Jeffrey, his sweet son … Nick looked up at the framed photo of Jeffrey on the bookshelves, forever frozen at the age of ten. And then, as if an invisible hand pushed it, it fell face down.

Goosebumps scaled Nick's arms.

"Dad?" Anthony stood beside him. "You okay?"

Nick took a deep breath and nodded.

"You don't look okay."

"I'm fine. How was your weekend at Zane's?"

"Great. He's helping me with a Christmas project."

Nick glanced again at the toppled photo. "That's good."

"And now I'm helping Kat with her project."

"Kat, huh? You two finally getting close?"

Someone laid a hand on his shoulder. Kat looked down at him. "Let's just say I don't want to kill him on a regular basis anymore."

Some good news. Finally.

Small compensation for the tornado swirling through his marriage.

*

"It's a sweet tree," Abbie said. She surprised Willie by decorating a balsam fir in his living room while he was picking up Nick and Kat.

"My very own Christmas tree. Never had my own before."

"Really? Cool. I want to put some fir branches on the mantle with candles, and maybe I'll frame the kitchen archway with lights and fir."

"You're turning this place into a real home. Barton wouldn't recognize it."

Barton. Abbie felt a twinge of guilt. This was the first time she thought about Lyle in weeks. It was almost a year since he was killed. Almost a year since she and Lyle stood beside Nick and Jessie at their wedding.

Willie grabbed his jacket. "We better go. Aunt Mary's made a special Welcome Home dinner for Nick and Kat, and we're expected."

*

171

Kat came down for dinner with Bertie. He moved gingerly, his ribs hurting. They were the last ones to sit down, with one exception. Jessie's place was empty.

Mary made lobsters for everyone, melted butter at each place setting. Baked potatoes, broccoli au gratin, Caesar salad and garlic bread rounded out the special dinner. Kat was beginning to love Mary's cooking.

Abbie asked about London. For the first time, Kat dominated the dinner conversation, explaining their trip and all the incredible things they did. She kept glancing at Nick, hoping he'd join in on the conversation, but he merely picked at his lobster. His silence and Jessie's absence cast a pall over the meal. Eventually, they all stopped talking, even Kat.

Mary put down her fork and cleared her throat. "I'm tired of all the long faces around here. It's Christmas. We should be thankful for our blessings. We need some holiday cheer." She waited. Silence. "I see. Well, you're going to get in the mood whether you like it or not. Listen up. This house is in sorry shape. Christmas Eve is only two days away. I need everyone to pitch in and help."

"I'll help," Bertie offered.

"Thank you, Bertie." Mary looked around at the others. "Sad the only person to speak up is the walking wounded. You'll ALL help. Out back," she continued, "there are two trees in buckets, the blue spruce for the living room, the Fraser fir for the study. Decorations are in storage on the fourth floor. And Violet and I could use help in the kitchen. Now I want to see some happy faces around here."

"Aunt Mary's right," Willie said, winking at Abbie. "Who'd like to go for a drive around Manhattan after dinner to look at the Christmas lights?"

"Great idea." Mary turned to Nick. "You'll stay here with me. I want to talk to you and Jessie."

*

Jessie sat across from Nick at the island in the kitchen. She was in no mood for another fight, so she hoped this would be quick. Even the candle Mary lit annoyed her. Who needed atmosphere when you weren't on speaking terms?

Mary pushed the brandy towards Nick and gave Jessie a cup of Chamomile tea. "I have something to say, and you're both going to listen." She looked from one to the other, her dark eyes intense. "The

172

fighting stops now. Do you hear me? You're ripping this home apart, making everyone miserable. It's Christmas. The season of peace and joy. All we've had around here is anger and jealousy." She looked pointedly at Jessie. "Whether you like it or not, Kat is Nick's daughter, and she's here to stay. As she should be. She's no threat to you or that baby."

"I'm not going to listen to—" Jessie said, rising.

"You will listen!" Mary waited for Jessie to sit again before turning her attention to Nick. "Jessie isn't being honest with you, Nick. Harrison Alder telling her she's too old—"

"Mary, don't—" Jessie again interrupted.

"Hush!" She turned back to Nick. "—too old for that role really got to her. Fear of aging happens to all actresses and most women in their thirties."

"Dammit, Mary—"

"I said HUSH! Anyway, Jessie now she thinks she's over-the-hill and you won't find her attractive anymore."

"That's ridiculous—" Nick began.

"Of course it is," Mary drowned out Nick's voice, "but that's not the point. She's worried about getting older. She's upset about your focus on Kat and Bertie. And she's worried about your baby. That's a lot of upset and worry for one pregnant lady, whether it's justified or not. Do you agree, Nick?"

After a beat, Nick nodded.

*

Josh or no-Josh, it had been easy for Harrison Alder to say no to Jessica Kendle McDeare. He'd never liked the woman, despite Bill Rudolph's devotion to her. But Bill was gone, and the Board of Directors had turned the reins of Rudolph's company over to Harrison. Now he made the big decisions.

Sure, Jessica was great for the box office. But after years of playing second banana to Bill, Harrison wanted to make the company his own. He wanted to find his own Jessica Kendle. He already had his next Andrew Brady.

It was time to clean house, and the sweeping had begun.

Nick McDeare had no power over him.

Especially since Harrison did nothing wrong.

*

173

Mary now turned her fury on Jessie. "As for Bertie, that boy has had one miserable life. Somehow, he's survived it. I see a lot of good in that kid. Kat sees it, too. Nick's provided the help Bertie needs. I don't know why Nick's doing it, I'm just glad he is. And if you weren't filled with crazy mixed-up hormones, you'd be happy to help him, too. Nick is doing the right thing. So put away your jealousy of Kat and Bertie. Nick loves you more than anyone in the world. You know it's true. When you're in your right mind.

"One more thing. Anthony came to me before dinner and asked if you were getting a divorce. I didn't think he even knew that word. But that's what your fighting is doing to him." Mary was suddenly exhausted from her tirade. "This time last year we were getting ready for your New Year's Eve wedding. This year your son is asking about a divorce. Think about that. I'm going to bed. And tomorrow I don't want to hear a cross word between the two of you."

*

Nick refilled his snifter and looked up at Jessie. "For the record, you're a classic beauty. Your look doesn't age." He hoped to get a smile out of her. Too much to ask, apparently.

"You don't understand how the theater works for women."

"You're right. I don't."

She rubbed her temples. "What's happening to me, Nick? Can a baby make this much difference in my moods?"

"Mary said you were like this when you were pregnant with Anthony."

"She said I was difficult. But I don't remember fighting with Andrew this much."

"Maybe Andrew was more accommodating than I am. He was the saint. I'm the sinner, remember?" He drained his brandy in one gulp.

"I hate when you say that."

"It's the truth."

"Not according to Mary. She thinks you're a saint for rescuing Bertie."

"But you don't, right?"

The candle in the center of the island flickered out. They both stared at it before locking eyes. Silence hung in the room.

"Nick, I-I don't know what I think. What's worse, I don't trust what I think. But Mary's right. It's Christmas. We shouldn't be

174

fighting. We both said some pretty awful things. And, Nick. About Bertie. You have to understand how terrified I am of losing this baby, after the scares I had when I was pregnant with Anthony. If I had it to do over again, I'd do exactly the same thing. You were gone. I was scared."

"I don't want you to lose that baby either, Jess. But your fear was unfounded. Bertie's father wouldn't—"

"Stop. Please. I don't want to fight anymore. Can't we forget about this and try to have a nice Christmas? For Anthony's sake?"

And for Kat's sake. "Sure."

"Let's go up to bed, Nick. It's been too long. I've missed you."

"I've missed you, too." Nick came around the island and kissed his wife. "Let's go."

*

Nick was up early, working on his gift for Jessie in the sitting room. Both doors were locked. He wasn't in the best of moods, but this project couldn't wait. As he made progress, his sour mood lightened.

He and Jessie tried last night. They really tried to forgive and forget. Usually making love after a fight was sizzling, but not this time. This was an hour or so of sex, no 'overexertion.' Well, not much. Followed by a midnight raid of chocolate-chocolate chip ice cream and crunchy peanut butter. The ice cream was the best part of the night.

By the time he came downstairs he was ready to get started on decorating. He found Luci in the kitchen helping Mary, and Anthony was feeding Monty. Abbie and Willie sat at the island, finishing breakfast. Nick grabbed an apple and a muffin. "Come on, Willie. Might as well get started."

They dragged the trees into the house. Beginning in the living room, Nick got on his stomach, inching the base into the snug holder while Willie held the bulky fir. The holder was ancient and a pain in the ass. "When is this house going to move into the twenty-first century?" he muttered.

"It's crooked, Nick. Tilt it to the left," Willie advised. "... the left, not the right ... the LEFT."

"Stop yelling. I can hear you."

"That's too far. Back to the right an inch ... an inch, not a foot!"

"You want to get down here and do this?"

The tree almost toppled over. Willie jerked forward to catch it.

"Get off my ankle!" Nick barked, trying to pull his foot free.

Willie leapt off, momentarily losing his balance. The tree fell on Nick.

When Nick finally crawled out from under the monstrosity, he glared at Willie. "You should come with a warning."

Hearing a snicker, he looked over his shoulder. He had an audience. Abbie, Mary and the kids stood in the study doorway, looking amused. He stalked from the room, bumping into Finn Cagney in the archway.

"Mary insisted I come for Christmas. I think she feels sorry for me," Finn's eyes swiveled from Nick to the prone Christmas tree. "Looks like you could use some help."

*

Luci enjoyed helping Mary that day. It had been years since she experienced any kind of Christmas. By late afternoon, the entire house was decorated, and the kitchen was warm with holiday smells.

The day was also depressing. Luci was forced to watch Anthony spend all his time with McDeare, calling him 'Dad.' She gave the boy his gifts and was touched when he handed her a wrapped package. Instead of opening the gifts, however, he put them under the tree in the study, explaining he'd save them for Christmas. Then he went back to helping Nick McDeare.

Who was the Spanish-looking kid? Birdie? No one bothered to introduce them. McDeare paid him a lot of attention. So did his brat.

And the old Irish guy. Fig? Fing? Mary said he was Kat's teacher. So this Fig taught Kat at home while Anthony was forced to go to that school where the other kids made fun of him.

The arrival of a baby would only make things worse.

But Luci knew that would never happen.

*

After a horrible night's sleep, Jessie's foul mood gave a return performance on Christmas Eve morning. She came downstairs grumpy, and she stayed grumpy. Her stomach was upset, the smell of bacon making her gag. She excused herself and went back upstairs.

The gifts she'd bought were wrapped and under the tree in the study, including Nick's present, a signed first edition of Dickens' *A CHRISTMAS CAROL.* But other than the book, she wasn't happy with the gifts she'd chosen. Her heart just wasn't in it this year.

To make matters worse, Nick had taken over their sitting room for his gift-wrapping, locking the doors. Only Nick McDeare would need a whole room for himself. Why couldn't he use his office?

*

Nick loved the warmth of the study at night during Christmas. The aromatic fir tree with its multi-colored, old-fashioned lights and hand-made ornaments. The mistletoe hanging in the archway. The flickering bayberry candles. The plastic illuminated Rudolph in the window. The red and white poinsettias. A fire blazing in the grate. Eggnog and Mary's frosted cookies and Violet's dreaded fruitcake. Even the weather cooperated, a gentle snow drifting to the ground outside the steamy windows. It was the kind of Christmas Nick envisioned as a child.

"These gifts are from your parents, Nicholas," the housekeeper Priscilla instructed the eight-year-old boy. "You can open them tomorrow. Christmas morning. They send their love and wish they could be here."

"Where are the gifts from Santa?" Nick asked.

"You're too smart to still believe in Santa."

Nick was crushed. No Santa? He stared at the expensively wrapped presents under the expensively decorated artificial tree. "Can I open one present tonight?"

"You know the rules. Now, off to bed."

Anthony no longer believed in Santa, so the family decided to open gifts on Christmas Eve. Nick sat back and watched the kids go at it, making a glorious mess. Shreds of colorful wrapping paper and ribbon made the room look like Broadway's Canyon of Heroes after a ticker-tape parade. Sporting his new bejeweled collar, Monty dove through the chaos, ripping paper into bite-sized pieces. Even Hamlet made an appearance, wrapped around Kat's shoulders and wearing a new turquoise collar which matched his eyes.

Anthony announced that his gift to the family wouldn't be ready until tomorrow morning. Whatever it was, he'd been working on it for months.

Abbie and Willie arrived late from his place. They were in high spirits, having already shared a bottle of wine. Violet Bodine didn't crack a smile. Nick got the feeling Violet wasn't pleased with her son's newest choice in girlfriends, despite knowing Abbie for years

177

Jessie seemed to rouse tonight, pleased that Nick loved her gift of *A CHRISTMAS CAROL*. He promised she'd like his gift just as much, but like Anthony, it wasn't ready until tomorrow morning.

Bertie seemed overwhelmed. The kid had probably never seen a family Christmas before. "By the way, Bertie," Nick said. "Finn has agreed to home-school you while you're here."

"How long do you think that'll be?"

Nick glanced at Jessie. He spoke to Child Protective Services, wanting to make their current arrangement permanent, to take on Bertie as their foster child. After what happened to the boy, he wouldn't be returning home. CPS told him Susie Jacobs and her husband had offered to take Bertie in. Plus, Bertie was a touchy subject with Jessie at the moment. With the arrival of Kat and a new baby on the way, Nick didn't want to push it. Yet. "Not sure. I'm working on it."

Kat was quiet, as usual. Hard to read. She only gave gifts to Bertie and Mary, although she gave Anthony the collar for his dog.

Nick pretended it didn't bother him.

It did.

*

Abbie sat with Willie on his couch late that night. The Christmas tree lights twinkled back at them in the darkened room. They sipped brandy, their feet up. She couldn't stop thinking about Violet and the disapproving looks she shot at Abbie. "Your mom isn't happy—"

"Shhh." Willie put a finger across Abbie's lips. "I don't want to talk about my mother tonight."

"But she—"

Willie smothered her words with a kiss. A fiery kiss. The kind that sent a tingle down a girl's body. She slid her arms around his neck and returned that kiss.

When he guided her down on the cushions and stared into her eyes, she was ready.

Oh, she was definitely ready.

*

It was after midnight. Everyone was in bed but Nick. When he stopped in his office to turn out the light, he was surprised to find gifts on his desk. From Kat.

The first was a large framed photograph taken in the tea shoppe on that snowy London day. He and Kat smiled at the world, Nick's arm slung around his daughter's shoulder, the ginger cat Oscar on their laps. Down in the corner, Kat had written, 'Ta very much – Love, Kat.' Kat adored the British version of 'thank you' and used in constantly, becoming a joke between them.

Nick ran his fingers over the glass. The image brought back that extraordinary week in London. No controversy. No arguments. Not a nasty word spoken. Nothing but a father watching his daughter have the time of her life.

Beside the photo was a small wrapped gift. Nick tore off the paper. Inside was a gold chain-link wristwatch. And not just any watch.

Nick and Kat found a charming jewelry shop in one of London's antique markets. Nick spotted the watch immediately, while Kat fell in love with a thin gold chain-link bracelet with a nameplate. She toyed with buying the bracelet and having it engraved, a memento of their trip to London. Nick talked her out of it, convincing her it was a cheap knockoff, secretly buying it when she was in another section of the store. When he got home, he had the nameplate engraved:

Kat - London - Dad

Although Nick wasn't into jewelry, he was drawn to this watch, to its tight fit, to its unique antique design. His only timepiece was a pocket watch, handed down to him by his birth mother.

Lifting the watch from the box, he ran his thumb across it. Flipping it over, he discovered it was engraved:

London - Love, Kat

Nick started to laugh at the irony of the situation. Like father, like daughter.

Taking the stairs two at a time, he stopped by Kat's bedroom. She was spreading her new duvet across her bed. "Ta very much for this!" They both laughed. "This is going to be the best night's sleep ever. And ..." She held up her wrist, the gold bracelet catching the light. "A cheap knockoff, huh?"

"Hardly."

She fingered the bracelet, peeking up at him. "You signed it 'Dad'."

Nick held up his own arm, the watch proudly displayed. "You signed it 'Love'."

Interesting they both had the good sense to exchange these gifts quietly. It took so little to rile Jessie these days.

"When did you get the duvet?"

"I went back the day you were at the National Ballet."

Nice, McDeare.

Nick spun around.

Lyle Barton.

"What's wrong?" Kat asked.

"… Nothing."

"I'm getting better at reading you. You're lying. Come on. Tell me."

Tell her.

Genuinely shaken, Nick chose his words with care. "I thought I heard …" He sunk down on the chair by the bed. "There are things that go on in this house which most people would find bizarre."

"Like doors opening and closing on their own? Or hearing a man's laugh? Or seeing silhouettes of people who aren't there?"

"You've seen …?"

Kat nodded. "Who is it?"

Nick locked eyes with his daughter. "Andrew." The word fell from his mouth before he could stop it. "He's been around here for a long time. I think being separated all our lives connected Andrew and me in an unusual way. It's a long story."

"You are a gifted writer, Nicholas," his first Composition professor gushed. *"Your writing is far advanced for a twelve-year-old. This boy you write about. I can literally see him. Hear him. He's real. I want to know more about him."*

So did Nick. The fair-haired boy who looked like Nick had been a living breathing creature in his head for as long as he could remember. Wherever Nick went, the boy went. Was he an alter-ego? An imaginary friend? Nick finally had to write about him.

Nick would never forget the day, only a few years ago, when he discovered he had a brother. Andrew Brady. And that this brother was the boy who had haunted Nick's youth.

"If you know it's Andrew, why did you look so spooked just now?"

"I heard a voice. But it wasn't Andrew. It was Barton." Nick cleared his throat, embarrassed, suddenly aware he was telling this to a twelve-year-old.

But Kat appeared to take it in stride. "He's here, too? What does it mean?"

"I'm not sure."

Kat scooped up Hamlet and slid under the duvet. "I wish my mom was here, like your friend, so I could hear her again."

He tucked the duvet around her and the cat. "I know you do."

"Will you tell me the whole story about Andrew and you?"

"One day." He yawned, heading for the door.

"Thanks for telling me. For trusting me."

Nick smiled at his daughter. "Night, Kat."

"Night."

Merry Christmas, McDeare.

*

It was the worst Christmas Luci ever had. She sat alone, missing Anthony, no tree, no lights, no candles, no special food.

Her gift from Anthony was a red knitted hat, scarf and mittens. It was her only gift.

She imagined what it was like at the McDeare home.

Which only depressed her more.

And which made her more determined to make sure this was the last Christmas the McDeares ever enjoyed.

CHAPTER 16

"Nick, where did you get the watch?" As Nick slipped into his robe, the gold links on his wrist caught the early morning light, drawing Jessie's attention. She was asleep when he came to bed last night.

"A Christmas gift from Kat."

"I didn't see you open it last night."

"She gave it to me when I went up to say good night."

"Can I see it?" Nick removed the watch and handed it to her before heading into the bathroom. It was beautiful. And looked expensive. Why did Kat feel the need to give it to Nick in private? Flipping the watch over, Jessie read the engraving. Of course. London. Their oh-so-special private trip.

"Come on." Nick returned and slipped his hand in hers. There was a look of mischief on his face. "Close your eyes." She did as she was told as he led her into the sitting room. "Okay, open them. Merry Christmas, Jess."

Nick promised her a special Christmas gift, and here it was. No wonder he locked the door. A corner of the room was transformed into the baby's nursery. A nursery with all the bells and whistles a McDeare baby deserved.

"Oh, Nick! ... It's-it's stunning. Where ...? When did you get all this?"

"I've been shopping for months. In every city on the book tour. I'm surprised you didn't hear me cursing yesterday when I struggled to put that damned crib together. It took me five hours."

Jessie couldn't believe her eyes. An ornate dresser for clothes. A rocking chair. A changing table with shelves above it. Colorful mobiles. A music box. A small machine that projected moving stars and clouds on the ceiling. Soft downy blankets. Stuffed animals. Everywhere she looked she found another delight. But the centerpiece was the antique carved black walnut crib. "I can't believe you did this. I never would have thought you—"

"—could be a baby decorator?"

Jessie laughed out loud. "Something like that."

Nick, too, laughed. "To be honest, I surprised even myself."

*

Kat woke up to the aroma of bacon frying. Even Hamlet had his nose in the air. Burrowing further under her new duvet, she snuggled with the cat.

She'd dreaded Christmas, knowing it would be difficult this year. And it was. She missed her mother. But it was also fun. Nick managed to keep her mind focused on the present instead of the past.

Nick. The trip to London changed Kat's feelings about him. Well, not just London. It was also the way he rescued Bertie. That was incredible. And last night when he told her about Andrew and Lyle Barton, it not only showed he trusted her, it revealed another side of Nick. He saw and felt things he rarely discussed. Beneath that tough-guy façade, her dad was a man of many dimensions.

Her dad. She was actually referring to Nick as her father.

Time to get up and eat some of Mary's awesome bacon before Abbie polished it all off.

*

Abbie could have stayed in bed all day. Waking up beside Willie made life seem wondrous for the first time in years. She was happy, genuinely happy.

They had coffee, bagels and orange juice in bed, wondering what the others would say when they finally made their way across the back yards. Abbie prepared herself for the wrath of Violet.

Oh, the hell with it. This was the situation, and Violet would just have to get used to it. After all, her son was a forty-one-year-old man.

Abbie pulled Willie back down under the covers. They forgot about the food, about the time, about Christmas, about everything …

*

Christmas Day raced by for Nick. First, Anthony's gift was waiting when everyone came downstairs. The boy lined the main hallway with framed photos of the family. Anthony and Mary spent most of the long night hanging them. The two gremlins must have hidden until they saw Nick go to bed.

The entire family was represented in the display, even Kat. And Lyle Barton. The man who whispered in Nick's ear last night in his daughter's room.

Christmas dinner was always an event, and Mary never disappointed. A standing rib roast with horseradish and bouillon gravy. Nick was ravenous and ate with gusto for a change. Everyone was in a good mood.

Over Crème Caramel, Mary made an announcement. "Nick and Jessie, I called Jean-Louis at Le Chanteclair, and he's reserved a table for you on New Year's Eve. My gift to you for your first anniversary."

Jessie looked at Nick. "Do you think it's okay for me to go out to dinner?"

"Of course it is. You have to get out of this house, honey." Nick squeezed Jessie's hand and nodded his thanks to Mary.

*

With Christmas over, Nick was anxious to get started on the Josh Elliot investigation. Jamal, the bartender at the Golden Calf Bar, however, was laid up after emergency oral surgery. He was out until the new year. Nick cursed, sure this was some kind of diabolical plot manufactured by Andrew.

At least Nick and Willie finally caught up with the coroner. Dr. Malachy was as cold and pale as the bodies he examined. Bill Rudolph's cause of death was myocardial infarction. In other words, a heart attack, common in a man that age. With the exception of broken blood vessels in the corneas, there was nothing unusual. No tissues or organ samples were preserved, but blood was taken and stored. Rudolph was an AB-negative blood donor.

"Now we pray the blood isn't needed until we get some answers from the bartender," Nick said as they headed back to the car. Reaching for the door handle, he added, "Jamal better have—" Nick slid on a patch of ice, going down hard.

Leaning over from the driver's seat, Willie peered down at Nick. "My fault again, right?"

*

Three days later, Jessie sipped mint tea in the breakfast nook. Mary and Luci were cleaning out the pantry, its contents spread all over the kitchen.

Nick tromped down the stairs from his office, looking glum. "You're not going to believe this. Liz called. I have to fly to Vancouver on New Year's Eve."

"Our anniversary? No!"

"Book sales are down in Canada, so I have to hit three cities." He looked at Mary. "Sorry about your dinner gift. We'll have to take a rain check."

"Can Linden Publishing do this to you?" Jessie was beyond disappointed. "At this late date?"

"They can, and they are. My first event isn't until the second, but all the flights are booked on the first.

Jessie had an idea. She speed-dialed Marcie Rudolph, asking if Nick could borrow Bill's plane and fly on the first. Marcie laughed. The plane was theirs. It wouldn't be official until the reading of Bill's will, but Nick certainly didn't need permission to use his own plane on the first.

*

On his way to meet Kat in the fifth-floor gym, Bertie ran into the cleaning lady on the stairs. He stopped to introduce himself. "Luci, right?" The woman nodded. "I'm Bertie Castro," he said in Spanish. "I saw you that day we were decorating for Christmas but never got a chance to talk to you. Where are you from?"

Luci opened and closed her mouth several times. She shrugged, which totally confused Bertie.

Bertie tried again in Spanish, "Where are you from in South America?"

The woman looked at him, her dark eyes large, before hurrying down the second-floor hallway.

What the hell? Bertie climbed the stairs and hustled into the gym. His ribs were sore but healing, and his face was almost back to normal.

Kat was at the barre. He joined her, slipping seamlessly into their warmup routine. "I just saw Anthony's pal Luci in the hall. She's one weird lady."

"Agreed. She gives me the creeps."

"Anthony said she's from some South American country. But when I asked her where in Spanish, she couldn't speak the language."

Kat stopped what she was doing. "Really? Interesting."

*

185

Luci couldn't wait to get out of the McDeare house. The chance meeting with the Spanish kid unsettled her.

On the train ride home, she went over the details of her conversation with the boy. She was being silly, she decided. Overreacting. Birdie – was that his name? - Birdie probably thought she was just shy.

She wouldn't have to go back to the McDeare home until next Tuesday. It would be forgotten by then. She hoped.

*

Jean-Louis led the McDeares to a private table in an alcove of Le Chanteclair. "Champagne?"

"Sparkling water," Nick countered. "With a bourbon on the side for me.

Jean-Louis winked. "I read about the baby. Congratulations. I will be right back."

Nick reached across the table and took Jessie's hand. "You're stunning tonight, Mrs. McDeare." Dressed in a cream silk dress, a teal silk wrap around her shoulders and her hair swept up, she took his breath away. Nick wore a three-piece charcoal suit with a deep violet shirt and matching tie. It had been a long time since they dressed for an evening out. It felt good.

"This time last year I was wearing white and you were wearing—"

"—a penguin's suit." Tails. The one and only time he wore tails.

"You and Lyle complained non-stop." She started to laugh.

Nick joined her laughter. "Barton in tails. The king of the ink-stained pocket." Nick's high spirits faded as he thought of his friend.

"I miss him, too." Jessie squeezed Nick's hand. "And on that note, I've been thinking about names for the baby. I have an idea. But if you don't like it, we'll forget it. How do you feel about … Lyla Mary? For two of our favorite people."

Nick found himself choked up. Lyla Mary. He cleared his throat and looked down. Then looked away.

"You don't like it?"

He shook off his emotion. Or tried to. "I love it." He finally met her gaze. "I love you."

Their drinks arrived. Nick lifted his bourbon in a toast. "To Lyla Mary."

"And to us."

"Happy Anniversary, Jess."

*

"Wait," Willie ordered as Jessie and Nick got out of the car after dinner. "No lights."

Jessie followed Willie's gaze. Every floor of the brownstone was dark. Even the outside lights were off. "A power outage?"

Nick glanced up and down the street. "The other houses have lights."

Willie slid his hand inside his coat. Dear God, his gun. "Wait here."

"No," Nick said, "I'm coming—"

"I outrank you right now, Nick. Stay here."

Jessie felt the first flicker of fear. She clasped Nick.

His hand still in his coat, Willie crept up the stairs, unlocked the door and stepped inside. He was back a moment later. "You were right. Just an outage."

Breathing a sigh of relief, Jessie and Nick hurried up the steps and pushed into the vestibule.

The lights suddenly came to life. "Surprise!"

*

"Willie deserves an Academy Award," Nick said to Mary. "What a performance. How'd you pull this off? Even the kids didn't give it away. And how'd you make the food without our knowing?"

Mary shrugged. "Violet made the food at Willie's, with my help. As for the kids, they have a healthy fear of my temper. And the guests were told they'd be cut off in the future if they blabbed." She winked. "Jessie's not the only one who knows how to work an audience."

They were in the living room. The furniture was pushed back against the walls. A five-piece combo played Broadway hits. Fifty or so people milled about, drinking champagne and devouring appetizers. Many were dancing, including Kat and Bertie. A handmade sign, obviously done by Anthony, was strung over the mantle. 'Happy Anniversary, McDeares!'

Nick looked for Jessie. She was talking with Nora, her theatrical dresser. And Quill was here! Quill Llewellyn, Jessie's last director on Broadway. Everywhere he looked he saw a face that made him smile.

"Hello, Nick."

Nick spun around. Brianna Fontaine stared back at him. Bree's fiancé, Yves Leveaux, was at her side.

"We should apologize for crashing your party," Yves said in his thick French accent. "We dropped by to wish you a Happy Anniversary—"

"—and your daughter Kat insisted we stay," Bree finished for him. As usual, her face was impossible to read. But there was no mistaking the quotation marks she put around 'daughter Kat'. "Kat said you mentioned me when you were in London together."

"She told us she's living here now," Yves added. "Congratulations. A beautiful young girl."

Nick changed the subject. "Congratulations on the Pulitzer, Bree."

"It was a surprise."

"But well earned," Yves said. "She almost got herself killed on that story."

"So," Nick continued, fishing for conversation. "How was the Middle East?"

"Volatile, as usual." Yves put his arm around Bree. "We're glad for a break."

Bree fixed her hazel eyes on Nick. The woman hadn't changed since he first met her in Hong Kong all those years ago. Another lifetime. Short dark shaggy hair. A crooked little smile that used to drive Nick mad. She still carried the slight scent of incense that reminded Nick of lazy nights under an Oriental moon. Of crackerjack days as they unearthed corruption in the Far East. As Nick penned *THE GREEN MONSTER*, his award-winning novel.

"So when are you two going to tie the knot?"

"Actually," Bree said, "we got married in Paris a couple months ago."

Nick caught Jessie watching them. There was a history between Bree and his wife that he didn't want to resurrect. Not with Jessie's current state of mind. "Well, congratulations and welcome back. Excuse me." He sidled over to Jessie, who was talking with Quill.

"You have rotten timing, my friend." Quill shook Nick's hand. "A baby? I just asked Jessie to play the title role of Princess Di in my new musical. Opens in London mid-April."

Jessie slipped her arm through Nick's. "He's not happy I'm pregnant."

"Well, of course I'm happy for you," the Scottish director said. "It's just that I'm having a hell of a time casting this role. I'm in a blind panic. May have to delay the opening. It was supposed to be a vehicle for Vicki Dorchester, hot Brit star – do you know her? – but at the last minute the backers said she was too old. Jessie would be perfect. You ARE Diana!"

"Did you hear that, Nick?" Jessie murmured. "Vicki Dorchester is too old."

"And you're not." He winked at her.

"But I'll be very pregnant. You don't know how sorry I am, Quill. I'd love to play Diana."

"I'm over here negotiating to bring it to Broadway. Besides looking for my star."

Conversation faded as attention was drawn to Kat and Bertie singing around the piano. "Dear Lord," Quill said, "who are those babies? They're magnificent."

"That's my daughter and her friend."

Feeling Jessie's eyes on him, Nick's collar tightened.

"Absolutely magnificent," Quill repeated, pushing through the crowd to get a closer look.

They were singing the song that was featured at Nick and Jessie's wedding. Sung during their first official dance. 'Can You Feel The Love Tonight?' from *THE LION KING*. Nick listened to the beautiful lyrics, remembering their wedding ceremony one year ago tonight. Lyle Barton gave a toast as they ... Barton ... He saw Lyle ...

... *crumpled on the ground in the front yard of a house in Ohio.*

Nick shoved the memory away. He couldn't, wouldn't, think about it tonight. His gaze landed on Bree across the room. She nodded, as if to say, "I remember, too." Brianna, another friend who helped put Gianni Fosselli and his enablers away.

Nick looked down at Jessie, who was watching him. There were tears in her eyes. She, too, remembered. It was the song ... "Dance with me, Nick."

*

Quill introduced himself to Kat and Bertie. Kat was in awe of the director. A famous Broadway director wanted to meet her.

"I just grilled your father about the two of you. He filled me in on your training. Your voices are superb. And I saw your dancing earlier. Bertie, they're casting replacements for my Broadway production of *WEST SIDE STORY*." He handed Bertie his card with a number scrawled on the back. "Call that number in a couple of days. It's the casting director. In the meantime, I'll talk to her. I want you to audition. At the very least it will be a great experience." He turned to Kat. "And you, young lady. I might have something for you later in the year. Now I have to run." He disappeared into the crowd.

Kat looked at Bertie, her excitement bubbling over. They threw their arms around each other, ran to the back porch and let out whoops.

*

"It sure didn't take you long to start raving about Kat and Bertie to Quill," Jessie shouted, pulling back the bedspread.

Nick rinsed his mouth and turned off the bathroom sink. Leaning on the counter, he exhaled slowly. It had been a late night, everyone wanting to stick around to usher in the new year. He was tired. The last thing he wanted to do was fight with Jessie.

Coming back into the bedroom he tossed his towel on the chair and climbed into bed. "I raved about you, too."

"When? I didn't hear it." She slid in beside him.

Nick rubbed his tired eyes. "Let's not fight. I'm leaving tomorrow."

"Who's fighting?"

"How's the baby?"

"Fine."

Nick flipped onto his side, rubbing her belly. A small mound replaced her usually taut muscles. That mound was his child. Their baby. Lyla Mary.

"How did Brianna end up at the party?" Jessie asked.

"She said they just happened to drop by, and Kat invited them."

"Of course. Kat."

Nick's hand halted. "Jessie, stop it. Stop trying to pick a fight."

"I'm not."

"You are. It was a wonderful evening. A fabulous way to spend our anniversary. We're going to have a beautiful baby girl, a miracle. AND Quill would give anything to have you play Diana. Life is good. Can't we just celebrate tonight?"

She sighed and curled into his arms. "I'm just upset because you're leaving tomorrow."

"Me, too."

"Your career has taken a toll on us lately."

190

"Our careers are part of who we are, Jess. We knew that when we got married."

"But yours always takes you away from me."

"You would have taken off for London in a heartbeat to do that play if you weren't pregnant."

"You'd come with me."

"Wrong. I'd be at the villa in the Caribbean working on my next book."

Jessie pulled away and sat up. "When did you decide to set your next book in the Caribbean? And why is this the first I'm hearing about it?"

"I told you."

"When? I think you're confusing me with your daughter."

Nick opened his mouth to argue, then snapped it shut. She was right.

"I'm your wife, Nick. You used to tell me everything. But since Kat--"

"Well, I'm telling you now." Punching the pillow, he turned his back to her. "Good night, Jessie."

*

Jessie hurried down the back stairs to the kitchen the next morning. "Where's Nick?" she asked Mary.

"Just leaving." She pointed to the hallway.

Jessie caught up with him at the front door, garment bag slung over his shoulder, briefcase in hand. "Wait. I don't want you to go away mad. I'm sorry about last night, Nick. Please. I won't be able to stand it if you leave while we're fighting."

Nick dropped the bags. "I'm sorry, too. And you were right about—" He seemed to be grasping for words. "Never mind. We'll do better when I get back. Promise." Pulling her into his arms, he pressed his lips to hers. It was a slow, moist, probing red-hot kiss.

What she called a Nick McDeare Special.

*

Luci was surprised Mary wanted her to work on New Year's Day. Until she saw the mess from the party. It would take them all day to get the house back in shape. Mary put her to work washing the crystal, a boring job.

There was no sign of the Spanish kid. And Mary said McDeare just left for Canada.

191

"Luci, I have to drop off leftovers at the senior center. Mrs. McDeare is in the study, reading. Could you keep an eye on her for me? Maybe give her a cup of tea? I just boiled the kettle. The kids are upstairs." Mary went to the intercom and pressed a button. "I have to go out for a bit, Kat." Clicking off, Mary grabbed her coat and basket of food. "I won't be too long, Luci."

Luci couldn't believe her luck. It was as if fate paved the way for her, giving her its approval. She poured some hot water into a mug and added a peppermint tea bag. She then got the vial with the abortion pills from her purse.

Raoul told her there were two pills to be taken on consecutive days. Luci didn't have time for that and was giving the McDeare woman both at the same time. What difference did it make? It would probably just make the abortion quicker.

As she struggled with the child-proof lid, Luci heard the kids in the third-floor hallway. Giving the bottle one final twist, the lid broke free. She pulled the capsules apart as Kat and Birdie came downstairs into the kitchen. Emptying the pills' contents into the mug, Luci tossed the empty plastic pieces back in the bottle. Again, the lid wouldn't turn. She hated these stupid bottles. The kids swung to the refrigerator, then settled into the corner table in front of the window.

Now, what to do with the bottle? Her skirt had no pockets, and her purse was across the room. Luci glanced over her shoulder. The girl was watching her. Desperate, Luci opened the drawer in front of her and jammed the pill bottle into it, closing it quickly.

Stirring the mug, Luci went to the McDeare woman in the study. "Mary asked me to make you tea."

"Thank you, Luci, but I just had some juice."

"I'll leave it here. Tea is calming. Good for you and the baby."

She returned to the kitchen and resumed cleaning the crystal. That girl was still watching her. Luci's eyes darted to the drawer. She had to get that bottle. But if she did, the girl would see her. And being an arrogant little bitch, she'd probably rip it from Luci's hands.

Luci's cell rang, making her jump. Mary had forgotten about the linens in the dryer. Would Luci take them out, iron them and put them away?

With the brat STILL watching her, Luci went to the basement. She'd have to wait until those kids left the kitchen to get that bottle.

*

192

When she came downstairs with Bertie, Kat caught the expression on Luci's face. The woman looked both scared and guilty. She was fussing with a mug of tea, the string from the tea bag hanging over the rim. And then she shoved something into that drawer before leaving the kitchen with the tea. The way Luci kept glancing at Kat sent up a red flag.

Waiting until she heard Luci go all the way to the basement, Kat sprung up and opened the drawer. A pill bottle? She read the label. "Oh my God."

"What?" Bertie asked.

A wail came from the study. "Mary? MARY?"

Stuffing the pills into her pocket, Kat bounded into the study, Bertie on her heels. Footsteps pounded up the basement steps.

Jessie was on the floor, crying. The mug of tea was on the coffee table. Blood covered the sofa cushion and rug. Kat crouched beside the distraught woman. "Bertie, call nine-one-one."

Bertie ran to the kitchen to get his cell in the breakfast nook.

*

Luci also heard Jessie and rushed upstairs. Relieved to find herself alone in the kitchen, she ran to the drawer and jerked it open. No pills! That brat must have seen her put the pills into the tea and taken the bottle.

Birdie burst into the room and grabbed his phone.

In a panic, Luci snatched her coat and purse and ran for the front door. Out on the street, she bent over a trashcan and lost her breakfast. Her hands were shaking. Her heart was pounding.

Ten minutes later she was on a subway home to the Bronx.

*

"Oh, God, please no. No. Please, God." Jessie was sobbing. "Nick. I need Nick."

Kat's mind raced. Nick was in the air, on his way to Vancouver. She wouldn't be able to reach him until he landed. Mary was out. Willie wasn't back from the airport yet. She didn't know where Abbie was.

Putting an arm around Jessie, she whispered, "You're going to be okay. Here. Hold my hand. Squeeze it if you need to." Spotting the mug, she remembered Luci carrying it towards the study.

"An ambulance is on the way," Bertie returned to her side.

"Where's Luci?" Kat asked.

"I think she left. What's up with her?"

"Take this mug. Don't drain it. Wrap it in saran and put a rubber band around it to seal it. Then hide it."

"What the hell? You've been reading too many murder mysteries."

"Just do it, Bertie. Please."

He grabbed the mug. "Anything else?"

Anthony. He didn't need to see this. "Anthony's up in his room. Pack his overnight bag and take him to Zane's house. The address is on the bulletin board in the kitchen. Close the study doors on your way out. Hurry." She turned back to Jessie. "Help's on the way, Jessie. Try not to worry."

"I'm losing her ..." she cried. "Oh, God, I'm losing her. Nick ..."

Kat pulled out her cell and called Mary.

*

As Nick emerged from Vancouver International Airport, his cell rang. "McDeare."

"It's Mary. Come home. Jessie's had a miscarriage."

194

CHAPTER 17

The flight home was the longest six hours of Nick's life. He was a prisoner in an airless silver tube.

Mary didn't tell him much. Just that Kat got Jessie to the hospital quickly, but it was too late.

Too late.

"You're too late, Nick." Lindsay wouldn't look at him. "You promised you'd be here when our son was born. You promised."

Nick couldn't take his eyes off his newborn, Jeffrey Nicholas, nestled in his wife's arms in the hospital bed. "I got here as fast as I could, Lindsay. It's a five-hour flight from LA. You're two weeks early."

"You always have an excuse. When are you going to take responsibility for your family? All you care about is writing and selling books."

Nick cringed at the memory. He arrived too late to get Lindsay to the hospital. To be with her when his son was born ... and ten years later when his son died ...

"I'm sorry, Mr. McDeare, but your son Jeffrey died early this morning. It was a peaceful death. He slipped away in his sleep ...

Jeffrey ...

Lindsay rubbed salt in Nick's wound. "You selfish bastard. You're so wrapped up in your career you couldn't even come home to be with your son when he died. He kept asking for you, Nick. He cried out for you."

"The doctor said he died in his sleep."

"Get out!

Wanting to jump out of his skin, Nick shed his seatbelt and began to pace the plane. But the images kept flashing through his brain like some horror flick. And at the end of the reel the screen froze on a tiny innocent child.

Lyla Mary.

*

Luci sat in the dark at her kitchen table. How did everything go so terribly wrong?

She had to get out of here. Eventually, they'd come for her. Anthony didn't know where she lived, but Nick McDeare would figure it out. She knew his reputation, how skilled he was when hunting down a target. She knew his history too well.

But where could she go? She had no family, no friends to rescue her.

The police would watch the airports, waiting for her to turn up. She could disguise herself. But they wouldn't let her on a plane without identification. If she used the name Luci Ruiz they'd trace her. Or maybe arrest her as an undocumented. But if she used her real name ...

There was nothing to keep her here in the city. She had no job. No friends since Raoul shut her out.

And what about Anthony? When he found out what she did he'd hate her. McDeare would love telling Anthony about it, watching him turn on his old friend. It would rip Luci's heart out. That boy was all she had left in the world.

Which meant she had nothing.

*

Jessie opened her eyes. The bedroom was dark. A figure sat in a chair nearby. Kat. What was Kat doing in her room?

Then she remembered. Tears cascaded down her cheeks. She lost the baby. Lyla Mary was gone. Burying her face in the pillow, she sobbed. For her baby. For herself. For the injustice of life.

"Can-can I get you something?" Kat asked. "A cup of tea maybe?"

"No," Jessie mumbled. "Is ... Nick ...?"

"Not yet."

"I'm here." Nick moved to the bed and sat down.

Kat quietly left them alone.

Nick stared down at her, his eyelids heavy, his eyes rimmed with red. "I got here as fast as I could." He cupped her face in his hands. "I'm so sorry I wasn't here." His voice was choked.

Jessie's eyes drifted to the windows. It was dark outside. "What time is it?"

"Around midnight."

A new day was about to begin. Without Lyla.

"Honey, what do you need?" Nick asked. "What can I do?"

Jessie looked at her sad husband. "Nothing ... There's nothing either of us can do ..." She brushed a tear from Nick's cheek. "You would have been proud of Kat today. She took charge when ..." Tears spilled from her eyes. "I'm sorry, Nick. It's my fault. Getting so upset about things. My blood pressure ... I should have taken better care of myself."

"Nothing is your fault."

"I ate cake at the party ... no sugar, remember? And a glass of champagne ... I shouldn't have ... I let you down ... our baby ..."

"No, sweetheart, you could never let me down." She felt his lips brush hers. "Never. I love you so much."

"Tired ... so tired ... and sad ..." She needed to sleep. To shut out this wretched day. It would all be waiting for her when she woke up. She'd think about it tomorrow ...

Tomorrow. At Tara.

*

Kat eavesdropped from the doorway. She had to know what they said to each other. To understand their relationship. To help her understand Nick. She'd been with Jessie every moment since she found the woman on the study floor. Jessie never stopped calling out for Nick. Now here he was.

She watched as Nick stood up, a silhouette in the darkness. He remained still for a long time before looking towards the sitting room. Moving as if he were made of stone, he disappeared into the room, closing the connecting door behind him. Creeping down the hallway, Kat hid outside the open door of the room and peeked in.

A single light on the bar cast the walls in shadow.

Nick stood in the middle of the room.

Kat spotted the outline of another figure sitting on the couch. Mary.

*

This wasn't happening. Nick silently repeated the mantra. It wasn't happening. It wasn't ... This was just another crazy dream. He'd wake up to find his pregnant wife sleeping peacefully beside him.

197

Except it WAS happening. Jessie was no longer pregnant. He should have been here. Maybe together they could have saved the baby. Lyla.

Jessie blamed herself. Dear God, she felt guilty about losing their baby. It wasn't her fault. None of it was her fault.

Nick dropped his head in his hands. Twisted his hair in his fists until it hurt. Squeezed his eyes shut to stop the pounding of his temples. Swallowed to keep the bile down.

"Dammit ..." His voice grew louder, making his head hurt even more. "DAMMIT. D-A-M-M-I-T!"

With a roar he grabbed the fireplace poker and slammed it down onto the baby's dresser. He did it again. And again.

He moved on to the crib, striking it, pounding it until it was reduced to kindling. He swung wildly, destroying everything within reach. Gasping for air, blinded by tears and rage, he hurled the poker towards the grate, not caring what it hit. The sound of breaking glass shattered something within him.

He collapsed against the wall, covering his face with his hands, sobbing.

*

Mary pushed herself off the couch and approached the distraught man. "Nick."

Nick swung around. He swiped at his tears and looked away. "Leave me alone, Mary."

"I can't. Come on. Sit down."

"I don't want to talk."

"Then we'll just sit and be quiet. Come on." Putting her arm around him, she led him to the couch. He slumped down, running his hands through his hair, hiding his face. Mary went to the bar and poured him a brandy. She brought both the glass and the bottle to the coffee table. "Here. Drink."

Mary watched as Nick drank some brandy, wincing as he swallowed. He probably hadn't eaten all day. Good. The brandy would loosen his tongue.

Going to the fireplace, she stepped over a shattered vase, grabbed the poker and put it back in place. Lighting the wood in the grate, she watched as it caught. The room was unusually cold. Andrew? If Andrew was here, she was going to need his help. She said a silent prayer to her absent friend.

Dropping down into the easy chair, she watched the fire crackle. Snow swirled outside the windows. The bar light gave a cozy atmosphere to the cavernous room, the splintered nursery receding into the shadows. Silence hung in the air.

"How do you do it, Mary?"

"What?"

"Remain stoic through all the tragedy in this house."

Mary sighed. "Because I believe beyond a shadow of a doubt that everything in life happens for a reason."

Nick snorted. "There's a reason our baby didn't make it?"

"It may take a while before we know the reason, but there is one."

Nick drained his glass. Mary reached for the bottle and refilled it.

"Trying to get me drunk?"

"If it will get you talking, yes."

A book fell from the shelves across the room, landing face-up. Mary exchanged a look with Nick before rising and picking it up. It was a biography of Albert Einstein, open to the end of a chapter, a single quote on the page. "Hmph." She handed the book to Nick. "Read it. Out loud."

Nick looked skeptical but took the book. "'We cannot solve our problems with the same thinking we used when we created them.'" He slammed the book shut and tossed it on the coffee table. "Your point?"

"Andrew's trying to tell you something. He's been here for months, but I couldn't figure out why. Now the answer's obvious."

"You know about Andrew?"

She sat back down. "You aren't the only one Andrew visits. That boy was like my own son. So are you."

Nick took another slurp of brandy and sat back. More silence.

"Tell me something. Why haven't your parents come for a visit?" Mary asked. "To meet Jessie. Or attend your wedding."

He shrugged. "They're busy. My dad's a—"

"—world-renowned surgeon in the Air Force, I know. You've told me. No one's too busy to see their son get married. Were they at your first wedding?"

Nick again drank. "No."

"Uh-huh."

"I hate when you do that."

"So does Jessie."

"Then why do you do it? He sounded annoyed.

"Because I know you're not telling me everything. Time to come clean, Nick. About your parents. And your childhood. When you first showed up in this house you were sporting a chip on your shoulder the size of the universe. No one is that bitter about being adopted if they had a loving upbringing."

Nick glared at Mary. "What difference does it make? It's in the past."

"What difference? Your past is affecting the present. I've been watching you for months, Nick. I see what's going on. Your memories are resurfacing. You keep trying to stuff them back into the vault and ignore them, but it's not working. And it's eating you alive."

"You can get inside my head now?"

"When will all of you realize I see everything that goes on around here? This house, this family is my life. I love you, all of you. I may not have all the college degrees you have, but I'm people-smart. I know you now, Nick. Really know who you are. Which is why I see what's going on with you. We all have a past we have to face at some point. Your problem is how you're dealing with it. Think of that quote. You're trying to solve old problems the same way you always have. Clamming up. Shutting down. When you bottle things up, they explode when you finally release them. Just ask what's left of that nursery."

Nick refilled his glass and went to the grate, kicking the remnants of the vase aside. He stoked the fire.

Mary watched him. "I've ticked you off. Must have hit the bullseye.

Nick turned around, leaning against the mantel and staring into his glass. Mary waited. "My dad wanted someone to carry on his name."

"They told you that's why they adopted you?"

"It was obvious."

"Go on."

He shrugged. "That's it."

"No it isn't."

"Why are you doing this?"

"I have my reasons. Tell me about your childhood. And don't sugarcoat it. Be honest. What was it like?"

Nick paced towards the windows and back. Mary waited. "My parents weren't around much. I was ... alone most of the time. With an aloof housekeeper. And a dog." He halted, angry again. "Look, what's this about, Mary?"

"You don't see the connection? These memories resurface at the exact same time Kat drops into your life. Come on, Nick. You have the brains to figure out the most complicated murder case, but you don't see this? Don't kid a kidder."

"Stop talking in riddles."

"Okay, I'll spell it out for you. Kat shows up at your door, a lonely little girl who misses her mother, who latches onto a cat like it's her baby. Remind you of anyone? Maybe a lonely little boy who latched onto a dog? Funny. You've mentioned the dog often, but not your parents. But back to that quote ... So here are all these painful memories haunting you, and what do you do? Instead of finally facing them head-on, you do what you always do. Squelch them. But you opened old wounds, Nick, and they make you angry now, so you take it out on Jessie, who had an easy childhood—"

"I take it out on Jessie? Jessie's the one who's been starting the fights—"

"And why was Jessie fighting with you? Because of Kat. Because you're trying to give Kat what you never had. What every child deserves. The same is true for Bertie. You commiserate with the boy, understanding better than anyone what bad parenting can do to a child. Your focus has been on the kids - understandable, in my opinion - and not on your pregnant wife. And Jessie's been jealous. Hence, the fights. Don't you see, Nick? You own part of the blame for the turmoil in your marriage because you refuse to face your past." She joined him at the fireplace.

"Yeah, well, I'm to blame for everything." He turned back to the fire.

"What does that mean?"

"Nothing."

"You're doing it again. Deny, deny, deny. Stop it. It's getting old. Tell me. What are you to blame for?" Grabbing his arm, she spun him around. "What are you to blame for?"

He shook off her hand. "This is pointless—"

"Tell me!"

"You want a list? Never being there for the people I love. Never. Not once. I promised myself when I was a kid— ..."

He tried to turn away, but she got right in his face. "Promised what?"

"That I'd be ... a good father ..."

"You are!"

He finally met her eyes, his voice a whisper. "Tell that to Jeffrey." Nick returned to the couch.

*

As Kat listened, she remembered something Anthony said the day they ran away from school.

"Dad said finding his birth family ended up not being about saving Jeffrey. It was about Jeffrey saving Dad."

Mary told Nick that everything in life happened for a reason. Kat had made this new family upheaval all about her. But these changes affected Nick just as much. Yes, their father/daughter situation was about Nick coming to Kat's rescue, but what if it was also about Kat helping Nick?

*

"It always comes back to Jeffrey," Mary stated.

"Yes, dammit. I wasn't there for Jeffrey's birth. Or his death. Or for most of his short little life. And Jeffrey was just the beginning. I got Anthony kidnapped. Lyle killed. And Kat, dear God, Kat. She comes here and is immediately confronted with my past, discovers she has a dad who spent most his life taking what he wanted, not caring about anyone—"

"Okay, that's enough!"

"Using women like--"

"Enough!" Mary sat down next to him. "No one is that special. Not even you. You don't spin the world on its axis, Nick. You don't call the shots. Jeffrey? I wasn't there. I wouldn't know. But I DO know about the rest. Gianni kidnapped Anthony, and neither you nor Lyle could prevent that. Lyle's death? Gianni killed him, not you. And Lyle chose to be there, right by your side. As for Kat, I've had a front row seat for that relationship. She came to this family broken from the loss of her mother. She had a chip on her shoulder that matched yours. So you made it your mission to piece her back together. And you have, Nick! You've honored her dead mother, and you've connected with her in a special way, just like you connect with all kids. Whether she knows it or not, Kat loves you, Nick. She loves you. You did the same for Anthony when you first arrived. He was one sad little boy, missing Andrew, the only father he ever knew. You gave him the love and attention he was craving. Anthony worships the ground you walk on."

"And our innocent baby? Try explaining that. I wasn't there for her either."

Mary took a deep breath and exhaled slowly. "I suspect she's with Andrew right now. And with Jeffrey. It wasn't her time, Nick. It's not our place to question God or the Universe or whatever you want to call it. It just wasn't her time."

Nick's eyes filled with tears. It must be the brandy. And exhaustion. And a deep sadness he feared he would carry for the rest of his days. Still, Mary's words salved his wounds somewhat. Reaching over, he took her hand, wishing he could express what he felt at that moment. Some writer he was.

"I love you, too, Nick." She brought his hand to her lips. "And now I'm going to bed. I don't ever remember being this tired."

Nick watched her leave. Shivering, he plodded back to the grate, hoping the fire and the brandy would chase the chill away. A chill that permeated his very core.

He felt a presence at his elbow. Kat looked up at him. "I'm sorry about the baby."

Nick took a gulp of brandy. "Jessie said you were a big help today."

She shrugged. "I did it for you ... I, um ... I heard you.

"Heard what?"

"You and Mary. Just now."

The hits just kept coming. "You were eavesdropping?"

Kat nodded.

"You shouldn't have—"

Kat hurled herself into his arms, surprising him. Hell, shocking him.

Setting his glass on the mantel, he wrapped his arms around her, kissing the top of her head. This girl was his daughter, his flesh and blood. She had come out of nowhere, changing his life forever.

"Mary's right," Kat said, looking up at him. "You're a good father. I'm proud to have you as my dad."

Nick was overcome with emotion. This day had been too much. Brushing her hair with his fingers, he smiled down into those amber eyes. "Back at you. You're an awesome kid, Kat."

"Mary says I'm a carbon copy of you. And I've learned never to argue with Mary. She's always right."

Out of the mouths of babes.

"Can I ask you something?" Kat asked.

"Sure."

"What was Jeffrey like?"

"Why do you want to know?"

"He was my brother."

Nick understood. She wanted to know about her family. "One day soon, you and I will have a long talk. I'll tell you about Andrew and Jeffrey and anything else you want to know. Promise."

*

No one noticed Jessie standing in the connecting doorway to the bedroom. She heard almost everything, watched it all unfold. Closing the door quietly, she slipped back into bed.

Guilt swept through her, as if she witnessed things she wasn't supposed to see. A voyeur. Watching her husband break down so completely. Hearing Mary dissect Nick's past. Jessie knew her husband was a private man, but why didn't he tell her about his childhood? Then again, she never asked. She wasn't curious. She assumed everyone had a decent upbringing, like she did ...

"Have you always lived a privileged life? Do you ever come down from your Ivory Tower and get a taste of life beyond the castle gates?

Nick's words.

Jessie suddenly felt like an outsider in her own marriage.

Mary understood Nick more than his wife did. Mary sensed his moods, knew what he was thinking, had the smarts to know exactly what to say to the man. Kat was a mini-Nick, a younger version of her buttoned-up, brilliant, acid-tongued father. Their bond was forever, as evidenced in the other room. As for Anthony, the boy was crazy about Nick. Nick had the answers to everything, loved him no matter what he did, and would always, always be there for him. They spoke a language all their own.

Jessie and Nick came to their marriage as equals. Both at the peak of their careers. Both feisty and flexible and passionate. What happened over the past year?

Kat happened, for one thing. Nick's daughter, a child he had with another woman, was hard for Jessie to accept. She didn't want to feel this way. She wanted to love Kat as much as Nick loved Anthony. Jessie had to accept Kat and make it work. Otherwise her marriage was over.

She and Nick were at a turning point. They couldn't take back the angry, hurtful words, but could they fix what was wrong? Get back to who they used to be? Could they move on from the loss of their child?

Jessie didn't know the answers to these scary questions. The only thing she did know was she loved Nick McDeare.

She would love him forever.

*

Back in her room, Kat undressed. Pulling out the vial of abortion pills, she turned them over in her hand. She couldn't tell her father about Luci tonight, not when he was hurting so badly. She hoped he'd have more strength to face the truth after a night's rest.

Despite her exhaustion, Kat sat down at her laptop.

Dear Mom,

It's dawn. I just spent the last few hours with Dad. That's right. Dad. Not Nick. And I learned a lot. Nick McDeare is a good man. He had a bleak childhood which created the loner he became as an adult. His parents hurt him badly, and it affected him in different ways. But one of the good ways is that it made him want to be a good father. And he is, Mom. He is. That's what I want to tell you tonight. You don't have to worry about me anymore. I'm going to be okay. Good night, Mom. And thank you for sending me to my dad ...

Your Kat forever

*

Nick undressed and slipped into bed next to Jessie, trying not to disturb her. He was drained, every move an effort.

Jessie was asleep, curled into a fetal position, her pale hair fanned across the pillow. Even in the darkness he could see that her eyes were swollen from crying. She looked so vulnerable. It broke his heart.

He wanted to hold her, but he didn't want to wake her. He wanted to tell her again how sorry he was. How he'd do anything to make it up to her. How she was his universe, his reason for getting up in the morning. But ... was it too late? Had things gone too far? The future was unknown, bringing tears to his eyes again.

The only thing he knew for sure was that he loved her.

He'd always love her.

CHAPTER 18

Jessie slipped into her robe and went to the window. It was early, only a little past eight. Flakes of snow drifted to the ground, several inches of white coating the sidewalk and bare branches of the trees. Winter had arrived in full force.

She glanced at Nick, asleep in the big bed, his arm tossed over his head. The blankets were barely disturbed, unusual for them, proof of their exhaustion. She didn't even hear him come to bed.

What should she do now? Take a shower and start her day like every other day? But this wasn't like any other day. She felt lost without the baby growing inside her.

Wandering down to the kitchen, her body took on a life of its own. Her mind was numb.

Mary sat in the breakfast nook, Monty curled at her feet. The dog looked as sad as Mary. Could dogs sense people's moods? Did they feel the atmosphere in the air?

Jessie poured herself some coffee, her first in months. Her legs felt heavy, and there was a weight on her shoulders that threatened to topple her. She dropped down across from Mary.

Mary squeezed her hand. "You'll get through this. We all will."

Jessie wasn't so sure.

"I saw you last night, Jessie. Standing in the doorway to your bedroom."

Jessie warmed her hands around the steaming coffee.

"Are you going to talk to Nick about it?" Mary continued.

"No. Not until Nick brings the subject up. He told you about his childhood, Mary. Not me."

"But that's because I—"

Abbie came through from the back porch. "We stayed last night until Nick got home. Then we thought you two needed privacy. How are you this morning?"

"Tired."

"How's Nick?"

"Hurting," Mary said, "like Jessie."

"In fact, I'm going back to bed." Jessie rose, coffee in hand, and climbed the stairs. She didn't feel like talking, but she had no intention of going back to bed. Sleep only brought dreams that cut through her, bringing on more tears.

Curling into the window seat in the sitting room, Jessie stared out at the back yard. Abbie's lone footprints marked the distance between the two brownstones. The twin plum trees were bare. Mary's bird feeder was deserted, the adjoining fountain an avian skating rink. The landscape was frozen and depressing, matching Jessie's mood.

She wished she could switch off her brain. Shut out the world. Make the last five months disappear.

"Some ugliness finally touched you. So what did you do? You hid in this house for two years."

What was she supposed to do now?

*

Nick opened his eyes and glanced at the clock. Four hours sleep. Blindly reaching for Jessie, he was surprised to find her gone.

He rolled onto his side. His head ached, and his stomach was queasy. He should get up. Take a shower. But he couldn't get his legs to move. Instead, he closed his eyes again …

Nick stared down at the inky waters of the Potomac. The Capitol dome and Washington Monument were illuminated in the distance. A passenger plane descended over his head, its engines roaring, coming in for a landing at Reagan International Airport. Life went on as usual in Washington. But not for Nick. Not without Jeffrey. If his son couldn't live, Nick didn't want to live either. He was alone now. No one would miss him. His whole sorry life needed to end here tonight on the Fourteenth Street Bridge. In those frigid waters.

A kid walking his golden retriever recognized him, halting his death wish. Said he wanted to grow up to be a successful writer like Nick.

A successful writer who killed himself.

If that kid hadn't chosen that particular route on that particular night to walk his dog ...

Nick's eyes flew open, a tear leaking onto the pillow. His focus zoomed in on his wedding ring and gold watch on the bedside table. Entwined together.

Swinging his legs to the floor, Nick pushed himself to his feet. He took a long shower, hoping the hot water would soothe his aching muscles. It didn't. He skipped shaving and drying his hair. What was the point? Dressing methodically, he slid the wedding ring on his finger and clasped the watch on his wrist.

Nick stood in the middle of the room. His brain was fuzzy, his eyes raw. What should he do next? The nursery. He'd made a mess of the nursery. Trudging into the sitting room he surveyed the damage. Nothing had escaped the swing of the andiron. The furniture was reduced to kindling. The stuffed animals were ripped apart, their insides spewed across the floor like sea foam.

Catching movement out of the corner of his eye, he spotted Jessie sitting at the window. He crossed the room, his legs moving on their own. She didn't seem aware of his presence. "Jess?"

She didn't move, just continued to stare out the window. "What am I supposed to do now?" she mumbled. "I've been pregnant for months. My job was to take care of the baby ... What now?"

"I was just asking myself the same thing." Sitting down beside her, he reached for her hand. "Jessie, last night you were blaming yourself. This isn't your fault, honey."

"Nick ... please. I can't ... talk about this yet. I need some time ... to sort things out. I'm sorry. We'll talk later, okay?"

Nick swallowed, the lump in his throat a boulder. He did his best to hide it. "Sure." Rising, he left the room.

*

Kat told Bertie what she suspected about Luci. Also, a little of what happened last night with Nick. Not everything. Some of it was too private.

They were in her room, the door closed. Hamlet sniffed at the sealed mug of tea. "No, baby." Kat stroked the cat. "Don't touch that, okay?" It was time to tell her dad about Luci. It couldn't wait any longer. She grabbed the tea and pills. "Come on. Let's go."

They found Nick in his office, standing at the window, the door open. He looked awful. His damp hair hung in his face. His cheeks and chin were shaded with stubble. There were deep circles under his red-rimmed eyes. He looked up as they sat on the couch.

"Sorry to bother you right now, but there's something you need to know."

*

Nick turned the vial of pills over in his hand as he listened to Kat's explanation about what took place yesterday afternoon with Luci. "You saw this, too, Bertie?"

The boy nodded. "But I didn't put it together the way Kat did. I guess I wasn't paying as much attention. Kat's been suspicious of Luci for a long time."

"Why, Kat?"

She shrugged. "There's always been something about her I didn't trust. I thought it was odd the way she latched onto Anthony, an eight-year-old boy."

But what's her motive? Nick mused. Why kill their baby? What was in it for her? "It doesn't make sense."

"Not much about that lady makes sense," Kat stated. "She's supposed to be Spanish, but Bertie says she can't speak the language."

The fog in Nick's brain lifted a little. His radar went up. "What?"

"I tried talking with her in Spanish," Bertie explained, "and she kinda froze me out and ran off."

"Well, she definitely has an accent." Kat folded her arms. "If it's not Spanish, what is it?"

"Italian?" Bertie suggested.

Italian. The word sent a chill down Nick's spine after all he'd been through with Gianni. He needed to think this through. And in his present state of mind, he needed help. He pulled out his cell. "Willie? Where are you?"

"Downstairs with Abbie and Mary."

"Can you come up to my office?"

"On my way."

"And bring coffee." Clicking off, Nick turned to the kids. "I'll take it from here. No matter what happens, you thought on your feet yesterday, kiddo." He touched Kat's shoulder. "Thanks, both of you."

*

"So what can we do to help Nick and Jessie?" Abbie asked Mary.

210

Mary had been contemplating that very subject all morning. "They need to get back to work."

"You mean they need to be busy?"

"No, I mean work. Their work defines them." She stood up. "I have an idea. Follow my lead." She grabbed a box of garbage bags and a cardboard box from the pantry.

They mounted the stairs, Monty tagging along, and went into the sitting room. The sight of Jessie sitting at the window surprised Mary, but it made her mission that much easier. "Don't mind us. We'll try not to disturb you." She grabbed the remote for the big screen and hit MENU. Choosing *HEARTTAKES,* the orchestra began the Overture.

"What are you doing?" Jessie asked.

"Cleaning up this mess." Mary approached the destroyed nursery.

"Why are you putting on *HEARTTAKES*?"

"I need something to get my mind off things while we do this. And listening to one of your shows with Andrew will make me feel better."

"Mary, I appreciate your doing this, but I really want to be alone right now." Jessie raised her voice over the music.

"I'm sorry, honey. If we're disturbing you, go downstairs or into the bedroom."

*

"Let's talk this through," Nick said after filling Willie in on Luci. He was having trouble getting his brain to function. "Let's start with the fact that Luci told Anthony she was from South America, but she doesn't speak Spanish."

"Maybe she was born somewhere else, and her family relocated later."

"Maybe." Nick gulped some coffee, upsetting his stomach even more.

"I worked in Little Italy when I first made detective. I always thought Luci sounded Italian. What do you think? You're the guy who speaks a dozen languages."

Including Italian. Nick dropped down into his desk chair. "Luci was pretty quiet around me. She left no impression, including her accent."

"Was she quiet around everyone? Or just you?"

Nick shrugged. "To be honest, I never paid much attention to her. Even that night she came to dinner, I barely remember her being at the table." He and Jessie were fighting that night. As usual. He'd been focused on that. "She can't be Italian," he decided. "If her accent was Italian it would have scared the hell out of Anthony, after what he went through with Gianni."

"Not necessarily. He's an eight-year-old kid. Granted, a highly intelligent kid. But it's been my experience that at that age, all languages and accents blend together. I could never get a kid to positively identify an accent when questioned."

Nick was frustrated. "No matter what her accent is, it still doesn't explain why she'd want Jessie to lose the baby."

"Maybe she didn't. Maybe those pills were for her. Maybe she's pregnant."

"I'm getting tired of 'maybes'. Besides, Kat saw her put the pills into the mug." Nick poured himself more coffee, over his stomach's objection.

Willie paced to the window. "What do we know about Luci, really?"

"Next to nothing. Only what she told Anthony."

"All that food she made for him. Day after day. I thought that was weird. It was like she was trying to bribe him."

"Gianni did the same thing." Nick forced himself to drink more coffee. "It made me sick the way he tried to buy Anthony's love—" He sat up straight, his brain clear for the first time all morning.

"What?"

"Damn, how could I be so stupid?" Nick turned to his laptop, pulling up old files. He forced his aching eyes to scan the list of topics, looking for one in particular. He hit ENTER. Willie watched over his shoulder.

A photo popped up on the screen. "I wondered what happened to her after Gianni died. But at that point I didn't think it mattered. I was wrong."

There she was. Their answer.

Lucianna Santangelo. AKA Luci.

Gianni Fosselli's sister.

Anthony's aunt.

*

212

Annoyed, Jessie tried to block out the sounds of *HEARTTAKES*. She wished Mary and Abbie would go downstairs. Would leave her alone.

She knew every word, every lyric, every dance step of the musical by heart. Closing her eyes, she saw it all in her mind. Andrew's face as they sang their signature duet. Their voices in pitch-perfect harmony. The endless applause when they finished. She felt the heat of the stage lights. The smell of the stage, of painted wood and old air-conditioning. Andrew's scent, part stage makeup, part virility, and always with him when he performed. The look in his eyes as they shared the moment. So many moments in their careers.

She and Andrew were such a team. A duo unparalleled. Broadway's sweethearts, loved by the masses.

Jessie sighed. Her sidekick was gone, the lights dimmed forever on their unique chemistry. No more duets. Only solos.

She ventured back onstage last year without Andrew. Terrified, she feared there would be no magic without him at her side. But with Nick's constant support, she triumphed. She stood on her own. Commanded an audience by herself. Reduced grown men to tears with her voice. Earned sold-out houses.

God, what a high. How she missed it. She felt alive onstage. Exhilarated. It was the most satisfying job in the world. How lucky she was to love her work. She wouldn't be who she was without her career. She worked hard all her life and earned her accolades.

Remembering, she felt a modicum of peace for the first time all morning ...

With Nick's constant support ...

*

Nick's patience was wearing thin. After dropping off the mug of tea and pills at the police lab, Willie drove them to Grantham Academy. The family had been sloppy when they hired Luci. They didn't get her vital information, blindly trusting the woman's friendship with Anthony. Nick and Willie needed Luci's home address.

After keeping them waiting fifteen minutes, the headmaster ushered them into his office. "Are you feeling all right, Mr. McDeare?"

Suddenly aware of how he must look, Nick fished for an explanation. Willie stepped in. "There's been a death in the family," Willie interjected.

"I'm so sorry. Are you here for Anthony?"

"Yes," Nick said. "And we also need Luci's address."

"Who?"

"Uh ..." Nick realized he didn't even know Luci's last name. "I'm sorry. I'm drawing a blank right now. The woman who worked in the cafeteria. She's a close friend of my son's."

"Why would you need her address?"

"Luci's working for the McDeares now," Willie said smoothly, "but she's off today. The housekeeper, who keeps the staff files, is sick. We'd like Luci to watch Anthony while the family makes the necessary arrangements for—"

"Of course. Let me find it for you."

"In the meantime, can we get Anthony?"

*

Kat sat at her desk, working on short stories for her first writing class. Two of them she wrote before she came to New York. They required a serious edit. But the third was brand new. She started writing it an hour ago, and the first draft was already finished. It literally flowed from her, almost writing itself. With some more work, she would be happy with it. Very happy.

She was no Nick McDeare, but it could be the best thing she ever wrote.

*

Nick and Anthony sat in the back of the car. The connecting window between front and back was closed, giving them privacy. After being shuttled off to Zane's yesterday with no explanation, Anthony had questions. Nick told him what happened, leaving out any mention of Luci.

"You mean the baby's ...?"

Nick nodded, not trusting his voice. Anthony's eyes welled with tears as Nick pulled his son into his arms.

"Why-why do so many bad things happen to us, Dad?"

"I don't know." "Nick cleared his throat several times. "Mary says everything happens for a reason. And sometimes we have to wait a long time before we know that reason."

Anthony sat up. "Do you believe that?"

"... I'm trying to."

"You've been crying. I can tell. That makes three."

"Three what?"

214

"Three times I've seen you cry. Jeffrey, Lyle, and now Ly-Ly-_"

"Lyla."

"So I'm not a baby for crying?"

"If you're a baby, I'm a baby."

They held each other silently the rest of the way home.

*

Jessie drifted off while listening to *HEARTTAKES*. She dreamed, but they were not the dreams she feared. Instead, she was onstage—

"Mom?" A voice woke her.

Her son stood in front of her, Nick a few feet behind him. Anthony hurtled into her arms, sobbing.

"He knows," Nick said quietly. His eyes were bloodshot. His shoulders sagged.

Pulling Anthony onto her lap, she rocked him. Thank God for this boy. He was a gift, and she cherished him.

Jessie watched as Nick left the room. He looked as heartbroken and exhausted as she felt. Her poor husband. If only she had the energy to comfort him. She could barely comfort her son. Or herself.

Her dream came back to her. Thinking about it gave her strength.

Which told her all she needed to know.

*

Luci lived in a dilapidated four-floor walkup in the South Bronx. Though the neighborhood improved over the years, it was still an eyesore.

"Luci? It's Nick McDeare." He pounded on the door. Silence.

"Luci," Willie said. "open up. We just want to talk."

Nick pounded again. And again. "Open the door, Luci."

Locks turned across the hall. A skinny elderly woman with thin pale pink hair gripped the door frame. A talk show blared from a TV in the background. She stared at Nick. "I know you. Where do I know you from?"

Nick leaned against the wall, closing his eyes. The last thing he needed was to be the lead story in tomorrow's gossip columns. 'Nick McDeare Has Meltdown in Bronx Apartment Building.'

"I definitely know you from somewhere," the woman continued. "Anyway, Luci's in there. Been there since she got home yesterday afternoon."

"How do you know, ma'am?" Willie asked.

"Who're you?"

"Police." Willie produced his shield. "How do you know she's in there?" he repeated.

"When her door opens and closes it causes my own door to rattle. There's a wind tunnel or something. And I don't go anywhere. So I know what I'm talking about. What'd she do?"

"Nothing. We just want to talk to her. It would be best if you went back inside. Appreciate your help."

The door slammed in their faces. Rattling Luci's door.

Nick was frustrated as hell. "Open the door, Luci. Your neighbor just confirmed you're home." He pounded on the door again. His hand was starting to throb. "We're not leaving until we talk to you. We'll camp out here overnight if we have to."

Silence.

Nick hurled his body against the door, willing the locks to snap. "OPEN THE DOOR!"

Willie grabbed his arm. "Nick, stop. We don't want—"

"Dammit, Barton, this is no time to go soft on me." He again tried to break the door down.

"... Barton?"

Nick halted, breathing hard. "What?"

"You called me Barton."

Nick collapsed against the door, combing the hair out of his eyes. What was happening to him? The hallway began to spin. His stomach threatened to rebel.

The locks turned across the hall again. The door opened. "Nick McDeare. You're Nick McDeare."

Nick opened and closed his eyes, trying to focus.

"Here." She held out a key. "Luci and I exchanged keys a few months ago. Just in case."

"Nick? You okay?" Willie took the key from the woman. "Nick?"

"I'm good." Nick pushed himself upright as Willie inserted the key into the two locks. The door swung open.

They entered cautiously. Willie's hand made contact with the gun under his coat. As a precaution.

No Luci.

Nick scanned the small place. A combined living room and kitchen. The kind of apartment you rented while looking for something better. Framed pictures of Anthony were scattered everywhere. Also pictures of Gianni and an older couple. Luci and Gianni's parents? There was a large framed photo of Luci's dead son on the wall. Eduardo Santangelo, the kid who actually pulled the trigger and killed Andrew. He did it for his Uncle Gianni. And because the mob ordered the hit.

Nick and Willie moved on to the tiny bedroom.

They found what they were looking for.

Luci was on the bed, her unblinking eyes staring at the ceiling. She wore a red wool scarf, hat and gloves over a dull brown dress.

Willie approached her cautiously and felt for a pulse. "I'm no coroner, but I'd say she's been dead for twenty-four hours."

An empty vial of pills was on the floor. Nick rolled it over with his foot. Sleeping pills.

"I'll call it in." Willie pulled out his cell.

Nick looked around the sad little room. A note was taped to the faded mirror:

Nick McDeare stole everything from me. My brother Gianni. My son Eduardo. My nephew Anthony. And now my life. I hope he rots in hell for what he's done.

"Get in line, lady."

Nick ripped the note from the mirror and stuffed it in his pocket.

*

Propped up in bed, Jessie picked at her dinner tray. Now that she could eat whatever she wanted, nothing appealed to her. There was just too much ache in her heart.

"Jess?" Nick stood inside the bedroom door.

Jessie pushed the tray aside. "I was getting worried. Mary said you and Willie went somewhere. It's been hours."

"Yeah, well, that's what I want to talk to you about." He sat beside her.

"If it's more bad news I don't want to hear it."

"I'm sorry, honey. You have to hear it. It's about … what happened to you."

"Please, Nick—"

"Luci is dead. She killed herself. Willie and I found her in her apartment." Jessie collapsed against the headboard, stunned. "The police were called, and we both gave statements. Which is why I'm so late."

"What does this have to do with—"

"I'm getting to that." He took a deep breath. "Luci is—was-- Gianni's sister. Lucianna Santangelo."

Did she hear him right? Gianni had a sister? Wait ... My God. Eduardo's mother.

"Now comes the hard part ... Luci caused your miscarriage."

Jessie stopped breathing. Luci caused her ... Dear God. Would Gianni Fosselli ever stop ruining her life? Even from the grave?

"She put abortion pills in the tea she gave you."

"The tea? The tea she brought me in the study right before—"

"Yes. The tea and the vial of pills are at the police lab. We'll have the results tomorrow—"

"But, Nick—"

"Kat saw the whole thing—"

"Nick---"

"Luci knew Kat was onto her. That's why she killed herself—"

"Nick, listen to me!"

"What?"

"I didn't drink the tea. Not a drop."

CHAPTER 19

"You didn't drink the tea?" Nick felt the air go out of his tires.

"No. I'd just had a glass of juice. It upset my stomach, so—"

"My God." He sat forward, dropping his head in his hands.

"Kat told you Luci drugged me?"

"She saw Luci put the pills in your tea."

"And Luci killed herself, thinking she—"

"She wanted you to miscarry, Jessie. Whether you drank the tea or not is irrelevant.

"You're not hearing me. If Kat hadn't told you about the tea, Luci might still be alive."

Nick straightened up, staring at her. "You're not blaming Kat for—"

"Kat's the one who—"

He shot to his feet, teetering. "Luci was Gianni's sister, Jessie. She wanted to hurt us. She thought she succeeded. She killed herself because she got caught."

"Kat's actions are why—"

"That's enough!" He lurched from the room to the sanctuary of his office, slumping on the couch.

"Dad?" Kat sat beside him.

She just called him Dad. But he was too angry to celebrate. "I'm not in the mood to talk, Kat." His stomach growled, a hungry beast.

"That's what you said to Mary last night. Before you talked."

Last night? His conversation with Mary happened only last night? He'd lived a year since then. His stomach growled again. When was the last time he ate? "My stomach's doing the talking for me."

"Let's go downstairs before Monty thinks we got another dog." Kat stood up. "I haven't eaten yet, and you definitely need food."

*

219

"Nick's a mess, Abbie. A mess." They'd ordered a pepperoni pizza and were eating it in Willie's living room. "He called me Barton."

Abbie paused mid-chew. "Wow." Nick was scary on the rare occasions he fell apart. Mr. 'I'm In Total Control' became the original Bowery Bum, minus the brain cells. "Losing the baby has knocked the stuffing out of both Nick and Jessie. Mary says they need to get back to work. That it will help."

"We still haven't interviewed that bartender at the Golden Calf."

"And that idiot kid will only talk to the Celebrity Reporter."

Willie chuckled. "You were right, by the way."

"About what?"

"That we shouldn't delete the Gianni files until you were sure there were no more specters out there."

Abbie didn't want to be right. Not about that. "At least that's the end of the Fosselli family tree." She picked off a piece of pepperoni and ate it. "Maybe you and Nick can do that interview tomorrow. Hopefully, he'll feel better after a good night's sleep."

"Tomorrow's a busy day. Bertie's big audition. Plus the usual stuff."

"Stuff?"

"Stuff. I'm back in chauffeur/security guard mode. I'm becoming a split personality."

*

Nick and Kat ate in the breakfast nook. Baked potato soup with shredded cheddar, bacon and chives. Garlic basil bread. And a tossed salad with more crudités and toppings than lettuce. Courtesy of Mary.

Although it was only a little past nine, the house felt like midnight. Everyone was in bed, exhausted after the past twenty-four hours. The kitchen was dim, the recessed stove bulb and Tiffany lamp over the table creating pools of light in the quiet room. A three-quarter moon lit the back yard, a winter backdrop for the flurries drifting to the ground. Across the way, lights shone in Willie's apartment.

The soup was perfect for Nick's wounded stomach. Everything hit the spot. It was as if Mary had an x-ray of his ailing digestive system.

Kat speared some salad. "So what happened with Luci?"

Nick swallowed some bread. "Not now."

"Don't shut me out. Please. I'm part of this."

220

Let Kat be a friend as well as a daughter. She's up to the task, believe me. She's got your genes in her.

Barton's words again.

And then it hit Nick. It finally made sense. Why Lyle Barton was here. What he was trying to tell Nick.

Nick looked across the table at Kat. This girl. His daughter. Smart. Intuitive. A silent creature who observed what went on around her. He mentally saluted Barton. "Luci killed herself. The irony is Jessie's miscarriage happened naturally. She never drank the tea."

Kat choked on her salad. "I wasn't expecting that." Fork in hand, she stared out the window. "This is my fault. If I hadn't grabbed those pills and told you—"

"You did the right thing. Luci wanted that baby dead."

"That's what I don't understand. What did she have against your baby?"

"Congratulations. You ask the most important question." Nick grabbed the bottle of bourbon on the counter and poured a drink. The first swallow burned. The second sedated. "Your suspicions about Luci were dead-on. She's Gianni Fosselli's sister. Anthony's aunt. With a long list of grievances. That's the connection. Jessie kept Anthony from Gianni for years. Gianni killed Andrew, and I killed Gianni when he kidnapped Anthony. Luci's son was murdered by the mob when I got him arrested for being Gianni's triggerman. She hates us all. Except Anthony."

Kat sat back, clearly stunned. "Wow."

"Listen to me, Kat. This is important. Anthony can never know who Luci really was. I'll tell him she died, but not that she was his aunt. Even the cops don't know her true identity." Nick burned Luci's suicide note. "It's too much for the kid, after everything he's been through. He'll never trust his own judgment again." Nick shook his head, taking another sip of bourbon. "It's the first time I ever lied to him. I'm not comfortable with it, but—"

"—it's the right thing to do," Kat finished for him.

"Anthony doesn't remember much about his weeks with Gianni in Ohio. Gianni and his sister were in touch during that time, according to the cell phones we seized. I don't think Anthony even knows Gianni has a sister. And he has no memory of that last night when Gianni ... and Lyle ... were killed."

"That's weird."

"He says Andrew protected him from it." Nick had a flash of Anthony on the ground in Ohio, his expression trance-like. "Andrew made sure he didn't see the carnage around him." Nick plugged the memory, refusing to go there.

*

Kat was distracted during class the next morning. Bertie was at his Broadway audition, and it was all Kat could think about. He'd been gone over two hours, which had to be a good sign. Finally Finn dismissed her, and they both went downstairs. Abbie and Mary sat at the island.

Bertie slumped home an hour later, sans his usual humor and animation. "I didn't get it. I made it through three cuts, but then I was let go."

"How many dancers were left after you were cut?" Abbie asked, grabbing another slice of homemade coffee cake.

"Seven."

"And how many started out?"

Bertie shrugged. "Maybe a hundred. But get this: they'd all been through the cattle call, so they'd already made the cut. For some reason Quill Llewellyn put me right through to this final audition."

"He saw your talent on New Year's Eve. Quill has a sharp eye for it," Abbie said. "You did well, Bertie. You came really close to getting cast. I know I don't look like a dancer, but I went to Juilliard with Jessie and Andrew, and I've been through enough auditions to know what I'm talking about. So cheer up. You're only fourteen. Lots of time to star on Broadway."

Mary grinned. "And the timing is perfect, with Susie Jacobs and her husband coming for an early dinner tonight. Thank God I talked Jessie out of canceling. This family needs to come out of the fog of grief, if only for one night."

*

Everyone was gathered in the kitchen, munching on Mary's appetizers.

Mary studied the faces around the island. They were all making an effort for Nick and Jessie's sake.

Bertie was in better spirits. Susie confirmed what Abbie said. He came very close to getting cast in a Broadway show at the young age of fourteen. His talent was to be celebrated.

Both Nick and Jessie were quiet. Mary heard their fight yesterday, knew Nick once again slept on the third floor last night. She also knew Jessie made some big decisions in the last twenty-four hours. But did she inform her husband yet?

Abbie and Willie were in their own little world. They were the one genuine speck of joy in this sad household. If only Willie's mother could accept the inevitable.

"I was an investment banker," Max Jacobs said. He was a big burly guy with a full beard and wire-rimmed glasses. "Until nine-one-one, when the towers fell. My brother was a firefighter and died that day. That's when I decided life is too short to do something I hate. Now I'm a contractor. Construction. And I get paid for doing what I love. Which makes me lucky."

Susie slung her long arm around her husband's shoulders. "On that note, I have some news. You know I spent time in California recently. Well, I was looking for teachers for my new school. The Jacobs School for the Performing Arts. All the arts. I bought the two buildings beside my studio. Max started renovation a month ago. Students will have to audition. Of course, you two," she looked at Kat and Bertie, "have an inside track. But I want to put an emphasis on talented kids who can't afford to study. Or who come from troubled backgrounds. There are so many of them out there, slipping through the cracks. Look at Bertie. If I hadn't seen him dancing on that street corner for spare change, a massive talent might not get the training he deserves."

"The Andrew Brady Foundation could offer scholarships," Jessie suggested, perking up. "I'll talk to the board of directors about it."

"Fantastic, Jessie. I'd love having you and Andrew associated with this." Susie turned to Kat and Bertie. "More news. A woman I danced with in Moscow is now running the summer arts program at Interlochen in Michigan. Interlochen is tops, very hard to get into. Many students go straight to Juilliard after training there. I told her about you, and she's saving spots for you this summer. Training is vital for your resume. It's the first thing a director looks at. Now, the tuition isn't cheap, but maybe you could get scholarships. Jessie, do you think the Brady Foundation could—"

"Forget it." Nick sipped his bourbon, avoiding Jessie's stare. "I'll take care of it."

Mary rolled her eyes. Now Nick and Jessie were dueling over who would finance Kat and Bertie's training?

*

Jessie, Nick and Mary sat in the study. Susie and Max went home hours ago. Anthony and Bertie were upstairs. Willie had driven Kat to her first writing class, Abbie tagging along.

Jessie swirled brandy in her snifter, enjoying the fire. She kept thinking about Susie. Choreographers and critics always described Susie's dancing as feline. Well, Susie the Cat was living out her nine lives. From star dancer at Juilliard to professional ballerina to gifted coach and teacher. She would influence countless young lives, guiding their destiny through her signature school. AND she seemed to have a successful marriage.

Jessie glanced at Nick. He lounged on the couch, his feet on the coffee table, his brandy balanced on his stomach. He'd been quiet all night. "Where are you, Nick? What are you thinking about?"

His eyes came back into focus. "Hmm? Uh, I was thinking about what Max said. About feeling lucky to be able to do what he loves." He took a sip of brandy. "Which led me to thinking about my new book."

How ironic. She was thinking about Susie, and Nick was thinking about Max.

"And you still plan to set the book in the Caribbean?"

"Yep."

Jessie went to the bar and poured more brandy. "There's something we need to discuss."

Mary pushed herself out of her recliner. It had been a long time since Jessie saw her move that fast. "I'm going to bed. You two talk."

The front door slammed. Kat appeared in the study arch. "Class was awesome. Drake Gideon is incredible. I'm going upstairs to work on my story."

*

Nick watched Jessie amble from the bar to the fire. For someone who wanted to talk, she was taking her time.

"I spoke with Quill today. He still hasn't cast the role of Diana. He offered it to me again." She turned around and faced him.

Nick pulled his feet to the floor and sat up. "In London?"

"Yes. I haven't accepted. But he knows I want to do it. I said I needed to talk to you first."

Nick rose and paced to the windows.

"Try to understand, Nick. I need to work. Losing the baby was devastating."

"You weren't the only one who lost that baby."

"I know. I didn't mean—" She came up behind him. "My career defines me. Just like yours does. Our devotion to what we do is one of the things that attracted us to each other." She moved to his side. "I've been doing some soul-searching the past couple days. And I realized you were right."

"About what?" He was still trying to digest the idea of her going to London.

"About living in an Ivory Tower. About remaining aloof from the ugliness of the world." She perched on the windowsill in front of him. "I had a wonderful childhood, Nick. My dad loved me and took good care of me. Then Andrew took over the job. And now you inherited it. When we got married, I thought my clingy, needy days were behind me. But I slipped right back into the same pattern, especially with the pregnancy. I don't like who I've become. I need to find the Jessie you fell in love with. The woman you married. I think getting back onstage is a start."

"With this role? In London?"

"Yes."

He slid a hand in his pocket and shook his head. "I can't go with you, Jess."

"I'm not asking you to."

What in the hell? Frowning, he stared down at his wife.

"Listen to me." She laid her hands on his chest, her touch gentle. "You were my support system throughout the show last year. I relied on your encouragement, your belief in me. I leaned on you. It was the only way I could get through it, to have the courage to go back onstage without Andrew. I need to know I can do this on my own. No one there to catch me if I fall. Do you see what I'm saying?"

"You're saying you don't want me with you."

"I always want you with me. But this is one thing I have to do by myself."

Nick drained his glass. "Then do it." Taking a step backwards, he went to the bar and refilled the snifter.

"You're angry."

"No. Just weary."

*

Weary? "You mean tired."

"I mean weary."

His tone scared her. So did that word. "Nick, if you don't want me to do this, just say it."

"You asked me to stay out of your career. That's what I'm doing." There was no emotion in his voice. Was he giving up on them?

"You know how much I love you, Nick. You mean everything to me. I don't want to do anything to jeopardize what we have."

"Go, Jessie. Do what you have to do."

"Tell me the truth, Nick. You're okay with this?"

"Yes." A gulp of brandy. "When do you leave?"

"The end of the week."

Nick choked, coughing hard into his fist. "That soon?"

"Rehearsals start next week for an April opening. I'll be back in August to get ready for the New York run."

He nodded. She wished he'd shout. Curse. Throw things. Anything but this icy façade.

"We have to decide what to do about the kids."

Going to the fire, he stared down at the flames. "They can stay here with me."

"…If that's what you want."

"It's not about what I want. It's what's best for them. They've both been through a lot. They don't need their lives disrupted again."

It meant she'd be separated from Anthony. But if she was being honest, Jessie knew her son would prefer being with Nick. "You'll visit a lot, right?"

"If I can."

"What does that mean?"

"I have my own career to take care of."

She wanted to put her arms around her husband. Show him how much she loved him. But his demeanor warned her not to. This was the old Nick. The man who was an island unto himself. The loner who showed up at her door two years ago. He was scaring the hell out of her. "I … understand you're upset. I hit you with this out of the blue and right after we lost—" She approached him. "But once you have time to digest this, I hope you'll see I'm right."

She waited for a response. Nothing.

"We knew we'd be separated at times because of our careers. You have your book to write, and I have my play. But we can get through this. I know we can."

He finally nodded, his back to her.

Jessie prayed Nick would come around once he had time to think about it. She had to believe that. She had to! "Well ... I'll go call Quill."

"It's four in the morning over there."

"I promised to call no matter what time it was. His production is hanging on my decision."

Nick again nodded, pacing back to the windows.

*

Kat never went upstairs. Eavesdropping was her downfall and always informative. It made her mom crazy. So she listened to Nick and Jessie's conversation around the corner in the hall.

She almost got caught when Jessie suddenly left the room. Ducking behind the open door of the study, she flattened against the wall as Jessie breezed by.

Creeping back to the edge of the arch, she peeked in at Nick.

He stood staring out the window, still as a statue, glass in hand.

Kat wanted to go to him, but her better judgment prevailed. He'd be furious if he knew she'd heard his conversation with his wife. That she eavesdropped again.

She looked up at the portrait of the two brothers over the fireplace. *Please, please, Uncle Andrew. Help my dad.*

Tiptoeing down the hallway, Kat climbed the front stairs.

She would never understand her father's love for that woman.

Jessica McDeare was a selfish bitch.

*

Nick cracked an eye open. A slight headache lurked behind his temples.

Where was he? Right. The study. He fell asleep on the couch after consuming a half bottle of brandy. One of these days he had to get a grip on his drinking. Maybe when he could go twenty-four hours without getting slammed by a cannonball.

Shades of pink streaked the inky sky through the windows. The snow had stopped. The house was silent. Pushing himself upright, Nick ran his hands through his hair and rubbed his eyes. He smelled coffee. Mary must be up.

227

Stumbling to the kitchen he was surprised to see Kat and Bertie in the breakfast nook, notepads, books and iPads in front of them. A pot of coffee had just been brewed. Mary must be around somewhere.

"What are you two doing up?" Nick filled a mug and slid in beside Kat.

"We're behind on our assignment with Finn," Kat explained.

"I'm behind," Bertie corrected, "Kat's helping me."

"Bertie just told me," Kat said, eying Nick, "Susie offered him a home with Max and her last night."

"She's done traveling, now that she's got her teachers," Bertie explained. "And, well, she's been a kinda mom to me. She can't have kids of her own. I guess I'm the closest thing."

Nick had hoped Bertie would eventually live here. With them. "What about school?"

"Susie's having me home-schooled, so I have more time for dance." He cleared his throat. "You know I'm grateful for everything, But I think I've imposed enough."

"It was no imposition, Bertie." So that was that. At least Nick knew Bertie would have a healthy home life. "We'll miss you around here, but Susie's a good woman. I'm happy for you. No matter what, you always have a home with us. That room upstairs is yours."

"Did you run this by Jessie?" Kat wore the smug expression that made Nick want to smack her.

Nick shot his daughter a look and took a sip of the hot coffee.

"Can I ask you something, Mr. McDeare?"

"Sure. And we agreed you were going to call me Nick."

"Okay. Nick, then." He took a moment. "Why'd you do all this for me? I mean, I'm nobody. Just a friend of Kat's. You've been so great to me, more than anyone. So ... Why? Really."

Nick weighed skirting the subject with a trite platitude. But always, always he returned to his ironclad mantra: never lie to kids.

"Because I was once you."

"Me? I don't think so."

"Hear me out." Nick took a moment. "When I was your age, I lived in Tokyo. I know. Sounds glamorous. It wasn't. I was a loner. A gawky kid with a passion for writing. One night when I was walking home from class I was jumped by a gang. A stranger found me and got me to the hospital before I bled out."

228

Nick could still feel the stabbing pain of his broken ribs. "A couple days later I started a new writing class. The professor was brilliant. He became my mentor. Encouraged me. Was tough on me. To this day, no one influenced who I am as a writer more than Alexander Gideon."

"Gideon?" Kat asked. "Any relation to—"

"Yep. Your writing teacher is Alex's son, Drake." Nick again paused, collecting his thoughts. "About a year after I met Alex, he told me he was the man who rescued me that night. How do you repay someone who literally saved your life? Alex told me how. By paying it forward one day."

"And that's what you did? With me?"

Nick nodded. "I was happy to do it."

"Where's Alex now?" Kat asked.

"Retired. Living in Italy. He's earned his rest."

"Did they ever catch the guys who beat you up?" Bertie asked.

It had been three years since Nick encountered trouble on that dark road. Hustling across the campus quadrangle, he heard a voice. A voice with a thick Boston accent. Scanning the usual crowd outside on this warm spring day, Nick spotted a guy flirting with a beautiful Japanese girl. The flattop threw his head back and laughed. A high cackle. Nick ducked behind a dumpster and watched. The couple separated, the man moving off at a quick clip. Nick followed.

The pursuit ended at a duplex a few blocks from the university. A young couple was moving into the upper unit. They nodded to their new neighbor, who went inside. Spotting the mailboxes along the curb, Nick checked the names inside.

New tape with the names Mr. & Mrs. Bill Wernet.

Old tape sporting the name Jack Flaherty.

Gotcha!

"That's a story for another day."

"With you," Kat chortled, "everything's a story for another day."

"Always leave them wanting more."

CHAPTER 20

Leaving Kat and Bertie to their studies, Nick went upstairs to talk to Anthony. The boy was in his bedroom, getting ready for school. He looked like one sad kid. Nick's news wasn't going to make him any happier.

"Come sit with me. I have something to tell you." Nick dropped down on the bed. Anthony joined him. "There's no easy way to say this. It's about Luci. She ... died, Anthony."

Anthony's face went slack. "How? Why?"

Nick shrugged. "She wasn't well. She died in her sleep." That part was true at least, considering the boatload of sleeping pills she swallowed. God, he hated this.

"She never told me she was sick."

"I don't think she told anyone."

Anthony was silent for a while. Nick gave him time to let the news sink in. Tears welled in the boy's blue eyes. "Why does everyone I love die?"

Anthony's words kicked Nick in the gut. "That's ... not true. I'm still here. And your mom—"

"You know what I mean."

He did. Too well. But he didn't know what to say. Anthony was learning too many of life's hard lessons at an early age.

"I have to finish getting ready, or I'll be late." He stood up. "Yablonski will make me stay after school." Anthony went back to the desk, packing his books in his leather bag. Nick didn't like the way the boy shut down. He seemed to do that a lot lately. "Don't you want to talk about this?"

"No. I just want to go to school and get it over with."

Nick felt like a shit. This couldn't go on.

Jessie was leaving, putting him in charge of the kids. Okay, he'd take charge. Nick pulled out his cell. "… Mrs. Harwell? This is Nick McDeare …"

*

"That's right, Jeremy." Jessie was on her cell as she sorted through her clothes for London. Her agent was fighting her on the details of her contract. She was having none of it. "I want to be back in New York mid-August with some down time before rehearsals for the New York run. And I want Nora Connor for my dresser. She's been with me forever. Those are the last of my terms. If they don't like them, tell them no." She clicked off and tossed her cell on the bed.

"Jessie found her chutzpah again." Abbie stood a few feet away. "Mary told me about London. Congratulations, girl."

"You won't believe the hassles with the unions, ours versus the British."

"That's what agents are for."

"And I just dumped it all in Jeremy's lap. Plus, there's another problem. The British press is ticked Quill hired an American to play Diana. And that's where, hopefully, you come in. I want you to come with me. As my publicist/assistant."

"Me? I wouldn't know where to begin—"

"That's not true. You're great at this kind of thing. Hell, you didn't even need an agent for your commercial bookings. You got them all on your own. You're smart, articulate and you understand the business inside-out. You know my actress persona better and longer than anyone. I'll pay you whatever you want. Please, Abbie. I can't handle the PR on my own. And Jeremy can't do it from New York."

"Mary also told me Nick isn't going with you. Everything okay with you two?"

Jessie stopped packing. "He says he can't come with me. Because of researching his new book."

"But you asked him to come, right?"

Jessie stared at the floor. "It's complicated. And I'll tell you everything. But first, say you'll take the job. Please!

Abbie pushed some clothes aside and sat on the bed. "There's Willie to consider. Our relationship is just getting started."

"Relationship vs. career. Why don't men have this problem?"

"They do. But it's a no-brainer for them. They always choose career."

Jessie paced, biting a hangnail. "What if Willie went with us? I'm going to need a security detail in London, especially if the public's hostile."

Abbie's face lit up. "Two girls alone in London could use some security. Especially if one of them is a huge star. If Willie's included, I'll take the job."

"This is perfect! Except for one thing. Nick."

"Start talking."

"Okay, I'll fill you in, and then your first assignment is to find us a large place to live. Lots of bedrooms. For all of us."

"And I need to talk to Willie."

"I should probably talk to Nick about Willie, too." She thought about it. "Oh, hell, he won't care. He hates having security all the time. Besides, things are pretty ... fragile ... between us at the moment."

*

"Mrs. Harwell, I respect your opinion. I do." Nick said, pouring on the charm. They were in a Chelsea diner, having breakfast. "Under normal circumstances, I would agree with you. But Anthony and Zane are being terrorized at that school."

"He's right, Mom," Zane said. "The kids are horrible to Anthony and me."

"They pick on us all the time," Anthony added.

Jane Harwell looked down at her son. "It's really that bad?"

"It's awful, Mom. AWFUL!"

"I spoke with Finn, my daughter's tutor, this morning," Nick continued. "He's excellent and is willing to take the boys on. Home-schooling is the wave of the future. Look, if it doesn't work out, you can always send Zane back to school."

The woman smiled. "You're a hard man to refuse, Mr. McDeare."

"Call me Nick. Since we're forming our own PTA over breakfast."

*

Willie enjoyed watching Nick McDeare in action. They were finally interviewing Jamal Baptista at the Golden Calf. Having told Nick the kid was in awe of his famous self, McDeare played the celebrity. He even dressed the part in black leather jacket and boots.

"They were here at the bar for about an hour," Jamal said, sliding a bourbon on the rocks across the bar to Nick. "It was early, so

232

the place was pretty empty. Mr. Rudolph was a regular. Met a lot of people here, so I always paid attention to him. He always drank Remy."

"What about Josh? The other guy?"

"He had some pussy drink. You know. Tom Collins or Whiskey Sour."

Willie grinned at Nick. "Water on the side?"

"As a matter of fact, yeah."

"Was it a friendly conversation?" Nick asked.

"I think it was a business meeting, but I can't say I actually heard what they were talking about. I had a stack of glasses to wash, so the water was running."

"Did Mr. Rudolph ever leave Josh alone?"

"No-well, yeah, briefly, to take a call. But he was only a few feet away."

"With his back to Josh?"

"Sure. It looked like a private call."

"Did either man take any pills while they were here? With that water on the side?" Nick sipped his bourbon.

"Pills? You mean aspirin?"

"Or prescription?"

"Oh, I see what you're getting at." Jamal looked pleased with himself. "You want to know if this guy messed with Mr. Rudolph's drink."

"You're a smart kid," Nick said, feeding the bartender's ego. Willie swallowed a grin. "Did he?"

"Not that I noticed. But when Mr. Rudolph took that call, I grabbed the time to refill the bar stock. I knew they wouldn't need anything for a few minutes. But I didn't see any pills. Just eye drops."

"Eye drops?"

"You know. The stuff you buy in a drug store to get the red out."

"Elliot's file said he had eye problems," Willie mumbled to Nick. "Did he use them while he was here?"

"Yeah. A couple times. He had that little bottle on the bar the whole time, tossing it from one hand to the other, taking the lid off and on. And he chewed on his stirrer. Bit it down to nothing. A real nervous Nellie."

Willie met Nick's eyes. Why was the guy nervous?

"Who else was here that day?" Nick asked. "Any customers who might have seen something?"

"Just one old lady. A regular. She comes in every day and sits at that table by the windows. Always orders a Cosmopolitan and flounder with spinach. As I said, it was early. Mr. Rudolph always came in when it was quiet."

Willie went over to the table Jamal indicated and sat down. From that vantage point, she could easily see the two men. But could she see if Josh did something to Bill's drink? Maybe. Back at the bar, Jamal supplied the lady's name.

"What about employees?" Nick pursued.

"They're not allowed to hang near the bar. At that hour they're usually folding napkins over in that alcove."

Willie glanced at the alcove in the far corner of the room. Not much chance they'd see anything from there.

"Okay." Nick pulled out his card. "If you think of anything else, give me a call, okay?"

"Sure thing, Mr. McDeare. Anything to help. Maybe I can trail you on a case someday."

"Maybe. Thanks again, Jamal."

*

Nick and Willie sat at the island in the kitchen, indulging in one of Mary's magnificent Monte Cristo sandwiches. The boys were wolfing down hot dogs in the breakfast nook, celebrating their release from the Institution of Hell.

"Well, that was a bust," Nick said, polishing off his sandwich.

"What was a bust?" Kat came down the stairs with Finn and Bertie. They happily accepted sandwiches from Mary.

Ignoring Kat's question, Nick turned to Finn. "The boys are all yours."

"I'll talk to them now," Finn said. "See where they're at in their classes." He joined the boys in the breakfast nook.

"We should talk to that woman." Willie looked in his notebook. "Carmella Hutchison."

"I agree. It's worth a shot."

"What was a bust?" Kat repeated.

"You don't need to know everything, Kat." Nick took his plate to the sink.

"Too bad Jamal didn't see any pills," Willie continued. "Instead, all we got were eye drops."

"Eye drops?" Kat sat at the island.

"Kat," Nick admonished, "Enough. My God, you're nosy."

"Not nosy. Curious. And interested in learning from the best."

Nick exchanged an amused look with Willie. "Don't pull that cr—" Nick glanced at the boys, who were listening despite their conversation with Finn, "that line on me."

"We know what you were going to say, Dad," Anthony grinned.

"Anthony, Finn's time is valuable. Focus, okay?"

"Um, the eye drops?" Kat sat beside Nick.

Willie laughed out loud. "I give you points for persistence, Kat."

"Good. So explain."

Nick knew she wouldn't give up until he answered her question. "We're investigating a murder. We thought a pill was put into the dead man's drink. Instead, the alleged killer was more interested in moisturizing his eyes every ten minutes."

"Maybe that's what he used. Eye drops. I just read an article about a wife who killed her husband with eye drops. They found the evidence in his blood."

Nick looked at Willie, the wheels turning.

Kat continued, "There's some chemical in eye drops that can cause—"

Nick and Willie bolted for the car out front. Stopping at a drug store they bought five different kinds of over-the-counter eye drops. While Willie double-parked, Nick ran upstairs and gave the drops to the coroner. Dr. Malachy promised to test Bill's blood and get back to him ASAP.

Back in the car, Willie brought up the subject of Jessie's trip to London. "Abbie called while you were with the coroner. She and Jessie need my answer fast, but I want your okay first."

Nick frowned. "What are you talking about?"

"Wait ... Jessie didn't talk to you about ...?" Willie exhaled slowly. "Jessie and Abbie want me to go with them to London. For security."

Abbie was going to London? When was that decided? And now Willie, too? Nick shook his head.

Nice, Jessie. Nice.

*

With Abbie's help, Jessie was packed for London. Abbie also secured a penthouse suite at a top-of-the-line hotel in the Covent Garden area. Five bedrooms. Eat-in kitchen. Restaurant with room service on the ground floor. And her own personal maid and butler service. It was extravagant, but she wanted to pamper herself. Besides, she could afford it. Jeremy had negotiated an outrageous salary.

"Are you going away?" Anthony stood in the doorway.

Surprised, Jessie fished for an answer. She wanted to tell the family with Nick present. "Um, was there something you wanted, sweetie?"

"Dad got Mrs. Harwell to let Zane be home schooled."

Typical Nick. Making decisions without her. "Well ... that's wonderful."

"Why are you packing?" Anthony backed up. "Are you getting a divorce?"

"No, sweetie. No ... Where's your dad?"

"He and Willie went somewhere."

Damn. What should she do? Anthony bolted for the door.

"Anthony, wait!" She went after him. "Come on. Let's go find the others, and I'll explain. I'll be right back, Abbie. Could you call Donald Atkins, our pilot, and tell him we'll need the plane on Friday?"

Taking her son's hand, she went down to the kitchen. "I have something to tell everyone."

*

"I remember the case. I was lead investigator," Lt. Mario Manganaro told Nick and Willie. They were in Mario's cluttered office at Midtown North, the door closed. His partner, Bernie Loman, lounged in a chair, texting on his cell.

After visiting the coroner, Nick insisted Willie drive them to Midtown North. He wanted to discuss the Elliot investigation with the two cops. Besides, Nick wasn't yet ready to face Jessie. Not when he was this angry.

Nick looked around Mario's office. Formerly Barton's office. How many hours had he spent sitting here drinking bad coffee and plotting Gianni Fosselli's demise?

Loman stuffed his cell in his pocket. "Remind me. What does our old case have to do with Josh Elliot?"

"I've got the old file right here." Mario stared at his computer. "George Penfield, the stage manager of your wife's show last year, was convicted of trying to poison her with ricin." He continued to read. "Penfield claimed Josh Elliot was funding him. That Elliot gave him the money to buy the ricin. But there was no proof. Just a lot of calls from an unknown person to Penfield from what turned out to be a throw-away cell. Without collaboration of Penfield's story we couldn't subpoena Elliot's bank records."

"I think we can get the records now," Nick said.

"What's changed?"

"Jessie." Nick cleared his throat. "She found out Elliot was involved with Penfield after the fact. She promised to keep quiet if Josh left town for good. Andrew Brady, her first husband—"

"And your brother," Loman added.

"Right. Andrew and Josh were close. You have to understand my wife. Jessie always strives to do what she thinks Andrew would want. Always. And she didn't think Andrew would want his friend in jail, no matter what he did. My brother was a forgiving sort." St. Andrew. The good brother.

"As opposed to you." Loman chuckled.

"I believe in justice." Sinner Nick. The bad brother. "So Josh relocated to California, and Jessie said nothing. But if Elliot did indeed kill Bill Rudolph, who was like a father to her, I think she'll be happy to put him away. Plus, Josh broke the deal by coming back to town."

Nick was banking on Jessie doing the right thing. The way he saw it, she owed him. Big time.

*

Jessie sat with Mary in the breakfast nook. When the front door slammed, she braced herself. Nick plodded into the kitchen.

"I saved your dinner." Mary nodded towards a plate on the stove.

"Thanks, Mary." He came around to face Jessie. "You're taking Abbie and Willie with you?"

"Did Willie tell you?"

"Yes. Nice way to find out. You could have discussed it with me first."

"I'm sorry, Nick. You weren't around. I'm pressed for time."

"I have a cell."

"I'm sorry. Really."

"I need a favor."

"Sure."

"I want you to tell two detectives what you told me about Josh Elliot being behind your ricin attack last year."

Jessie sighed. This again. Josh Elliot. "Why?"

"We need Josh's bank records to prove going after Bill Rudolph isn't the slime's first deadly adventure."

Jessie rubbed her forehead. "Do you know for sure Josh killed Bill?"

"Not yet."

Nick wasn't going to like her answer. "Until you know for sure, I don't feel comfortable opening that chapter again."

Nick's eyes narrowed. "Comfortable? You don't feel comfortable? Josh broke your agreement by coming back to town. That's not enough for you?"

"I just want to leave the past in the past. I need a fresh start."

Nick slammed his hand down on the island, making Jessie and Mary jump. "Not everything is about you, Jessie."

"Dad?"

Nick swung around. Anthony stood a few feet away.

"Could I talk to you?"

"Not now, Anthony." Nick realized he was yelling. Damn. He forced himself to calm down, softening his tone. "Sorry. Sure. Come on."

*

Anthony was too worried to sleep. He curled into a ball, Monty at his side.

He was scared his parents were getting a divorce, no matter what they each said earlier.

"Hey, sweetie." His mom stood in the doorway. "I couldn't sleep, so I thought I'd check on you." She came over and sat on the bed. "Anthony, please don't worry about your dad and me."

"It's weird you going away for so long without Dad."

"I need to work in London, and Dad needs to work here. This is going to happen at times. Our careers are important to us."

"But you never left Daddy Andrew."

"That's because we worked together. Nick and I have different careers." She pulled the blanket up around his shoulders, like she used to when he was little. But he wasn't little anymore. He was almost nine.

238

"Where's Dad?"

"Watching TV in the study."

"Still?" His mom nodded. Dad reassured Anthony there was no divorce, but something was wrong between his parents. Something terrible.

His mom took his hand. "Anthony, I'm sorry you're upset I'm going away. Maybe you can come over for a visit by yourself. I can show you London, just you and me. Dad showed Kat, and I'll show you. Would you like that?"

Anthony nodded. He'd rather Dad showed him London. But he didn't want to hurt his mom.

*

Willie rolled onto his back in the dark bedroom. "You should have seen him, Abbie. Nick had no idea what I was talking about."

"You shouldn't have said anything until Jessie had a chance to talk to Nick." She lifted up on one elbow. How could Jessie have screwed up so badly?

"How was I supposed to know Jessie hadn't told him?"

She rubbed Willie's chest. "I should have warned you to wait. I'm sorry. What a mess."

"I felt like I was kicking a dog when he was down."

Abbie curled into Willie's arms again. "Jessie hasn't handled this whole thing well. Of course, she's still reeling from losing the baby."

"This doesn't feel right, Abbie. Our trotting off to London and Nick staying here."

"It's what Jessie wants. And Nick, too, I guess. He has a book to write."

"Well, just between you and me, I think it's ripping Nick to shreds."

"Nick is tough. He'll bounce back."

She hoped.

*

Nick sat alone in the study, his feet propped up on the coffee table, his dinner plate untouched. It was late, past eleven. The fire in the grate was dying down. The house was quiet, everyone in bed long ago.

239

He flipped channels on the TV and sipped his bourbon. Was this what life would be like when everyone left town? Sitting alone night after night watching mindless TV?

He was in a foul mood. Discovering Jessie intended to take Abbie and Willie with her to London was a blow to his ego. She needed everyone's support but his. And what if Nick needed Willie here? Maybe that was part of Jessie's plan. Without Willie, Nick wouldn't get involved in any dangerous investigations.

Jessie also told the family about the play. Again, without him. It confused the hell out of Anthony. Nick did his best to reassure the boy that all was fine. Which was another lie. He hated himself right now. And he was furious with Jessie for putting him in this position.

Glancing up at the portrait of the brothers, he wondered where Andrew was these days. He'd been silent for weeks. Was this what he wanted, to destroy Nick's marriage to Jessie? Why would he want them to separate after he worked so hard to bring them together?

The television turned off.

Had he accidentally hit the OFF button?

The lamp on the bar went out.

Okay, that was no accident.

Andrew. "For God's sake," he whispered, "stop playing games and tell me what you want."

A photo fell off the mantle. Nick struggled to his feet and picked it up. Even in the dim light he could see it was a picture of Nick and Jessie on the couch in this very room. They were laughing. Nick remembered the night Anthony took it. They were joking about what a circus their wedding was going to be.

Nick ran his fingers across Jessie's face. They looked so happy together. How had they lost that magic? How could so much damage be inflicted on a marriage in such a short time?

"Okay, Andrew, I hear you. But you better talk to Jessie, too."

*

Jessie pressed on with Anthony, hoping to pull him out of his dark mood. It had been a long time since they talked like this. "Focus on being home-schooled with Zane. That's something to look forward to. This is no time to be sad."

"I'm happy about that. But I'm sad about Luci."

Anthony's words startled Jessie. So Nick told their son about Luci. Without Jessie's input. The lack of communication between Nick and Jessie was out of control. "Don't be sad about Luci, Anthony. She doesn't deserve your kind heart. She wanted to hurt me. And she hurt you by not telling you she was Gianni's sister."

Anthony's eyes grew larger. "Gi-Gianni? His sister?"

He didn't know. Dear God, Anthony didn't know Luci was his aunt! Damn Nick. He should have told her he— She had to fix this. Make it easier for her son somehow, even if it meant lying. "Anthony, listen to me." She took both his hands.

Anthony scooted up to a sitting position and pulled his hands away.

"Her real name was Lucianna Santangelo, and she was Gianni's sister. She wanted to be close to you – I'm sure she loved you, honey - but she blamed Dad and me for so many things, including killing Gianni, so she had to pretend to be someone else. When her true identify was revealed, well, she knew the charade was over. That's why she killed herself."

"Killed herself? But Dad said … No! You're lying! I don't want to hear anymore. Get out. Get out!" He put his hands over his ears, screaming at her. "GET OUT! You're a LIAR!"

CHAPTER 21

Nick heard Anthony all the way down in the study. He took off running, scaling the stairs two at a time. Kat and Bertie hovered outside Anthony's bedroom door.

Anthony stood on his bed, shouting at the top of his lungs. Monty crouched beside the bed, growling at Jessie, who backed away from the angry dog. Mary stood in the middle of it all. "Tell her, Dad. Luci was my friend. She wasn't Gianni's sister. You wouldn't lie to me. TELL HER!"

"Anthony, stop yelling, okay?" Nick approached the boy, keeping his voice calm. "Stop yelling at your mom, and we'll talk."

"Not until Mom gets out of here. I'm glad she's going away. She's a LIAR!"

"Don't talk to your mother like that!"

"Tell her to get out."

Nick glared at Jessie. "You told him?"

"I thought you told him. I didn't know—"

"You should have asked me."

"You should have told me!"

"You mean it's true?" Anthony screamed.

"I can explain," Nick said.

"NOOO!" Anthony wailed. Nick grabbed him, pulling him from the bed, Anthony punching and kicking. "You said you'd never lie to me! I can't trust anyone, not even you!"

Monty bared his teeth at Nick, ready to spring. Ready to protect Anthony from any perceived danger.

Nick stared at the dog, memories of that last night in Ohio slamming his brain. Pain shot across his temples. His stomach threatened to rebel.

Gianni let Anthony go, the boy looking dazed and falling limply to the ground.

Nick let Anthony go, the boy slipping from his grasp to the floor.

The memory played out in his mind's eye. Nick watched in horror, a spectator.

With a snarl, Monty leapt at Gianni, fangs bared. Gianni stumbled back, arms flailing. His gun went off, a spark of light.

Gianni toppled to the ground under Monty's weight, springing free with a vicious kick to the dog's belly. Yelping, the dog rebounded and crouched, ready to launch himself at Gianni again, who was back on his feet.

Barton slumped to the ground, clutching his chest.

Nick finally moved, ripping his own gun from his belt and firing. Gianni clapped a hand to his heart. Opening his mouth, he tried to speak. No words. Just a trickle of blood. He staggered and fell to the ground, a look of surprise stamped on his face.

Barton lay where he fell, hands clutching his chest. Nick frantically stripped off his coat and pressed it to Lyle's chest, trying to staunch the flow of blood. "Hang in there." Sirens wailed in the distance. "Help's on the way." A sob welled from Nick's gut, a silent heave of anguish as he watched helplessly.

Barton's eyes slid to Nick. "Gianni?"

"Dead."

"You ..." Barton gulped for air, drowning, a fine mist of blood pumping out of his mouth, "... best partner ... friend ... I ..."

A lump lodged in Nick's throat. He didn't have friends. Not until Lyle Barton.

Barton's face went slack. His body relaxed. He was gone. Nick's friend was gone.

Nick froze, adrift in a time capsule.

*

As Anthony stared up at his father, he heard Daddy Andrew's voice. *It's okay to remember now, Anthony. You're growing up. You can handle it. Your dad needs to get past this. He always helps you, right? Now you can help him ...*

For the first time, Anthony saw it. Tears fell as he saw it all. The front yard of the house in Ohio. The spooky moon and the shadowy bare trees. Monty protecting him, attacking Gianni. The gunfire. Gianni dead. His mother, sobbing. Lyle, bleeding on the ground. His dad, panicked, trying to save his friend.

"Dad?" Anthony whimpered, pulling himself to his feet.

His dad didn't move.

"It's okay, Monty," he cooed to his dog. "It's Dad. He's not hurting me."

Anthony wrapped his arms around his father. "Dad?"

*

Hearing his son's voice, Nick broke free from the memory.

"Dad? ... I remember, Dad. About Ohio."

Mary spoke ... "Anthony's okay now. Let's leave them alone."

Jessie's voice, cracking with emotion ... "No. I need to be here. To hear this. I was there that night, too."

"I want to talk to Dad alone." Anthony buried his face against Nick.

Nick was incapable of moving. Of talking. His knees threatened to buckle.

"Come on, sweetie." Mary again. "Nick will tell you everything later. This is between the two of them. Let's leave them alone." The sound of the door closing.

Spent, Nick half-slumped, half-collapsed onto the bed. The pain in his head threatened to crack his skull open.

Anthony sat beside him, his face wet with tears. "I saw it, Dad. What happened that night. Daddy Andrew helped me remember."

Nick stared at his son, things finally coming into focus. "Andrew was here?"

Anthony nodded. "He showed me Lyle's death wasn't my fault. Or yours. It was Monty who caused the gun to go off. It was Monty trying to protect me."

"Monty ..."

"He said something else. He wanted me to remember so I can help you get past this."

"Get past what?" Guilt over killing Gianni? Nick felt no guilt. The creature deserved to die.

"Maybe he thinks you miss Lyle too much. And he wants you to get past it."

Wise words from the little man sitting beside him.

In the end it was all so simple.

*

Jessie went into her bedroom, shutting the others out. She was hurt and felt alone. So alone. She crawled onto the bed, sobbing.

No matter how hard she tried she would never have the bond with Anthony that Nick had. There was more to being a parent than blood. She saw it with Andrew, and now with Nick.

Jessie loved Anthony. And she loved Nick.

But tonight she was an outsider in this family.

The tears flowed freely. She couldn't stop them. She cried for her son and for her marriage. She managed to harm both in recent months.

In a rare moment of clarity, Jessie realized how selfish she could be. How selfish she'd been throughout her life. She'd been a spoiled child and a spoiled wife. Jessie always came first. Before her father. Before Andrew. Even before her son.

Somehow Nick saw past it when they met and fell in love. Maybe because he was no stranger to self-absorption. Their love was greater than the sum of their parts. Jessie would stake her life on that fact.

This divide had to end. Tomorrow she would try to put the pieces of her broken life back together.

Was a production in London worth the loss of her family?

*

Nick and Anthony laid against the headlboard, Monty stretched across the foot of the bed. They talked about what just happened, about Luci, about Jessie going away, about everything but the elephant in the room.

"Why'd you lie to me, Dad?"

There it was. Finally.

Nick rubbed his eyes, willing his headache away. "Because I was afraid if you found out who Luci really was it would damage you forever. And I didn't want that for you."

"What do you mean, damage?"

"You've been through a lot in your young life, but you've always bounced back. We all thought Gianni and everything related to him was finished. Then here comes Luci, and it starts all over again. I was afraid she was one thing too many, that her lies would make you never trust your judgment about people again."

"Will it? Damage me?"

Nick slung his arm around his son's shoulders. "That's up to you. You can let it make you bitter and angry and suspicious of everyone. Or … you can let it go and be grateful for what you have. A family that loves you. This fabulous home. The best friend a guy can have in Zane. A challenging new sister. A fabulous grandma in Mary. And an awesome dog. I know what I'd choose." He looked down at his son. A smile crept across Anthony's face, and he wrapped his arms around Nick. "I'm sorry, Anthony. I was wrong not to tell you the truth. I keep forgetting you're growing up. You can obviously handle anything. And I swear on Andrew's grave I will never lie to you again."

"Pinky swear?"

"Hmm?"

"It's the biggest promise you can make. Zane and I use it for important stuff. Give me your hand."

Nick forked over his appendage. Anthony curled his pinky finger around Nick's pinky. "Now squeeze and say you 'pinky swear.'"

Nick obeyed his son. "I pinky swear I will never lie to you again."

Anthony hugged Nick tighter and yawned. "Would you stay with me until I fall asleep? I'm not being a baby, I just--"

"I was going to ask you the same thing." They slid down, and Nick closed his eyes. He was exhausted.

His cell woke him early the next morning. Trying not to disturb his sleeping son, he crept out of the room. "McDeare."

It was the coroner. The test results were in. Tetrahydrozoline was found in Bill's blood, a chemical in over-the-counter eye drops. It also explained the broken blood vessels in Bill's corneas.

As a result, Dr. Malachy amended the cause of death. "According to his medical records," the coroner continued, "Rudolph had high blood pressure – nothing drastic – but enough to cause a stroke or heart attack with the ingestion of tetrahydrozoline. Especially given the high dosage administered."

Nick thanked the doctor and hung up. It was time to get Jessie on board, whether she liked it or not.

*

Jessie was just leaving the bedroom when Nick appeared in the doorway. They stared, neither speaking for a moment.

Not sure where to begin, she murmured, "The bathroom's all yours."

Nick stepped towards her, his expression intense. What now? "Jess, you have to tell the cops about Josh Elliot. I just got new information that points to his guilt. With your background statement, we've got him."

Josh again? Jessie bit her tongue. She needed to fix things with her husband, not resurrect old fights. "And without it?"

He shrugged. "It's a crap shoot."

Jessie swallowed. "Okay, Nick. I'll talk to them." It was a small step in bridging the gap between them.

Nick's face relaxed. "Thanks."

"Is it possible for them to come here? I'll give them all the time they need. It's just that, with my leaving tomorrow, I'm—"

"I'll ask them." Nick headed for the bathroom, stripping off his shirt.

"Can we talk?"

"Now?" He paused. "I have a full day. How about tonight?"

She nodded. "Tonight." She'd take what she could get. Anything to make things right again.

*

When Nick came down to the kitchen, Mary was waiting for him. "I want you to sit down and eat every bite of food I put in front of you. I found your dinner plate from last night. Untouched. You're going to make yourself sick. Now, sit."

Nick knew it was hopeless to argue with her. As he forced down Mary's asparagus and cheddar omelet, he made phone calls, the first to Marcie Rudolph. By the time Willie joined him, he had their day planned out.

*

Kat finished her five miles on the Nordic Track up in the gym as Bertie worked out at the barre. "I'm going to miss you, Bertie."

"I hope so. But I'm only a text away. And I'll still be hauling your fat bod into the air at ballet."

Kat laughed as she mopped her face with a towel. Hamlet rose from the table by the windows and stretched. She rubbed the top of the cat's head. "When are you moving to Susie's?"

"Couple days. Max is renovating a room for me."

"You're sure you'd rather live there instead of here? You know Dad would love to have you."

247

"You and your dad need time together without any outside interference.

"And with Jessie in London, there won't be any."

"Kat?" Jessie stood a few feet away. "Can we talk?"

Good God, do you always sneak up on people? Kat shrugged, exchanging a look with Bertie.

"Should I leave?" Bertie asked.

"We won't be long. Thanks, Bertie."

"Sorry, Kat," Bertie whispered before leaving the room.

Jessie moved to the table. "Let's sit." She stroked Hamlet, who backed away and curled into a ball on Kat's lap. "I want to start by apologizing to you. I haven't given you a fair shake since the day you arrived. I'm sorry. Really sorry."

Excuse me? What are you up to, lady?

"You see, I always had Nick to myself. I was the only female in his life, and I liked it. Then you came along and, well, things changed. I was jealous, Kat. It's that simple. I was jealous of Nick and your mom, and I was jealous of you, of Nick's devotion to you."

Am I supposed to believe this drivel?

"I never meant to become your enemy, Kat. Far from it. I want you to be happy here. This is your home."

You're up to something. What exactly do you want?

A frown creased Jessie's perfect forehead. "Why don't you like me?"

Kat crossed her arms. "I don't like the way you treat Dad."

"You're calling Nick 'Dad' now?"

"I've been calling him 'Dad' for a while."

"I should have noticed."

"Yes. You should have."

Jessie took a moment. "So you don't like the way I treat your father. Why?"

Kat snorted. "Where do I begin?"

"Granted, I wasn't myself when I was pregnant, but—"

"You're selfish, Jessie. You always think of yourself first. Like this trek to London. Do you know how hurt Dad is that you don't want him along? You want Abbie and Willie, but not him."

"I explained to Nick why I needed to go without him, and he understood."

"Did he? Maybe you don't know him as well as you think."

Anger flashed across Jessie's face. "You want to hurt me. To get back at me. I get it. Do your worst. But I'm apologizing, Kat. I know I've been selfish. I'm trying to make up for it."

"Make up for it by apologizing to Dad, not me. You and I won't have a better relationship until you have a better relationship with Dad."

Jessie pursed her lips. Her eyes narrowed. She was definitely angry. "Tell me something. What's your definition of a marriage?"

"I don't know. I haven't been around married people much. Maybe your bad behavior is normal. If it is, I'll pass."

Jessie stared out the window. When she looked back at Kat, there was a steeliness in her eyes. "First of all, my relationship with your father is our business, not yours. It's between Nick and me. Secondly, I'm extending an olive branch to you. I'd like to start over. To at least be friends. I respect the closeness between you and Nick, and I'll support it, even cheer you on. If that's not good enough," she shrugged, "there's nothing more I can do."

She stood up. "The ball's in your court now." She marched from the room, her heels clicking on the wooden floor.

Kat looked at Hamlet. "Who was that woman?"

*

"Josh killed Bill. There's not a doubt in my mind," Nick said to the two detectives. He and Willie were again in the chief's office.

Mario looked at his partner. "What do you think? Lay it out."

Bernie shrugged. "It's circumstantial. Unless the lady in the bar saw something."

Mario looked up Carmella Hutchison's contact info. "We'll talk to her. After Nick's wife."

"Correction. Willie and I will talk to her." Nick snapped a cell picture of the info on the computer. "We've been to the bar, seen the layout and know what to ask." Loman raised his eyebrows. "What, you don't trust me? Barton's allegiance isn't good enough? And my own reputation?"

After a beat, Mario nodded. "Okay. Call us when you're done." He looked at Loman. "Continue."

Bernie shifted in his chair. "So Nick talks to Rudolph's wife. She says her husband never used eye drops. The bartender verifies Elliot had eye drops in the bar that afternoon. Rudolph turned away for a phone call, presenting opportunity. Motive? Josh Elliot benefitted big time from Bill Rudolph's death. If Jessica Kendle backs up the stage manager's claim about Elliot's involvement in the ricin incident, we'll get those bank records. Then we talk to the D.A."

"One more thing," Nick said. "Bill's partner, Harrison Alder. We don't know if he was in on it. He set up the meeting with Rudolph and Elliot. And because of Bill's death, Alder is now running the organization."

The two detectives locked eyes, a silent conversation taking place.

"This has to be coordinated, so Alder doesn't tip off Josh Elliot." Mario said. "We wait on this until we have a warrant for Elliot. Maybe even flip Alder."

"I want to be there when you question Alder. I know the man," Nick added. "Also when you arrest Elliot."

Mario shook his head. "Barton said you were pushy."

*

Jessie found Anthony on his computer in his bedroom. "Can we talk?"

"Uh, sure." Anthony remained focused on the computer. A photo of Nick and Kat filled the screen. They were backlit at the window in Nick's office.

"That's fantastic, Anthony."

"Yeah? I'm saving it for Kat's birthday. Whenever that is."

"Honey, why I came in here ... I just ... I want to apologize for last night. I didn't know Nick hadn't told you about Luci and—"

"It's okay. I know it wasn't your fault. I'm sorry for calling you a liar."

Jessie felt her shoulders drop a few inches. "And you understand why I'm going to London for a while?"

"Yeah. Dad explained it."

"I'm glad he could do that for you."

"He says we're going down to the villa as soon as school's finished. Even Monty's going. It'll be fun."

Fun. Already her son was moving on with Nick. Jessie forced the dark thoughts from her mind. She had to stop thinking like this. After all, it was her decision to leave. And she wanted everyone to be okay with it.

"Anthony, look at me, honey." He turned those huge blue eyes on her. "I love you. You know that, don't you?" He nodded. "And you love me, too?"

"Yeah."

She pulled him into her arms and hugged him tight.

He wriggled away. "Mom! I'm too old for that stuff now."

"You're never too old for a hug from your mom."

"You are when you're a GUY."

Jessie left him alone with his photos, not completely satisfied with the conversation. Maybe this was all she should expect from an eight-year-old boy, a child who was forced to grow up too fast.

So. She talked to both kids and did what she could to make things better. Two items to cross off her list. Jessie took a deep breath. The toughest mea culpa was yet to come. Nick.

As she came down the stairs the doorbell rang. Mary ushered Lt. Manganaro and Sgt. Loman into the living room.

*

"Mrs. Hutchison?"

"Yes. Come in, Mr. McDeare. Captain Bodine."

They entered the impressive lower Fifth Avenue apartment. The impeccably dressed woman ushered them into an ornate study and offered them coffee.

"We're sorry to bother you," Nick began, donning his genteel society persona. This woman fit the mold perfectly.

"No bother. I'm a widow, so life is simple. Charity and church. Besides, I'm a huge fan of your books. I've read many in the Golden Calf over dinner. That's what you said you wanted to talk about when you called. The Golden Calf?"

"Yes." Nick sipped his coffee. "Did you know William Rudolph, the producer?"

"A bit. Enough to exchange pleasantries with. My husband knew him well. We were both patrons of the arts. I often saw Mr. Rudolph in the Golden Calf."

"He was in the bar the day he died. Do you remember that day?"

"Oh, yes. I remember it because of that fact. He was with an actor. I can't remember the man's name, but he was big on Broadway at one time. In fact, he starred with your wife in a show. It didn't look like they were the best of friends. I never saw Mr. Rudolph smile once."

So far, so good. "Anything unusual about their meeting, other than it didn't look friendly?"

"Not really. Well, there was one thing. I noticed it because Mr. Rudolph is so fastidious. A natty dresser. Polished shoes. Creased trousers." She giggled, an odd sound for such an austere woman. "Anyway, I remember thinking it was a good thing Mr. Rudolph didn't see the other man spill something on the bar. At least, I think he spilled something. Mr. Rudolph was on his phone at the time."

"You're certainly observant. Do you always people-watch?" Willie asked.

"When I forget my book, yes."

"Did it spill where Bill was sitting? Across that area of the bar."

"Well, he certainly was fussing in that area." Again the giggle.

Nick caught Willie's eye. Things weren't looking good for old Josh Elliot.

*

After class with Finn, Kat told Bertie about her conversation with Jessie. "The woman is definitely up to something."

"Maybe she's genuinely sorry, Kat. Give her a break."

"Why? She never gives me one."

They headed downstairs for lunch. Kat smelled chili.

"She just did. She admitted she was jealous. That's not easy. Look, whether you like it or not, Jessie is your stepmother. Fighting with her will only antagonize your dad. So swallow your pride and get along with the woman."

Get along with Jessie? Impossible. But Bertie was right. Kat didn't want to upset her dad.

"The way I see it," Kat concluded, "I don't have to worry about it right now. Jessie will be gone for six months. A lot can happen in that time."

*

Nick and Willie rode the elevator up to Harrison Alder's office with Manganaro and Loman. It had been a long but productive day. Carmella Hutchison was a solid witness. Jessie gave the detectives what they needed to get Elliot's bank records. The bank records provided proof of Josh's financial investment in the ricin incident. A DA was on board. And a judge had issued a speedy arrest warrant. Sgt. Loman had friends in high places. Who said the wheels of justice turn slowly? Today they moved at lightning speed.

Nick should be on top of the world. He wasn't. Maybe because it happened so quickly. Maybe because it seemed too easy.

They bypassed the guard-dog-secretary and pushed into Alder's inner sanctum. Harrison looked up from his desk. "What the hell? Who are you?" He glanced at the detectives.

Nick made the introductions – with over-exaggerated courtesy – before perching on the edge of the man's desk. As pre-arranged, Nick would take the lead, with Willie's assistance. "Josh Elliot killed Bill Rudolph. It's a fact. The only thing we don't know is if you're in on it."

Alder started to laugh. "You're nuts."

"Is that a no?" Willie asked, his face serious.

"Of course it is." Harrison shot to his feet.

Nick glared at the man. "Did you set up Bill with Elliot?"

"What do you mean 'set up'?"

"We already know you arranged the meeting between the two men. Marci Rudolph confirmed it. But did you know what Josh was planning to do?"

"What the hell are you talking about?"

"Elliot put a chemical in Bill's drink that afternoon that caused his heart attack."

Harrison Alder's face fell. He slumped back into his chair.

"Well?" Willie pushed.

Harrison reached for his cell. "I'm calling my lawyer."

"Go ahead. We'll wait." Nick stood up and faced the man. "But you could make this a lot simpler if you just tell us the truth. That is, if you're innocent."

"Of course I'm innocent!"

Alder appeared to be having an inner debate, his cell still in his hand. He exhaled slowly, ran a hand through his thinning hair and looked from one face to another. "If I tell you the truth, I'm not in any trouble, right?"

"Let's just say we'll take your candor into consideration." Mario spoke for the first time.

"Okay." Harrison tossed his cell and came around the desk. "Okay. Here's what happened, and I swear it's the truth. Josh called me out of the blue when he got back to town. We've known each other since college. He asked if I could get Bill to agree to see him. Bad blood between the two since Josh quit the show last year without notice. And there were rumors that Josh had something to do with the ricin planted on Jessie Kendle's prop. I never bought into that story."

"Buy into it. It's true." Nick informed him. "We have Elliot's bank records."

"Dear God." Again, a swipe through his hair as more blood drained from his pasty face. "Josh wanted to meet at Bill's apartment. Bill said no and suggested the bar. Josh called me after the meeting and said it went well. That they'd talked about Josh doing the lead in *EARLY SPRING*."

"He lied. He knew Bill wouldn't live to refute his story."

"That's all I did. I swear. I set up the meeting." Alden tossed his glasses on the desk and rubbed his eyes. "Damn. He played me for a fool."

"How?" Willie asked.

"Josh wanted that role badly. When we first talked, I told him if it was up to me the role was his. But Bill wanted nothing to do with him. When Bill died, the board of directors turned the company over to me, and I ... gave the role to Josh. Damn. I was such a fool!"

Nick locked eyes with Manganaro, who nodded. Alden was telling the truth. He was a pawn in Josh Elliot's master plan.

"Okay, Alder," Mario barked. "Here's what we want you to do."

CHAPTER 22

Josh Elliot cabbed down to Harrison Alder's office. It was past six, the sun long gone. Josh hated winter on the east coast. The days were too short, the weather too brutal.

Whatever Harry wanted, it sounded important. He said it had to do with *EARLY SPRING*. Everything was always life-or-death with Harry. A crisis every five minutes. He actually threatened to cancel Josh's contract if he didn't show up in the office within an hour. Something had the little man riled.

Josh emerged from the elevator, nodded to Harrison's secretary and pushed through the office door. Nick McDeare stood beside Alder. "What the hell are you doing here?"

"Joshua Elliot?" a deep voice boomed.

"Yes." Two men stood behind him.

"You're under arrest for the murder of William Rudolph."

*

On the drive home, Nick was quiet. They'd gone to Midtown North to celebrate with Manganaro and Loman. Josh Elliot huddled with his lawyer, who told him the DA would have a hard time proving any of this to a jury. Nick knew the case wasn't airtight. But with the previous ricin incident, which the DA was convinced he could get admitted, the future prospects for Josh Elliot looked grim. No matter what happened, Elliot wouldn't be starring on Broadway anytime soon. Not according to Harrison Alder. That in itself was a victory. Nick had learned over the years that without an audience, without a character to portray, actors were relegated to the dustbin.

Nick stared out the window morosely. Snow flurries whipped around the car. The windshield wipers clacked furiously to provide visibility. Pedestrians bundled against the fierce wind, ignoring traffic lights, their footing precarious, their umbrellas flipping inside-out. The sidewalks and gutters were a graveyard of broken umbrellas.

Where was the usual high Nick felt at the end of a case? The satisfaction of seeing an investigation through to a conclusion? Righting a wrong was what Nick lived for, what had fueled him for decades.

The Japanese authorities didn't care if Nick found the man who jumped him. After the first year passed with no resolve, the incident went into an unsolved case file, to be forgotten. Nick felt like putting his fist through a wall. He wanted the bastards to pay.

Nick spent the following month keeping an eye on Jack Flaherty, waiting for his moment. It never came. He mentioned the situation to Alex in passing, who jumped on it. "The authorities won't investigate this man? You're a journalism student. Go to the papers with your story. Shout Jack Flaherty's name at the top of your lungs. Don't be a sheep. Make a difference in this world!"

Nick followed his mentor's advice, ultimately writing his first feature article in The Washington Post at the age of seventeen. Other American outlets picked up the story and ran with it. Three weeks later, Flaherty was arrested, also selling out his loser friends.

Nick took Alex out for an expensive dinner to thank him. Lesson learned. Celebratory pattern established.

"What's up?" Willie glanced over at Nick.

"Just tired."

They rode the rest of the way in silence.

*

By the time Nick got home that night, the house was quiet. This was becoming a pattern. He'd promised to talk with Jessie, but his legs refused to climb the stairs. It had been a long day. He was exhausted.

Mary left him a plate of roast beef, mashed potatoes and asparagus with a note attached, ordering him to EAT. He sat alone at the island, feeling empty. Had the joy gone out of his investigations? After all these years, was he now merely an author of suspense novels? Had he suffered one too many body blows recently, altering his course forever?

"Hey." Kat sat on the stool next to him.

"You're up late." Nick pushed a piece of beef around on his plate.

"I was worried about you."

"No need."

"Thanks."

"Sorry. I didn't mean—I'm just tired."

"So did you get the guy with the eye drops?"

Nick chuckled. She was relentless. Like him. "Yep. Your tip set it in motion."

"Wow, glad I could help. I asked Mary about your investigation after dinner. I figured if anyone knew the details it was her."

Nick grinned. "You're definitely starting to navigate your way around here."

Kat helped herself to a spear of asparagus. "Jessie apologized to me this morning."

Nick stared at his daughter. "For what?"

"Lots of things. But mostly for being jealous. Of both Mom and me."

Interesting. "Were you nice to her?"

"I'm always nice."

"No, Kat. You're not. Were you?"

"I don't like the way she treats you. And now she's going to London tomorrow. Without you."

"She has to work."

"Not in London. She can work here."

Nick agreed with Kat, but he couldn't let her know it. It would only throw kindling on the fire. "You go where the work is. Right now, for her, it's in London."

"So you're excusing her. Again."

Nick slammed down his fork. "Dammit, Kat, you can be so unforgiving."

"Like you."

"I—" She was right. But it didn't soften his anger. At Kat or his wife. "Stay out of my relationship with Jessie. It's complicated enough without your interference. This is between Jessie and me. Understand?"

Her shoulders sagged. She slid off the stool and headed for the stairs.

"Wait." He reached out for her. "Come here." Sitting her back down, he stared into her chastened young face. "I don't mean to be harsh with you. But you have to back off with Jessie and me." He sighed and resumed eating.

"I'm not going to Interlochen with Bertie. I've decided to stay here. With you."

Nick swiped his mouth with a paper towel. "Don't, Kat. Don't pass up this opportunity. Opportunities come once, then they're gone forever."

"It's not what I want."

"What do you mean?"

"I've been thinking about what you said about passion. I'll always love dancing. The piano. The stage. Performing. But my passion is writing. When Drake told me he thought I was gifted, it meant more to me than a hundred standing ovations. He said my story is good enough to be published right now." Her face changed completely as she talked about writing. She was animated.

"What's the story about?"

"You and me."

Whoa.

"Don't worry. No one knows it's us. It's about a father and daughter bonding over their mutual love of London."

"They won't know it's us? Are you kidding?" My God. "Can I read it?"

"You really want to?"

Nick nodded. While Kat ran upstairs to get her story, Nick buried what he didn't eat in the bottom of the trash. He also rinsed his dishes and put them in the dishwasher. Since he and Mary would now be co-parenting, he better stay on her good side.

"Here." Kat held out the pages.

Nick slid into the breakfast nook and read slowly. When he finished, he looked over at his daughter, perched on a stool. "It's good, Kat. Really good. London comes alive in your words. And your characters are multi-dimensional. Real people."

"What about the relationship between the father and daughter?"

He gave her back her writing and sat beside her. "You 'showed' me their love instead of telling me. One of the hardest things to learn. And not easy to do. Drake's right. You have a gift."

Kat picked up an asparagus spear left behind on the island. She wouldn't look at him. Was she embarrassed by his words?

"You make me proud."

She still wouldn't look at him. Was she crying? Kat held the asparagus up, examining it. "Well," her voice was barely more than a whisper, "I have your writing genes in me."

"And your mother's."

Now he saw it. Her eyes were moist, threatening to spill over. Dropping the asparagus, Kat threw her arms around him, her tears dropping onto his shoulder. He rocked her, wishing he could have done this when she was a baby. He missed twelve years of his daughter's childhood. He intended to spend the rest of his life making it up to her.

*

"I'm not going to London, Abbie." Willie came out of the bathroom and turned off the lamp. "I just called Jessie and told her."

Abbie jolted upright in bed. "What? Why?"

"Several reasons." He slid in beside her. "First, my main job is protecting the kids. If someone wants to hurt Nick or Jessie, they'll do it through Anthony or Kat. And the kids are here, so I should be, too."

"Another reason's Nick, isn't it?"

He smiled at her in the dark. She was starting to understand him. He laid down, pulling her into his arms. "I've never seen him this low. We got Josh Elliot today, someone he's hated forever, but it didn't seem to mean anything to him. I think too much has happened in the last few weeks, and he's not handling it well."

"But how does your being here make a difference? I mean, it's not like you're besties."

"I'm not Barton, and I never will be. Nor do I want to be. You said yourself Nick's a loner, and Barton was his only friend. But with Jessie gone, he's going to need someone to hang with besides two young kids."

"You're giving up six months in London to hang with a loner?"

"Don't say it like that, Abbie. I told you, there are multiple reasons for staying."

"Am ... I ... one of those reasons? Do you need time away from me?"

"Not from you. From us. I think we could use a cooling off period. Some time to step back and reassess." Were they falling in love, as he suspected? Or were they just a moment in time? "I need to ask you something."

She looked hesitant. "Okay ..."

Willie took a moment. "Why did it take you so long to go to bed with me? ... Make love with me? You told me you hopped into bed with other men pretty fast. What was different about me that made you hesitate?"

Abbie looked away. "It wasn't hesitation exactly. It was ... I realized early on that my feelings for you were—I began to realize ..."

"You never have trouble spitting words out. This must be big. Should I prepare myself?"

Abbie looked up at him. "No." She sighed. "I realized my feelings for you were genuine, different from the others, which made me not want to screw it up. If I slept with you too soon, and then you dumped me, I would have been devastated. So I waited until ... I don't know." She shrugged. "You think we need time apart?"

So she felt it, too. That spark between them. Thank God. "What we have won't change with a little distance. Not if it's real."

Alarm flashed across Abbie's face. "So you think it isn't? And this is the easiest way to break up, right? When we're apart."

He couldn't help laughing. "You can be such a drama queen. I didn't say that."

She sat up. "Now I'm a drama queen?"

He sat up, too. "I think I love you, Abbie. Is that good enough for you?"

"Really?"

"Really."

Abbie stared at him, a goofy grin on her face. "Well, okay then." She flopped back down. "So where's my goodbye sex?"

Willie laughed hard. Being with this woman was like playing a fast game of Ping-Pong. It was hard to keep his eye on the ball. "You sure you're up for it? My goodbye sex is legendary.

"Am I up for it?" Abbie rolled her eyes. "Fire when ready, Gridley."

*

Her dad's praise meant everything to Kat. It was as if she'd been holding her breath for months, waiting for this moment. And with the mention of her mother, everything she was holding in was released, tapping an overflowing well. It was the first time she really cried since she moved to New York. Her tears turned to sobs. Her shoulders heaved with each gasp for air.

260

"It's okay, baby girl. It's okay." Her dad's voice was gentle as he held her, kissed the top of her head, combed her hair with his fingers.

Kat cried because she knew her mother was gone. Really gone. She'd never see her again. She cried because, after twelve years of missing father-daughter events, of avoiding the curiosity of classmates who asked where her father was, of pretending she didn't need anyone but her mom, she finally had a dad. A man who was proud of her. A man she loved and wanted to emulate. And she cried because she was tired. It took so much energy to be tough, to not let anyone get the better of her. Especially Jessie.

"It all caught up with you, didn't it? The brick wall crumbled."

She nodded and burrowed her face against his sweater. "How'd you know?"

"Think back about a week ago. You watched a lunatic destroy a nursery with a fire poker and bawl like a baby."

He made her laugh through her tears. How'd he do that? He lifted her chin. She stared into his eyes, a mirror of her own.

"I know how much you miss your mom, how much you're hurting."

"I know you do."

"We are who we are, you and me. Guarded. Sarcastic. And tough. You're tough as nails, Kat. It took a hell of a lot of strength to start over in a new city with a new family. I'm surprised it took you this long to face it."

"I love you, Daddy."

"Daddy?"

"Right now you seem more like Daddy than Dad.

"I'll take that as a compliment."

"You take everything as a compliment."

"Not from you."

"True." She grinned, her tears finally finished.

A wide smile spread across his face as he pulled her back into his arms. "I love you, too, you little smart-ass."

*

Jessie closed the last suitcase and scanned the room. She was ready. That is, if she even went to London. It was up to Nick.

"All packed?" Nick stood inside the bedroom door. He looked tired. Spent.

"You're late. It's almost midnight."

Nick closed the door. "Sorry."

"Is it over?"

"Yep. Josh was arrested." He sat on the bed and tugged off his boots. His attitude was flat. So was his voice. "You wanted to talk?"

"Are you okay, Nick?"

"Yeah. Just beat. Long day." Even his eyes were dull.

Jessie wanted to shake him. Anything to see some life in him. "Maybe this isn't a good time."

"There is no other time. You're leaving tomorrow."

"You're still angry."

"No. Resigned."

"Listen to me, Nick." Jessie sat beside him. "I'll cancel everything right now. Just say the word. I mean it."

"Don't be ridiculous. You signed a contract."

"I don't care. You matter more."

"Jessie, this is me you're talking to. I understand contracts better than most. I'm fine. The kids are fine. Go. We'll be here when you get back."

"Will you?"

Nick's eyes slid to hers. She couldn't read him, which terrified her. What was he thinking?"

*

Dear Mom,

This will be my last letter. Thanks for listening all these months.

Dad is taking good care of me, and I'll take care of him. He never gave up on me, despite my snarky attitude and acid tongue. Despite whatever personal hell he was going through with Jessie. He won me over, day by day. The more I learned about him, the more I understood myself. He continues to fill in the missing pieces of my jigsaw puzzle. I think maybe I helped him, too. I hope so, anyway.

You were and are a great mom, and I'll always love you. You gave me the freedom to explore who I am, who I want to be. You encouraged me, protected me, laughed with me. You reminded me the world is full of endless possibilities. And so it is. My journey of discovery goes on ... May it never end.

Rest, Mom. You've earned your peace. I will carry you with me always. Until we meet again one day ... Love, Kat

A man laughed. Kat distinctly heard a man's laugh.

The fur on Hamlet's back stood on end, his blue eyes fixed and enormous.

Kat scanned her bedroom. "Uncle Andrew?"

Something brushed Kat's cheek. Did her uncle just kiss her?

Hamlet bounded off the desk, his body suspended momentarily as his paws paddled the air like some cartoon caricature. Finally he dropped to the floor with a thud, his motion a blur, his yowl trailing behind him as he skittered to the inner sanctum of the bathroom.

Kat's laughter matched her uncle's. This was one crazy house.

*

"What do you want me to say, Jessie? I told you I'm okay with this. I understand your need to work. This play is a great opportunity, the role of a lifetime. Go with my blessing."

"Really? Because nothing is more important to me than you are, Nick. Nothing."

"But you still want to go alone."

"I have to. I have something to prove to myself."

"But Abbie and Willie don't count in your quest to be alone."

"Willie isn't going. He says the kids need him here. He's right. I can hire someone over there."

Willie wasn't going? When did that change?

"Nick?"

"Hmm?"

"For God's sake, talk to me."

"Sorry." He rose and emptied his pockets. "I'm tired. It's been a long couple of days. Jam-packed with surprises," he added sarcastically.

"That's it? That's all you have to say?"

He shrugged and removed his watch.

"I give up." Jessie got to her feet. "I apologized to Kat. Apologized to Anthony. I'm trying to fix things with us. And I'm getting nowhere. I'm willing to give up this play for my family – as you pointed out, the role of a lifetime – and no one gives a damn. So be it. I'll see you in six months." She marched into the bathroom, slamming the door. The shower turned on.

Nick desperately needed sleep. Tugging off his sweater, he glanced around the cluttered room. Tomorrow night all this luggage would be gone. More importantly, Jessie would be gone, too. Nick would be left with a lonely oversized bed in a lonely oversized bedroom.

Dropping down on a chair he rubbed his weary eyes. He felt ... empty. Was this how Jess felt in the face of the family's callous attitude towards London?

Without an audience, without a character to portray, actors were relegated to the dustbin.

Nick suddenly felt like a shit. Jessie was offered a stunning role in a new play at exactly the right moment. She needed to heal. They both did. He'd hoped they could heal together. Apparently not. But he had no right to stand in the way of her health or success.

Pushing himself to his feet, he stripped off the last of his clothes. Slipping into the bathroom, he joined his wife in the steamy shower.

Jessie swept her wet hair out of her face. "Look, sex isn't going to fix things, Nick. It's too late."

"I'm here to apologize." He reached out, stroking her cheek. "I'm sorry, Jess. I've been a jackass about this. Losing the baby ... and then your decision to go to London ... It was—"

She came into his arms, burying her face against his wet chest. "Thank God, Nick," she whispered. "Thank God. I thought I lost you."

She almost did, but she didn't need to know it. It wasn't until this moment that Nick realized how close their marriage came to failing. They still had things to work out. Apologies to be heard. Promises to be made. And a long separation to endure. Nick had learned the hard way that nothing is forever. He wanted his marriage to be the exception.

Jessie looked up at him, her blue eyes so vulnerable. He traced her cheekbones with his thumbs and covered her mouth with his, 'showing' her instead of telling her how much he loved her.

Scooping her up, he pressed her back against the tiles, his hands roaming across her slick silky skin to peaks and valleys he hadn't felt for far too long.

Jessie exhaled, a long low audible sigh.

And with one smooth slow thrust, they began their healing process.

Three hours later, they were rewarded with their favorite medicine.

Chocolate, chocolate-chip ice cream and chunky peanut butter.

*

MacArthur Airport on Long Island was quiet at this hour of the morning. The sun was bright. The air, crisp. Nick stood with Willie, Mary, Kat and Anthony on the tarmac as the private plane taxied towards the runway. Bertie had bowed out, knowing the family needed their privacy to say goodbye. Nick's last moments with Jessie aboard the plane were bittersweet. He wished her the best, but he also wished like hell she wasn't going.

"Great weather for flying," Willie said, squinting at the horizon. "You'd never know we had blizzard conditions last night."

Nick nodded, his eyes following the silver speck as it positioned itself at the end of the runway for takeoff. "Why didn't you go with them, Willie? Really?"

"What? And miss all the fun here?"

Nick cracked a smile. "Let's go." Mary and the kids climbed into the car as Nick reached for the door handle. When he looked back up, the plane was airborne, banking to the left towards the open waters and the shores of England.

Willie guided the car into Manhattan and straight to McGowan's. The lunch rush was over when they settled into the corner booth by the window.

"How'd you find this place, Dad?" Kat perused the menu.

"Barton introduced me to it. It's a cops' bar. Friendly and safe." He could still see Lyle, groaning over the food, acknowledging friends, talking shop.

"Wow, Dad, your picture's on the wall." Anthony was impressed.

"That's our Wall of Fame." Gil O'Brien stopped by their table. "His picture's next to his old pal Lyle's." He leaned over and shook Nick's hand. "Hey, Nick, how ya doin'? And who do we have here?"

"This is Mary, my adopted mother. Willie, my newest partner in crime. And my kids, Katrina and Anthony. Meet Gil, the proprietor of this place."

Over mile-high corned beef on rye, French fries and half sour pickles, Kat learned all about her Uncle Andrew from those who loved him best. And, as promised, Nick painted a detailed picture of her brother Jeffrey.

Anthony sobered as Nick spoke about his son.

"What's the matter?" Nick asked the boy.

"Why did he have to die so young?"

"Everything happens for a reason. Right, Mary?" Kat polished off her sandwich.

Mary winked at the girl as she smeared more horseradish on her rye.

"What reason could there be for a little kid dying?" Anthony asked. "Gianni deserved to die. So did Luci. Dad, I've been thinking about Luci. What do you think she wanted from me?"

"Maybe just to be close to you. To love you. You were her only family."

"That's sad."

"The Fossellis were born with a cloud hanging over them. Their lives were sealed at birth."

"So who we are as kids makes us who we are when we grow up?"

"Not exactly. Remember our conversation the other night in your room? When I told you that you had a choice about your reaction to Luci? This is what I meant. Our childhood is the framework for who we become. Some people carry it with them their whole life, like the Fossellis. Others use it as a springboard and learn from it. Grow from it."

"What did you do?" Anthony popped a French fry in his mouth.

Nick pulled out his wallet and peeked at Kat, who was watching him. "Yeah, Dad, I want to know, too." There was a challenge in her smug gaze.

Damn her habit of eavesdropping. More than anyone else, Kat knew Nick's history. Well, except for Mary.

Nick glanced at Mary. She eyed Nick as she chewed her sandwich methodically. The hint of a smile passed between them.

"Well, Dad?" Kat persisted.

Nick turned to the waiter. "Check, please."

EPILOGUE

The next day, Nick was in his office catching up on email. He spent a sleepless night on the study couch, not yet ready to face his empty bedroom. He'd gotten a text from Jessie in the wee hours, saying they'd arrived. A text? Really, Jessie? Abbie had called Willie, and they talked for an hour. Nick resisted the urge to call his wife that morning and sent a brief text instead. She wanted to do this on her own? He'd let her.

His cell buzzed. Brianna Fontaine. She must have read in the paper that Jessie left for London. And she wasted no time getting in touch again. He chuckled at the woman's brazen style. Marriage didn't change her at all.

"Hey, Bree. What's up?"

"I just got a call from the American embassy in Baghdad. Yves is missing."

Nick's smile faded, and his stomach lurched. "What did they tell you?"

"He went out with an interpreter two days ago to get some shots of the locals and never came back. *The Times* is sending me to Baghdad tonight to look into it."

"Do you want me to come with you?"

"I can't ask that of you. It's too dangerous. You have kids to consider now. Two other reporters are going with me. They worked with Yves. Know him well. That will help."

"If you need me, call. I'll be on the next plane out. I mean it. I'm indestructible. You know that better than most."

"Thanks, Nick. That means the world to me. If you still have contacts over there, could you tap them to see if they've heard anything?"

"I'll get on it today. Stay in touch, okay?" He hung up, feeling sick at heart. These things never ended well. Bree was strong, but was she resilient enough to handle losing Yves? Nick was all too familiar with Brianna Fontaine's vulnerable core. The irresistible combination of tough and fragile was what attracted Nick to Bree in the first place. He made a mental note to check in with her daily.

There was a knock on his open door. "Is this a good time?" Bertie asked.

"Uh, sure. Sit down." Nick moved the clutter on the chair by the desk. "What can I do for you?"

"I'm heading over to Susie's now and wanted to say thanks again."

"We'll miss you, Bertie. You know I hoped you'd join our family, but you'll be happy with Susie. Around here you could get lost in the crowd."

"Things worked out for the best, I think. You and Kat need time together without me around. And it's probably best if Kat and I aren't living under the same roof, considering."

"Considering?"

"How I feel about her."

Nick was confused. "I don't understand."

Bertie chuckled. "I didn't think you did. Kat thinks of me as a friend, but I, well, I ..."

Christ! Bertie was attracted to his daughter. He wasn't gay? Nick started to laugh. How could he have been so wrong? His gaydar was way off these days.

"What's so funny?"

"Nothing. It's just ... Never mind."

"Wait. Did you think I was gay?"

"No. Well, yeah."

Now they both laughed.

"I think the ballet threw me."

"Goes with the territory. But it's also my secret weapon. Helps me to move in on the chicks without them realizing." Bertie's face turned crimson. "Oh, God, Nick, sorry. I wasn't talking about Kat."

"Yes you were." Nick leaned forward. "But hands off my daughter until she's much older. Understand?"

"Yes, sir. Uh, you won't tell her, will you? About how I feel?"

"No. It's our secret. For now."

*

Jessie spent the day unpacking. She and Abbie ordered dinner from the restaurant downstairs and then went for a walk. When people began to recognize her, she retreated back to her suite. The metro newspapers were full of articles about her being cast as Diana. Neither the press nor the fans were happy. They wanted their beloved princess played by one of their own.

She almost called Nick twice, just to hear his calming voice. But that would show her neediness. She needed to prove she could handle the pressure on her own.

Around eight that night, Quill showed up at her door. A tall, dark-haired, foreign-looking man with mesmerizing chocolate-brown eyes stood beside him. Actually, there weren't enough adjectives to describe the handsome man. His gaze was disarming.

"I thought you might like to meet the actor who will be playing Dodi Fayed in *DIANA*," Quill said.

"I'm Moni Mizrahi," the man said in a thick accent, extending his hand. "We have a lot in common. You're an American playing a Brit. I'm an Israeli playing an Egyptian. We can fight public discontent together."

Jessie couldn't help smiling at the charming man. "Please. Come in."

*

Nick spent the next few days organizing his office. Mary was griping that it was a sty and refused to let the girls clean it.

He came across the garbage bag filled with Barton's things. Sitting down, he ran his hand across the plastic. Was he ready for this?

If not now, when?

He reached inside. There wasn't much. Barton's small brown leather notebook and pen with his name engraved on it. His wallet. And framed photos. One picture was particularly good. Lyle and Nick stood at the office window, backlit, talking. The last photo knocked the wind out of Nick. It was of Kat and Nick. In the same room. In the same positions. And with the same lighting as the photo with Barton.

How did this picture get in here? Nick had tucked the bag away and forgotten about it.

He put the two pictures side-by-side. They were mirror images of each other.

"Anthony? ... ANTHONY!"

"What?" The boy cannonballed into the room. "How'd you get that picture?"

"Did you take it?"

"Yeah. But I never printed it. Or framed it."

A chill danced down Nick's spine.

Time to move on, McDeare. Without me.

*

Andrew Brady accomplished his missions. Nick and Kat cemented their father-daughter relationship. Jessie reconnected with her acting roots. And Nick faced his grief and guilt over losing Lyle Barton. Best of all, Andrew was able to tap into his long-neglected acting skills. Reenacting Barton's voice, manner and intent was all in a day's work for a celebrated actor like himself.

So Jessie was off to London to wow the Brits, and Nick was bonding with his kids in New York.

But the collateral damage was considerable. The chasm between Nick and Jessie was more than a mere ocean …

***

About the Author

Deborah Fezelle received her theatrical training in the Drama Division of the Juilliard School in New York City. She's worked on Broadway, at the Kennedy Center in Washington D.C. and at other professional theaters around the country. Penning her first play at age ten, Deborah continued to write as a hobby over the years. Her younger sister's untimely death inspired the original book in the Nick McDeare series, THE EVIL THAT MEN DO, co-written with Sherry Yanow. The duo also wrote a sequel, A  WALKING SHADOW, two web dramas and five plays, all directed by Deborah. FULL CIRCLE marks her solo debut with the series. An Air Force brat, Deborah grew up on various bases around the country. After living in Manhattan for twenty-five years, she returned to her native Ohio to care for her mother. Deborah now makes her home in the beautiful foothills of North Carolina.

www.ingramcontent.com/pod-product-compliance
Lightning Source LLC
Chambersburg PA
CBHW070842250626
47159CB00003B/892